# UTTERLY

PAULINE MANDERS

Published in 2018 by Ottobeast Publishing
ottobeastpublishing@gmail.com



Cover design Rebecca Moss Guyver.

ISBN 978-1-912861-00-2

A CIP catalogue record for this title is available from the British Library.

*Also by Pauline Manders*

Utterly Explosive (2012)
Utterly Fuelled (2013)
Utterly Rafted (2013)
Utterly Reclaimed (2014)
Utterly Knotted (2015)
Utterly Crushed (2016)
Utterly Dusted (2017)

To Paul, Fiona, Alastair, Karen, Andrew, Katie and Mathew.

# PAULINE MANDERS

Pauline Manders was born in London and trained as a doctor at University College Hospital, London. Having gained her surgical qualifications, she moved with her husband and young family to East Anglia, where she worked in the NHS as an ENT Consultant Surgeon for over 25 years. She used her maiden name throughout her medical career and retired from medicine in 2010.

Retirement has given her time to write crime fiction, become an active member of a local carpentry group, and share her husband's interest in classic cars. She lives deep in the Suffolk countryside.

ACKNOWLEDGMENTS

My thanks to: Beth Wood for her positive advice, support and encouragement; Pat McHugh, my mentor and hardworking editor with a keen sense of humour, mastery of atmosphere and grasp of characters; Rebecca Moss Guyver for her boundless enthusiasm and inspired cover artwork and design; David Withnall for his proof reading skills; Emma Bennett for allowing me to spend a short time behind the scenes as a temporary waitress; Mark Brewster for patiently answering my fishing questions; Sue Southey for her cheerful reassurances and advice; the Write Now Bury writers' group for their support; and my husband and family, on both sides of the English Channel & the Atlantic, for their love and support.

# CHAPTER 1

Chrissie rested back into the Ford Mondeo passenger seat. The early morning daylight tinged hard grey as Clive drove smoothly along the single-lane road leading away from the Harwich Port Customs and Passport Control buildings.

'And remember to *drive on the left side of the road*,' she murmured moments later, as they passed road signs now also warning of two-way traffic. She glanced at Clive, his face less careworn, more deeply tanned than on their outward journey. Yes, she thought, the week's holiday had been good for body and soul, but she couldn't help noticing how the tightness around his jaw and frown lines deepened with every mile they travelled onto the mainland and edged closer to Suffolk. 07:22 blinked from the dashboard display.

A sudden ringtone cut across the quiet engine hum, the strident sound distorted and amplified by the car speakers.

'Yes?' Clive sounded clipped, efficient, but his face spoke tension and irritation as he answered the call on the hands-free system.

Chrissie sighed and closed her eyes, her head easy against the headrest. Now what, she wondered. She knew she was bound to hear both sides of the conversation and her question would be answered, but Clive's first call so soon? She hadn't expected it.

'Sorry to call so early on your first day back, but….'

Chrissie recognised the cheese-grater qualities of Detective Sergeant Stickley's tones.

'Something's come up?'

'Yes. We've had a call. A woman's body has been

found in a car near Tattingstone,' the voice seemed to drift, 'Are you driving at the moment?'

'Yes, we've just left the ferry, haven't got home yet. Hell, Stickley, it's not even eight o'clock. You go to the scene. Report back to me.'

'I have, and I am. That's why I'm calling. It's, well this one's unusual.'

'Unusual? A body in a car? How?'

'The car is in a paint spraying booth.'

'So?' Clive seemed to fire the word.

'I don't know how much you know about spraying booths, but this one doesn't only pass clean air through it,' Stickley's voice dropped, 'it's also got another feature.'

'Come on, Stickley. Less of the drip feed. Just tell me.'

'It can heat the air as well, like an oven function – to cure the paint.'

'An oven function?' Clive murmured.

'It was jammed on at 140 degrees Fahrenheit.'

*Oh my God*, Chrissie's inner voice screamed. Her head spun with Fahrenheit to Celsius conversions. By her reckoning 140° Fahrenheit must feel as if you were breathing air almost fifty per cent hotter than your own body. What would it do to you?

For a minute the soothing hum from the engine filled the Mondeo.

'Have you called the SOC team? The Duty Pathologist?' Clive finally asked, his words flat, emotionless.

'Yes, they'll be here soon.'

'Do you have any idea if it was the heat that did for her, or could something else have killed her?' Clive's even tones dragged Chrissie back from her thoughts. 'We'll be driving past the turning to Tattingstone shortly. Can you give me the exact location?'

'What? You can't drive straight to Tattingstone now,' Chrissie blurted across Stickley's directions, her eyes now open, agitation rising. 'Clive, I need to get home first. I'm due in the workshop this morning. I've a business to run.' There was no point in adding she didn't want to go anywhere near the shocking find.

He didn't seem to be listening. Impassive lines had set hard across his face. It told her the holiday was over. He was back in detective inspector mode. This was business as usual with his DS.

With each tree and hedgerow flashing past, she felt their break recede and her thoughts accelerate. Those lazy glasses of wine and tastings of Gouda, chocolate and darkly aromatic coffee seemed a lifetime ago; Amsterdam another planet. To her mind, the journey back from the ferry should have been part of the holiday, but Stickley's stark announcement had just changed all that. She'd imagined opening the front door of their cottage in Woolpit; a pile of post on the mat and her laptop sitting on the narrow kitchen table, its inbox full of unread emails. Only then had she planned to shed her holiday mantle.

Hell, it had taken her long enough to get into holiday mode, and now she'd been catapulted back. What happened to the gentle re-entry? Another mile and she wouldn't be able to recall half the Dutch masterpieces she'd seen or the names of the places she'd visited.

'Clive, how am I supposed to get to work?' she said, exasperation sharpening her voice as he turned off the Harwich road and headed towards the smaller A137.

'This won't take long, Chrissie. If I take a look at the scene now, before the SOC team are crawling all over it with their paraphernalia, I'll get a better feel for it. We don't have to stay long. I just want first impressions. The crime scene photos and forensics will give me the rest. So - just first impressions, then we'll drive home. OK?'

'But you're never only half an hour. You'll get dragged in. You know you will. We should have come back yesterday,' she finished, more to herself than to him.

He didn't answer. She knew she was starting to sound like a petulant child. Any more whinging and she'd lose the moral high ground. Instead she fixed her eyes on the changing terrain as the car smoothed down the hill from Lawford, across the low flat bridge over the River Stour with its fingers of muddy estuary, and then up the short steep climb out of Brantham and into Suffolk.

'Tattingstone is on Alton Water, isn't it?' she queried, unable to keep her mind from drifting back to the imagined paint spraying booth, the looming reality threatening her composure. She tried not to picture sunburned skin, but couldn't help conjuring up something between a bloated pink sausage and… what? The charred husk of an over-baked potato? Oh God! She hoped the unfortunate women had died from something else. Something fast.

'I don't think I can do this, Clive.'

'Do what? Wait in the car for thirty minutes?'

'No. I mean,' she swallowed her irritation, 'you know exactly what I mean.'

'Then do something practical. Phone Ron, let him know we're running late and you might be held up a little.'

Clive was right. Keeping busy was how she coped when stressed, but it didn't help to be told that, and not now when she wanted to be bathed in his sympathy and understanding. She guessed he was too busy steeling his own reactions for what lay ahead than to empathise with hers.

Ron, the Ron he'd suggested she phone, was an elderly carpenter – Ron Clegg, *Master Cabinet Maker & Furniture Restorer*. He hadn't always been her business partner; he was her assigned trainer when she was first apprenticed from the Utterly Academy carpentry course, close on three years ago. Their bond would always be one of trainer and student despite their easy friendship; he arthritic and in his early sixties with a lifetime of carpentry experience, she in her early forties with minimal carpentry experience but an accountant's career behind her. She fished her mobile from her bag and pressed the workshop's automatic dial number.

'Come on Ron, answer. You're always there this early,' she murmured, as Clive slowed and turned onto a narrow lane. Three or four sleepy cottages huddled near the junction and then they were driving past, the lane taking them between flat fields of harvested wheat and barley, not another house or farm building in sight. The land sloped downwards, the lane gently turning.

'Hello?' Ron's voice spoke quiet suspicion.

'Oh hi, Ron,' she rushed, relieved he'd answered at last.

'Mrs Jax? Is that you? Are you all right?'

'Yes, yes. But something's come up. We're off the ferry OK but Clive's had a call from work and, well, the scene is on our way home and he has to go there now. So,' she let her voice hang in the air, 'well I'm stuck in the car while…,' she took a deep breath, 'so I could be a bit late getting to the workshop.'

'Are you saying your car's broken down, Mrs Jax?'

'No, no. I'm in Clive's car.'

'Yes, but where, Mrs Jax?'

They turned another corner and caught unbroken views

of Alton Water, the grey early morning light reflecting off its smooth calm.

'Hey, I think we may have just about reached it. Alton Water. It's a lake, no a reservoir and kind of eerie at this time in the morning. And that must be Stickley's car–'

She broke off as Clive drove on. 'Over there!' She'd spotted a police car parked on the verge of what was now more of a track than a lane. A collection of outbuildings and a couple of damaged cars, their dented metal already rusting, breathed desolation. The overgrown hawthorn and brambles beyond blocked any further view of water.

'Did you say Alton Water, Mrs Jax? Isn't that near Holbrook? I'll be driving past there when I take the corner cupboard I've repaired back to Mr Stone. I said I'd drop it by, first thing. Around nine.'

'Really, Mr Clegg?'

Chrissie could hardly believe her good luck. She tapped her phone's loudspeaker mode. 'Clive can give you the directions,' she said, her words intended for both Ron and Clive.

She watched the position of the Mondeo on the dashboard satnav, barely taking in Clive's words. He reached forward and adjusted the scale. The bright blue expanse representing Alton Water filled the screen like a giant ink splat, shrinking and expanding as he altered its size. The shape squirmed like a reptilian fish – large head, thin tail and jagged fin-like frills rippling along a lithe body.

'Are you OK, Chrissie?'

'What? Yes, I'm fine,' she said too quickly, 'Why, shouldn't I be?'

'Well in case you weren't listening, Ron said he'd pick

you up from the public car park on the west side of Alton Water in about thirty-five minutes. Here.' He tapped a P on the satnav screen. 'This track'll be blocked with SOC vans shortly. It's best Ron doesn't try and drive down here. The car park is only a few minutes away. You'll be OK walking to it won't you?'

'Of course. It'll do me good.' She stared at her phone. It was in her hand, still on but the call already ended by Ron. Was it possible to lose minutes of your life? Blank out and just not know? Stress, it was taking control. She needed to get a grip.

While Clive got out of the car and walked over towards the outbuildings, Chrissie opened the car boot and swopped her summer sandals for sensible canvas pumps, pulled her oldest pair of jeans from her case and grabbed a sweatshirt. It would do for work. She shivered. The air wasn't exactly cold, but it would take time before the mid-August sun warmed her enough to feel comfortable in a short sleeved tee. Back in the Mondeo again, she changed from her light cotton travel slacks, her petite size for once proving an advantage in the confines of the car. But she couldn't sit still and wait. Action, her stress-buster, spurred her on.

She slung her soft leather bag over her shoulder and headed on foot back up the track, away from what she imagined was the crime scene. She decided to walk to the point where she'd last seen the water before the dense hawthorn and brambles hemmed in the track and blocked her view. Once she had the water in sight, if she kept it to her right and followed the shoreline, then she'd be able to find the car park.

There was plenty of time, but anxiety quickened her pace as she wondered if the dead woman had been dragged down the track, driven or come willingly. Her gaze dropped to ground level, but what was she expecting to see? 'Stupid me,' she murmured and looked up, at last seeing the water. It seemed to hold her eyes, the far shore snaking in and out, following the contours of what she figured was really a flooded streambed and its tributaries. A glance to the right and she saw a dead straight shoreline – the low dam across its south-east end.

The track they'd driven down turned back up the gentle slope to the fields and eventually the A137, but a path of hard-trodden earth led from the bend and down towards the water. Chrissie, her eyes on the view rather than the ground, followed the path. It was a short cut through a belt of overgrown vegetation, most likely adjoining some kind of boundary road encircling the reservoir. At the very least, she hoped it would lead straight to the water's edge.

'This must be a cycle path.' Her route had brought her to a narrow tarmac way. The earthy path continued on the other side, slightly offset and leading down towards the water. She supposed it made sense; walkers and cyclists sharing some of the same tracks, but she was faced with a dilemma. Should she follow the path down to the water or walk the cycle track, keeping the water on her right hand side?

'The water,' she decided and strode across the tarmac only glancing down as she spotted clumps of hairy-stemmed meadow cranesbill, the purple-blue flowers brushing against her legs as the footpath narrowed. Something white caught her eye and she paused, irritated to see it was litter blown amongst the wildflowers and nettles. She stooped and peered. The words *Nieuwe Spiegelstraat*, and then in larger loopy print, *Chocolatier* were written on a small crumpled white paper carrier bag. Hadn't she seen that name somewhere before? In Amsterdam? Of course, it had been only yesterday, Saturday morning in the Museum District. She'd walked with Clive along the very same *straat* to a boutique chocolate shop where they'd bought freshly made chocolate truffles. How strange? Someone had bought high-end Dutch chocolate from the same exclusive location as her, travelled the same sea miles, and then discarded the Dutch luxury chocolatier's carrier bag near the edge of Alton Water. What were the chances of her finding it? She reckoned they were millions to one.

Feeling slightly otherworldly and spooked by the coincidence of her find, she pressed on along the path.

'Wow,' she murmured as an unbroken view of Alton Water opened in front of her. She sat on a section of old fallen tree trunk and drank in the scene. The ground sloped gently to the water's edge inviting her to roll up her jeans and paddle, but reeds clogged the shallows. She imagined her feet sinking into cloying clay or softly yielding silt. Scary. Even the pink clumps of great willowherb and swathes of blue water pimpernel jollying the brackish edge, couldn't tempt her to dip her hand into it.

So, why was there a path to this point? Certainly not for swimming. She decided it must be somewhere private to sit, simply to enjoy the solitude.

For a moment she concentrated on the faintly metallic scent of the water. Feeling calmer at last, she retraced her steps back to the cycle path and walked along it for the best part of a mile, only to reach the car park minutes before Ron drove in. She waved and hurried to his old van. Smiling with relief, she opened the passenger door.

'Thank you so much, Mr Clegg. I really thought I was

never going to make it to work this morning.'

He nodded a greeting. 'That's quite all right, Mrs Jax. In fact I think it may have worked out quite well.'

She glanced at him as she settled into the passenger seat. The morning sun now held some warmth and it shone through the windscreen, highlighting his thinning hair and catching the slight frown creasing his kindly eyes.

'I've been thinking while you've been away on holiday, Mrs Jax. I reckon we should take a look at one of those modern vacuum press systems.'

'Really? Aren't they very expensive? I mean, can we afford to spend money on something like that?'

It wasn't what she'd expected. Maybe a casual enquiry about Clive's call, but not something about spending large sums of money. He was usually so careful, so resistant to change. A knot of anxiety tightened in her stomach. 'Oh God, I'm getting wound up again,' she breathed.

This time she searched his face and caught the smile. She laughed. Ron was distracting her. Trust him to realise she would react immediately and all thoughts of Clive's case would fly out the window. 'You're joking, right?'

'Kind of. But I'm serious. I want to take a look at a vacuum press system that's up and running.'

'And?'

'So, I've arranged to drop by at Willows on the way back to the workshop. Is that OK with you?'

'Willows? Well yes, I suppose so.' She let her voice drift as her thoughts ran on. Willows & Son was pretty much on their route back to Wattisham and the Clegg & Jax workshop. 'It'll be nice to catch up with Nick.'

# CHAPTER 2

Pat, the firm's secretary poked her head into the carpenters' office-cum-restroom. 'Hey Nick! There're some people coming to see you.' She turned to leave. 'They'll be here in about thirty minutes, OK?' She tossed the words over her ample shoulder as the door swung too. Nick was alone again.

'What?' Nick looked up from the drawings he was studying. His head felt heavy. A pulse throbbed deep within his forehead, and when he moved his eyes, they ached. Ugh. He shouldn't have drunk those chasers last night. What had he been thinking?

But he hadn't been thinking; he'd been reacting. When faced with a rather cute waitress offering complimentary vodka shots, sudden bravado had taken hold and he'd tossed one back. His strict rule of only drinking bottled water while fronting the vocals for the band had been shattered, and so after the final set he'd downed a second. His attraction to the waitress was immediate, and it had turned out to be one hell of a gig. He was pretty sure he had her number scribbled somewhere on his tee-shirt. He frowned. His tee was in a heap of dirty laundry and her name was...? Yes that was it - her name sounded something like Grace or Gisela. But this couldn't be the girl. So who had Pat just announced?

The whine of a table saw and sanders sounded through the wall from the Willows & Son workshop. It gently bruised his ears while a kernel of curiosity grew. Who was coming to see him? He'd worked for over a year for the firm as a fully trained carpenter, but he reckoned he was still too new for clients to ask for him by name.

Another mug of black coffee might help he decided, and glanced around the room. The shabby mix of plastic stacker and threadbare fabric chairs was uninviting. Filing cabinets and a dulled stainless steel sink and drainer stamped additional purpose on the space. He laid the drawings on the table, switched the kettle on and pulled over a pad of paper. It was time to double-check the quantity of French oak the foreman was going to order for a staircase and banister rail. Nick needed to think through exactly how he was going to use the wood. But his calculations were laboured and slow, and his brain felt leaden. He reckoned he had half an hour maximum before Dave shouted through from the workshop for help. There were stacks of pale cherry wood doors to make for bespoke kitchen cabinets. And to add to his troubles, hadn't Pat just said people were coming to see him? It was all too much. Bloody vodka, he should have stuck with the beer.

'If Nick isn't expecting us, he might not be here.'

Nick recognised Chrissie's voice milliseconds before the door swung fully open. 'Hey Chrissie!' he called above the sound of the sanders, but the bigger surprise was the sight of Ron at her shoulder. 'Mr Clegg? What are you doing here? Is everything all right?'

He stood up, pushing back the plastic chair. He caught Chrissie's brief nervous smile. What the hell was going on? He scrabbled in his brain to make sense of it.

'It's OK, Nick. We've come to look at the Willows vacuum press. I phoned last week to arrange it. I thought someone would have told you. I spoke to Pat a bit earlier today and brought it forward to this morning,' Ron said.

Nick was taken aback. 'Well I kind of heard. About two

seconds ago. But I didn't know it was you or what it was about.'

'If you're making tea, we could kill for a cup,' Chrissie murmured, then frowned and continued hesitantly, 'well not kill exactly, but you know what I mean.'

He was used to reading Chrissie. They'd been friends since the early days at Utterly Academy. That had been four years ago. She'd been like the older sister he'd never had. He could usually tell when something was wrong. Was it the quick nervous smile or her embarrassment by the word kill in her casual throwaway phrase? Superficially she looked good with a pleasantly tanned face and sun bleached tones highlighting her short blonde hair. But she obviously wasn't relaxed. At least not how he'd expect her to be after a great holiday.

'You've just got back from Holland, right? Did you have a good time?' He hoped he wasn't stepping on sensitive ground.

She nodded in reply.

'And Clive? He's OK too?' He caught a flicker of emotion cross her face, and then it was gone. Something was definitely wrong. He'd known her too long to play games, and he wasn't in the mood to tiptoe around avoiding her feelings. His head hurt too much.

'But Chrissie, you could have asked me anytime about our vacuum press system. You haven't mentioned it once in the last six months. Why now? Something else is going on. At least that's what your face is telling me.'

'What are you on about, Nick? There's nothing more than that mug of tea you promised… as well as the vacuum press, of course,' Chrissie shot back.

'It's me who's the one really wanting to see the vacuum

press,' Ron said in his quiet calm manner. 'It hasn't been a good start to the day so far, Nick. Mrs Jax hasn't even managed to get home yet. I had to pick her up from Alton Water, so I thought as we were both in the van and passing this way, a visit might fit in nicely.'

'Yes that's right. Clive was called to a case just as we left the ferry at Harwich. So you see, a mug of tea–'

'Yeah, yeah I get it.' At least Nick thought he got it. Chrissie was obviously stressed about something and Ron was distracting her. The trouble was, in his experience it didn't always work. Sometimes she needed to talk first.

'The kettle's just boiled. It won't take a minute,' he said as he flicked it on again and busied with mugs and tea bags, 'So what was the case he was called to?'

'Some unfortunate woman. Found dead in a car in a paint spraying booth. The hot paint-curing function was still running.'

'What? Are you being serious? Did you actually see her?'

'Milk but no sugar for me thanks, Nick,' Ron murmured.

'Yes, I am being serious and no, thank God I didn't get to see her. But the poor woman – can you imagine? She must have been slowly cooked. It's sick.'

'Best not dwell on it, Mrs Jax. They're bound to catch whoever's responsible. It sounds so horrible the public will help on this one. Somebody will come forward, someone will have seen or heard something.'

'Mr Clegg is probably right, Chrissie.' He waited a moment and changed track, 'So on a more cheerful note, tell me about your holiday. I can see you've caught the sun.'

'We had a great time. You should visit Amsterdam if you get the chance. But how about you? You look as if you're going down with something.'

He knew she was fobbing him off.

'Just a bit tired, that's all. I was singing with the band yesterday; a gig at a private function over at Freston.' He caught her blank expression. 'It's a couple of miles after the road takes you under the Orwell Bridge. We had a fantastic view over-looking the Orwell.'

'And not a million miles from Alton Water,' Ron murmured.

'So you had a late night and you're feeling rough. I think I'm getting the picture.'

Before he could deny his implied hangover, the door opened and Dave appeared, red-faced and flustered.

'Come on, Nick. What are you still doing in here? I've been expecting you through in the workshop. Oh hi, Chrissie. It is Chrissie isn't it? So what is this, a morning coffee group or something?'

'No, Dave. You've met Ron Clegg before, haven't you? Workshop over towards Wattisham? He's come to see our vacuum press.'

'Yes, Nick was just telling us about it,' Chrissie said without missing a beat.

Ron stood up stiffly and shook Dave's hand.

Nick's cheeks burned. Dave had been his trainer at Willows when he was the apprentice. He was used to Dave's blunt ways, but as a rule he was kindly and caring. So why act like this in front of visitors? He felt humiliated.

'Willows was lucky to keep Nick. I've heard several joineries would have been more than happy to have him,' Ron said quietly. His words cut through the rarefied scent of stale tea, sweat and wood dust.

Dave grinned. 'Absolutely. He was the best apprentice we've had. That's why I need his help.'

'Come on then, let's go and take a look at our vacuum system,' Nick mumbled and led the way through to the workshop.

It didn't take him long before he was absorbed in explaining and demonstrating the portable bag press system. He opened a special polyurethane bag and placed a curved mould inside. 'This is just a demo, so we'll use a bit of offcut going to waste.'

He slipped a straight strip of thinly cut wood into the bag and balanced it on the curved mould, or former, as he preferred to call it.

'And the pump sucks the air out of the bag?' Ron murmured.

'Yeah, but to prevent air-trapping I've placed the former on a baseboard with grooves.'

'And then of course you connect the pump.' Chrissie shot an impatient glance.

'Not before I've sealed the bag.'

'So how long do you keep the vacuum going?' Ron asked.

'Normally we'd be using several laminates together – so I'd say until the glue between the laminates has set. The glue gives the strength. It's what helps to keep the shape afterwards. Look, I'm not going to show you the whole process now. I just wanted to demonstrate how easily the vacuum bends the wood.' He connected the system and switched on the vacuum pump.

'It's like a magic show,' Ron whispered, as they watched the polyurethane bag collapse and shrink back against the wood balanced on the former. The bag pulled and pressed down on it, slowly bending it tight against the curved shape. Pockets of air close to the mould gradually collapsed and vanished, sucked away as the pump motor whined.

'You can speed up the glue drying process by using a heat pad,' Nick added.

'That was really helpful. Thank you. But we best not take any more of your morning,' Ron murmured. He looked thoughtful as he said goodbye.

'It's brilliant!' Chrissie smiled.

'See you after work for a pint on Friday, OK?' Nick called after her as they left.

'Yes sure. The Nags Head,' she called back.

He reckoned she was almost her normal self again and glanced around the large modern workshop housed in the single storey industrial unit. It felt light and airy as dust extractors, hooked up to the bench saw and planers, hummed and whirred. Dave was planing a length of wood on the far side of the workshop. Work was backing up. Just as well he hadn't gone overboard with information about the vacuum press. The details could wait until Friday, that's if Chrissie was still interested.

'Come on, Nick. This pale cherry isn't going to make itself into unit doors by itself,' Dave called.

'Yeah, yeah. I'm coming.'

•••

Nick stripped off his tee and boxers and tossed them onto the pile of dirty laundry. The air was stifling. Having a room up in the roof space didn't help. The tiles above had caught the full fury of Tuesday's August sun, while the summer air in the double garage below rose gently. All the heat from above and below had compressed into his attic room. It sapped his energy.

At times like this, when he returned to Woolpit after a long day at work, he wondered if it might not be more comfortable to move back in with his parents. They lived less than eight miles away in a modern designed house in Barking Tye. But at twenty-four he craved independence and had mastered the art of effortlessly deflecting his over-attentive landlady.

The room he rented stretched over a double garage and was separate from the main house. Outdoor wooden steps gave him a private entrance, but there were limited facilities. He had to use the toilet in the main house. However at the end of his room there was an apology for a shower squeezed next to a sink and electric water flow heater.

He reached into the tiny shower compartment, adjusted the controls and stood under a stream of cold. It seeped through his short dark hair, dripped from his chin and gullied down his back. Slowly, he washed away the day's sweat and cooled his throbbing head.

When he emerged from the shower, his room seemed hotter than ever. He threw open the door to the outside steps and towelled his hair dry. What had Chrissie said yesterday about the temperature in the paint spraying booth? He forced it from his mind.

'Fresh tee and boxers,' he murmured and the thought turned his mind to what he'd worn earlier in the week.

'Hey, she was Grace… or Gisela,' he said, remembering the gig. Her name and phone number should be on his camel-coloured tee. Nothing had been washed, so it should be just a matter of delving through the pile.

It didn't take him long to retrieve the stale cotton tee, a grubby beige in the natural light. Haphazard spidery writing stretched along the inside near the hem. He squinted at the numbers. Were those 3s, 5s or 8s, and was that a 4 or a loopy 9? It was hopeless. He reckoned there was a formula to work out the number of permutations from a line of interchangeable numbers. It was going to be massive; more than he'd be able to try ringing or texting. The pang of frustration surprised him.

So what was her name? He concentrated on the writing.

'G a c e l a,' he said, sounding out the letters. And then it came back to him. She had been called after a gazelle; a gentle soft-eyed creature, a type of small antelope. Except her mother had chosen the Spanish name for a gazelle – *gacela*. Her black eyelashes and rich dark brown hair fitted with a Spanish ancestry, so he'd been surprised when she'd said none of her relatives were from Spain, or so she'd been told.

The pang bit again. It was the attraction of the unattainable, he realised as he pronounced her name, running his tongue around the sounds. Before, when he thought he had her mobile number, he was happy to delay any contact, even to feign indifference about whether he saw her again. It was the art of appearing to be cool. But now, with only a name and a jumble of numbers for her mobile, he might never be able to contact her. Is that what he wanted?

Confused by his reaction and claustrophobic in the attic's heat, he retrieved his mobile from his jeans and pressed Matt's automatic dial number. 'Who'd have thought,' he muttered as he waited for his friend to answer.

'Hi Nick.' The rich Suffolk accent seemed to match the

warm air.

'Hiya. Who'd have thought I'd be calling you to find a girl's number? It's bloody hot,' he added and wiped his forehead with the back of his hand.

'Not where I am, mate. So where are you?'

'In my room. It's up under the roof, remember? It catches the heat all day.'

'Yeah, right. So this girl?' There was a pause. 'Why'd you say *who'd 've thought,* like that? You know, 'bout me findin' a bird's number for you?' The peevishness in Matt's tone was obvious.

'I didn't mean I thought you couldn't find it. You're doing things like that all the time. It's your job. No – I meant I never thought *I'd need* you to find a girl's number for *me*.' Nick hoped he'd emphasised the words *I'd need* and *me* sufficiently. But that was the thing about Matt, words were often taken literally and innuendo missed. Nick waited, listening to the silence on the call.

'Matt? Are you still there?'

'Yeah, yeah. I were just thinkin'. What's her name, then?'

'I only know her first name. Gacela. It's Spanish for gazelle,' Nick explained and then sounded out the letters for him.

'Yeah, and what else?'

'That's it.'

'Scammin' hell! All you've got is she's named after a kinda Spanish goat?'

'No, a gazelle. It's a sort of antelope.'

'OK, an antelope, then. But you're kiddin' me, right? You must have more? An email? A picture on your phone?'

'If I had more….' He caught back the *I wouldn't be*

*asking you* and added, 'I could find her number myself.'

'Oh yeah?'

'Well maybe not.' Seconds ticked by. 'Matt? Are you still there?'

'Course I'm still here. Where else'd I be? I already said I were thinkin'. See the thing is, with an unusual name, well it narrows me search.'

'So is that a yes you'll find her number for me?'

'Yeah, I'll have a go, but I'll be needin' a couple of pints first and you'll 'ave to tell me all you've got on her.'

'OK, OK. Where are you?'

'Bury. About to ride back, yeah an' Woolpit's on me way.'

'White Hart then? See you in the bar?'

'Cool.'

Nick tossed his mobile onto the bed. What was he doing? It must be the heat. He'd only met the girl once, but if anyone could discover Gacela's number, then Matt was pretty much the best in the business. Funny how things turned out; how a good mate from his carpentry course could have morphed into such a computer geek.

# CHAPTER 3

A light breeze played across Matt's sparse ginger beard and dark sandy hair as he ended the call. He paused for a moment and considered Nick's request. 'So it's a Spanish bird now, is it?' he murmured.

He was used to the constant turnaround of Nick's girlfriends, but it was unusual for him to talk about them. Generally it was a no-go area, so there must be something special or different about this one. In the early days when he'd first met Nick, there'd been some bird who'd broken his heart. At least that's what Chrissie said. Matt had nodded, pretended to understand, but he'd never quite got it, the broken heart bit. And since then, well Chrissie said it explained why he didn't want to risk getting hurt again and why his birds, except she called them girlfriends, never lasted long. Matt had nodded again, but he still didn't get it. The way he saw it, with all those different birds Nick was just a lucky bastard.

Matt shrugged, slipped his mobile into his denim jacket, rammed his helmet on and started the scooter. So what's so special about this one, he wondered as he eased away from the Balcon & Mora office where he traced people and located addresses. 'Yeah, has to be coz she's Spanish.'

A sudden windy gust barrelled an empty lager can along Bury St Edmunds' Whiting Street. He wove past the can, twisted the throttle hard and let the Vespa's 125cc engine surge with an urgent whine. For a hundred yards he revelled in its power. His old two-stroke Zip had been OK, but this more powerful retro-styled second-hand four-stroke was a different beast. 'Cool,' couldn't do it justice. 'Awesome,' he breathed.

Matt chose the back roads, threading along quiet lanes as he headed east through Blackthorpe and Beyton, towards Woolpit. It had been a warm dry summer and the combine harvesters had left grey stubble fields stretching for miles. Wedges of natural woodland obscured some of the view while the huge clear Suffolk sky pressed down and flattened the gently rolling land. It barely took him twenty-five minutes, as he skimmed between hedgerows of hawthorn and bramble, before the road bore left into Woolpit.

'Yeah, the White Hart,' Matt murmured, already picturing his glass brimming with cold lager. He rode past historic Suffolk-brick houses and small shops huddled alongside stuccoed timber frame cottages. He parked at the side of the road, stowed his helmet and walked the last fifty yards, quickening his pace at the thought of a clean-tasting thirst-quencher.

He found Nick already in the pub drinking a beer. It was easy to spot him - he stood head and shoulders taller than the handful of other drinkers who sat on bar stools or leaned against the scrubbed-pine counter. The air hung warm and heavy with the smell of ale. Matt grinned and half-waved.

'Hiya, Matt,' Nick called, 'Great timing. A pint of lager, please,' he added, turning to the barman.

'I thought the deal were a couple of pints,' Matt muttered, now standing beside him.

'Yeah well, not all in one sitting. I need you with your wits about you.' He handed the pint to Matt.

'Yeah, the full two pints, Nick. That's….' Matt started to make the conversion into litres in his head.

'Stop. I've heard you on this before with Chrissie, and

yeah I know you know the exact amount. Probably down to the last trillionth decimal point. Let's go and sit over there where we can talk.'

'Yeah OK, mate.' He gulped a mouthful of lager and followed Nick to a pine table near the old brick fireplace. This time he drank more slowly, savouring the flavours before placing the glass on the table. He shed his denim jacket, windmilling an arm and his jacket in the effort.

'Hey, watch out, the specials board's behind you!'

'Oh yeah, sorry,' he mumbled and glanced over his shoulder at the chimney breast before sitting down. The chalk writing on the specials board had smudged across Tuesday's puddings listed on the bottom corner.

'So what more do you need to know?' Nick sat with his legs outstretched.

Blatant body language was easier to read than faces. Matt reckoned sitting with your legs out straight, if you were Nick, meant you were deadbeat. He'd heard Chrissie say *you look pretty relaxed* when Nick had sat like that while they'd all been drinking in the Nags Head, in Stowmarket. It took him a moment, but he figured he was watching relaxed deadbeat.

'When did you meet this bird, then?' he asked.

'Sunday.'

'Like Sunday two days ago?'

'Yeah. Look, I've written it all down for you.' He pulled a folded scrap of paper from his pocket and tossed it onto the table.

'It don't look much.' Matt reached for the paper, unfolded it and read; *Gacela. Looks Spanish, sounds local. Dark brown hair, dark eyebrows. Waitress at gig in Freston, 18th August.*

‘Frag and burn - you aint written much, Nick. So what you reckon for her age? And her hair - long or short? I need a photo. And more about her.’ He watched his friend sip beer. What was going through his mind? He waited, hoping for a clue.

‘You mean you want stuff about her like her interests and friends, in case she posts on say… music sites or about her friends. Right?’

‘Right. Have you looked on the band’s Facebook page or website? You know, maybe someone posted a photo of the gig and she’s in the shot?’

‘Shit, I didn’t think to look.’

‘What?’

‘Sorry, mate.’

‘Yeah, well take a look an’ let me know. You text me, right?’ He thought for a moment. ‘See what I don’t get is why you think she’d fancy you when she never gave you her number. I thought givin’ out your number were like a sign. You know, tellin’ someone you fancy ’em without actually sayin’.’

‘Yeah, well she wrote it on my tee-shirt but I can’t make out the numbers.’

‘Scammin’ hell! Why aint you said before? Where’s your tee?’

‘In my dirty laundry. And before you ask, I’m not giving it to you.’

‘Then for blog’s sake, use your phone and send me a picture.’ He took a couple of long gulping swallows, almost draining his glass before setting it down on the table. ‘Of the numbers, I mean. A photo of the numbers.’

‘I got what you meant, Matt and if that’s a hint for another pint, I haven’t noticed.’

‘But….’ He gave up processing the *not noticing the noticed* hint as two blokes, glasses in hand, ambled up to the specials board. Their presence drove a wedge into further talk. While the two drinkers stood and made choices between *local Red Poll beef burgers* and *chickpea pancakes with yellow lentil & squash dhal*, Matt let the gentle babble of lounge bar voices wash over him, and sifted through Nick’s words. Surely it was the Freston venue and the caterers he needed to focus on.

‘Is it true?’ Nick’s voice cut into his deliberations as the two blokes moved away. ‘Hey Matt, is it true? Chrissie said old Smithy asked you to help out one morning a week in the computer lab? With the September freshers?’

‘What? Oh yeah, I’ll be back at Utterly again. Like a kinda volunteer assistant for the Computin’ & IT department.’ His mind flipped into *non-search* mode as the topic changed.

‘Awesome. I’m guessing volunteer means no pay?’

‘Yeah, Mr Smith said there weren’t no budget for me. But that’s OK coz I get to use their computers, and the rest of the time I’ll be at Balcon & Mora. There’s plenty of work for me there.’

‘Well, it sounds great. I’m getting another half of Hell Cat. It’s this week’s *vat on tap* ale. What about you? Another lager?’

‘Yeah, but I thought….’

He watched as Nick picked up their empty glasses and weaved between the smattering of drinkers standing near the scrubbed-pine counter.

‘Malware,’ Matt sighed. He and Nick were sitting at the most exposed table in the pub. He let his mind drift back to Utterly. Utterly Academy in Stowmarket. The only good thing to have come out of that disastrous carpentry course was meeting Nick and Chrissie. That was before he'd discovered carpentry wasn't his thing and he was more comfortable with computing. At least the Computing & IT course had given him out-of-hour access to the library, and now with the volunteer job, also the computer lab.

'Are you working tomorrow?' Nick asked, as he put full glasses on the pine table.

'What? Oh yeah. At Balcon & Mora.' Matt pulled his thoughts back on track. But the specials board troubled him. It attracted too many glances which seemed to take in him as well. He felt exposed. It wasn't the place to talk about tracing missing people, addresses and contact details. 'So how's the band?' he asked.

Nick pulled out his phone and showed him photos of previous gigs. They talked keyboard riffs and drum solos.

'Well, I'm wiped out. It's an early night for me,' Nick said and downed the rest of his pint.

'I figured you were beat,' Matt muttered, 'oh yeah, and relaxed.' He was pleased he'd read the outstretched legs correctly.

They walked from the pub into the warm evening air. A faint sweet scent, almost like roses, drifted from a large half-barrel planted with pale pink geraniums.

'Nice here, aint it,' Matt breathed.

'Hmm. Nags Head, Friday?' Nick asked.

'Yeah, see you there.'

'If you get anything before then, you know… on Gacela, let me know.'

'Yeah.' Matt waved and headed for his scooter, his thoughts once again on the Freston venue and the caterers.

The Vespa was a fifty yard walk away, back along the

road, past parked cars and houses encroaching on narrow pavements; but he barely noticed. Even his ride into Stowmarket to the modest bungalow he called home, was a dim memory by the following day. He filled his mind with other things; it was in *search mode*, and so mundane aspects around him were temporarily pushed into the background.

Some things, however were so familiar, they had become permanently invisible.

They were the household things he'd known since his earliest memories, such as the bright blue of his bedroom walls which dulled through his childhood and had slowly morphed into their current shade of dirty Mediterranean smog. To his mind's eye, they were the blue they had always been. It was his bedroom.

And his mother; she was Mum, the mum she had always been - cold, distant, and to him unfathomable. He didn't question it; he accepted it, just as he accepted the unkempt state of the bungalow. It was his mum's – infused with her cigarettes and as inhospitable as ever. So when he called, 'Bye, Mum,' over his shoulder on Wednesday morning as he left home, he no longer saw her dyed dirty-blonde hair changed from an earlier platinum, and he was still no more able to read the lines on her face than when he was a small child.

•••

Matt parked his Vespa in one of the back alleys behind the Buttermarket shopping area in Bury St Edmunds. It was still early Wednesday morning. The outside stucco-facings of the buildings gave them a more modern feel than the tilt of the old windows suggested. He felt an uncharacteristic spring in his step as he climbed narrow stairs to the first-floor offices of Balcon & Mora.

*People Tracing* had been printed in neat black lettering on the open door to the pint-sized waiting room, and Matt paused to inspect the words.

The people tracing, as stated, was internet based and largely for debt collecting agencies. In the past he'd been tempted to trace for more interesting targets than disorganised people with small debts, but Damon Mora, his boss, had made it quite clear he was in no hurry to branch out.

'Oh hi, Matt,' Damon said, appearing from his office and halting mid-stride. 'You're early.'

'Mornin',' Matt muttered, 'yeah, I reckon it's me Vespa.'

'Ah yes, a beast under a retro body. Look, come in and make yourself a coffee or–'

'Chocolate milk?'

'Right. I've got to go out. I'll only be twenty minutes, so catch up on this morning's news sites and we'll start work once I'm back. OK?'

'Yeah, OK.'

He watched Damon hurry past. Slight build with pale skin and mousey hair, Matt reckoned he must be in his late twenties or just about hitting thirty. He looked neat and clean in light-weight denim jeans and tee-shirt. 'So where's he off to in such a hurry?'

The office was cramped, with a trestle table for Damon's desk and hard drives and back-up storage stacked in the legs and against a far wall. By contrast, Matt's area was a narrow table set against the wall with barely space for a monitor screen and keyboard. He headed straight to it. He figured he had twenty minutes maximum to check out a few things before Damon returned. He switched his computer on and entered his password.

'Gacela,' he murmured. The band's website and Facebook page seemed a logical place to start and it only took him a moment before he was scrolling through Facebook pages. 'Mega,' he breathed. He'd been right. A photo of the band playing at the Sunday gig emblazoned the screen. 'Yeah, there's Nick, an' Jake alright,' he murmured as he squinted at the figures grouped together in performance. He could just about make out Adam on bass close to Jason on drums. Denton the keyboard player, had been caught with his face turned away from the camera, but the shot had caught the atmosphere of the evening, with coloured spotlights at the back of the stage, and the microphones standing sleek against the lighting. He read the title of the photo. *Jake, Nick Adam, Jason & Denton playing at Freston Village Hall, Sunday August 18th*.

He clicked on the *like* and *comment* box below the photo and read the drop-down messages. There was nothing left by a Gacela or anyone with a name or handle remotely resembling a gazelle, antelope or goat. 'Scam,' he muttered and Googled Freston Village Hall.

Armed with a contact number he keyed it into the office phone.

'Hi, I'm enquirin' about the gig at Freston Village Hall on Sunday,' he said in his best clear Suffolk. 'It is the village hall I'm ringin', right?'

'Yes, yes. If it's a booking for the hall you're wanting, you'll have to wait while I find the diary,' a man's thready voice answered, 'I'm not at the hall you know. I do the bookings from home.'

'Right.' He waited, willing the man to hurry. The last

thing he needed was Damon to return part-way through his phishing call.

‘Yes… I’ve got the diary. Now what date did you say?’

‘The $18^{th}$, it’s the Sunday just gone. I wanted to ask. The caterers were amazin’. Do you have a name or contact for them?’

He listened, as the sound of pages turning and paper rustling filtered through his hand piece.

‘Hyphen & Green, but they didn’t make the booking so there’s no number. Yes, Hyphen & Green it says on here.’

‘Thanks,’ Matt said, ending the call and keying the caterers’ name into Google search. Luckily only one entry with that name came up in Suffolk, and it was based in Ipswich, so he reckoned it was a safe bet. He keyed in the number and waited.

‘Yes?’ The woman’s voice sounded harsh.

‘Hi, is that Hyphen & Green?’ Matt asked smoothly.

‘Yes, how can I help you?’ The tone seemed a little softer.

‘I’m from the Freston Village Hall. I don’t know if you can help me but I’m lookin’ for somebody called Gacela. I think someone with that name left something of theirs behind on Sunday. Would you, by any chance have a Gacela workin’ for you?’ He’d prepared the patter.

‘Who is this calling? I don’t think I caught your name.’

‘Ah, well that’d be Jim,’ he said, hoping the name would sound about right.

‘Jim who? I don’t recall it being a Jim I dealt with before. And what’s she, I mean this Gacela, left at the hall?’

‘Designer, no sorry, prescription sunglasses. The name’s in the glasses case – but I’ve no idea if it’s a first or last name, or an opticians. I thought I’d start with you. The guests at the party – well that's goin' to be a nightmare and take forever,' he wheedled, relaxing into his role-play.

'But I don't think I've seen… no not wearing glasses.'

'Well no, you wouldn't have, would you. Not if she left them here,' Matt reasoned.

'Hmm….'

'Hey, but that's great if I've tracked her down. Can you get a message to her? Or better still, can I contact her? Or she could contact me, I mean the village hall.'

'Hey, just a minute. This isn't about glasses and Gacela is it? It's about that poor girl's death. You're a reporter aren't you? You just want to talk to one of our waitresses and get a story from someone who knew her. We've had lots of enquiries since it was splashed all over this morning's news. But I've got some news for you, I don't like time wasters. Now leave us alone.' The call ended abruptly.

'But what about her glasses?' Matt spluttered into the dead line.

It was time to click on a news site.

# CHAPTER 4

Chrissie turned up the volume on her car radio. She knew Clive would be making a statement to the press later that morning, so the headlines for this earlier Wednesday news slot were unlikely to incorporate his latest press release. There had been very little said so far in connection with the dead woman, and she wasn't really sure what she was expecting to hear at this hour.

*And now the eight o'clock news brought to you by…* a voice on BBC Radio Suffolk announced.

She slowed as she drove, ready to concentrate on the newsreader. *The body of a woman found dead in a car near Tattingstone on Monday has been named as Juliette Poels. She is believed to have lived in Manningtree and worked for an Ipswich based business. The Government has announced….*

'What?' Chrissie hissed in exasperation. 'Is that all the poor women gets? Barely four seconds on local radio before they move on to the next government fiasco?'

She accelerated, a sudden flash of exasperation spurring her. She swung the yellow 1981 TR7 onto the Wattisham Airfield boundary lane and flew past chain-link fencing and wild hedgerows.

Clive had said the woman died horribly, and then he'd clammed up, refusing to say more before he'd left for work that morning. But if she died so horribly, how come she only gets a few moments of airtime, Chrissie wondered. At least they'd released her name at last.

Another couple of seconds and the *Clegg & Jax, Cabinet Makers and Furniture Restorers* notice came into view. 'Shykes,' she hissed, slammed on her brakes, turned sharply and rattled and bounced along the rough track to the old barn workshop. By the time she drew up between Ron's old van and the firm's smarter ex-Scottish Forestry Commission van, exasperation had morphed into anger. When she pushed the heavy old barn door open, she was on the boil.

'Good morning, Mrs Jax. So what's bitten you this morning?' Ron asked mildly.

She didn't try to deny it. She was too irritated by the brevity of the news bulletin. 'It's that dead woman they found in her car near Tattingstone. They named her on the news as I was driving here.'

'Well, they were bound to name her one of these days, Mrs Jax? What's wrong with that?'

'Nothing, except that's all they did, well almost all they did. There was no hint of whether the police think she was murdered. No appeal for sightings of her before her body was found. No reference to the paint spraying unit.' She let her voice drift. She reckoned she'd said enough to make her point.

'But don't the radio people just read out the police statement?'

'Yes, I s'pose so. But… oh, you're being so reasonable, Mr Clegg. I want people to care. I want Clive to whip up a damned sight more interest when he meets the press later this morning, you know, really get the public on board.'

'Pardon me for saying this, Mrs Jax, but aren't you getting too drawn into this? I know you were there with Clive when he was called, but… well that's probably all I should say,' Ron murmured.

'But you're forgetting I walked around outside near

where she was found. I wandered down to the water while I was waiting for you. I felt the atmosphere. It connected with me, made me care. Don't you see that?'

'Ye-e-s, but Clive may not, and you know he doesn't like it when you interfere in his cases. And another thing, you still haven't said her name. Don't you think it's maybe the shock and your curiosity spurring you on, rather than a… feeling of connection with this woman, Mrs Jax?'

If Clive had said this, Chrissie would have gone ballistic, snapped back with a cutting remark and denied her insatiable curiosity. But this was Ron talking. Quiet, considered Ron. He'd worked with her for close on three years and… well she hated to admit it, but he was probably right.

'Juliette Poels. Her name was Juliette Poels,' she said tightly. 'I'll put the kettle on and make some tea. Do you want another?' She glanced across his workbench.

'That would be nice, if you're making.'

She was conscious of his eyes following her as she scooped up his mug.

The old barn felt insulated from the modern world by its weatherboarding walls and the wormed beams spanning its roof space. The scent of wood, polish and dust hung in the air. Bottles and tins of beeswax, stain, oils and glues crowded the shelves and exuded a feeling of timelessness. Just the sight of them calmed her. Even the sturdy profiles of the pillar drill, band saw and wood lathe stood solid, like guards against intrusion. She took a long deep breath and composed herself. Ron was right. She had an insatiable curiosity once it was aroused.

'So what do you suggest I do, Mr Clegg?' she asked as she fussed over the kettle and mugs.

‘Do what you normally do, Mrs Jax. Find something else to absorb your energy and engage your curiosity. Find another project. Throw yourself into that.’

But what could possibly absorb her attention enough to completely expunge Juliette Poels? ‘Any ideas for a project?’ she asked, unsure if she wasn’t already drawn in too deep.

‘Well, there’s the vacuum press. You could look into that a bit more. And of course there’s the Dutch mid-eighteenth century games table which came in yesterday. It’ll remind you of your holiday.’

‘Dutch? Really? I hadn’t realised. You were dealing with the customer while I was concentrating on ordering wood.’ She put down her mug, slipped from her work stool and crossed the barn to the furniture waiting in neat order in the far corner.

‘You mean this?’ she said, running her hand over the surface of a three feet wide table standing on six elegantly turned legs. ‘It’s teak isn’t it? Now that’s unusual, I would have expected… maybe walnut. Yes, and the shape of the hinged fold-over top is quite… well it looks very much in the Dutch style. Bold and curvy, and with a deep shaped apron following the curves.’

‘Yes, circa 1740, Mrs Jax. I suppose with Amsterdam being a huge trading centre back in those days, they’d have imported all kinds of exotic wood. It would explain the teak.’

‘Well it looks in pretty good nick. So how does it need repairing?’ she asked, picturing Amsterdam and its old canals.

‘One of the legs you swing out to support the unfolded top requires some attention, and also the drawer.’

‘Ah,’ she said as she pulled on the brass drawer handle, ‘the runners aren’t running and it looks as if the drawer base is split and broken. So tell me, how did it get here from Holland, and how long ago?’ She caught his look and smiled. ‘I know, you’re right. I’m hopelessly inquisitive.’

‘I’d have said you’re unwaveringly curious, Mrs Jax,’ he murmured.

They decided Chrissie would concentrate on repairing the Dutch games table. ‘Did you give the owners a rough estimate, Mr Clegg? How did you leave it with them?’

For once Ron had been organised enough to take a name and phone number. ‘I’ll ring Mrs De Vries once I’ve taken a closer look at it,’ she said, part of her question about its background already answered with the Dutch sounding surname.

Time flew as Chrissie threw herself into the games table repair project. When four o’clock signalled the end of the working day, she was surprised. Where had the hours gone?

It wasn’t until she drove back along the rough track and onto the Wattisham Airfield boundary lane that she thought to switch on her car radio. Oh no – she hadn’t given Juliette Poels another thought all day. ‘And Clive’s statement to the press?’ she breathed.

Shocked by her ability to push the dead woman to one side, she turned up the volume and searched across the channels, hoping to catch a news update. There was nothing. She needed to be on the hour if she was going to learn anything. Of course there were always the news sites on her laptop at home, or failing that, Look East on the TV. At least she could get the internet as well as a phone signal in Woolpit.

‘Bloody fibre optic cables and copper wires.’ It was a

well-known fact. The workshop might as well have been on the far side of the moon, for all the measurable megabits per second it received. It was time to concentrate on the road. Juliette Poels would have to wait.

Twenty minutes later she parked outside her Victorian end of terrace cottage. A sultry breeze carried a hint of late flowering honeysuckle from a trellis close to her front door. She slipped her key into the lock, let the mild heady fragrance play across her nose for a moment and stepped into the close airlessness of her narrow hallway. She threw her keys onto the table. There was no need to call up the stairs, Clive, are you home? The floorboards would have creaked and his tread would have sounded through the ceiling, and besides, the cottage was too small not to be aware of the presence of another. She headed past the living room and into the kitchen. The cramped space felt safe, reassuring, a little on the warm side.

'Hmm, iced tea.' It was exactly what she fancied; she'd pour herself a tumbler from the jug she'd left in the fridge.

With her cold glass filled to brimming, she settled at the undersized kitchen table and opened her laptop. It didn't take her long. The news sites were headlining *The Paint Spray-Shop Murder*. It seemed reporters had taken to using a catchy handle for the killing.

'Good old Clive,' she murmured between faintly sweet sips of clear minty lemon tea. He must have played up the imagery conjured by some well-chosen words to the reporters.

Phrases jumped at her from the screen. Quotes like, *found dead in a car* and *we suspect foul play,* along with *car body repair shop* and the *paint curing oven had been running for several hours*. If there had still been any doubt the *we are treating this as a murder investigation* dispelled any misunderstanding.

'Good, and he's appealed to the public for sightings,' she said firmly.

Juliette's face stared from the screen, displayed along with the appeal. Her stark piercing eyes looked intently from beneath a dark fringe. Shoulder length hair framed wide cheek bones and a heart-shaped face. She struck Chrissie as quite young, probably in her early twenties. And there was a kind of sadness about the passport-like mug shot, as if not only the observer but also the sitter knew her fate.

'Poor woman,' Chrissie sighed, and scrolled through more news sites. She was searching for video clips of Clive giving his press report. She liked the warm proud feeling it always gave her when she watched him talking to the media, and besides, if she found a clip she could play it back to him when he got home. She guessed he wouldn't have seen one yet.

She was onto her second glass of iced tea by the time she heard the front door latch turn and Clive stride into the hallway.

'Hi,' she called from the kitchen, 'there's cold beer in the fridge, if you'd like one.'

She listened to his footsteps, fast and light past the living room and into the kitchen. She'd expected the weary end of day tread; the *I need a cold beer and to collapse on the sofa* kind of walk. 'Is everything OK?' she asked.

'Yes, sure.' He gave her a fleeting kiss on the cheek, 'How's your day been?'

'Fine, thanks. I'm afraid I missed your press meeting, but luckily I've found a video clip. You come across really well. Hey, grab a beer and let's go and sit down and watch it.'

She waited while he took a bottle from the fridge. Weary stress lines around his mouth were eclipsed by a focussed frown; *my mind is on the case* kind of focussed frown. She'd seen it before. It was bound to be about this case.

'Come on then,' she said, gathering up her laptop and leading the way into the cosy sitting room.

It was dominated by a modest two-seater sofa and armchair. A low coffee table and geometrically patterned rug of burgundies, midnight blue and beige distracted the eye from a plain sea of upholstery. They settled next to each other on the sofa, Clive resting his head back and drinking his beer straight from the bottle, while Chrissie balanced her laptop on her knee.

'Right, here it is,' she said and ran the video clip.

He pulled a face when the picture froze at the end, ready to repeat the play. 'No, don't set it off again. Once was quite enough.'

'Ah, don't say that. The camera likes you. And you've got just the right mix of serious and approachable. Yes, I'd say bordering on sexy.' She caught the smile in his eyes.

'Hmm... but it's not meant to be about me. It's about what I'm saying.'

'Or not saying,' she said slowly.

'Well you'd hardly expect me to spell out all the gory details.'

'Were there many gory details, then?'

'Hmm,' he nodded. 'I've spent quite a long time with the pathologist. He's been telling me what happens when your body gets overheated.'

‘Really? What did he say?’

‘OK, if you’re sure you want to hear. I reckon it goes something like this. At first she would have felt hot - her mouth and throat drying as she breathed the stiflingly hot air. To begin with she would have sweated, that’s her body’s way of keeping her temperature down. And as she sweated, she’d have lost more and more water and salt. But she wouldn’t have been able to keep that going. Her blood chemistry would have gone crazy with the dehydration and salt loss. Then there’d have been headaches and dizziness – you can imagine.’

‘Horrible.’

‘Yes, but it gets worse as she got hotter. Her heart would have pumped like crazy, trying to get the reduced volume of concentrated blood around to her brain, muscles and organs. There’d have been heat cramps, severe confusion, and overwhelming exhaustion as she struggled to breathe. Her kidneys would have failed. And finally….’

‘Finally?’

‘Yes, in the end the cells in her body would have died. The pathologist told me our cells die at about 45° C. That’s about 112° F in old money, and the paint curing cycle was jammed on at 140° F - a hotter setting than they normally use.’

‘Oh my God.’

‘Exactly. However much she struggled to stay cool and alive, she was definitely going to die if her body temperature rose to 45° C.’

For a few moments they sat in silence, Chrissie remembering how warm she’d felt less than an hour earlier, a beaker of iced tea in her hand. The temperature in her kitchen could only have been in the low twenties, and that had felt hot enough.

'It sounds terrible,' she whispered. 'Could she have already been dead before someone switched on the oven?' she asked, hoping her suffering had been less.

'Well that's the interesting thing. Estimating her time of death is somewhat skewed by the oven temperature. Normally a dead body slowly loses heat at a steady rate dependent on the temperature around it; hers of course was gaining it. Her core temperature hadn't had time to reach the 140° F setting, but….'

'But what?' she asked, impatient to hear more.

'Well, the odd thing is she was sitting in the driving seat. But if she been alive when she drove the car in, then you'd have expected her to get out of the car and try to escape from the curing booth.'

'Not if the car was locked or if she was tied up. Maybe she was drugged? There has to be a reason she was still in the driving seat,' Chrissie argued.

'Precisely. But the car wasn't locked and we didn't find any ties. There were marks on her forearms and her nose was broken – but the question is, was all that from warding off an attacker or bashing at the steering wheel in heat-confusion as she tried to escape? Her skin was in such a shocking state from the high temperature, the pathologist couldn't really say.'

Chrissie processed Clive's words. 'Toxicology? What about the toxicology?' she murmured.

'And that's another problem. The pathologist says the tests are going to be bloody difficult to interpret. It's back to the temperature problem again and all those substances and chemicals released into her body when the cells die.'

'So what d'you think happened? Hey, before you tell

me, I'll need something stronger than iced tea.' She closed her laptop and hurried into the kitchen. She knew Clive was on a roll and she was breaking the flow of his thoughts, but she'd maxed out. Too many shocking images, too many unanswered questions. The stark graphic detail of it all made her feel she'd taken a body punch. She needed a breather, a couple of minutes in the corner between rounds.

She opened the fridge and reached for another bottle of beer. It would do for Clive, but she needed something a little stronger. A glass from the half-full bottle of sauvignon would hit the spot. She cast around for a clean glass. And then her eye caught the box of Dutch chocolates, tucked high on a shelf above the printer reserved for a stack of printer paper and cookery books. So that's where Clive popped them. Almost out of her eye line. Well it was too bad, she'd seen them now and they were exactly what she needed. A chocolate hit. Why hadn't she thought of them sooner?

Armed with the cold bottle of beer, a small paper carrier hanging from two fingers and a glass of wine cupped in the rest of her hand, she joined Clive on the sofa.

'Thanks. I see you've found the chocolates,' he said, taking the bottle from her hand.

She sipped her wine. 'You didn't have to hide them. Hey, you were about to tell me what you think happened that night, you know – at the body repair place.'

'Ah, right. Well… she was found in her car and I think she drove it there herself. I think something happened while she was at the body repair place – an argument, a fight or she was pumped full of drugs. I'm guessing she was rendered unconscious, put back in her car and then her car was pushed into the paint curing booth.'

'But why? And if she was dead or almost dead, why not throw her in the reservoir instead? It's so close,' Chrissie reasoned.

'If you're talking about what was easiest, then why not just lock her in the boot, and then push the car with her in the boot into the paint curing booth? The forensics from the building, both inside and outside the booth, haven't shown blood splatter or signs of a scuffle. I think the fact she was sitting in the driver seat meant she was either willing or already unconscious. It sends a message.'

'Sends a message? To who?' Chrissie reached for the paper carrier and pulled out the modest 100gm box of Dutch chocolate truffles.

'I'm guessing the message had something to do with the car body repair business, either locally or in East Anglia. I've been talking to the organised crime division.'

'Right.' Her mind spun with questions. Without thinking she opened the box.

'I figured you wouldn't be able to resist those once you'd found them,' Clive laughed.

'Hmm, so tell me, if I choose the Sicilian lemon truffle, is that a sign? Am I sending a message?' she said as she bit through the gloriously rich chocolate and into a creamy lemon centre laced with hints of limoncello. 'Try one,' she added, handing him the box.

'Hmm,' he murmured and picked out a champagne truffle.

'Oh no!' Chrissie yelped.

'What? What's wrong?'

'Nothing, well maybe nothing. I'm so stupid. I should have told you. On Monday, after I left you at the crime scene, I wandered down to the water. I saw a paper carrier like this one. It had been chucked away amongst the bushes. I'm pretty sure it was from the same Dutch chocolatier. At the time I thought it was kind of spooky, you know - a weird co-incidence, but I forgot about it, until now.'

'Where exactly was this? The area around the building and the track were searched. I'm damned sure they didn't find anything like that.' The concentrated frown consumed his face.

'Well I found a path, probably an unofficial one. It cut down from the bend in the track and headed straight to the water's edge. Oh yes, and on route it crossed a cycle track.'

'Hell, I think we may have missed that. I'll get Stickley onto it first thing. Thanks Chrissie.'

She knew he was watching her. 'It's OK. I can't tell anyone anything because you haven't really told me anything at all. I mean you ran through what happens to someone when they get massively overheated. But that's not sensitive or confidential information. And as for the events which took place in the body repair shop that night – well you don't seem to have a clue.' She smiled. The wine and chocolate were smoothing the horror.

'Now hold on there, Chrissie. Just a plain *I'll keep my mouth shut about this* would have done. No need to….'

She smothered a giggle as she caught his indignant tone.

'Oh I get it. It's payback time, isn't it? I shouldn't have put the chocolates up on that shelf.' His smile reached his eyes.

'Well maybe not such a high shelf,' she corrected, openly laughing. 'Now, do you want a rose-water and champagne truffle, or a praline and jenever truffle? Do you think that's basically a praline and Dutch gin truffle?'

# CHAPTER 5

Already it was Thursday and Nick felt the week slipping away. He listened to the ringtone and waited, a soft pulse sounding in his ear. He'd delayed phoning Matt until after work so he'd be free to pick up the call. He drummed his fingers. 'Come on, Matt. Answer!'

'Hi,' a guarded voice murmured.

'Hey, is that you? Matt?'

'Course it's me. Are you ringin' 'bout that bird's number?'

'Well, yeah. It's been a few days. I thought you might have something by now. Are you OK? You sounded kind of odd just then.'

'Course I'm OK. I'm at the Academy. I were tryin' to get me pass for the library and computer lab.'

'But it's,' Nick checked his watch, 'it's late for the Academy. It's well after five. And anyway, isn't it still closed for the summer? I thought you said the students weren't back for a week or two.'

'Yeah, but I rang the admin office earlier. Spoke to some bird called Glynnis. She said she'd be here, but she aint. They've all gone home.'

'Glynnis? I don't remember a Glynnis.' Was he losing his touch? First Gacela's number, and now a girl in administration wiped from his memory?

'She wears them big fashion frames, yeah and she's always got bright lips. Remember?'

'Ah yeah,' Nick murmured, sifting through a litany of girls with bright lipstick and statement glasses, but still not remembering. 'She must have started since I left.'

‘Don’t think so, Nick.’

‘Hey, well that’s not why I’m ringing. Have you worked out Gacela’s number yet?’

‘Ah yeah, the Spanish goat.’

‘No, Matt. We’ve been through this. It’s Spanish for a gazelle.’

‘Right, well anyhow, I blew up your photo and I’ve kinda got some of them numbers now. Cool idea, writin’ on the inside of your tee like that.’

‘Hardly. It hasn’t worked out too well so far.’

‘Nah, it’s neat. Now for them other numbers, well I’ve weeded out what they aint.’

‘So it leaves us with what they might be?’

‘Right, but it’s a scammin’ high number of possibles when you add up all them different combos to try.’

‘So, where’s that leave me, Matt?’

‘I dunno, mate. I’m still workin’ on it and it aint goin’ to be quick. I’ve started runnin’ some of them combos through Google search and a reverse phone directory. But see, unless her phone number is on her on-line profile, it’s a phishin’ hell linkin’ her with it. So it’s been bloggin’ difficult prunin’ me list of numbers.’

‘Meaning?’

‘I can only prune off them numbers when I know they aint her.’

‘Right. So…?’ Nick tasted defeat.

‘We could try just ringin’ ’em?’

‘What?’

‘Well I could come round your place – you got signal in your room, right?’

‘Yeah, but–’

‘OK then.’ The line went dead.

Nick let Matt's voice hang in the air for a moment and collected his thoughts. This was crazy. He'd only met the girl once and it was hardly a big deal. It had been OK to stand Matt a couple of pints to decipher scrawled numbers on his tee-shirt, but an evening spent cold-calling a list of possible numbers? Apart from anything else, it made him look desperate. And sad. He was Nick, for God's sake. He never had problems finding girls.

But if he wasn't going to spend the evening with Matt cold-calling, what were his options? Did he want to slide back into the mid-week cycle of showering, eating, listening to music, catching up on the latest DVDs, maybe ringing some mates, a beer, and then turning in for an early night before work the next day?

'Beer,' he muttered. 'Now that sounds good. I need a beer.' But it was too late to put Matt off. He'd already be on his way; he'd never hear a ringtone through his helmet.

'No,' Nick sighed. He needed a beer but he wasn't going to sit with Matt in the pub for the whole world to watch while he plumbed the depths in girl searching. He'd get in some lager and beers instead. It wouldn't take him a moment if he nipped out now. The Woolpit's general store usually had a basic selection. This way they could cold-call in the privacy of his hot, stuffy roof-space room.

By the time Nick heard the sound of the Vespa's four-stroke engine as it popped harshly, then chattered quietly outside, he'd had time to prepare for the evening ahead. He stepped out onto the small wooden staging at the top of his outside stairs, and feeling resigned to his fate, watched Matt park the scooter. Mild anxiety already ate into his mind. What if someone reported his own mobile number as a nuisance call? What was he supposed to say if anyone answered when he rang?

'Hiya,' he called down as he leaned on the wooden rail, an opened beer in his hand. There was a light breeze up at his level. He waited, letting it play across his face, feeling it soothe away some of his tension. Would Matt and he be breaking any kind of law, he wondered.

Matt couldn't have heard or seen him as he pulled his scooter onto its parking stand and stood in front of the double garage doors. He didn't look up, but pulled off his helmet and spoke to a figure just out of Nick's sight line below.

'Come on Mais. We'll stop off for a burger later.'

'Oh shit no!' Nick wailed. Matt had brought Maisie. What the hell had he done that for? With just Matt, the evening might have even turned into a bit of a laugh. But now it was going to be really humiliating – far beyond cringe-worthy and toe curling. It was about to crash into the sweaty armpit of minger. He was going to look like one sad loser in front of Matt's girlfriend, and by next week, half of Stowmarket would know. He could almost hear Maisie telling her mates about it. He made a rapid decision.

'It's OK, Matt,' he called down, 'I've changed my mind. No need to do any searching. At least not on my behalf.' There, he'd stopped it dead. Killed the project.

'Hiya, mate. I didn't see you standin' up there. What you just say?' Matt called back.

'I said,' and this time Nick firmed up his voice, 'I said, forget it, mate. There's no reason to search. I've changed my mind.'

'Oh hi, Nick.' Maisie stepped into view and pulled off her helmet. Wisps of bleached hair stuck to her forehead and clung to the shape of her head. Longer tendrils gave her a wild look, knotted by the wind where they'd escaped her helmet on the ride.

'I should think that Vespa's a bit faster than the old Zip,' Nick said, smiling now he'd pulled the plug on the search.

'Yeah, it's right cool. And the colour's kinda cute,' she said as she followed Matt to the outside stairs.

'Yeah. Mais says it's purple mist, but I'm not too sure. I thought it looked a bit pink, but she says no.' He had the hint of a woolly Viking about him as he lumbered up the first few steps, baggy cargo shorts, scrappy ginger beard and dark sandy hair catching the breeze.

Nick saw Maisie's raised eyebrows and the unambiguous shake of her head behind Matt. 'Bubblegum – blackberry bubblegum?' Nick suggested hastily.

'See, I told you,' Maisie said, as she started to climb the stairs.

'So what you sayin' about not searchin''?' Matt asked, as he reached the staging at the top.

'What? Not searchin'? Did you just say we're not searching, Matt?' Maisie screeched, and then prodded at him as she reached the staging. 'It aint fair, Matt. First you say we'll be tryin' to ring this girl to get me a waitressin' job. And now you're sayin' forget it?' Her voice rose another octave.

'A waitressing job?' Nick felt reality slipping.

'Yeah, Maisie wanted a lift an'… well then I remembered she'd mentioned waitressin' once. You've got the contact. I saw an openin' for her.'

'An opening?' Nick echoed.

'Yeah. I reckoned she could give them numbers a go,' Matt muttered.

'Really? You mean Maisie makes the calls? Well… if

she’s sure, but don’t hang around out here. Come inside. Grab a can. There’s beer if you’d prefer.’

‘Cool,’ Maisie squawked. ‘See, Matt – Nick knows how to make a girl feel she’d be great as a waitress.’

‘How’d I not make you feel you’d be great as a waitress, Mais?’

‘Hey,’ Nick butted in, ‘you know I haven’t got the whole number, don’t you Maisie? I mean, Matt has told you, hasn’t he?’

‘What? You aint said nothin’ ’bout that. Matt?’

‘No, but it’s goin’ to be one of them numbers I got.’

‘So how many numbers you got then, Matt?’

Maisie’s squeal drowned Matt’s answer. Whatever the figure, it was lost to the evening air.

Ears ringing, Nick felt the project take another nosedive. He definitely wasn’t going to risk asking Matt to say how many again. Instead he mumbled, ‘We could help by ringing some of the numbers. You know, share them out between us, if you’d like?’

‘Really?’ Maisie squeaked. Nick was rewarded with a close-up vision of bleached hair as she flung her arms around his neck. ‘Ta, you’re a real nice guy, Nick,’ she said, looking at Matt.

‘Right, well that’s settled then. Grab a drink, and Matt – share out the list, mate.’

While Nick settled on the bed, his back awkward against the sloping ceiling, Matt sat on the floor and leaned against the bed. Maisie chose the open door area and adopted a cross-legged sitting position; her back supported by the edge of the door frame, her face flushed and fine strands of hair lifting in the light breeze from outside.

Nick held his sheet of A4 paper. It was covered in

closely printed phone numbers. He glanced at his friends. Their A4 sheets looked just as dense with numbers as his.

'Hell,' he breathed.

'So what you think I should say?' Maisie asked, a steely quality hardening her tone.

'Yeah, what's the script, Matt?'

'Just kinda say *hi, is that Gacela?* If they say no, then ring off. If they say why you askin', then say somethin' like *I've been given Gacela's number by Hyphen & Green. I'll be one of the waitresses for next week, or I might be but I want to know what it's like workin' for Hyphen & Green first.*'

'And if it's Gacela and she says yeah that's me?' Maisie shot at him.

'Then just say you want to know what it's like workin' for Hyphen & Green.'

'Right,' Maisie said softly.

It seemed simple enough, but Nick felt his stomach churn as he tapped in the first number on his list. He supposed it was just a case of first-phishing nerves. Fifty calls under his belt, and he reckoned he'd be brutalised, hardened, punch drunk.

The air in the attic room grew hotter, more humid. At first, Nick found Maisie's strident *are you sure you aint Gacela* repeated every few minutes strangely distracting. And then her voice took on a rhythm of its own, blending and merging into the background with Matt's *are you Gacela*, like a harmonised catchy riff in the chorus of a song. He reckoned an angry voice said *no I'm not Gacela, now piss off* every four minutes. It seemed to take on the form of a musical canon, the words repeated in rote. He opened another bottle of beer. Matt pulled the tab on another can of lager.

'What?' Maisie shrieked out of the blue, 'You're Gacela? But that's amazin'. And with Hyphen & Green?'

The room's humid air stilled. Nick held his breath, Matt's mouth gaped. Everything changed. Anticipation was palpable.

'So, what they like to work for? Coz I wanta check if they pay OK before I say "yeah I'll give it a go", right?' Maisie nodded as she spoke, her eyes focussed on the floor, her attention obviously on the call. 'No, I aint no reporter,' she squealed.

Matt shifted, tension evident in his movement.

'How'd I get your name? Nick gave it me. He says he knows you, right?' she continued.

Nick cringed, felt his face burn.

'Yeah, OK.... I'll get back to Hyphen & Green.... Yeah thanks, an' I hope I get to waitress with you too.... What? Nah, tell 'em I'm Maisie.' She ended the call.

'Well that were easy,' Matt said and grinned.

Nick blinked, the situation had spun beyond his control. At least Maisie hadn't given him the phone saying *yeah it were Nick who gave me your number; he's here with me now. Say hi, Nick.*

He winced at the thought. 'Yeah, well done, Maisie,' he said.

'She sounded kinda stuck-up at first, said I had to go through the Hyphen people. Mind you, she lightened-up when I said I knew you, Nick. I'd say she came over quite friendly after that.'

Maisie drained the rest of her can, frowned and then added, 'Why d'you reckon she asked if I were a reporter?'

'Flamin' malware, Mais. How'd we s'posed to know?'

Matt muttered.

'Maybe she thought I were a scammer an' didn't like to say? Anyway, I'll tell the Hyphen people I've spoken to her when I ring 'em in the mornin'. I'm definitely goin' to ask for a job. Hey, I'm starvin'. Can we go for a burger now, Matt?'

'Yeah, OK. You comin' as well, Nick?'

'No thanks. I'm beat.' He pulled a weary face.

'Hey Nick, Gacela came over all interested when I said your name. I reckon she fancies you. You should give her a call. You've got all her number now,' Maisie said dropping her voice and handing him her A4 sheet of paper.

'Thanks. Yeah, maybe sometime,' he muttered.

A few minutes later Nick stood on the staging and watched Matt ride away with Maisie, blonde wisps lashing around her helmet and arms around Matt's waist. It took a few moments to get his head around the twisting turn of events. He had the number now but he was still a loser. The last thing he needed was Maisie thinking she was matchmaking.

By Friday morning, Nick felt grounded, calmer. A deep night's sleep nurtured by several beers had restored his equilibrium. If it wasn't for the slight muzzy feeling behind his eyes, the evening before could all have been a crazy dream. For a girl he'd only met once, Gacela had created far too much embarrassment and discomfort. Nothing about her so far had been straightforward or predictable, and Maisie's involvement had only helped to shatter her special magic. Surely it was a warning; one he'd be wise to note. He realised he'd decided, sometime between Matt and Maisie leaving on Thursday evening and his waking on Friday morning, that he wasn't going to call Gacela. He no longer wanted to.

Feeling strangely liberated as he drove to work, he barely took in the newscaster's voice or the blaring music on his car radio. His mind was on kitchen units and biscuit joints. He was back to normality as he parked in the Willows car park.

'Morning, Nick,' Dave called, as he drew up alongside.

Nick wound up his window and got out of the old Fiesta. He glanced across at Dave's Series 2A Land Rover, its weathered bodywork a matt bronze-green. 'Your Series 2 makes my old Fiesta look smart,' he said as he waited while Dave jumped down and slammed its door.

'Oi, less lip! You're missing the whole point. It's about how original the paintwork looks. Hey, did you catch that story in the news about the *Paint Spray-Shop Murder*? It's not the time to be thinking about a re-spray, Nick.'

'Yeah, I vaguely heard something but I haven't been following it. Have they caught the killer yet?'

'No, and in the meantime it seems the car paint-spraying business is taking a bit of a hit. Some kind of knee jerk reaction - a logjam while they rush to get their paint-curing systems serviced. No one wants to risk invalidating their insurance.'

'No, I suppose not,' Nick murmured, his mind flipping back to Chrissie and her visit to Willows with Ron. She'd mentioned a case Clive had been called to on their way back from the ferry. Something about Alton Water, a dead woman and a paint-curing booth, but he hadn't given it much thought since. He'd be seeing Chrissie in the Nags Head later. 'Friday already,' he murmured.

'Hey, that friend of yours, the one with the detective boyfriend – she'd know what's happened, if you asked her.'

‘You mean Chrissie? I doubt it, Dave. She doesn’t talk about Clive’s cases.’

‘Oh well, probably best not to know. It’d likely only give you nightmares,’ Dave said, disappointment running through his voice.

‘So why are you so interested? No, let me guess. It’ll be your off-roading mates. The Land Rover fraternity, right?’

They walked companionably to the side door into the workshop. Nick had always found Dave easy to talk to, but he was pretty sure any insider snippets, however small, were off-limits while the murder investigation was still on-going. He should have phoned Chrissie, should have shown an interest, and for a moment he felt bad.

‘Has Alfred put you with me today?’ Dave asked, as he followed into the carpenters’ restroom-cum-office.

‘I hope so. I wanted to help fit those pale cherry doors. After all, I’ve made enough of them over the last few days.’

The air smelled stale and the room felt busy. Tim and Kenneth crowded around the stainless steel sink and drainer as they poured boiling water onto teabags in mugs. Alfred fussed over the work schedule at the table that served as a desk.

‘Nick, the oak won’t be in for the staircase until the middle of next week so you’re with Dave today. It’s a holiday on Monday so you’re with him fitting the cherry wood kitchen units Tuesday and maybe Wednesday as well next week. You best get on the road soon, it’s a bit of a drive to Nacton, OK?’ Alfred said, looking up from the worksheet as if he could read their minds.

‘Yeah, OK Mr Walsh. That’s great!’ Nick replied, and then grinned. The day was turning out just fine.

# CHAPTER 6

Matt sat and considered his options. It was Friday and he'd been tracing names for most of the morning. The air hung warm and heavy in the Balcon & Mora office, while somewhere behind, an electric fan whirred on Damon's desk. The walls seemed to be closing in on him. He needed a break and something Maisie had said the previous evening during the Gacela search was still bugging him.

*Why d'you reckon Gacela asked if I were a reporter?*

It struck him as odd. He'd made hundreds of calls for Balcon & Mora searching contact details for their debt agency clients, but few, if any had ever asked if he was a reporter. So why when he rang Hyphen & Green, phishing to see if one of their team had left some prescription sunglasses at Freston village hall, had the woman on the phone been so quick to accuse him of being a reporter? And then Gacela had also asked Maisie if she was a reporter.

'Is everything OK?' Damon asked, his words cutting into Matt's thoughts.

'What?'

'You've stopped searching names. You've gone kind of inert.'

'It's fraggin' hot, Damon, and I were just thinkin' 'bout stuff. That's all,' he said without turning round.

'Right, water break time,' Damon said.

The rumbly stutter told him Damon was standing up, pushing his office chair backwards across worn carpet as he got to his feet. 'I need a coffee. So what stuff were you thinking about, Matt?'

'Aint you always said coincidences don't exist in our

business? It aint a fluke when things seem connected?'

'Yeah, that's right. Why?'

Matt watched Damon switch on the kettle. His pale face topped by mousy hair looked as if it hadn't seen the sun in months. Even the blue of his denim jeans seemed washed out, his tee-shirt a faded shade of neutral. Only his tawny eyes and brisk movement distinguished him from the sepia of his office.

'Do you think I sound like a reporter when I do me phone phishin'?' Matt asked.

'Only when you're pretending to be a reporter. Why?'

'So if I don't say out straight I'm a reporter, you wouldn't think I were one?'

'No. Where are we going with this, Matt?'

'If I don't sound like a reporter and me girlfriend don't sound like one, an' people from the same place keep askin' if we're reporters – well that aint no coincidence, right?'

'I wouldn't have thought so. Sounds like they're expecting reporters. So who or what are we talking about here, Matt? And what the hell have you been nosing around this time?'

'But that's me point, Damon. Me nosin' round and sniffin' stuff out. It aint no fluke when I keep turnin' up weird stuff, right? It has to mean it's somethin' 'bout me. It's what I'm meant for.'

'What you're meant for?'

'Yeah, I reckon it's me nose. A kinda gift.' Matt watched Damon's face as he spoke. The straight brow and tight lips were impossible to read. He blundered on, feeling his way, 'I could nose around for Balcon & Mora. I reckon I'm always turnin' up weird stuff, so why not do it for Balcon & Mora? Official.'

'Weird stuff? What are you talking about? Something illegal?'

'Nah, it's just I reckon I'm cut out for more than internet searchin' for defaulters on card payments. See, the office door says *People Tracing*.'

'But people tracing for credit card debts is what we do, and the point is it pays.'

'Yeah, but the words on the door aint so specific. It suggests we do more than debt, and it don't say internet only. The way I see it, I get paid for how many I trace. The rest of me time is me own. See I figure I could be takin' on projects. What you say, Damon? We could write more on the door.' The office air was stifling. A bead of sweat broke from Matt's temple and trickled past his eye and into his beard.

Damon stood, arms akimbo, his face inscrutable.

'You've certainly got a talent for sniffing out trouble, but I don't recall *trouble* bringing in any money. Kudos and a call to tipoff the police - yes. Money - no.'

'Yeah but–'

'So what have you been poking your nose into this time? Come on, come clean.' Damon's voice sounded resigned, his eyes hawk-sharp.

'I-I....' Matt felt sick.

'I what?'

'I-I were checking out Hyphen & Green. They're a caterin' outfit and I were lookin' for a contact number for one of them waitresses a mate of mine fancies. It's a long story, but me girlfriend's thinkin' of workin' for 'em.' His voice trailed. How to find the words for what lurked in the depths of his mind?

'Here, you look hot. Drink something.' Damon tossed

him a bottle of spring water.

The bottle clipped his chest, rolled onto his outstretched arm and landed in his lap. Phoosh! Fine spray erupted into his face as he loosened the cap.

‘DOS-in’ malware!’ Matt spluttered.

‘That’ll cool you down. So from what you said earlier, it’s the Hyphen & Green outfit who were worried about reporters, right?’

‘Yeah.’ Matt wiped his face with the back of his hand.

‘So do a search, find out about them. I’ve a contact on the Eastern Anglia Daily Tribune. A little investigative research might be worth something to an ambitious reporter. See what you turn up.’

‘Really? No kiddin’? But that’s cool. Thanks, Damon.’

‘It’s OK. But if names for the clients start backing up, then you drop the project until we’ve cleared the names. Got it?’

‘Got it.’

‘And the writing on the door stays the same.’

‘Yeah, *People Tracin*’.’

Matt glowed, his forehead throbbed. He gulped the bottled water and pulled at the neck of his tee-shirt. The words

BREAK THE CODE

DISCOVER THE WORLD

were printed boldly across the sweaty blue cotton. No matter there was a travel company logo plastered all over the short tight sleeves. The stretch had distorted its name beyond recognition.

Damon seemed to regard him for a moment and then focussed on his chest.

‘If you feel the urge to change anything you could

always cross through the DIS on discover and write UN. No, better still, score through the whole word and write EXPOSE. I'm talking about your tee-shirt. Just leave my door alone.'

'Mega!' It was official; he was a researcher for investigative journalism. It was so secret it wasn't even written on the door. In an instant he was Robo Nose, a comic-strip hero with a computer screen for a magnifying glass and a virtual world to probe. He was.... Something pulled him up short. He didn't need to make-believe Robo Nose. He was Matt Finch, nearer twenty-two than twenty-one and with a Computing & IT qualification under his figurative belt. He could wear his own skin and nose, thank you.

He turned his attention back to his computer and keyed in the Companies House website address. Seconds later the gov.uk site filled his screen. From there it was easy, just a matter of typing Hyphen & Green in their search box.

It all popped up: the registered office address; its status - which was active; its type - which was private limited since 2011; and the nature of the business - which was catering. Even the names and addresses of the company officers, along with their year of birth were listed. Matt concentrated on each nugget of information in turn. The office address matched one of the directors' addresses, Sophie Hyphen of 222A Longbottom Road, Ipswich. She had been appointed in January 2011.

'Must be a small outfit, if she's workin' from home,' Matt murmured as he found the location in a dense residential area on a quick Google Maps search.

There were two more names listed, both directors; John Brown and Kinver Greane. Matt put together a timeline using appointment and resignation dates. Sophie Hyphen and John Brown had started the catering company two years ago in 2011. Kinver Greane joined eighteen months later towards the end of 2012. And then John Brown, one of the original two directors, resigned seven months later in May 2013. That was now almost four months ago. Was Kinver Greane the catalyst behind John Brown leaving?

'Let's 'ave another look at Kinver,' Matt mumbled, 'Now that's interestin', his nationality's listed as Dutch but he's got a UK address. Tuddenham St Martin, that's just north of Ipswich.'

And John Brown? Matt checked the address. It was listed as Poachers, Flodden Drive, Bury St Edmunds. Using an address and year of birth, Matt trawled through Facebook and LinkedIn.

'How's it going?' Damon asked.

'What? Oh yeah – I were lookin' at a John Brown, he's one of the directors an' also a chef. It says on LinkedIn he were trained in some fancy kitchens in Bury an' Sudbury. He's posted recipes and shots of food on his Facebook page. But he aint posted nothin' since he left Hyphen & Green, beginin' of May. There's a link to a foodie blog. I've checked it out, an' that's gone silent an' all.'

'So John Brown left Hyphen & Green under a cloud in May?'

'I don't know about no cloud. There's two more directors. Sophie Hyphen an' Kinver Greane. The Greane bloke's Dutch. That's all I got so far. I were just about to check the news sites.'

'Hmm, if Greane's Dutch, I suppose Brown might have left to work in Holland. You could see the attraction if Greane has contacts there. Amsterdam would seem a damned sight more exciting than Bury.'

'Yeah, well I don't speak no Dutch.' Matt clicked on *favourites* and started working through the Eastern Region news sites. Plain *John Brown* in the search box was a disaster. 'Frag!' There were thousands. He should have narrowed the search parameters, and when he did, there were still hundreds. It was exhausting. There was nothing to link them with Hyphen & Green.

'Hey this could be somethin'.' The face of a young teenager stared from his screen. A short paragraph accompanied the picture of a *John Brown* and predicted a *bright future* for the *youngest ever winner* of the *Bury St Edmunds Spring Baking Competition, 2005*. When Matt did the maths, he figured the fourteen year old winner was the same person as Hyphen & Green's John Brown. He had the same year of birth. That would be 1991. It was also Matt's year of birth, a co-incidence he chose to shelve. 'Yeah, this has to be 'im.' The cooking association was too much of a coincidence. He copied and pasted the article and photo into a file he'd named Hyphen & Green.

Next he typed Hyphen & Green in the news site searches. There weren't many results, just the occasional passing reference naming them as caterers at social events such as weddings, a mayoral occasion and something to do with an Oyster Fishery opening ceremony on the River Colne and Mersea Island, near Colchester. A headline leapt from the screen. *The Paint Spray-Shop Murder*. Why this in a search result for Hyphen & Green? Matt swigged more water and read on.

*The police are still piecing together the last known movements of part time waitress Juliette Poels. She failed to turn up to work at a private function in Woodbridge on*

*Saturday 17th August. A spokesperson from Hyphen & Green, an Ipswich based catering firm, said "It was unlike her, she's usually so reliable." The police believe she was still alive on Saturday. They are appealing for help in piecing together her movements between early Saturday morning and when she was found dead at a car body repairers near Tattingstone, Alton Water on Monday morning 19th August. The police are asking the public to come forward with any sighting of her during this period.* The report was dated 22nd August 2013. It had headlined only yesterday.

'Scammin' crazy. That's why she thought I were a reporter,' Matt murmured.

'Have you found something?'

'Yeah, Damon. One of their waitresses were found dead on Monday.'

'Food poisoning?'

'Nah, she were Juliette Poels, the woman in the Paint Spray-Shop Murder.'

'What? The police'll be buzzing around like mad. They're bound to sniff out anything remotely suspicious, including you, if you've been nosing around. Drop Hyphen & Green. Now! Got it?'

'Yeah, but–'

'Drop it.'

But he didn't *get it*. Would the police look up Hyphen & Green on the Companies House website? They'd likely do a background check on Sophie Hyphen, Kinver Greane, and all their current waiting staff. But what about John Brown? Would they even know he'd been part of the firm? He'd left almost four months ago.

Without really thinking, Matt opened Google Maps and

typed in John's address. He was curious. The bloke and he could almost be each other. Same year of birth, same love of food, same.... Was that where the similarities ended? Tumble Weed Drive, Flower Estate, Stowmarket didn't quite match Poachers, Flodden Drive, Bury St Edmunds.

'Maybe it's a bungalow, like me mum's,' he muttered as he scanned and zoomed on satellite and street level views. Except nothing quite fitted or made sense. The street views ended short at the start of an unkempt gravelly track, blocked by a five bar metal gate. The satellite pictures suggested something like a rough grassy area laid out in plots, but the image pixelated on maximum zoom. A cemetery? Allotments? He was intrigued. Could he take this further? Damon had said not to.

'Any new names to trace?' he mumbled.

'Not yet.'

The day started to drag. It was unbearable - still only a little after two o'clock, and the temperature in the office already hotter than the morning. Bored and restless, he clicked on Sonic Rider. If there wasn't another project to take the place of Hyphen & Green, he'd catch a comic-stip. But he felt too unsettled. His mind wrestled with unanswered questions. He itched to know more. Distractedly, he clicked again on Sonic Rider.

'Hey, Matt. If you've nothing more to do, go home. Enjoy what's left of the day,' Damon said.

'What? You're OK with that?'

'Yes. You're fidgeting. And watching comic-strip clips doesn't count as work. Don't forget I've got remote administrator access to that computer. So don't try to fool me. Go home. See you on Monday, OK?'

'I thought Monday were a Bank Holiday. Are we

workin' Monday?'

'What? Sorry I'd forgotten. No, of course we're not working – so have a good one! See you Tuesday.'

Matt didn't argue. He had a plan. If he left the office early he'd have plenty of time to weave a longer route out of Bury. A route taking him past Flodden Drive.

'OK then. Bye, Damon.' He hunched his shoulders to shield his face, grabbed his denim jacket and bustled to the door. He wasn't going to risk Damon reading his mind as well as his work computer, or calling him back. With Flodden Drive his focus, he hurried through the small waiting room and lumbered down the narrow stairs. As soon as he was outside he stood, sweating and panting. The pulsing inside his head slowly eased while the dry August warmth and faint breeze cooled. He just needed to catch his breath, collect his thoughts and decide what he'd do if he actually found John Brown.

Feeling less sweaty, he kept to the shady side of the street and ambled to his scooter. It didn't take him a moment to swop his jacket for the helmet stowed in the top-box behind the saddle. Seconds later he'd fired up the Vespa. He eased away gently, the 125cc four-stroke engine chortling and tittering as he rode along narrow streets and headed away from the central shopping areas. He followed Cannon Street as it cut between small Victorian and Edwardian terraced houses, passed the Old Cannon Brewery and fed into a busy roundabout. He knew where he wanted to go and pictured the Google satellite view in his mind's eye. But how was he to get at the no man's land corralled between the Football Ground, the A14, the busy Compiegne Way and Northgate Street? He hadn't planned on getting off his scooter and walking anywhere.

He circuited the area, this time more slowly, but he couldn't get closer. Frustration grew. 'Let's try this'un,' he muttered as he spotted a car-width's gap hiding between the houses. It was roughly tarmacked and obviously meant for cars. He scanned for a notice; something, anything saying *Private. Flodden Drive*. There was nothing.

Revving gently, he manoeuvred onto the rough surface. He straightened his back and rode slowly, his eyes darting right and left. The lane led between a house and the start of a neighbouring terrace. He passed its side brickwork, then a wall and backyard. The lane turned sharply to track behind Northgate Street. It was an access route to the rear of the properties.

'Blog spot!' A city of allotments and sheds hid on the far side of the lane. That's what he'd seen on the satellite views. He relaxed. This was going to be OK. No one was going to try and stop him riding along here.

'So where's Flodden Drive an' Poachers?' he muttered. The location had to be somewhere near. He sensed he must be closing in.

For ten minutes, he rode in hunting mode along the lane, scanning up and down, and side to side. There was nothing to suggest a house named Poachers or a Flodden Drive, only walled and fenced-off backyards with tall gates and rickety bolted doors. He passed a couple of old warehouses but no names, and then he spotted earth trails, the horticultural roadways leading from the lane into the allotments on the far side.

'I aint goin' in there,' he breathed. But so far his search had been fruitless. Was it to be a ride straight back to Stowmarket or an incursion along the trails? They were wide enough for vehicles. The deep ruts where car tyres had channelled away the ground told him car access was permitted. And it meant he wouldn't have to walk if he....

Yeah - he'd ride in.

He turned off the lane and onto the widest track. Ahead, a patchwork of oblong plots tiled a vista of flattish land. It stretched across acres, textured by shrubs, fruit trees, tall weeds and sheds. Rows of vegetables and fruit canes spelled order while heaps of compost and rubbish assaulted his senses.

'Frag!' He'd taken his eye off the ground. The Vespa's tyres spat soil and small stones. The front wheel caught in a sun-baked rut. The back wheel followed. Ahead the trail turned sharply to the right. He steeled his nerves and followed the rut. 'Frag!' He wasn't going fast enough. The scooter couldn't pull him round the bend. He wasn't going to make it. His back wheel slewed sideways.

He felt the jolt and held on tight. His body lurched back. The handle-grip throttle rotated. The four-stroke engine crackled and roared and the Vespa leapt forward. Together they cleared the rut, landed on scrappy short grass and accelerated towards a shed.

'Oh no!' Throttle off, front brake, rear brake – he made an emergency stop. 'Frag!'

'What the hell are you playin' at?' shouted an angry voice.

Matt sat, legs astride the Vespa, both feet firmly on the scrappy grass. He felt sick, his hands icy cold. The 125cc engine idled gently.

'I said what the hell are you playin' at? An' don't sit there all intimidatin' like. I aint scared of no young'un on a pink scooter.'

'What?' Matt pushed up his visor. The word pink had

penetrated. He took in an elderly man standing in front of the scooter. He wore a flat cap. It cast shade on an angry weathered face.

'I said–'

'I heard. Them ruts are scammin' lethal, mate. And me scooter aint pink – it's blackberry bubblegum. It's special edition. Kinda retro.'

Something in the man's manner changed. He pushed back his cap and scratched his head. 'I had a scooter back in the sixties. It didn't look like that. So, what's your name? Where're you goin'?'

'I'm lookin' for Flodden Drive. Is it up this way?'

'You're on Flodden Drive, but I aint heard it called that in years. Yeah, it were known as that on account of the floodin'. This were old flood meadows.'

'Right. So where'd I find somewhere called Poachers?'

'Poachers? That'll be the name of someone's shed, I reckon.'

'And John Brown?'

'We don't use full names round here. John, you say?'

'Yeah, he'd be about my age.'

'There's someone they call Mr Risotto. He'd be your age, maybe older. Not his real name, mind. He cooked up some rice dish with his herbs and a pike caught in the Lark a year back, last summer.'

'The Lark?'

'Yeah, it were the river causin' the floodin' all them years ago.'

'So where'd I find Mr Risotto?'

The man shrugged and pointed in the direction of the rutted track. 'You keep on that way and take a right. There's more allotments up there. You'll find plenty of herbs on Mr Risotto's plot. I aint seen him in a while, mind.'

'Thanks mate. I go through a metal gate, yeah?'

'A metal gate? Only one I seen is on the main track from the road, and that were stolen last winter. Metal thieves. Our tools are easy pickin' here unless we watch out for each other. Keep out the ruts.'

'Thanks, mate.' He eased away and rode slowly, careful to keep to the side of the main track.

He followed the man's directions, this time noticing how neatness and order neighboured barren and neglect. He had no idea how to recognise a herb, but if the man hadn't seen John Brown in a while, he reckoned he was lookin' for something overgrown, untidy.

'Hey, that's Poachers,' he breathed. He drew to a halt and stared at a wooden shed. A faded name board hung from a nail on its door. An unkempt mix of spindly plants had overrun the plot. The soil looked arid, the plants weakened by neglect, wilting and dying for want of a good watering. He got off his scooter, kicked down its parking stand and pushed a path through thigh-deep tangle.

He circuited the shed with difficulty. It measured about eight feet by four, blackened with wood preservative. There were no windows, just the single door.

'Hi! John Brown? Are you in there, mate?' he called.

He stepped closer to the door and considered his next move. It wasn't going to open if he just stood there. He grasped the handle and twisted. It turned stiffly. Just a little push…. A pungent fetid smell seeped from the shed. 'Ugh.' He half-twisted away and leant his shoulder to the door. It opened a fraction more and then met resistance.

'John? Is anyone in there?' He pushed the door harder.

Foul air knocked him back.

'Oh my blog!' He'd caught a glimpse inside.

# CHAPTER 7

'So what are you doing this Bank Holiday, Mrs Jax?' Ron asked.

It was Friday afternoon and they were taking a break, sitting with mugs of tea in the old barn workshop, the door wedged open for more ventilation. A faint breeze circulated, carrying a cool scent of teak and tiny black flies.

'I don't know why they call them thunderbugs. It doesn't feel like it's going to thunder,' she said and blew a couple of the minute insects off the workbench.

'They'll be from the fields. Harvesting always causes this.'

'I know, but they usually settle on something pale or yellow, not a wooden workbench.' For a moment she pictured the photo of her dead husband Bill, the one of him sitting astride a gate smiling, the wind catching his hair. She hadn't looked at it in a while. Not really looked, but when she had she'd noticed the tiny black insects had crept between the framed-glass and photo. The field in the shot had been awash with bright yellow dandelions. They'd been happy times.

'You're looking very serious, Mrs Jax.'

'I was just thinking about the past and the present; how it's best to keep them separate in one's mind. If we owe it to remember those who've passed, then don't you think we owe even greater consideration to those still here?'

'You're sounding very philosophical. Are we talking about the murdered woman or the Bank Holiday, Mrs Jax?'

'What?' She felt her cheeks burn. She hadn't thought about Juliette Poels all day, at least not since she'd kissed

Clive goodbye as he left for work. She glanced at Ron. He was obviously waiting for an answer.

'Kind of both. I thought I'd try my hand at making chocolates. Hey, what's so funny? What have I said?' She watched him smile and then shake his head.

'Nothing, Mrs Jax. It's not what I was expecting you to say. So are you both making chocolates this weekend?'

'Hmm, it'll probably just be me. I thought I'd do a bit of chocolate-type research first, something slightly different from thinking about wood and glue. I expect Clive will be busy working this case. I'm not sure about Bank Holiday Monday, though.'

She sipped her tea and contemplated Mrs De Vries' games table. Ron seemed to read her thoughts.

'So how are you going to repair the leg that swivels out?' he asked.

'Unfortunately I've got to sort out the swivel mechanism as well as the leg. Come on, I'll show you.'

She slipped off her stool and led the way to the antique Dutch games table. She'd positioned it upside down on a large workbench. Its top, carefully protected by a dust sheet now rested on the bench while its legs pointed into the air.

'Look – the swivel mechanism which lets you pull out this leg to support the folded top has been damaged. Here,' she pointed, 'where the stretchers turn around the dowel pinning the bottom of the leg to its bun foot. I think when people sit at the table there's a tendency to rest their feet on the stretchers. I mean it's a simple swivel mechanism but it's vulnerable down there at the bottom of the leg.'

'So how will you go about replacing the broken dowel?'

'Looking from this angle I'd say I should be able to ease the bun foot away from the stretcher and off the dowel.

Then the leg'll lift away from above. Once I've repaired the leg and stretcher, and I've replaced the dowel, it's just a case of re-attaching the bun foot.' She knew she'd made it sound simple, but theoretically the split in the leg could be mended and the dowel replaced. Getting it all to swivel easily might be a bit trickier.

'And the drawer?'

'I've found a nice piece of old chestnut to match the damaged lining.' She was about to say more. She'd checked the continental fashions and tastes in wood in the 18$^{th}$ century but a shrill ringtone cut her short. She pulled her mobile from her pocket and read the caller ID.

'Clive?'

'Hi, Chrissie. Sorry to call right now, but I'm going to be home late. There's been a development in the Juliette Poels killing. Another body's been found. I thought I'd better let you know before I get too tied up to call again.'

'What? Another woman?'

'No, it's a man this time.'

'What?'

'Sorry, I can't say more, but don't go talking about this to anyone. OK?' He ended the call. She hadn't even had time to say goodbye.

'Is everything all right, Mrs Jax?'

She glanced across at Ron, caught the concern in his eyes. 'I don't know. It's just, well it's just Clive's bloody job. Every time I'm stupid enough to hope we'll have a quiet evening together, it's as if I've tempted fate and he gets called to a case. He'll drop some hint about the case, just enough to whet my appetite before saying *now not a word about this to anyone*. Then he's gone before I've had time to say goodbye.' Her voice climbed half an octave with the injustice of it all.

'You can't blame him for what's going on out there, Mrs Jax.'

'I know, but....' She saw there was no point in explaining. Ron, of all people understood how she needed to probe and delve. And when her curiosity was fettered by confidentiality and silence, the frustration crushed her.

'Come on, Mrs Jax. Back to work. It's the best medicine.'

She had to agree. And so for the next hour she concentrated on Mrs De Vries' teak games table. Five o'clock came and went, then six o'clock approached. It was time to pack up.

'I'm having a drink down the Nags Head this evening. Nick will be there. If you're really serious about that vacuum press system, I reckon I can get him to agree to us trying one of our veneering jobs on the Willows kit. What do you say?'

'Good idea, Mr Jax.'

'Right, well I'm going to tidy up now. Do you want me to make you another mug of tea before I go?' She hadn't asked him what he was doing over the Bank Holiday weekend. She guessed he'd spend a large part of it working, just as she knew he'd be another hour at his workbench before he went home. His life was his work, a little like Clive, except Ron's work schedule was largely self-imposed.

It was still light and the early evening pleasantly warm as she drove her TR7 to the Nags Head in Stowmarket. She steered the bends with aggression, the soft top down and the wind pulling and tussling her hair. She felt released, exhilarated. By the time she drew into the pub car park, she'd shelved her frustration and was ready to unwind. A Special Edition Pink Vespa stood beacon-bright near the waste bins. She scanned around for Nick's beat-up old Fiesta. She spotted it, a less conspicuous dark blue and blending in, close against the panel fence.

'Great!' It was good to sometimes not be the first to arrive.

She hurried into the pub. It was Friday night hectic. The heavy door swung slowly behind, as the warm blanket of beery air enveloped her. Music blared from the jukebox. A gaggle of blokes laughed and drank at the bar. She blinked, adjusted to the indoor dusk and elbowed her way to the counter.

'A ginger beer, please. Oh yes, can I also make that a pint of lager, and a pint of Land Girl,' she said to the barman. She'd caught sight of Nick frantically waving an empty glass and pointing at Matt. They were standing beyond the jukebox.

She made her way from the counter, clasping the three glasses together. 'Hey you guys!' she called. Beer slopped onto the bare boards. 'Hey Nick, give us a hand, will you?'

She hadn't expected Matt to think to come and help without being asked; but Nick? He was usually the first to offer. She looked again and caught the body language. Something was wrong. Matt stood like a sack of potatoes, Nick's shoulders sagged.

'Right, this is as far as I go.' She set the glasses down on a small stained table. She hadn't even reached where the worn floorboards met the red quarry tiles in front of the empty hearth and chimneybreast. 'Hey, find yourselves a couple of chairs.'

She sat on the one chair at the table and waited while

they drew up more.

'Hiya, Chrissie. Thanks for the pint,' Nick said.

'Is everything OK?'

Nick didn't answer. She waited while Matt slumped onto his chair.

'Well whatever's wrong it can't be your Vespa, Matt. It was still gloriously pink and unscratched when I parked just now.'

'I thought it was blackberry bubblegum, not glorious pink,' Nick murmured. This time he grinned at her over his glass before taking a long gulp.

She sipped her ginger beer. So it wasn't Nick who had the problem. She sighed. 'Come on, Matt. What's wrong? What's happened?'

'That's the thing, Chrissie. I aint allowed to say. I been told not to go gabbin' 'bout it.' His Suffolk sounded dense. It was a bad sign.

'You know, that's exactly what Clive said to me when he rang this afternoon. He said *now don't go talking about this to anyone*.' She laughed quietly. It was a joke, a throwaway line, something to break the atmosphere.

Matt looked haunted.

'Now what have I said? Nick, do you know what's going on?'

'Only that Matt's spent most of the afternoon with the police.'

'What?'

'Why'd Clive tell you not to go gabbin' to anyone, Chrissie?' Matt muttered.

'He was giving me a reason why he'd be late this evening. He said there'd been a development in one of his cases. He gave me a bit of a hint and then said to keep it to myself.'

'Well, no one's told me not to talk about it. And as far as I can make out from what Matt's said, he's been looking into Hyphen & Green because I'd asked him to find the number for–'

'Yeah, he asked me coz he wanted to ring a bird he fancies.'

'She's a waitress I quite liked. I met her at the gig we played on Sunday. That's all.'

'Oh yes, *the good view of the Orwell* gig. So that's why you were hung over. But Hyphen & Green? What the hell's that?' Chrissie was losing the thread.

'It's the catering outfit she–'

'A Spanish goat–'

'She's called Gacela. It's Spanish for a gazelle.'

'Wooah stop! So Nick – you're interested in a Spanish waitress called Gacela. But why investigate the catering company if all you want is her number? It sounds like overkill. I mean it's a bit like investigating a nature reserve to find the pet name for a Spanish gazelle.' She directed her question at Matt.

'Ah well, that were down to me nose. Me investigative journalism.' He stumbled over the mouthful.

'Your what?'

'Me nose, Chrissie. Me nose. See Damon said if it were interestin' then he reckoned a reporter on the Eastern Anglia Daily Tribune would snap it up.'

'Snap what up?' It was too hot. She pulled at the neck of her tee-shirt.

'The Paint Spray-Shop Murder. Juliette Poels. She were a waitress for 'em.'

'What? For Hyphen & Green? And that's why you've

spent the afternoon with the police?'

'Nah, Chrissie. They already know she were a waitress with 'em. It were in the news.'

'Was it? So what else did you find out? Oh my God, it isn't something to do with this latest body is it, Matt?'

He didn't answer. He didn't need to; the way his shoulders hunched told her. The background of pub babble and chinking glasses filled the space.

'What latest body? You didn't say anything about a body.' Nick fired his question across the stained table.

'Well, I aint s'posed to gab 'bout it.'

'Yeah, just some of it,' Nick sneered.

'Hey, that's not fair. Leave him alone. Can't you see he's been affected?'

'Yeah sorry, Matt. But sometimes you're just bloody impossible. Sorry mate.'

'Hey surely they can't think you had anything to do with it, can they?'

'Nah, I don't reckon so, Chrissie.'

'So?' She willed him to say more.

'It's just – well the stink should've told me. I-I can't… it's like the whiff's still up me nose. See, I dunt hang round. Soon as I clapped me eyes on 'im I were outa there. That's when I called Clive.'

'Oh Matt. Are you saying you found the body? No, sorry, I shouldn't have asked that. Well I hope Clive was nice to you.' She was shocked.

'But where was this? Not another paint-spraying booth? You can say. I mean you could've been checking out somewhere to get the Vespa re-sprayed. So telling us would be like normal chat. Clive couldn't have meant no conversation at all, when he said not to gab about it.'

'Yeah, but flamin' scam, Nick. Why'd I want to re-spray me Vespa?'

'Right, I wasn't thinking straight.'

For a moment the conversation died. Ed Sheeran's voice rose from the jukebox while Chrissie let the memory of his YouTube acoustic boat session blend with his words. It transported her from the Nags Head to shots gliding along a canal. It was strangely soothing.

'Hey, Mais!' Matt's words pulled Chrissie back to the here and now.

A vision of a girl with bleached straggly hair waved at them across the crowded bar. She appeared slight beside the other drinkers. Skinny black, mid-calf chinos and retro 60s high-top pumps completed her look. 'Hi!' she squealed.

Maisie's excitement was obvious as she hustled her way to their table. 'I got the job! I got the job!' She raised her arm and punched the air in victory.

'What Mais?' Matt looked pale behind his blighted beard.

'Come on, Matt. I told you I were ringin' them caterin' people. Seems they need waitin' staff badly and see… well I got a quick interview and yeah, I'm on for Monday. A big do out some place in Wickham Market.'

'You mean with Hyphen & Green?' Nick asked.

'Yeah, well who else d'you think, Nick? But don't worry like coz I'll still get to meet Gacela, even though I'm back-of-house this time. Washin' up in the kitchen. Helpin' chef plate up. But I still get to wear the same outfit – black trousers, blouse an' the H&G apron.'

Chrissie watched Nick's face. There was something about the way he set his mouth, as if he was about to say something but thought better of it. He stood up, pushing his chair back.

'Well good for you, Maisie. What'll you have? Rum and Coke? Anyone else for a refill?'

'Ta, Nick. Hey Matt, you aint said much.'

'What? No I aint. So you're really doin' this? You're platin' up with Kinver Greane? Malware, Mais. Are you sure about this?'

'What are you on about, Matt?'

'I aint sayin'. But they've been in the news recent. That's all.'

'Ah, aint that sweet. He's jealous.' Maisie planted a kiss square onto his lips.

'Well done, Maisie,' Chrissie murmured. And Maisie's face told her. She knew nothing of Matt's delving into Hyphen & Green. Nothing of his afternoon with the police. Nothing of this latest dead body.

'So this is like a trial for front-of-house waiting, right? If they like you, you get to waitress?' Chrissie stood up to help Nick with the round of drinks.

'Yeah. If they like me then I get to wait at table and serve canapés.'

'Well, if that's what you want I'd suggest saying very little on Monday and you'll do fine. Just get on with your work. Be the hard worker they want. Go for the polite, clean, neat and tidy approach.'

'Hey thanks, Chrissie.'

Chrissie smiled and then trailed Nick to the bar.

'Maisie's no idea what's going on,' Nick hissed when she caught up with him.

'Well neither have we and I reckon she's safer that way.'

'If I say not to mention me to Gacela, then knowing

Maisie, she will.'

'More than likely. Hey, I know. I'll tell Clive she's doing some work for them. He'll know if we should....' She shouldered past a burly bloke, and joined Nick at the counter.

'So are you interested in trying something out on our vacuum press, Chrissie?

'You bet.' She knew it was code for no more talk about Gacela.

•••

The newsreader's voice droned from the far bedside table. Chrissie opened her eyes, felt too sleepy to focus and closed them again. The radio alarm must have triggered. So it was seven o'clock and time to get up. Except it was Saturday and her head felt muzzy. She turned away from the radio, snuggled into her pillow and tried to shut out the summer daylight, along with the voice.

'Hey, good morning, sleepy head!'

'Huh....' She forced her eyes open. It took a moment to centre her thoughts and adjust to the sideways view of her bedroom with its tall mahogany chest of drawers and narrow sash windows.

'I've made you a tea.' Clive's voice separated from the radio presenter talking in the background.

'Hmm, that's nice. You're up early.'

She caught the faint scent of toothpaste and shower gel, as he bent closer and placed the mug on a stack of books by the bed. They served as her temporary bedside table.

'Now don't drop off again or it'll go cold.'

'Thanks. Hey, you're dressed already! Has something happened?'

'No, no. But I told you last night I had an early start.'

'Did you? I'd forgotten.' She closed her eyes and let the memories roll.

She'd got back from the Nags Head, and thrown herself down on the sofa exhausted. Clive was out, still working his case and she'd felt disappointed and a little lonely. She'd mulled everything over, all that had been said, implied, or pointedly not said, and by the time Clive arrived home, the evening had as good as vanished. He'd looked shattered, too tired to cope with her hot-housed questions. Instead she'd given him a cool beer from the fridge and then they'd headed for bed. She couldn't be sure he'd said he had an early start, just as she wasn't entirely sure how well she'd managed to bite her tongue and suppress all the questions bubbling in her mind.

'Chrissie, you're dropping off again. Your tea will go cold.' Clive's voice pulled her back.

'Right.' She forced herself awake. There was something important he needed to know. 'I can't remember if I told you last night, but Maisie is about to start working for Hyphen & Green.'

'Maisie?'

'Yes, Matt's girlfriend. And before you say anything or get cross with anyone – Maisie tipped up at the Nags Head and told us. It was obvious Matt didn't know anything about it.' She watched him frown.

'No, Clive, we weren't talking about what you told me not to say. You know, the latest body in your Paint Spray-Shop Murder case? But it was in the news about Juliette Poels working at Hyphen & Green, so I thought you might want to know about Maisie.'

'What did Matt say to her?'

'Nothing very much that I heard.'

‘Hmm, well I’ll give him a call.’

Chrissie felt Clive’s eyes search her face.

‘What?’ she said.

‘I’m not stupid. I know you’ve been talking to your friends–’

‘That’s not fair.’

‘Well, maybe not all your friends. Just Nick and Matt.’

‘But Matt was in a dreadful state. He said you’d told him not to say anything. It wasn’t difficult to put two and two together and–’

‘OK, so you’ve been talking without naming names. But really Chrissie, Matt’s a potential witness in a murder investigation.’

‘And I didn’t say anything. Believe me. If you say not to say, I keep my mouth shut.’

‘OK.’ He kissed her.

‘So is this latest killing another paint-curing oven effort?’

‘God, you’re impossible, Chrissie. No it isn’t. The body was found in a garden allotment in Bury. You’ll hear more in the press release later today.’

‘So how….?’

‘How did he die? We’re waiting on the pathologist’s report, but I’m betting the garden fork sticking into his chest had something to do with it.’

‘Oh my God! So who was it? Do you have a name yet?’

‘That’s not so easy, but we believe it’s someone called John Brown. There’s a formal identification this morning. A relative is driving across from Norwich. Now stop asking me questions. You’re going to make me late.’ He tossed the last words over his shoulder as he moved towards the bedroom door.

‘Hey let me know what time you’ll be back. I’m cooking supper tonight,’ she called after him.

She listened as his footsteps hurried down the narrow stairs. She pictured him in the hallway, heard the che-chunk-swish as the front door opened, the clunk as it shut. He was gone.

‘Oh God,’ she murmured. Why did she let herself get drawn in? If she hadn’t asked, she wouldn’t have known, and now the image of a man with a fork thrust into his chest both sickened and compelled. It ranked up there in gruesomeness alongside the slowly roasted Juliette.

Anxious nausea gripped her stomach. She forced herself to sip the warm tea; a few more mouthfuls and the muzziness started to lift. Then she remembered. Clive had said he had Monday off. Chocolate making might distract her but she doubted it would be enough for Clive. No, she had to think of something else for Monday. Something he wouldn’t want to slip away from. Something Nick had mentioned in the Nags Head.

# CHAPTER 8

It was Saturday morning and Nick stood in the sun outside Jason's parents' home, or to be more precise, the double length garage squeezed alongside. The mundane atmosphere of Stowmarket suburbia closed in on him as he gazed at the estate of 1950s houses with cars parked in driveways and spilling onto the road. At least the garage had none of that feel. Quite the opposite. It was a music den crowded with Jason's drum kit, amplifiers, microphones and speakers. There was no natural light, just the comfort of an old sofa and an assortment of discarded kitchen chairs.

He'd known Jason since his schooldays, just as he'd known Adam and Jake. Drums, bass and guitar – they were the core of the band. Denton on keyboard had joined later.

'Come on, Nick. We need to run through the last set again.' Jake's voice pulled him back. It was time to hit those top haunting notes in Casanova Blue. The break was over.

He began to head back inside, but he didn't feel good. It wasn't anything to do with the beer he'd drunk at the Nags Head; if it was he'd have a headache. This was an empty unsettled feeling. Guilt. He'd been sympathetic with Matt about his afternoon spent with the police; but finding the body? He'd barely tried. He'd been too irritated by being misled. Maybe it was just the business about Gacela and Maisie. It was starting to get to him.

'Come on, Nick.'

'Yeah, yeah,' he breathed.

*Brr brr, brr brr!* Now what, he wondered as he checked the caller ID on his phone.

‘Chrissie? Hiya, is everything OK?’

‘Yes, all good. Hey, did you say something yesterday about the Great East Swim being on Monday? I was thinking I might come along with Clive.’

‘Really? That’d be cool. You do realise it isn’t the actual Great East Swim? I mean that was supposed to be back in June but it got cancelled. High winds again. This is like a breakaway swim by some of the swimmers.’

‘But it’s still on Alton Water isn’t it?’

‘Yeah. Look I’m in the middle of band practice at the moment but I’ll check the start times with Jason and get back to you. OK?’

‘Great!’

‘Bye.’ He ended the call. Funny, he thought. She hadn’t shown much interest when he’d mentioned it yesterday at the Nags Head.

Back inside the double length garage again, he waited while Denton tried different harmonies on a five bar intro to Give Me Ear. It was a melody Denton had penned; they’d all helped with the lyrics.

‘Sorry guys, this needs more work,’ Denton muttered.

‘Hey I’ve an idea. How about Jason wears his wet suit and goggles. We could sing *give me arms* or *give me flippers*. You know, change some of the words and turn it into a charity swim anthem. It’ll be a rave. No one’ll care if we miss a few notes. After all we’re only playing it at the post event barbeque, for God’s sake!’ Adam fingered a funky riff on his bass like a *de-dum*, as if to emphasise his point.

‘Why only me wearing a wetsuit?’

‘You’re the one doing the swim, Jason. The rest of us, well we could wear goggles or coloured swim hats. But wetsuits? You must be joking.' Nick felt he'd made his point.

# CHAPTER 9

Chrissie pulled into the side of the road and turned up the volume on her car radio. She wanted to listen to the one o'clock news. Her plans for Saturday were running late.

She'd dozed off sometime after phoning Nick. The next thing she knew she'd woken in bright sunshine flooding her bedroom, and the clock on Clive's side of the bed, the one with the digital face on the radio alarm, read 11:02.

Cursing, she'd leapt out of bed and quickly showered and dressed.

'I'll catch all the traffic and supermarket queues,' she'd moaned. It had taken longer than she'd anticipated but eventually the weekly shop was bought and loaded into her car boot, the soft top was down and warm air tugged at her hair as she drove home. She reckoned Clive's press release should have reached the news desks by one. The time on her factory original TR7 dashboard clock read a quarter past three. She checked her watch.

'Bloody clock's way out again,' she muttered. At least she wasn't running that late in her day.

*And now for the one o'clock news read for you today….* She turned the volume up a little louder. *The body of a man was discovered yesterday on garden allotments near Compiegne Way in Bury St Edmunds. The police haven't named the man yet but believe he may have lain undiscovered for several weeks. They are treating the death as suspicious.*

*Record numbers of people are flocking to enjoy the sunshine…* the newsreader's voice faded as Chrissie turned down the volume.

‘But I thought someone was driving from Norwich to identify him,’ she murmured.

It was too confusing. She pulled her phone from her leather bag and pressed Clive’s automatic dial number.

‘Hi, Chrissie.’ He sounded pleased it was her.

‘Hey Clive. How’s it going? I’ve just done the shopping. I caught the news on the radio while I was driving home. There wasn’t much said about the latest body. They didn’t even say his name. I thought you knew who he was.’

‘Ah… it seems we may have been wrong. John Brown’s family don’t think it’s him.’

‘What? So who is the dead man?’

‘That’s what we’re working on.’

‘So this may be nothing to do with your Paint Spray-Shop Murder?’

‘Yes, that’s a possibility, Chrissie. But the body was found on John Brown’s allotment and John Brown hasn’t been seen since May. Before that he’d worked for Hyphen & Green. I still think there’s a connection.’

‘Because Juliette Poels worked for Hyphen & Green as well?’

‘Yes, it’s another lead we’re working on right now. Hey, enough questions. Just let me get on with it. How’s your day going?’

‘OK,’ she lied.

# CHAPTER 10

'You've been right moody with me these last couple a days,' Maisie said, raising her voice.

It was Sunday and Matt sat facing her in the cinema cafe, a small pedestal table between them and another thirty minutes before the film was due to start. 'No I aint.'

'Yeah, an' every time I talk about this waitressin' job on Monday over Wickham Market, you go all quiet an' strop.'

'No I aint. I just don't want to gab about it, that's all.'

He wanted to explain, but the hard tone in Clive's voice when he'd called him on Saturday had left no doubt. 'Leave it,' Clive had said, 'don't say a word about your suspicions to Maisie. In fact don't even mention it to her. You could be putting her in danger. The less she knows the better.'

'But I could tell her not to take the job,' Matt had whined.

'Do you really think she'd take any notice without you giving the real reason?'

'Nah,' he'd mumbled and the call was over.

Clive's voice and the phone call repeated in his head over and over, as if on a loop. He sat and prodded the ice floating in his cola and waited for Maisie to say something.

'See, you gone all quiet an' moody again,' she breathed.

'No I aint,' he countered. His head hadn't gone quiet but he couldn't tell her about the noise inside; not without saying about the body, about his internet search, and about Clive.

'So how you gettin' to Wickham Market? I could take you on me scooter, if you like?'

'Nah, they'll give me a lift. An' it'll give me a chance to

get to know 'em others. Like Gacela.'

'They'll give you a lift?'

'Yeah, coz see they emailed me an information pack. Do an' don'ts. Things to do in the kitchen before the event an' about settin' tables. Like fillin' the salt an' pepper an' water jugs. There's loads. Even the menu.'

'So where you goin' to be picked up?'

'I aint sure. Ipswich somewhere.'

'If you forward me the email. I can drop you off where it says, if you like?'

'Yeah, OK. I'll send it to you when I get home.' Her voice softened, 'So, why you want to come all the way to Bury to see this film?' She nodded towards a poster of The Wolverine. Steel blades were pictured extending from the superhero's fingertips.

Matt held back, curbed his words. 'Coz I want to watch it on a big screen. It'll be great. All action and science fiction.'

He wasn't going to say the word *superhero*. Maisie didn't have any interest in his comic-strip heroes, didn't understand his obsession with them. They'd been the comfort blanket of his childhood. To his eyes The Wolverine was a superhero fantasy to hide in, somewhere to side-step the horrors of a dead body in a garden shed. As soon as the opening sequence rolled, he'd be up there, empowered to move with speed and superhero strength; handle smell with superhero skills; fight with tempered steel touch blades. And in the process, he'd escape and forget.

'You OK, Matt? You gone all quiet again. I reckon you're goin' down with somethin'.'

'Yeah, maybe.'

By the time Matt dropped Maisie off at her parent's house in Stowupland after the film, the evening had merged into night. The cloudless sky gave full view of the moon, no longer a perfect disc. 'A wanin' Gibbous,' he murmured, almost in Wolverine mode. He sat on his Vespa in the faint lunar shadows cast by a large beech, and waited until the door closed behind her. *Don't forget to forward the email* he thought. He twisted the handlebar grip and rode slowly past the playing fields cloaked in half-darkness near her home. As soon as he was clear of Stowupland, he gave the scooter more throttle and followed the Stowmarket road.

He parked his Vespa along the side of his mum's bungalow. He figured Maisie would have had time to forward the email from Hyphen & Green by now, and he hurried in, barely pausing as he passed the living room door. It was ajar, no light from inside, apart from the soft flickering and blare of a TV left on twenty-four hour watch.

'G'night, Mum,' he called. He didn't wait for an answer. He knew she'd be dozing on the sofa.

He pushed his bedroom door open and flicked the switch. A single low-wattage bulb glimmered as if it was a tiny moon, captured in its orbit and forever anchored to a point in the centre of his grubby ceiling. For a moment he was Wolverine. He blinked and he was Matt again, ready to settle on his bed and check for the email on his laptop. He flipped up its screen and keyed in his password.

'Ta, Mais,' he murmured, as he opened the forwarded *Hyphen & Green Wickham Market lunch event* with two attachments.

The body of the email was from Sophie Hyphen and was clear and concise. It gave her contact number and the venue address. *Please arrive at venue by 11:30. Guests will be arriving at 12:30. If you need a lift, Gacela can pick you up at 10:45 from the Copdock A14, A12 interchange Tesco car park. Please ring and arrange it with her if you want a lift.*

'Scammin' Trojan, she's given the Spanish goat's number. All that fraggin' effort to find it an' she's givin' it out!' He'd check the IP address of the sending computer and its location when he was next at Balcon & Mora.

Matt turned his attention to the attachments. There was a document called *Notes on Staff Training Wednesday 22.5.13*. He skimmed through, picking up on what Maisie had already told him, along with phrases like *pre-empt customers' wishes when needed*. 'Well Maisie aint no mind reader,' he muttered.

The second document, the *Wickham Market Menu* was simply bewildering. Roulades, tartlets, brioche, canapés and brûlée – what the DOS was all that about? One item caught his eye and his mouth watered. Chocolates. They had a special mention. *Coffee & Van Vervolgens Chocolates from Holland*. He made a note to mention them to Chrissie. She knew stuff about making chocolates, at least that's what she'd talked about on Friday at the Nags Head. He reckoned she'd be interested, might even have tasted some.

*Hi Mais*, he typed. *Thanks. I'll pick u up 10:00. Don't forget to ring or text Gacela for lift from Ipswich to the do. Xxx*

And the real bonus? He hadn't expected to catch a glimpse of the Spanish goat, but this was going to be something to tell Nick. He flipped his laptop screen down and reached for the stack of comic-strip books with the superheroes from his childhood. He needed to escape for a little longer. He reckoned he'd be OK by the morning.

# CHAPTER 11

Chrissie stood by the sink in front of her kitchen window and gazed at the sky. It held the promise of a sunny day; a definite blue in the early morning expanse of grey with as yet, no hint of a cloud. Yes, it had all the ingredients for a great Bank Holiday Monday.

She picked a couple of clean mugs from the drainer and sliced some bread, ready for the toaster. Clive must have finished his shower because she heard the boards creak above and then his footfall on the stairs.

'Tea, toast?' she called.

'Hmm, thanks.'

'Hey, aren't you eating it in here?'

'There isn't much space. You've got chocolate making stuff all over the kitchen table. I know you were explaining it last night but I dropped off during the *bean to bar, or not* dissertation. Sorry.'

'Right.' The word dissertation told her. She'd overdone her enthusiastic monologue. It wasn't exactly a slap on the wrist but she felt a pang of hurt. Was he saying she was boring?

'Ah good, it's marmalade or jam! For a moment I was worried it might be chocolate spread.' He looked pointedly at the jars she'd got down from the kitchen cupboard.

'Sorry, Chrissie. I wanted to listen last night, hear all about it, honestly. I just fell asleep, that's all. Why don't you tell me about it again while we have breakfast? I can probably take it in now.'

'OK, if you're sure.'

'Yes, but maybe in bite-sized instalments. Didn't you

say something about Alton Water and an open water charity swim? We don't want to be late for the start, right?'

She waited until they'd carried a stack of toast into the living room and laid out the butter, jam and marmalade on the coffee table. Armed with mugs of tea, plates and trays, they settled on the sofa.

'This is cosy,' he said.

'Right, well it's all about the cocoa bean. *Bean to bar* means you source the cocoa bean, say from Mexico, Peru or Somalia and then you have to go through the process of making it into a chocolate bar.'

'I don't remember you explaining it that briefly last night.'

'Yes, well you were asleep. It's about the process of getting your specially sourced cocoa bean to super-smooth chocolate melting in your mouth. There's some expensive equipment needed for grinding and then refining the ground bean liquor. But the point is you can control how much sugar and extra cocoa butter you add, and that way, with the bean you've chosen, you produce a personalised type of chocolate.'

'So do you need to buy some equipment?'

'Kind of. And don't forget the time consuming side of it as well. I'd need a better food processor for the initial bean grinding. And also a wet grinder – it has quartz grinding stones. You use it to refine the ground beans and sugar.'

'The so called *melanger*? I heard they're expensive.'

'So you were listening? Hey, were you pretending to be asleep last night?' She grabbed a slice of buttered toast from his plate.

'Oi!'

'No,' she said, holding his toast up high, 'this is the test.

Now, do you remember me mentioning *couverture* chocolate or were you already asleep?'

'I wasn't listening that hard. Must've dropped off by then.'

'OK.' She put his toast back on his plate. 'You can buy couverture chocolate from specialist chocolate suppliers. When they make it they grind the beans and sugar finer than regular chocolate and add extra cocoa butter.'

'Couverture? My schoolboy French suggests you cover or blanket–'

'Exactly. Melt and temper it, then use to cover and coat. So, all things considered, I've bought some couverture chocolate, a marble slab, some simple moulds, and I'm going to have a go.'

'Right, so that's what's on the kitchen table. Hey, you really are taking this seriously.'

She caught the inflection in his tone, read the signs. It was time to move on from chocolate.

'Yes.' She kept her voice silky, the smoothness of couverture chocolate. 'Now what do you think we should take with us to watch this charity swim?'

'Well, if we want to sit and watch, then I suppose those foldup chairs or a blanket.'

'And it's going to be sunny. Let's take my car. We can put the soft top down.'

'So forget the foldup chairs. Just the blanket if it's your boot. Hey, do you mind if I drive?'

She was surprised. Clive didn't usually want to drive her TR7. He'd always complained it was less gutsy through 0 – 60mph than his Mondeo. Of course he wasn't being fair, his was a modern car. So, did he really want to cast off the Mondeo and visit Alton Water in complete off-duty mode?

She figured not. It was more likely he was pandering to her TR7 preference but wanted to be in control of exactly where they drove. Either way, it implied he wasn't going to suddenly disappear with excuses he was needed by his colleagues in Ipswich or Bury St Edmunds.

'OK,' she said and relaxed.

It didn't take long to clear away breakfast. Chrissie found a sunhat to complete her summer guise of lightweight linen trousers and canvas espadrilles while Clive unhooked an undersized backpack from the hall coat rack. She thought he looked rather expedition-like, dressed in knee length shorts and trainers as he loaded the TR7 boot with a groundsheet blanket combo and sweatshirts to layer over their tees if the weather turned. He helped her put the soft top down.

'That should do us,' he murmured.

'I hope you know where we're going. My car hasn't got a satnav,' she said and sank into the passenger seat.

'I rather thought you'd map read, Chrissie.'

'In your dreams. Hey, Nick said to head along the Stutton road towards Holbrook. It's somewhere off to the left. He said there should be notices.'

'Or we could take the more scenic route under the Orwell Bridge - approach from the Holbrook end and follow the road towards Stutton.'

'Whichever – you choose. You're driving.'

Clive started the car, grated the gears into first and drew away with a jolt. 'I don't drive this yellow peril often enough,' he murmured. She winced, but from there on, it was nothing but seamless gear changes as they glided through Woolpit and onto the A14. Was he making a point? She wasn't sure, and rested back, letting the air blow across her face, pat and ruffle her tee-shirt and tug at her hair. But something else bugged her. It had been niggling through the weekend. She worked up to her question.

'Talking about chocolates this morning reminded me of something you said earlier in the week.' She raised her voice against the wind noise. Had he heard her?

'Clive? You said, when we were eating those Dutch chocolate truffles you'd hidden on the high shelf in the kitchen… you said something about the organised crime unit. I'm sure you said you'd been talking to them. Has anything come of it?'

He didn't answer, but she knew he'd caught her words by the way he raised one eyebrow.

'Well,' she ploughed on, 'I was thinking, if that poor chap had a fork sticking out of his chest, was it meant as a message for someone, like the paint-curing oven was a message?'

'What? Chrissie, sometimes I wonder if you ever let your mind relax. Just let go. You should try it once in a while. People have gardening accidents all the time and the equipment involved makes it sound melodramatic. It doesn't automatically mean someone's leaving a message.'

They drove in silence for a few miles before he added, 'But you're right. I did say something about the organised crime division. As it happens, they are interested, but so far it's all been a bit one sided. They get to hear everything from me but I don't get much back from them. Although I must say they seemed very keen to identify the garden fork victim.'

'So you still don't know who he is?'

'We're checking the usual things – the fingerprint database, dental records, missing persons and Interpol.'

‘And?’

‘So you have to remember the organised crime squad are into surveillance and undercover work. They’re a secretive lot at the best of times, gathering info from all over the place and then collating. It’s all about a bigger picture.’

‘And you’re just a small cog.’

‘Thank you, Chrissie.’ He sounded light, relaxed. She guessed it meant he wasn’t totally in the dark over his case.

With a flash of clarity she understood. He knew far more than he was willing to tell. His reaction smacked of the secretive, undercover style of the investigation unit he’d been so at pains to describe.

While Chrissie wrestled with Clive’s real meaning, the TR7 ran smoothly, eating the miles as Clive followed the A14. They skirted Ipswich and left the dual carriageway to drive under the Orwell Bridge. It made Chrissie feel very small, like a tiny creature passing into a gigantic open-sided concrete chamber, its supports soaring forever upwards to where the roadway spanned high above them in the sky. It held her for a moment, and then they were through, tracking the River Orwell before peeling off to head south to Alton Water.

‘Hey, there’s a notice for the charity swim. We carry on this way.’ She pointed across Clive as they drove through Holbrook and down the short sharp incline to the old mill house and then up the other side.

They followed the notices and turned onto a narrow road leading to the reservoir and the parking areas near the water sports and visitor centres. The air was filled with excitement as loudspeakers called the half-mile swim entrants to make their way to the start point.

'Come on Clive, it's about to begin. Meet me near the start point.' She left him to lock the car while she hurried past families with dogs on leads and straggling children. She joined the general flow as everyone headed for the water's edge and the grass expanse in front of the sports centre. Swim entrants were obvious in bright coloured swim hats and wet suits. Some looked ready for the water while others strolled with a nonchalant air, their wet suits only half on, the top-parts left to hang around their knees. A large knot had formed in front of the registration gazebo and more were clustering near the start point.

It took Chrissie a moment to take it all in. Her focus was on the two slipways into the water. She guessed they'd been constructed for launching the small dinghies she'd noticed stowed in rows near the sports centre building. Today, they were obviously doubling for the swimmers' entry and exit from the water. One slipway had banners saying START and the other FINISH.

'I suppose that must be the swimmers' route,' Clive said, slipping his arm around her and pointing across the water.

'What? Hey you startled me. You mean those buoys out on the water?'

'Yes.'

A series of large white buoys floated at intervals out on the water. She imagined a line connecting them and pictured a simple circuit. They were certainly easier to link than the Great Bear constellation. Just as well for the swimmers, she thought.

'I overheard someone say the five kilometre swim is three times around. The half-mile isn't even once. They cut out those distant five buoys.' Clive slipped his backpack off and pulled out his binoculars.

'You're making the half-mile sound almost doable. Hey, let's see if we can find Nick. I reckon he'll be with Jason. Do you know anyone swimming today?'

'Not unless you count Nick. But I thought you said Nick wasn't swimming.' Clive sounded distracted; his binoculars were set on the distant shore.

'He isn't. It's Jason, the drummer. Come on, they'll be near the start slipway.'

She led and Clive followed as she elbowed and dodged through the crowd. 'Hi, Jake!' She waved at the band's guitarist.

'Chrissie! It's crazy. It'll settle down once they're in the water.'

'Have you seen, Nick?'

'Yeah, somewhere over that way.' He gestured behind, further along the grassy area.

'Thanks.'

*Will the half-mile swimmers with registration numbers one to ten come to the start, please*, the loudspeaker boomed. Chrissie sensed the growing excitement as an inflatable dinghy positioned itself beyond the third buoy, the cut off point for the shorter circuit, while a small fleet of marshal and rescue dinghies started to patrol the outer waters.

*Boom!* A starting pistol fired and the first swimmers ran down the slipway and into the water.

The crowd cheered. Water splashed. Arms flailed. Heads wearing red swimming hats bobbed and glided along the water. Chrissie stood with Clive and drank in the atmosphere as the loudspeaker called successive groups of ten to start their swim.

‘I’ve got it now, Chrissie. If you want a yellow swim hat, you’ll have to enter the five K swim. They’ve colour coded the swimmers.’

Yes, but I don’t’ have to complete the five K to get the hat. Just register. Isn’t it exciting? Will you swim next year?’

‘What? Just to get a yellow swim hat? I suppose if you promised to wear it when you’re driving the yellow peril, soft top down–’

‘What?’ She poked him in the ribs. He turned to escape. She gave chase through the crowd and caught him in five yards.

‘Hey,’ he said, laughing, ‘did you see the *bicycles for hire* notice? Do you fancy doing a circuit of Alton Water? We can watch the swimmers from the cycle path. What d’you say?’

Twenty minutes later they were on hire bikes and cycling beyond the sports centre and towards the dam. They stopped to take photos of the swim.

‘You can only see about a third of the length of the reservoir from here,’ Clive murmured.

‘Hey, where does the runoff go?’ She peered over the other side of the dam, more interested in the fast flowing weir.

‘Probably to that mill we passed in the car, and then into the Stour.’

‘Right, of course the River Stour, with Harwich at its mouth.’

‘Yes, and kind of also the Orwell. The two rivers join the sea at the same point on the coast. Felixstowe one side, Harwich the other.’

‘So could you get by water from Harwich to here?’

‘It would have to be at high tide. Holbrook Bay is mainly mud flats. And you’d need something like a small kayak. But it’s not practical. Why would you want to do it?’

‘Just wondering,’ she murmured.

‘You could likely make it up the Stour and to Flatford Mill, and as far as Sudbury, though.’

They rode on, following the path as it skirted the shoreline. The loudspeaker blared in the distance as the sound of cheering travelled across the water. ‘It’s surprising how difficult it is to locate the exact spot where the sound comes from,’ she said as Clive stopped to get out his binoculars and study the opposite shore.

‘Yes, that’s an interesting point,’ he said.

‘Is that where the body repair unit is?’

He didn’t answer. They cycled on, but minutes later he stopped to take photos, mainly of the opposite shore. She sensed not to ask questions and concentrated on the views of the water instead.

It took them the best part of an hour, cycling along tarmac and in places, dirt track, before Chrissie recognised somewhere.

‘Hey, this is familiar. We’re passing the car park where Ron picked me up.’

‘Right, so we should be coming to where you found the chocolate wrappers.’

‘Yes, if I can find the spot again. It’s a big reservoir, Clive. What did they say at the hire place? 11 kilometres to cycle around?’

Memories of the drive from the ferry and Clive taking the call from DS Stickley flooded back. The awful empty end-of-holiday feeling was real again. She’d followed a narrow footpath through clumps of hairy-stemmed meadow cranesbill and down to the water's edge.

'Watch out for a narrow dirt footpath crossing the main track. There should be some clumps of purple-blue wild flowers. Oh yes, and nettles,' she shouted as she relived the fateful morning.

'Hey, do you mean these?' Clive called back over his shoulder.

She caught up with him. The thicket of hawthorn blocking the view of the water seemed familiar.

'What have you seen?'

He dismounted and bent to study something. She slid from her bicycle and focussed on what had caught his attention; the trodden broken stems of some knee-high purple-blue flowers. There was something else. A barely discernable compacted earth path, more like something worn by animal tread than a walker's boot. It headed from the side of the tarmac cycle path track and off towards the shoreline. She pushed at a low blackthorn branch, saw the nettles beyond and then a splash of the delicate purple-blue flowers, in pairs on tall stems and with jagged green leaves lower down. 'Meadow cranesbill,' she murmured. 'This is the way.'

She took the lead, pushing her bike ahead and then laying it on its side against a shrubby elm. 'Better leave the bikes here. They'll be safer. No one'll see them from the cycle path.'

She pressed on, and just as before, an unbroken view of Alton Water opened in front of her. 'Wow,' she said and sat on the old fallen tree trunk.

'What an amazing spot,' Clive said and perched next to her.

'It all looks so untouched. Are you sure the SOC team

and your sergeant came and checked this out?'

'Well, Stickley took some photos with his phone. He said he'd had a nose around and thought it was just somewhere people came to pee. There wasn't enough to justify the SOC team.'

'I don't get the smell of pee, and I don't see old paper tissues. That's usually the give-away.'

Clive stood up and moved slowly, eyes on the ground and visually raking to the right and left. He followed the path as it opened out and sloped gently to the water. Chrissie watched him from the tree trunk. His whole manner had changed. He was in sleuthing mode with binoculars trained on the far shoreline and phone snaps taken in panoramic view.

'So, what do you think?' she asked eventually.

'What do you hear and what can you see across the water?'

'Nothing very much.'

'Exactly. This is a very private place. Sheltered, secluded and with no overlooking habitation.'

'Can you see the car body repair unit from where you're standing, Clive?'

'No, but I can see the top of some kind of pipe or flue over there. I'm guessing it's related to the clean air ventilation system for the paint spray booth.'

'So what do you know about the car body repair unit?'

'It's part of a chain. You wouldn't guess it from the names, but they're all owned by one person.'

'And this one, what will happen to this one here?'

'It's still closed. The cars waiting to be repaired have been moved to one of their outlets in Hadleigh and the people who investigate workplace accidents are crawling all over the oven paint-curing unit.'

'And what's happened to the men working at this one, here?'

'There are only a couple of blokes. They've been interviewed and had all the background checks, but there's nothing to link them to Juliette Poels. We held them for as long as we could without charging them, but we couldn't find anything, so we've had to let them go.'

'But they must be involved in some way, Clive.'

'You'd think so, but Juliette's car had no damage and had never been repaired or re-sprayed. And there's no evidence she'd ever been to the unit before.'

'Then there has to be someone or something else common to Juliette and one or both of the blokes.'

'And that's the tedious part. We're going through all the names and registrations of customers and cars over the past few months. It's a lot to check out.'

'Sounds like you need the equivalent of the Facebook feature – *people you may know*. A list comes up based on your friends' friends, or people who went to the same school.'

'Hmm.'

'So, what's happened to them in the meantime?'

'They're swelling the workforce over at the Hadleigh unit. But don't worry, we're keeping an eye on them. Right? Back to the cycle path and the last couple of kilometres.'

'OK.' She stood up stiffly, reluctant to end the talk about the car body repair unit. She caught his glance. 'Was it only a week ago we drove back from the ferry?' she said mildly.

'Hmm, it's been a hell of a week. Now come on, back to

the bikes.' He led the way.

Minutes later they were pedalling along the cycle path.

# CHAPTER 12

Nick sat with Jake on the grass, enjoying the sunshine and watching the swimmers out on Alton Water. Heads in yellow swim hats bobbed in the distance as the 5 K participants swam from buoy to buoy circuiting the longer course.

'Hey, only a couple of stragglers wearing red hats left in the water, now. Much longer and someone'll have to go and fish 'em out,' Jake murmured.

'Well at least Jason is round and out. Any idea what time he did it in?'

'Not sure. Hey, did Chrissie find you?'

'No I haven't seen her. S'pose we better finish setting up. Jason may need some help with his drums. Come on, the barbecue starts in about an hour.'

A gazebo had been erected with a back but no front or side panels, and a low platform placed inside. It gave the band a stage to play on and a shady area to set their speakers, amplifiers and instruments. It all backed onto the dinghy storage area and was conveniently near enough to run some electric cables from the sport centre building.

'It seems Denton's found his level,' Jake said as they ambled over. He was playing on keyboard, left of stage, while a handful of fascinated young kids listened from the grass, the musical spectacle easier to follow than the swimmers in the distant water.

It felt effortless as Nick slipped into his pre-gig routine of sound checks and voice warm ups with Denton's harmonies. He relaxed. Last minute nerves evaporated.

'Hey, anyone want swim goggles?' Adam threw a

selection on top of the huge bass speaker. Nick grabbed a pair and slung them carelessly around his neck. He'd already found and discarded a sun-bleached cork panel floatation aid abandoned amongst the dinghies. For a crazy moment he'd reckoned it might work as a sloppy open jacket to wear for the gig. Then he'd caught the smell and tossed it back to lie where it had lain for months. Enough identifying with the event, swim goggles would suffice.

They ran through the hastily penned *Give me Flippers*, rolled it into the first number when no one was really listening, and then played it for real at the start of the second set. When it was four o'clock and time to end, shouts of 'Give me flippers,' landed it as the encore. The feeling of goodwill was electric.

They took their time packing up. Nick felt great. The crowd was happy, kids had bopped and arm-waved, parents had smiled and clapped. It was very different to their usual type of venue, not the cool image of the pub bar, nightclub or private function. But a charity event held some kudos and he suspected the *Give me Flippers* number almost guaranteed a return invitation. He'd noticed some faces amongst the jostle. Chrissie and Clive had waved in the second set, and there'd been a cute group of girl swimmers, students from the University of East Anglia, judging by the UEA tee-shirts clinging to their wetsuits.

*Ping!* A text alert focussed his thoughts. 'What?' he breathed, reading the text ID. Gacela?

He opened her message. *Hi! Do u want to meet for cocktails, 7:30pm, Sandlings Bar – Ipswich harbour front?*

Did she mean today? In a couple of hours? Cocktails? It sounded crazy, but he supposed it was just her style. Without really thinking he texted, *Do u mean today?*

*Yes*, came the reply. *OK*, he answered.

'You look as if you've had a shock. Is something up?' Jake asked.

'No, no. It's just a bit sudden, that's all. I need to get back, freshen up. Seems I have a date! Let's get the car loaded.'

He didn't know what he felt. Excitement, anticipation? But then she'd had that effect on him when they'd met just over a week ago.

•••

Matt waited on his scooter near the bus stop at the side of the car park. It was almost five thirty. He felt hot and eased his helmet off to allow the bright Bank Holiday sun dry his sweaty head. The distant drone of traffic on the A14 merged with his thoughts as warmth radiated from the sea of tarmac at his feet. He reckoned he had a few minutes to cool off while the sweat evaporated. Of course he'd need to don his helmet again. He knew that, but at least he could enjoy the freedom for a few minutes.

He recognised Gacela's pale blue Fiat 500 as it turned off the slip road and into the car park. It was quite distinctive as it approached; a glossy pastel bug on wheels. He waved. He could have spotted it anywhere.

Gacela drew up in the bus lane. The passenger door flew open and Maisie tumbled out, her blonde hair a riot of wisps and curls. She hugged a basket-bag along with her bundled up silky-black bomber jacket.

'Hi Mais,' he said as the vision of her dressed in all-black waitressing trousers and blouse approached.

He glanced at the Fiat again. He was curious. He'd barely caught a clear view of Gacela's face when he'd dropped Maisie in the car park earlier that day. She'd called something through the window to Maisie, but he'd been wearing his helmet and all he'd really taken on board was a girl with luscious dark brown hair. This time his view was better, and he held it square. Gacela stared back. For a second she seemed to appraise him, and then she looked away, checked her rear view mirror, indicated and moved smoothly back onto the slip road. So what had just passed between them? It certainly wasn't a smiling hello. He reckoned he probably wasn't her type.

'Well, how'd it go? Were it alright?' he asked, turning his attention back to Maisie.

'Yeah, but I'm starvin' an' I'm parched.'

'Didn't you like any of their fancy grub then?'

'Yeah, it smelled amazin' but the staff aint allowed it. See the customers 'ave paid for it and well, there weren't nothin' left over. I don't count fancy bread. Yuk!'

'But that's why you took your basket-bag thing. Like a doggy bag, right? Honest Mais, I thought you'd bring somethin' back.'

She hopped up behind him on his scooter. He drove slowly out of the car park, around the mini roundabout at its entrance and headed for the drive-through burger bar, a stone's throw away. They sat on the closely-cut grass near the mini roundabout and downed huge paper cups of iced cola and munched on burgers topped with extra cheese.

'So what's this Kinver Greane bloke like, Mais?'

'I don't know, he weren't there. Just some guy called Leon. You should've seen him slice a tomato. Like them TV chefs.'

'I thought Kinver were the chef.'

'Well he weren't today. I didn't get to ask, Matt. It were full on. No time for natterin'. And then all the clearin' away. Hey you try washin' those big pans sometime.'

'So did you spend the whole time in the kitchen?'

'A fair bit. Chef needed me helpin' with platin' up. He said I were neat with me hands. Yeah, I learnt to fan out carrots, make a plate look cute.'

Matt tried to picture a cute plate, gave up and moved onto safer ground. 'So what's this Gacela bird like?'

'She were real friendly in the car. Askin' me about what I done in the past. Yeah, and she wanted to know about Nick. I told her the band were playin' the charity swim gig today. I reckon she fancies him.'

'So what she say about herself, Mais?'

'Er… not much. I s'pose I were doing most the talkin'.' Maisie giggled, a self-indulgent *well you know me* kind of giggle.

'And Sophie Hyphen? Did you talk to the boss?'

'Might've. Just to say hi. Yeah, she were OK. Why all the questions?'

'No reason. Just hearin' about your day, Mais.'

'Ah, you're real nice.' She poked him affectionately in the ribs.

They ate and drank in silence for a few moments while Matt sifted through all she'd said. Something peeved him. It was no good; he was going to have to say.

'I'd hoped you'd get some of them fancy chocolates. Bring some back for me. Mais.'

'Yeah, well it were a bit hot an' melty, but the one I managed to snitch were amazin'. Sorry, Matt. I'll try for you next time.'

'Next time? So you workin' for them again, Mais?'

'Yeah, you bet.'

•••

Nick scanned the tables outside the cocktail bar. Bottle green umbrellas cast long soft shadows in the early evening sun while drinkers in jeans and summer-prints talked, laughed and sipped from glasses decked with fruit and mint leaves. The view was equally vibrant looking away from the tables and across the narrow road, with its low brick wall tracing the quayside. It transported him over the waterfront, the surface of the River Orwell reflecting a muddy blue sky with glinting surface highlights. The word Mediterranean sprang to mind. It was how he imagined it would feel; yachts, marina, sunshine and an outside table and drinks.

He'd never visited the Mediterranean. It was something on his to-do list, and the thought distracted him as he walked through the open door into the body of the cocktail bar. He spotted Gacela immediately. She sat on a tall stool close to the counter, her attention seemingly focussed on the bartender. Nick hesitated, an arm's length away.

'Hi, Nick,' she said, her interest barely wavering from the cocktail being mixed.

He was quick to pick up the signals. She might have made the first move with her invitation text, but he guessed she was telling him not to read anything into it. Except… she'd obviously been watching for him, her eye on the mirror behind the counter.

'Hiya, Gacela. Great idea - cocktails to end a Bank Holiday weekend. What are you drinking?'

'A Cosmo.' She maintained eye contact with the mirror as she spoke.

The bar tender smiled, removed the mixer-shaker cap with a twist, and lined up a cocktail glass on the counter. Next, with an imagined drumroll filling the dramatic pause, he poured cranberry coloured liquid into the cocktail glass with the flourish of a magic trick.

'It looks amazing,' Nick murmured.

'It is. Would you like a Cosmopolitan as well, sir?'

'No. I think... a Black Russian, and with plenty of crushed ice, please.' Nick hoped he sounded spontaneous, hadn't given himself away. But after Gacela's text, he'd had time to look up some cocktails and think them through. He'd rehearsed in his mind what to choose. A Black Russian – iced black coffee and vodka, served in a stocky tumbler glass and no surprises.

They carried their drinks outside and sat at a table under one of the bottle green umbrellas.

'So what've you been doing today?' she asked.

'Catching the sun and supporting a charity swim over at Alton Water with the band. How about you?'

'I guess it was ideal weather for open water swimming,' she murmured.

'Awesome. But you haven't said. About your day?'

'Me? Just the usual - carrying trays and plates, serving food, watching people getting steadily pissed while I'm slowly dying for a drink. So, as I see it, when I finally get a drink I say, "make it a good one".' She raised her glass to emphasise her point.

'Cheers,' he murmured and lifted his glass, caught her intense scrutiny and smiled. It felt odd. Normally a full-on gaze would have been an invitation, an unspoken lure. But this was different. The sexual chemistry was missing. Well not exactly missing, but there was something else to read behind those beautiful brown eyes. What was it? Slightly nonplussed he murmured, 'Where was your do, today?'

'A lunch party over in Wickham Market.'

There, she'd done it again, slightly obtuse, but at least this time she'd answered his question. He was intrigued.

'Tell me about it.'

'The lunch party or Wickham Market?'

'The lunch party, of course. I've driven through Wickham Market loads of times to get to the A12 and up the coast, that's if I'm coming cross country from Barking Tye.'

'So what's at Barking Tye?'

'My parents. Now come on, I've answered your question. Are you going to answer mine? About your lunch do?' He kept his words feather light, expecting a rush of irritation, but all he detected were smile lines near her eyes as she conceded he'd scored a point. He liked this girl, so refreshingly different to the groupies following the band.

While she told him about the venue with its sprawling thatched house, large lawns and marquee, he let his gaze drift across her dark maroon painted toe nails and minimal strappy sandals.

'Yes,' she said, breaking from her thread, 'when you've been on your feet waitressing all day in black pumps and sub-Saharan heat....' She wiggled her toes. 'Freedom, escape. They've earned it,' she murmured.

He laughed. He would have laughed at anything she'd said, even if it was only remotely funny. Perhaps it was just the vodka kicking in.

'Did they have music at the do? A band?'

'It was a sixtieth celebration. Very smart, Nick.'

'Are you implying a band would have lowered the tone?' He let amusement leach through his words as he played the indignation line.

'Well of course if your band had been available, perhaps

they'd have had a band.'

'Hmm, but we'd have still turned them down. I mean, the pull of Alton Water. It would have been no contest.'

'Posh parties do drugs too, you know. Probably more so.' It sounded like a throwaway line, but it jarred.

'What?'

She didn't answer, just avoided his surprise as she sipped her Cosmopolitan.

'Are there a lot of drugs at your catering gigs?' he asked, hoping to shift the focus back onto her.

'Well you were there last week at Freston. What did you notice?'

'You mean apart from you? I'm afraid I'm not into the drug scene, so unless it's obvious, I tend not to see it. How about you?'

Again she didn't answer.

'How about you, Gacela? Are you into the drug scene?' It was important, he had to know.

'I might have sampled once or twice in the past, but that's all history, a long, long time ago. Hey, you must have seen that guy with the party pills? I'm guessing ecstasy. I assumed he was with your band.'

'What? A dealer attached to our band? Well you can shelve that notion straight away. We're not big enough. We don't have roadies, technicians, backstage crew – just a few fans and a website. We're too small to draw the dealers and pushers.' He held her glance as he spoke.

'Good, because this is what I enjoy, Nick.' She sipped her Cosmo, 'a drink in good company at the end of a heavy day.'

'Cheers! I'll drink to that.' He raised his glass. Was she saying he was simply good company? What about a hint of something a little more intimate on the horizon? Of course being cast as a pot-smoking, crack cocaine-addicted singer or dealer would have been worse. At least he counted as good company. He guessed he should be grateful for that for the time being. But it set him thinking.

'Now, why are you frowning?' she asked.

'I was thinking about the rest of the band; we all drink too many beers sometimes, but nothing more. I don't think anyone even smokes weed.'

'You don't have to smoke it, you know.'

'I know, but–'

'You should take a trip to Amsterdam. They sell weed in all sorts of things. Quite openly. Cakes, biscuits, chocolate.'

'Hair shampoo?'

'No I think it's caffeine in hair shampoo.'

This time they both laughed and he sensed a subtle change in the way she sat. He let his eyes play across her and noticed the tension ease from her shoulders.

The fine silver chain hanging around her neck trailed a bunch of charm-like silver dragonflies, enamelled blackberries and leaves. He asked her about the significance of them, how she'd come by the necklace, about herself and her ambitions - but she fenced and dodged with her words as she spoke, never answering fully. She talked. Certainly she talked, but somehow he was always left with a feeling of mystery and wanting to know more.

'What do you do when you're not waitressing? Any other jobs?' he asked.

'Oh you know, a bit of this and a bit of that. How about you? Have you always wanted to work with wood?'

She seemed genuinely interested, encouraging him to tell her about himself. But when he got back to the subject of her, asking a simple *where do you live* was answered with, ‘I live in Ipswich. How about you, Nick?’

So by the end of the evening he’d told her about his early ambitions, how he’d dropped out of an Environmental Sciences degree at Exeter University, and his passion for carpentry. But what did he know about her? Not an awful lot, just the certainty that he wanted to see her again.

‘Hey, it’s been a great evening,’ he said.

‘We must do this again.’

‘Yeah, I’ll check when I’ve some gigs but are you OK for something mid-week?’

‘You never know, your gigs and my events might match, like the Freston gig. Let me know your timetable and then I can tell you.’

She hadn’t said, *and I’ll let you know my timetable*, but he wasn’t going to quibble. It was better than a vague *I’ll text you.* He reckoned, all things considered, the evening had gone well. He had a feeling he wasn’t going to be the one doing all the running.

# CHAPTER 13

Matt stared at his computer screen. It was weird. The whole Bank Holiday thing had put his week out of kilter. It might be Tuesday morning, the day after the Bank Holiday Monday, but to him it felt like a Monday, the first working day of his week. He sat in the cramped Balcon & Mora office, his back to Damon and searched for the contact details he needed in order to trace the names on his list. His search routine was beginning to sooth while a sense of order cloaked him as he worked.

*Beep-itty-beep! Beep-itty-beep beep!* The ringtone cut through the whirr of fans cooling the hard drives stacked under the desk. He reached for his mobile just as Damon said, 'No personal calls.'

'Yeah I know, Damon.' He checked the caller ID. It was Clive. Onto me already? Bloggin' hell! 'Hi,' he murmured into his phone, already self-conscious.

'Good morning, Matt. Just a quick de-brief report. How did Maisie fare at Hyphen & Green yesterday? Any feedback on Kinver Greane?'

'Yeah well, she said there weren't no Kinver Greane. Some bloke called Leon were doin' the cookin'.'

'Leon? Leon who?'

'I dunt know. She dunt say. But it seems 'e sliced a tomato like a right professional.'

'Hmm, and what else did she tell you?'

'Not much. She got all scammy when I kept askin' her 'bout stuff. Can't we just tell her she's like, under cover? It'd be a lot easier if she knew. Then she'd ask what you want.'

‘No Matt. We’ve been through this already. Maisie is safer if she doesn’t know. And besides, we’ve no proof there’s anything suspicious about Hyphen & Green. She’s not officially an informant. This is just a situation that’s arisen, an opportunity too good to pass up. Do you understand? Now tell me, will she be working for them again? Where and when is their next event?’

‘I dunt think to ask. But she forwarded me her first email from ’em, so if they send any more, I’ll send ’em on to you as well. That’s if you give me your email address.’

‘Excellent idea, Matt. And don’t forget, let me know if she tells you anything more, anything at all.’

‘What? You mean stuff like the chocolates were awesome?’

‘No, Matt. I don’t need to know things like *the chicken liver parfait with fig jam on a brioche canapé* was delicious. OK?’

‘Right.’

‘Good. Thanks Matt.’ The call ended.

Silence settled on the office. For a moment it weighed heavy, compressing the warm air and adding to the sudden feeling of claustrophobia. Matt, uncomfortable and troubled, laid his mobile on the desk. It was one thing to play at covert police operations and MI5-type surveillance, but having DI Clive Merry breathing down your neck was distinctly unnerving. And another thing, what the scammin’ hell was a parfait?

‘What was that about?’ Damon’s voice broke into his thoughts. ‘Hey Matt? Are you listening? Who were you talking to just now?’ An unmistakable edge had crept into the words.

‘It were Clive. DI Clive Merry.’

'What? The police? Are you in some kind of trouble?'

'Nah, I don't think so.'

'So what's it about, then? You did what I asked and dropped the Hyphen & Green investigation you started on Friday, didn't you? Juliette Poels, the murdered waitress worked for them, remember? Hey, why are you getting calls from the police? This sort of thing is exactly why I didn't want to expand the scope of our searches.'

Matt bit his lip. How much to say?

'Come on, Matt. You're going to have to tell me. What the hell's going on?'

'Well, after I left here on Friday, I went to what I thought were John Brown's address. But it weren't.'

'Who's John Brown? Remind me.'

'One of the directors, nah that's wrong, one of the ex-directors of Hyphen & Green.'

'Ah yes. But I'd told you to drop the investigation. How is going to someone's address an internet based search, Matt? Or am I missing something here?' His tawny-coloured eyes hardened as he spoke.

Matt's world began to spiral. He felt hot and sick. He knew if he stopped telling now, he'd never get started again. He plunged on.

'He were dead in his shed on his garden allotment, Damon. See I found him… dead. Lyin' there. An' that's when I rang Clive. I thought he were more into dead bodies than you.'

'What? You found John Brown dead? Are you sure? But this is horrible. Are you OK, Matt?'

'Yeah, I reckon so. Should I have rung you as well?'

'What? No, at least….' Damon turned his attention back to his keyboard and screen, clicked on his news feeds and read out, '*The body of a man discovered on Friday on garden allotments near Compiegne Way in Bury St Edmunds has still not been identified. The police have established that the body had lain concealed for several weeks. The death is still being treated as suspicious.* So that was you, right? This is a report about the body you found?'

'Yeah.'

'But I thought you said it was John Brown. Why haven't they named him?'

'I don't know.'

'So what did Clive want to know when he rang you just now? Who was the "she" you kept mentioning?'

'Please, Damon… slow down, will you? It's doin' me head in.' With a throat like sandpaper and a glue stick for a tongue, emotion took the day. His voice broke, 'See Maisie, me girlfriend, well she landed herself that waitressin' job. Remember me tellin' you about the phone call when they asked if she were a reporter?'

'Oh yes. So she got the job with Hyphen & Green, did she?'

'Yeah.' Matt rocked forwards, his head in his hands. He had Clive on his back, Damon on his case, and the vision of a garden fork sticking out of a man's chest spinning in front of his eyes.

'OK – coffee break. Yeah, I know you don't want a coffee, but I need one. Have some water or chocolate milk. Alright, Matt?'

While Damon fussed with the kettle and a jar of instant coffee, Matt tried to marshal his thoughts and corral them into compartments. He was grateful for the bottled water, his insides were churning too fast for chocolate milk.

'Right!' Damon said, settling into his office chair and

leaning back on the worn faux-leather. 'We're not a detective agency and we're definitely office based. But if the police won't pull your girlfriend off the case, and judging from the half of the conversation I overheard, she can't be told what's really going on, then I can't see any alternative but for you to follow her.'

'What?' Matt couldn't believe his ears.

'I think you should get on that scooter of yours and follow where she's going when she's waitressing. You need to make sure she doesn't end up in a car paint-curing oven, like that poor girl, Juliette Poels.'

'What? But I don't know how to track her when she's on the move, Damon. I'd rather do more online investigatin' of Kinver Greane and Sophie Hyphen.'

'No, Matt. I've already told you to drop the Hyphen & Green investigation. I expect the police are already questioning Kinver and Sophie. But following your girlfriend, unless she realises and objects, won't be stepping on anyone's toes, OK?'

'But–'

'No, Matt. You ignored me on Friday when I said to drop the Hyphen & Green investigation, and look what happened? You found a dead body.'

'Yeah but… so how'd I do this followin' or trackin' business, then?'

'Ah, now that's the interesting bit,' Damon laughed, 'we'll have to give that some thought.'

Matt swigged a mouthful of the bottled water. So what had just happened? Damon had been cross. It had been bad, but he hadn't sacked him. So it was OK. And now, Damon had just said *we'll* have to give that some thought. Matt reckoned he wouldn't have said *we* unless he meant it.

Damon didn't say things he didn't mean.

'So Damon, are we good now? Are *we* OK, again?' Matt asked, just to get it straight in his mind.

'Yeah, but lay off Hyphen & Green.'

It was a big ask. 'Hmm, OK, Damon.' But Matt knew he had one more trick up his sleeve; he could always do his online investigation of Kinver and Sophie using the Utterly Academy computers. He'd have to wait a week or two until the term started, but at least by then the dust would have settled.

'Hey, there's a news update,' Damon said, his eyes on his computer screen. 'I'm sending the link across to you.'

'What?' Matt read the webpage. *The police have identified the man found dead on Friday 23rd August 2013 on garden allotments near Compiegne Way in Bury St Edmunds. He is Dutch and has been named as Kinver Greane, a 38 year old part-time chef. It is understood that the police would like to interview a 22 year old man called John Brown as they believe he may be able to help them with their inquiries.*

'Scammin' hell,' Matt muttered.

# CHAPTER 14

Chrissie stood back to survey her work. She'd spent the past half hour trying to detach the bun foot from its turned wooden leg, the one on the Dutch games table with the broken dowel and swivel mechanism. It should have allowed the leg support to swing out to hold up the unfolded table top, but the stretcher and leg were damaged and the dowel fractured. She'd tried to ease the bun foot off by driving a slim wooden wedge into the gap below the swivel joint, but without success.

'Looks like I'm going to have to use a coping saw,' she murmured. Despite a faint movement of air from the open workshop door, it felt hot and oppressive as she walked past the thickness planer to the rack on the far wall. Various clamps and saws hung from it, and she selected a small frame saw with a fine replaceable blade. She pressed the blade sideways, testing the tension with her thumb. Yes, its teeth were pointing in the direction she wanted, right for cutting on the push stroke, not the pull. Satisfied, she held it up to her eye, looked along its length and gauged its alignment. 'Good.'

It would do the job.

She positioned the table so that it lay on the workbench exactly as she wanted, and then secured and protected the leg in the bench clamp. Holding her breath, she made careful, steady cuts in the narrow space above the bun foot.

'Yes!' Finally she'd made the last saw cut through the dowel.

'Well done, Mrs Jax. I wondered how you were going to do that. Not easy to keep the leg steady. If you'd had the table standing up on the workbench, its weight would have born down and made the saw cuts virtually impossible.'

'That's what I reckoned as well, Mr Clegg. Luckily I've had time to think about it over the weekend.' She held the bun foot up like a trophy, the wooden barn the auditorium for some gladiatorial struggle.

'I thought you were making chocolate.'

'Well that's what I'd hoped. And at least I made some progress on the chocolate front over the weekend.' She caught his frown and pressed on, 'You see I decided to drive up to Cambridge. There's an amazing specialist chocolate shop there. They gave me loads of advice and… well I thought I'd start by buying the basics and see how I got on.'

'Sounds sensible, Mrs Jax. So have you made any basic chocolate?'

'Ah, a bit of a change of plan, Mr Clegg. I spent yesterday cycling around Alton Water with Clive and watching a charity open water swim. So there wasn't any time for making chocolate. I've still got the paraphernalia all over my kitchen.'

'Alton Water? Wasn't that where the car body repair and paint sprayer was?'

He didn't actual say *the dead woman*, but Chrissie knew exactly what Ron meant and by implication, a whole lot more.

'Yes, and don't say it, the day wasn't a total off-duty experience for Clive.'

'What was he looking for?'

'I'm not entirely sure.' She could have added that she'd been thinking about little else. And if she was brutally honest, Clive's focus hadn't been on her, or hearing about her foray into the world of chocolate. He'd been impatient to get to Alton Water and its shoreline, particularly the waterfront on the same side as the murder.

'I'm guessing he had concealment, secret places and rendezvous on his mind,' she said under her breath. She wasn't going to admit he hadn't told her.

'You look very thoughtful, Mrs Jax.'

'Hmm.'

'Let me give you a hand slipping that stretcher off the broken dowel.'

They worked together, barely needing to speak as they moved the stretcher, rotating its cracked tongue around the dowel and lining it up with its neighbour's undamaged tongue above. 'It's a bit like a corner halving joint, Chrissie murmured, while Ron held it steady and she gave it a judicious tap with the wooden mallet. The stretcher eased down off the dowel.

'Neat,' she said.

'Lucky, more like.'

The rest was straightforward. Time flew as she freed the undamaged stretcher by sawing above it through the remaining spike of dowel. After that it was easy to remove the rest of the fractured dowel and drill out where its sawn ends were still buried in the top of the bun foot and the base of the table leg.

'Tea, Mrs Jax?' Ron's voice blended with her thoughts.

'What? Oh yes, that's a good idea. She put down her tools, and turned her hand to teabags and pouring boiling water.

'I'm going to use teak to make the new dowel. Teak rubbing on teak will probably wear best, don't you think. Mr Clegg?'

‘I reckon so.’

She sipped her tea and let her mind run on. Of course the repair would make more sense if she tackled the stretcher and leg first. The order mattered. Is that what Clive had been thinking about for most of the Bank Holiday Monday? The sequence of events around the murder?

Without much thought she voiced the question forming on her tongue. ‘If you were going to meet someone near the water’s edge at Alton Water, where would you park your car, Mr Clegg?’

‘Now that’s a strange question. What’s set you thinking about that, Mrs Jax? And anyway, tell me why I’d be meeting someone near the water’s edge.’

‘I don’t know. A spot of fishing, do you think?’

‘Are you allowed to fish there?’

‘I don’t know Mr Clegg. I’d have to check up on that. But say it was night time?’

‘You mean night fishing? Poaching?’

‘Well possibly, but what about something more romantic, or secretive?’

‘Courting? Back in my teens maybe, but I’m a bit out of touch with what the young’uns get up to now, Mrs Jax. You’d have to ask someone else.’

She glimpsed a wistfulness in his eyes as he sipped his mug of tea.

‘This is just theoretical, Mr Clegg, OK?’ she said softly.

‘Well… if we’re talking about near where the murder happened then I think I’d park my van in the car park where I picked you up. There isn’t really anywhere else to park. If it was night time, I suppose I’d stay in the van and wait for whoever I was meeting and then we’d walk to the water’s edge together.’

‘Hmm, except it would have had to be pretty late for it to be dark. The evenings are still light until close on nine o’clock. Hey, did you notice any signs saying if they close that car park at night?’

‘No, I can’t say I did.’

‘Hmm, I guess Clive will know.’

‘But I don’t think I’m following your line of thought. What are you getting at, Mrs Jax?’

‘Well I was thinking about the parking, the sequence of events. As I see it, if Juliette Poels drove to meet someone at a secluded spot near the water’s edge, she’d have had to park somewhere. If it was after the car park gate had been closed, then the track to the car body repair and paint spray place would have been the closest location. I suppose what I’m saying is, what if she wasn’t going to the paint spray place at all, but just happened to use its track as somewhere to park her car?’

She met Ron’s unblinking gaze with her own raised eyebrows and a *how’s that theory sound* kind of a look.

‘You might be right, Mrs Jax, but how can I put it… yes, you wouldn’t ask Clive to tell you how to repair Mrs De Vries’ games table, now would you?’

‘Who said I was going to run this past Clive? It’s still in the early theory stage.’

‘Hmm, but I know what you’re like, Mrs Jax. Once you’ve got the scent of an idea in your nose….’

‘But I’ve learned over the years, Mr Clegg. I know to tread lightly over this kind of thing with Clive. Once I’ve checked if the car park is gated at night, I can drop my theory into the conversation as if, well I can be completely spontaneous and there’ll be no suggestion of meddling.’

‘I don’t know, Mrs Jax. I think you’re asking for

trouble. Stick to what you do well. Solve cabinet restoration problems.'

For a long minute Chrissie struggled with the double edged sword of Ron's advice. So where was the line between mental problem solving and meddling? More to the point, where was Clive's line? Ron might have struck a chord, but it didn't mean she wanted to hear it.

'Hmm,' she sighed by way of an answer.

Before she could make a throwaway comment about how her mind was already working on patch-repairs for the stretcher, and scarfing and turning repairs on the leg, her phone burst into a strident *Brrring brrring!*

'Hey,' she said frowning, as she read Clive's caller ID. It felt spooky, as if she'd summoned him by the power of thought.

'Hi, Chrissie. Everything OK?'

'Yes, all good.' She bit back the *why, shouldn't it be* about to trip off her tongue.

'I've... there've been some developments. A Dutch policeman is coming over from Amsterdam and I'm meeting him at about eight this evening.'

'Really? Where?'

'Martlesham, the investigation unit. The DCI thinks it'll look more impressive than Landmark House or a Premier Inn. So I thought, as I'm going to have to hang around until eight for this meeting... would you like to drive over and we can have a bite to eat beforehand?'

'Well yes, that would be nice, but in Martlesham? Where?'

'I thought the Black Badger. It's the closest pub, and the food's pretty good. It's a regular for our lot. Is that all right?'

'Yes, I suppose so.'

'About six thirty then?'

'Err… a quarter to seven would be better for me.'

'OK, see you then. Bye, Chrissie.'

She glanced up to catch Ron watching her. 'What, Mr Clegg?'

'Nothing. It's just that I know that look, Mrs Jax.'

'I've no idea what you mean,' she murmured. But she guessed it had been written plain across her face. The flash of an idea usually had that effect.

Her plan had taken shape in the moment Clive suggested they meet at six thirty. She reckoned she'd need a little longer if she was going to drive the circuitous route from the workshop to the Black Badger via the Alton Water car park.

'Hmm,' Ron sighed, 'time I got back to work on Mr Hurst's refectory table. Those cupped table top boards aren't going to flatten by themselves.'

•••

Chrissie followed the dual carriageway as it swept across rolling countryside to the east of Ipswich. With the soft top down, the TR7 smoothed at a cool 50 mph. Any more than that, and the turbulence around her head would have been crazy and she wouldn't have been able to think. For once she felt relaxed. Her information gathering mission was complete and she had twenty minutes to find the Black Badger.

'Two birds with one stone,' she murmured as she thought back to the Alton Water car park. A man had been loading his car with a fishing tackle box, sun shade, rod, net and a folding canvas chair as she drew up.

'Does this car park really close at these times?' she'd

asked as she stood next to her TR7 and studied the notice near the open gate. ‘I mean, does someone really come round and close the gate at six o’clock? It’s six now and it’s still open.’

‘I know, it says six on the notice but it’s eight o’clock at this time of year. It used to be dawn to dusk, no overnighters, all on trust and no gate locking. But there’s always someone who has to spoil it for everyone else and over the years there’s been a spot of bother, so now the gate has to be closed overnight.’ The man collapsed his fishing kit trolley and packed it into his car.

‘Any luck today? Did you catch anything?’ Chrissie asked and nodded towards the fishing kit he’d been loading. She reckoned he was likely to be a regular, judging by the way he’d said the bit about there always being one to spoil it for everyone else.

‘Yeah, a few bream – only small ones. There’s not a lot of fishing here, hasn’t been for a few years. But the fish are just starting to appear again. I’ve seen a few carp, and we may get lucky with some roach. The water level’s a bit low at the moment, so round the water’s edge here, it should suit the roach.’

‘Why? What do you mean, it should suit roach?’

‘Roach lay their eggs on willow roots, and there are lots of willow trees around here. With plenty of fry, there’s a chance of more roach next year.’

‘That’s good. Is there any night fishing?’

‘No, and if you’re after large carp, there aren’t any. Really, there aren’t many who fish here, and most of us prefer early morning.’ He’d raised his hand in a half-salute, slammed his car boot shut and got into his car. He’d already driven away by the time she’d realised she hadn’t thought to ask where exactly along the bank he liked to set his rods and fish from. Could it have been the secret place, the one at the end of the hidden path crossing the cycle track?

It was an opportunity missed and she'd mentally kicked herself. Frustrated, she'd juggled the snippets of information as she drove back from Alton Water and crossed over the Orwell Bridge. By the time she cruised along the dual carriageway east of Ipswich, a degree of orderliness had taken hold of her thoughts. Her theories took a firmer shape as she coasted past the imposing telecom research laboratories with their roadside concrete buildings seeming to shriek *keep out*. She turned off a roundabout; an inner calm descended and she headed towards Martlesham Heath and the Black Badger.

She recognised Clive's Ford Mondeo in the narrow parking area to one side of the pub. A board swung from a bracket high on the brick building. The words Black Badger were painted on it, along with a dark four-legged creature with a paler head and charcoal stripe running from nose to ear. She glanced around. No building older than the mid nineteen-seventies met her eye. She tried to imagine it earlier, fifty years back in time. 'All fields or heathland, I suppose,' she sighed as she slipped into the lounge bar.

An overwhelming impression of burgundy upholstered dining chairs placed around dark chunky wooden tables conjured an aura of steak and chips. She glanced across the tables. A handful of people were seated but no one was eating yet. She turned her attention to the less cluttered area near the bar counter - only a few drinkers. She spotted Clive immediately. He must have seen her because he'd slipped partway off his stool and stood, one foot on the busy patterned carpet, the other resting on the barstool stretcher.

'Hi,' he said as she hurried over to him.

He looked cool in a pale short sleeved shirt, unbuttoned at the collar and smart enough to get away without wearing a tie. If there was anything to mark him out as a policeman, it had to be the haircut; short, neat, and only two centimetres longer than an army cut.

'Hi,' she said and kissed him.

'Any problems finding here?'

'No, but it's a bit of a surprise. I thought it would be in the middle of a quaint old village. Nothing looks more than forty years old.'

'It probably isn't. It's a newish development on what used to be an old WWII airfield. And before that I guess it was flat heathland. I think I'm probably sitting in the middle of a runway! What would you like to drink? Your usual?'

'Wow. And yes please, a ginger beer for me. Oh, and with loads of ice in it.'

While Clive caught the barman's attention, Chrissie carried some menu cards to a table.

'So why is someone coming over from Amsterdam to see you?' she asked when he brought over her ginger beer and his pint of ale.

'I don't know if you caught the news this afternoon, but we had a stroke of luck. We've identified the dead man in the garden shed in Bury St Edmunds. He's Kinver Greane, a thirty-eight year old Dutch man.'

'Really? Dutch?'

'Yes, he's known to their police. He's on their computer database. That's how we identified him. Through Europol. But the detective coming across isn't from Interpol or anything fancy. He's from the Korps Nationale Politie and, well it's more about co-operation and sharing information. Kinver was only a small-time criminal with a flair for cooking.'

'Sounds like a lot of fuss over a small-time criminal.'

'Yes, but he was murdered on our patch, remember.'

'So what happens now?'

'I should imagine our Dutch visitor will want to see the body. And of course he'll look at what we've got on the case so far. Hopefully the Korps Nationale Politie won't be able to spare him for any longer than a day or two. After that we can communicate electronically across the North Sea.'

'But have you got anything on him yet, Clive?'

'Oh yes, and this is the good bit, he's worked or been associated with Hyphen & Green for over a year now.'

'What?'

'Hmm, rather a coincidence, winding up dead and working for Hyphen & Green, don't you think?'

'Well yes, when you put it like that. So you think the dead waitress and this Dutch man are somehow connected?'

'Or were killed by the same people. It seems our Dutch friend, when he wasn't cooking, had a record of small-time drug dealing and related theft and assault.'

'What here? In Suffolk?'

'No, back in Amsterdam. I think that's why Europol identified him for us so quickly. But he's been "clean" since he's been over here; or rather he's managed to stay under the radar. Not quite the same thing, I suppose.'

Chrissie turned her attention to the menu card while she absorbed Clive's news. The air in the bar suddenly felt hot and close.

‘And John Brown? How does he fit into it all? You originally thought the dead man was going to be him.’ She spoke as she glanced through the lighter meal options. ‘I think I’ll have the Caesar salad with chicken.’

‘I guess the key question with John Brown is – is he still alive? And is he our killer?’

‘Killer or killed? I thought he’d disappeared. Are you saying he could have been murdered as well, Clive?’

‘Hmm… so you’re having the Caesar salad. I’m going to have… yes, a burger and chips. I’ll go and order.’ His voice sounded tight. The Dutch policeman’s looming visit had racked up the angst. The burger and chips said it all, a comfort food choice.

Chrissie watched Clive return to the counter. He held his back rigid as he walked, but moved his fingers continually, clenching them into a ball, then loosening them, straightening and clenching again. Poor Clive, two bodies delivered to the morgue in less than a week, and an international spotlight on one of them. She determined to be truly empathic, supportive and kind. And then her busy mind took over. What was the motive, she wondered. Was it only about drugs?

‘You’re frowning, Chrissie. Is everything all right?’ She’d barely noticed he’d come back from placing their food order. He slipped a table number sign onto the dark stained wood.

‘I was just wondering, do you have any evidence the waitress or John Brown were into drugs? Was Kinver Greane even still dealing? I know you’re saying drugs could be a motive, but how about a love triangle?’

‘What makes you say that?’

‘Well what if Juliette had gone to Alton Water for a romantic evening? The car park closes at eight o’clock. She might have parked her car on the track to the paint shop repair place, simply as somewhere convenient to park for longer, and then walked down that little path to the water’s edge.’ Chrissie maintained a relaxed tone as she elaborated her theory.

‘Are you talking about the car park the cycle path leads into, not far from the paint spraying unit? Stickley tells me they call it the Wonder car park after the Tattingstone Wonder.’

‘The Tattingstone Wonder?’

‘Yes some crazy folly; a fake tower a farmer built onto his farmhouse years ago. So how do you know when the car park closes?’ Clive’s tone wasn’t exactly sharp, but she heard the warning signs.

‘Ron,’ she lied smoothly. ‘Remember he picked me up from that car park? He’d seen the times on the notice. Winter - nine till four, and summer - eight till six or eight. He said something about it possibly being a bit of a problem for the fishing lot if they wanted a really early morning fish.’

‘Are you saying you think she had someone else in the car with her? John Brown? Or are you suggesting the person she was meeting also drove there, or even cycled there? They don’t close the cycle path, Chrissie.’

‘I-I was just throwing the idea into the pot, that’s all. Was John Brown into drugs?’

‘We’ve spoken to his mother, she’s quite worried about him, hasn’t seen him for weeks, and I believe her. Apparently he’s an asthmatic and she’s anxious he hasn’t got his inhalers with him. As for drugs, there’s no police record and according to his mother, he was too much into healthy food and cooking to take drugs.'

'Hmm, but she could just be saying what she wants to believe.'

'Maybe. She did tell us he'd tried smoking weed when he was about fifteen. It set him wheezing and he needed his inhaler.'

'Yes, I suppose that would put you off, but we're only talking weed. And Juliette, was she into drugs?'

'Not that we know. We're still interviewing her friends and working through the waiters and waitresses on Hyphen & Green's books.'

It felt hopeless. Overwhelming. She groped for something positive. 'Is there anything helpful back from the forensics on Juliette's car or from her biochemistry?'

'The pathologist thinks testing her urine and stomach contents are our best bet. He says she would have been very dehydrated as she heated up and her kidneys as good as shut down for a while before she died. On that reasoning, most of the urine in her bladder will have accumulated from earlier. Later, when her kidneys failed and her cells were dying - sodium, potassium, all sorts would have poured into her blood. Hopefully it hasn't contaminated her urine as much as her blood picture. With any luck her bladder contents might be able to tell us if….'

'If what?'

'If she'd taken Rohypnol, GHB, Ketamine. They're the so called date rape drugs. I know it's horrible but it would have made her more compliant, easier to kill.'

'But that's so premeditated. So evil.' Chrissie suppressed an involuntary shudder.

'Yes, the premeditation aspect is interesting; Juliette's

murder feels very different to Kinver Greane's. He had a garden fork sticking into his chest and there'd been a fight first. The preliminary post mortem findings are bearing that out. More spontaneous, less planned.'

Their conversation died as a lanky teenager hurried from the kitchen and set their plates on the table. Chrissie glanced at her Caesar salad. Sliced chicken fanned across a mountain of torn lettuce leaves. Garlicky sourdough bread croutons peeped from amongst the green while the aroma of olive oil and parmesan tickled her nose. Clive seemed instantly absorbed with his burger and chips. She followed his lead and concentrated on her food. The killings weighing heavy in the air could drift away while the flavours and calories soothed. At least for now.

# CHAPTER 15

It was Wednesday and Nick was surprised he hadn't heard from Chrissie. The last time they'd had a chance to talk freely had been in the Nags Head on the Friday directly before the Bank Holiday weekend, and that was only while they'd bought drinks at the bar. She'd been brimming with questions about the vacuum press and then divulged her chocolate plans, a flurried conversation full of restlessness and turmoil. He'd guessed it was probably a nervous reaction to hearing about Matt's discovery of a body in a garden allotment shed, and to Maisie's excitement about landing a waitressing job with Hyphen & Green. He didn't really count her call inquiring about the Alton Water charity swim the following day as a proper talk. He'd been too taken up at the time with band practice to ask how she really was. And then on Monday, at the Alton Water event, he'd spotted her in the crowd, nothing more. Was she all right?

'Probably busy getting caught up in Clive's case,' he said into his mug of tea.

'What? What you mumbling about?' Dave asked.

They were sitting on some steps in a garden. Midday sun beat down on the pergola arching over them, while climbing roses offered dappled shade as they ate their packed lunches.

'It's nice here. This house, the garden, Nacton. There's a lot of trees. It's kind of hidden, don't you think.' Nick's words seemed to float in the air.

'And the kitchen. Don't forget the kitchen units we've just installed. They're pretty special too. But that isn't what you said just now. You definitely mentioned something about Clive's case.'

'All these ornamental cherry trees… I can see now why they chose cherry for the kitchen units,' Nick persisted, gazing around the garden and trying to throw Dave off the scent.

'Yeah, they've probably got a thing about cherry trees. Now come on, Nick. You were going to find out the latest on the body repair place out near Tattingstone. You know, where that woman was murdered.'

'Hmm, you and your Land Rover friends. You're the automotive equivalent of Twitter.' He caught the smile creasing Dave's ample face. A summer tan blended with his thinning hair and wiped years from the blatantly inquisitive face now studying him.

'So what've you heard? Come on,' Dave asked, impatience oozing from every pore.

How much to tell, Nick wondered. 'Well, Chrissie's my source and she's the one I'm worried about. She was with Clive when he was called to the crime scene. She won't say anything about it because Clive's sworn her to secrecy. But the thing is I think she's struggling to keep cool about it all. I get the bit about her interest in our vacuum press as a distraction, but chocolate making… what's that about? It's weird; not her usual kind of thing. I'm worried she's losing it.'

'Chocolate making? That's comfort food, Nick.'

'Oh yeah, I hadn't thought of that. I s'pose you could be right. Anyway it proves my point. I reckon this paint oven death has got to her. I haven't dared ask how the investigation is going in case she goes all funny on me.'

It wasn't strictly true, but he guessed it was probably

enough to satisfy Dave for the moment. He bit into his cheese and pickle doorstop of a sandwich while Dave concentrated on a ham and mustard roll.

There was something else Nick had been thinking about, but he wasn't ready to share it with Dave. The whole subject was too fresh. He still had reservations about Gacela. She was steadily getting under his skin but he reckoned she only saw him as the singer fronting a band, a one-dimensional bloke. She'd been incredibly curious about him and he'd enjoyed the attention, a sign of her interest and no doubt part of a drug-vetting exercise on her part. But he'd been taken aback by the surprise in her voice when she'd said, 'You mean you really enjoy carpentry and working with wood?'

It was like a challenge, a throwing down of a gauntlet. He'd explained his passion for working with wood. He'd wanted her to share his enthusiasm and appreciate the artistry in exceptional craftsmanship, but he also needed to prove his own skill. Carpentry was the key to who he was and fundamental to where he saw his future. Music was important but it wasn't the thing about him she'd mildly dissed.

A way of impressing Gacela had dawned at some point during the morning. Alfred the foreman had texted to say the French oak for the staircase and bannister rail had just been delivered.

'Seems I'll be back at the workshop after today,' he'd said to Dave.

'Working on the French oak staircase? The key is to get your measurements dead-on accurate.'

Nick knew Dave was right. This was a double-edged opportunity to prove his skill. He needed to impress both

John Willows and the client. He just hoped to God the original measurements for the total staircase rise were accurate. That's when he got his idea. If he wanted to amaze Gacela with his carpentry skills and spark a genuine love of wood, why not make her a stunning gift? How about a wooden trinket box?

'The cottage where you're replacing the rotten stairs is on our route back to the workshop, isn't it? We could drop in on the way and re-measure if you're worried,' Dave had suggested.

# CHAPTER 16

Matt rubbed his eyes. He could tell it was daytime by the sunshine shafting through the thin faded curtains. Still yawning, he reached for his mobile and read the time and date display. *12:16 Wednesday 28 August.*

'Malware,' he groaned. He hadn't meant to sleep right through the morning. He'd anticipated waking at about ten o'clock. 'Malware,' he groaned with deeper conviction and buried his face in his pillow. But with twelve hours' sleep already spent recharging his batteries he wasn't ready to fall into a drifting snooze. Wakefulness ripped through his mind and with it a troubling unease.

'Trojan,' he breathed as he recalled Damon's advice to follow Maisie. That had been yesterday and for the time being he'd shelved the idea. It was easier not to think about the practicalities too deeply, at least not until Maisie emailed him with her waitress bookings. He sighed and let his arm dangle from the side of the bed so that his hand skimmed the threadbare carpet. His fingers brushed across familiar shapes and textures: discarded socks, a cotton tee-shirt, empty lager cans, something smooth slim and rectangular – his laptop. He scooped it up and rolled onto his back, now fully awake. 'Right then, let's see what you got for me.' He flipped up the screen and listened to the bungalow's sounds while the laptop came to life. He reckoned his mum was on the move, judging by the heavy footfall passing his door. He went straight to his emails.

'Glynnis? Now what she want?' He pictured her heavy-framed fashion glasses as he read, *Your paperwork and pass are ready for you to collect. I'll be in my office on*

*Wednesday, Thursday & Friday this week midday – 2pm. We'll be back to normal office hours next week when the Academy term begins on Monday September 2nd 2013. Sorry I wasn't here when you tried to call in last week. Must have just missed you. Glynnis.*

The sound of a toilet flushing diffused from along the hallway. He scrolled to the next email in his inbox. 'Hey, old Smithy's replied,' he murmured as he read, *Hi Matt, In answer to your question re timetables, I'd like you to help with the new intake of Computing & IT students in the computer lab on Thursday mornings. I've attached the Thursday programme for this coming term. Please remember you are expected to be in the lab well in time for the session start at 9:30am. HM Smith.*

There wasn't anything from Maisie. The unease gripping his guts eased. Trailing Maisie on her waitressing sessions could stay shelved for a little longer.

While the muffled sounds of his mother dropping the shower head passed through the thin wall between the bungalow's bathroom and his bedroom, Matt took stock of his situation. Apart from the Maisie concern, his timetable pretty much followed his previous routines. As a student he'd worked at Balcon & Mora part time on Monday and Friday afternoons, sometimes even later on Fridays. Since completing his course he'd been free to increase his hours, but he was by no means working fulltime for Damon. There simply wasn't enough work, unless expanding into surveillance was on the menu. And now the session he'd be working for Mr Smith seemed to fit neatly into his timetable without clashing with anything at Balcon & Mora. It was all turning out OK, and equally importantly his pass was ready to collect.

'Bloggin' hell!' It was 12:45. He needed to get up and out on his Vespa if he was going to catch Glynnis.

There was no point in showering. If he waited for his mum to finish in the bathroom he'd be late. He threw on a slate-coloured tee-shirt with the words CREATE A RESTORE POINT emblazoned across the front, stepped into baggy cargo shorts and forced his feet hurriedly into his trainers.

'Bye, Mum,' he called over his shoulder as he hurried down the gloomy hallway, one arm in his denim jacket, the other still free and swinging his backpack.

It didn't take him long to ride through the outskirts of Stowmarket and park his scooter in the Utterly Academy staff and student car park. It was off to one side of the old mansion block, built by Sir Raymond Utterly in Edwardian times. Modern additions sprawled behind and separate buildings had spawned into the grounds. Matt had never taken to the mansion's original pale Suffolk brick façade with the once fashionable chequered pattern of red brick threading through it. At least the main door had been modernised and replaced with plate glass. He headed for it and stepped into the cool elegance of the entrance hall with its pale marble flooring.

It felt deserted and silent inside without its student population, but he ignored the stillness and concentrated on Glynnis and the pass. He still had time.

'Bloggin' stairs,' he muttered as he unzipped his denim jacket and trudged up a couple of flights to the admin office. The door was open and Matt hesitated while he caught his breath. Glynnis had emailed so it followed she was expecting him. He walked in without announcing his arrival.

‘Ahh!’ She almost jumped from her office chair, ‘What do you think you’re doing creeping up on me like that? And why are you breathing all funny?’ She looked severe, her heavy fashion frames sporting a muted tortoiseshell pattern, her lips drawn tight.

‘It’s them stairs, Glynnis. Why aint your office on the ground floor?’

‘What? What’s that got to do with anything? You should have knocked or said something instead of just… appearing.’

‘Sorry, Glynnis.’

‘Right. It’s Matt Finch, isn’t it. I’ve got your pass and some paperwork for you to complete.’ She pushed back her chair as she stood up and walked across the office to a bank of filing cabinets along one wall. ‘We need photographs with the passes now. It’s a new requirement, and I’ve just realised the photo we’ve used for you is the one in our files from when you first joined us as a student. Before you grew that beard.’

‘Do it matter? Me eyes and nose aint changed.’

‘Hmm….’ She looked at him for a couple of seconds, ‘I suppose it’ll be OK, at least until you get a new photo taken. The photographer’s here next week, Monday and Tuesday afternoon. Just turn up and wait your turn. We’ll issue you with the new one once it’s been taken. OK?’

‘Yeah, cool.’

She handed him a sheaf of documents and his pass attached to a blue lanyard. He turned it over, felt the smooth plastic, read his name in print. He’d have described it as more of an ID card with photo and barcode than a badge or permit. The paperwork wanted a raft of contact details, and amazingly included a contract to sign. It was megatastic.

‘I weren’t expectin’ a contract from Mr Smith,’ Matt said, glowing.

‘It’s more of a volunteer, gratis type of arrangement. Take it away and read it through. Bring it back to me signed before you start on Monday.’

‘Yeah, cool.’

‘OK then, Matt. Thanks for dropping in.’ She slid the filing cabinet drawer closed with a clunk. It sounded final, the full stop at the end of a sentence.

He waited a moment, elation running high, but it seemed she was no longer aware of his presence. He didn’t know exactly what he was hoping. Maybe something like *congratulations you’re joining the staff, you’re one of us now*, but she said nothing. A blank screen.

‘Cheers,’ he breathed, deflated and reluctant to be moved on by an imagined fast forward sign, no longer of interest.

He slipped the blue lanyard around his neck and stuffed the paperwork into his backpack before retracing his steps along the corridor. Everywhere seemed deserted. There was no one to see his pass, but it didn’t mean he was ready to go home. On a whim he headed for the library. It made sense. He knew the code for its door lock and it would be somewhere to sit and collect his thoughts while he used their computers. If he was lucky someone might come in while he was there and notice the blue cord and shiny plastic.

‘Sweet,’ Matt murmured as he tapped in the number sequence for the lock and pushed the door. A quick scan around the bookcases and computer stations told him he had the place to himself. Disappointed, he headed for his favourite spot, the computer close to the wall near the corner. The old floorboards creaked a little in the silence as he plodded across, but the faint smell of wood and books soothed.

Ten minutes later he felt cooler and more grounded, but an undercurrent of angst about Maisie's waitressing job with Hyphen & Green still grumbled. Sophie Hyphen seemed the obvious person to search more deeply and while he was in the library it was an opportune moment. It had been difficult at Balcon & Mora with Damon sitting at the desk behind, breathing down his neck and watching his every keystroke through the administrator access. Originally Matt had found her address and details recorded on the UK Company House website. That had been before Damon had told him to stop his search, but today endorsed and bolstered by his almost-staff status, a fresh idea struck. If he looked up her address on an online directory like 192.com, then any additional names living at the same address would likely be listed. Malware! Why hadn't he thought of it before? Investigate the other people at her address and he might uncover something interesting. More to the point, he wouldn't be going against Damon's directive.

A few clicks and he was on 192.com and Sophie's address in Ipswich. 'Appin' crazy! There's a Lang Sharrard also livin' at 222A Longbottom Road,' he yelped. With a name like that his search had just been made a whole lot easier.

As he trawled through Facebook and LinkedIn, some basic facts became obvious. Lang Sharrard was Sophie's bloke. He was in his early thirties, had dark hair, a thin face and worked as a teacher at an Ipswich sixth form college. An initial news site check didn't pick up anything. 'So

Lang's keepin' his head down an' his nose clean.' The only thing of interest was a blog site link from his Facebook page identifying him as the blog's author.

'Seems 'e likes waterbirds,' Matt mumbled, incredulous as he scrolled through the blog photos of dark bellied Brent geese on the River Deben and Avocet roosting on the Deben Estuary mudflats. This avian world wasn't Matt's thing, and it didn't take long before he was ready to move on from the blog.

'There aint nothin' here,' he sighed, about to minimise the page when a photo heading caught his eye. The words Alton Water leapt from the screen. 'Is that a nightingale photo'd at Alton Water?' He stared at a small bird, larger than life on his screen but looking rather unremarkable; something which could have passed for a female robin.

'Alton Water?' Matt murmured, all of a sudden alert and focussed. 'Weren't that the place Chrissie were on about? Tattingstone and the dead waitress bird, Juliette Poels?'

Was the blog find important? Matt had no idea, but it was a coincidence and coincidences always warranted further investigation or action in the world of search. At least that's what Damon had drummed into him. On a whim he emailed Chrissie with the link to Lang Sharrard's bird watching blog. She'd visited Alton Water and might recognise the exact location of the photo. And she'd likely know more about nightingales than him.

'Oh scammin' hell.' He'd spotted a new email in his inbox. It was the one he'd been expecting from Maisie. He opened it.

It was her timetable for the catering events, or rather she'd forwarded her email from Hyphen & Green. A quick skim through told him it was for September, the month ahead, and Maisie's name was down for pretty much all the Friday and weekend events. Blog Almighty! He was going to be spending half his time skulking outside catering venues. At least it wouldn't clash with his Balcon & Mora and Academy timetables, but it wasn't his idea of a night out with a bird.

'Scammin' hell,' he breathed as he remembered his promise to keep Clive informed. He clicked on the forwarding symbol, keyed in Clive's email address and then sent it before he could change his mind. He also made a decision. He needed to talk to Maisie.

•••

It was mild and breezy later that Wednesday afternoon, as Matt waited for Maisie in the small market place in the centre of Stowmarket. He sat astride the blackberry bubblegum Vespa, and rehearsed the looming conversation. He'd had time to think about it in the library, but he still hadn't got beyond an opener on the lines of *thanks for sendin' me your waitressin' timetable, Mais.* Further words were unchartered territory and he reckoned he'd have to rely on his ingenuity and the eloquence of the moment.

'Hey, Mais,' he shouted as he spotted her approaching from the direction of Ipswich Street.

She waved and quickened her pace. She swung a plastic carrier bag as she walked and Matt guessed she'd likely bought something from the retro clothes boutique where she'd been working all day.

'Thanks for sendin' me your waitressin' timetable. Have you seen some of them places you have to go to are miles away, Mais?' He was surprised by his fluency and hoped he sounded cool.

'Hi,' she said and kissed him. 'Are we gettin' fish 'n

chips on the way back? They start servin' at six. If we go now we'll be at the front of the queue.'

'What?'

'I fancy some fish 'n chips, Matt. I'm starvin'.'

Just hearing the words conjured the smell of crisp golden batter and potatoes cut into gloriously long dangly chips, deep fried and salted. They were the ones he could dunk into tomato sauce.

'D'you mean the chippy in Stowupland?' he murmured.

She nodded.

'Yeah, but Mais – about this waitressin'. It aint a good idea. All that travellin'. It'll take forever. Cost a fortune.'

'I'm tellin' you it'll be great. OK, Matt? Now let's get goin'.' She sounded more thoughtful as she added, 'Yeah, I know some of them Hyphen & Green gigs are miles out, but see that's why I'll be gettin' a lift with Gacela. It'll be wicked, and the drop off an' pickup's the same place each time so,' she kissed him again, 'so-o-o-o if it's OK with you takin' me to the Ipswich roundabout, I promise I'll bring back some chocolates if I can.'

'Yeah, but Mais–'

'You can always sign up for some waiterin' yourself. What you say, Matt?'

'Flamin' malware. You gone soft in the head?' Matt sensed the conversation slipping from his grasp. 'C'mon, Mais. Let's get to the chippy.'

He started his scooter. The four-stroke engine gave a throaty pop and bang, the sound reflecting from the smooth stucco-faced Victorian and Edwardian-fronted buildings walling two sides of the old central market place.

# CHAPTER 17

Chrissie closed her laptop. Was it a clue? Was it about anything related to the case, she wondered. Matt's email with a link to Lang Sharrard's bird watching blog had been sitting in her inbox when she opened her emails. She needed to think, sip her mug of tea and think some more. The daylight in her kitchen started to fade, and the packets of couverture chocolate on the scrubbed pine counter took on dark forms.

'What a tangle,' she sighed. There were too many people involved, too many threads, and now Matt had added another name – Lang Sharrard. Did anything make sense? One thing was certain, it was Wednesday, Wednesday evening and Clive would be working late with Gert, the investigator from the Dutch Korps Nationale Politie. If it had been any other evening, she could have shown Clive the photo of the nightingale and asked if he recognised the exact location on Alton Water, but of course it was impossible. He was busy, under pressure and in the critical Dutch spotlight. The nightingale would have to wait.

However there was something she could do, and she flipped up her laptop screen and keyed *fishing permits Alton Water* in the search box. Moments later she was on the Anglian Water site reading about fishing. 'It doesn't look as if there's currently a lot of fishing at Alton Water, and there's no mention of night fishing at all,' she murmured. She read on, *further enquiries should be directed to the warden*. There was a contact number and she scribbled it down. She decided she'd phone in the morning and try to find out a little more.

Feeling buoyed by her plan, she rewarded herself by keying in *tempering chocolate* and escaped into the world of the chocolatier.

•••

Thursday dawned slightly overcast, and for once Chrissie found the inside of the old barn workshop comfortable, neither too warm nor too cool. She had started work on the lid of a writing box. Some of the highly patterned rosewood veneer had separated from the carcass wood so that it had lifted away like a smooth shallow dome. If she pressed the veneer with her finger she could flatten it back down onto the solid wood. At the edges of the lid, veneer had flaked away, exposing the carcass beneath. It was in a bit of a state, as Mr Clegg would have said, but it was something to be getting on with while the glue was still setting on Mrs De Vries' games table repairs. Also, in keeping with her principle of two birds with one stone, Chrissie reckoned the veneer on the writing box might be a project to try out on Nick's vacuum press.

*Brrring brrring!* Her phone's ringtone cut into the peace of the workshop. She grabbed it from her pocket. 'Hey thanks for getting back to me,' she said in a rush as she caught the words, Anglian Water.

'You left a message about fishing permits for Alton Water,' a male voice replied.

'Yes, yes. I'm interested in night fishing. I've been told there are some large carp, but I understand the car parks are locked at night, so how does that work for night fishing?'

'Large carp? There aren't any. Not at Alton Water. We've had a number of years with rather sparse fishing, and that's for any type of fish, although more recently we're starting to see carp again. But the big ones, the ones you'd want to track and night fish? No. Maybe try the Ardleigh Reservoir? OK?'

'Right, so there isn't any call for night fishing. Well thank you for that.'

'Anything else you wanted to know?'

'Well yes, early morning fishing. If I wanted to fish at dawn, get some fishing first light the car parks would still be locked, wouldn't they?'

'If it's the parking you're worried about, keys are available. There's an extra charge for a key to the car park, and there's a deposit of course.'

'Ah, that's a relief. It didn't really say anything about it on the website. So if I just fill in the form on the website and–'

'Yes, yes, and then contact me again.' He sounded distracted, as if his mind had moved on to other things.

'Well, thank you.'

The call ended.

'Whoa… so it's possible to get a key?' Chrissie's mind leapfrogged into possibilities and permutations of why or how Juliette Poels came to drive up the track to the car body repair unit, and who else might have been parking in the area.

'What's that you're saying about a key, Mrs Jax?'

'What? Oh, the Alton Water car parks, Mr Clegg.'

'And big carp? Did you say big carp? Don't tell me you've decided to take up fishing as well?'

'No, they don't have any big ones. And they lock the car parks overnight and, well I told Clive you'd seen it on the notice when you picked me up and wondered how the night fishermen manage.'

‘I did, did I?’

‘Yes, I thought it sounded better if it had come from you.’

‘You did, did you?’

‘Yes, Mr Clegg. So now you know about the key and that no one night fishes.’

‘Well thank you for that, Mrs Jax. I’ll remember if it ever comes up in conversation with Clive.’

She caught the smile, the barely perceptible curve of his lips as he turned his attention back to the refectory table with the warped wooden boards.

‘That glue must’ve set by now, Mrs Jax. You used hide glue, so overnight should have been plenty long enough.’ He tossed the words gently over his shoulder.

‘Ah yes, back to Mrs De Vries’ games table. I expect you’ll say these cramps were a bit of overkill, as well,’ Chrissie murmured, and then as an afterthought, ‘As you’re my official fount of knowledge about Alton Water, Mr Clegg why do you reckon the fishing is a bit sparse there?’

‘I don’t know. It used to be good. But if you ever find out the reason why it’s a bit sparse now, let me know if I’m the one who told you.’

She laughed. Ron never seemed to get rattled by anything. Perhaps she should take a leaf out of his book. She released the cramps on the stretcher and inspected the spliced repair. The replacement section of teak was now glued securely and bonded with the old wood. It was an invisible patch she’d cut into the original teak to strengthen the turning point. At least it would be invisible when she’d sanded it down flush with the old wood and stained and waxed it to match the rest of the old stretcher.

‘OK, now the leg.’ She loosened the rubber tie – a

length of deflated bicycle inner tyre she'd wound tightly around the table leg, binding where she'd glued the split back together. It worked well, exerting good even pressure on the curved surface without damaging it.

'Another invisible mend when I've sanded off this little bit of excess glue and waxed and polished.' She ran her hand over the repair. Yes, it was going to be solid and hopefully last the life of the table. The glue was as strong as the wood, not stronger, as with some modern glues.

When they stopped for a mug of tea, she showed Ron the glued leg repair. 'It's gone back together well,' she said.

'And of course if the leg fractures again, it'll split through the animal glue without splintering more wood. People tend to forget that's important when they're dealing with antiques. I reckon the forces on this leg are likely all wrong, in fact they were always wrong and that'll be in the design. If and when something has to give again in the future, it's better if it's in the line of glue than the wood splintering and breaking around the glue.'

'Well I'm hoping by replacing the dowel and repairing the stretcher, the leg will be protected, Mr Clegg.' She was about to add something about modern thick pile carpets not being one of the hazards back in 1740. A table leg dragged across todays' carpets met plenty of resistance.

*Brrring brrring!*

'Now what?' She reached for her mobile and checked the caller ID.

'Clive? Hi. Is everything OK?'

'Yes, yes. I thought it would be nice if we took Gert out for dinner before he goes back to Amsterdam, and I was wondering which day would be best for you.'

'For me? When is he going back?' Chrissie asked,

touched she was being included.

'He's catching the ferry first thing Saturday morning.'

'Tonight might be more relaxed than a Friday night, particularly if we're eating out. Anywhere nice gets really busy and booked up on Fridays. And, I expect he'll want an early start on Saturday if he's got a ferry to catch. So, I think tonight.'

'OK.' His tone was easy-going, unsurprised.

She had an idea. 'Hey, but Clive, if you've got work to discuss, you could bring him back to ours for dinner. I could cook if you like, or you could both talk and then we all go out and eat at the White Hart. It's an old traditional Suffolk pub. He should like it. What do you say?'

'That's great. I was hoping you'd say to bring him back to ours. I'll give you a call when we're leaving Landmark House. Steak would be nice. Bye.'

'Steak?' she echoed, but the call had ended.

She looked across at Ron, her eyebrows raised. He sipped his tea calmly. She knew he'd heard her half of the conversation and would guess her offer of dinner was driven as much by nosiness as hospitality. No doubt he was expecting her to fly into a panic about cooking and tidying the cottage. She waited for him to say something.

'There's a farm shop on your way back to Woolpit. Not too far out of your way. I've heard they only sell local meat,' he said mildly.

'Clive said he'd give me a call when Gert and he are leaving the new police offices in Ipswich. The Landmark House place. But I've no idea when that's going to be.' She heard her voice rise.

'Sounds like Gert is getting a tour of the county's police resources. It'll probably be the new investigation centre in

Bury St Edmunds, tomorrow.'

'Hmm,' she murmured, already deep in her own thoughts.

•••

When Chrissie took Clive's call to say he was leaving Landmark House and was on his way home with Gert, she knew she had about thirty minutes before his Mondeo drew up outside. She checked the time. Ten past six. For once she felt on top of the situation.

She'd already had time to tidy the cottage. It was brick end of terrace with a stone plaque in the brickwork, *Albert Cottages 1876*. Her home was less dusty and prone to spiders than the older timber frame wattle and daub constructions making up the heart of Woolpit. With only Clive and her, it barely needed more than a swift fly-round with the vacuum and a few flicks with a duster. It was the usual quick squirt of toilet cleaner and brush around the pan, a wipe over the basin and retrieval of Clive's hairs stranded in the shower tray.

Ron's suggested farm shop had come up trumps with steak from Suffolk-reared cattle, fresh salad, strawberries and some locally homemade meringues. Clive's request for steak meant minimal preparation and any cooking could be left until they were almost ready to eat: a pan of new potatoes to boil, salad to prepare.

She decided they would have their meal in the living room, the kitchen was too small, and besides, her chocolate making purchases were still in bags and packets on the scrubbed pine kitchen counter. As she cleared the books piled on the small Edwardian oak table pushed against one wall in the living room, she couldn't help but wonder about Gert. He was based in Amsterdam, Clive had distinctly mentioned it. If she was quick, she'd have time to get out her Amsterdam map and take a look to remind herself.

She pulled the table away from the wall and then had to shove and nudge the sofa to make more space around the table. With two extra pine chairs carried in from the kitchen, she laid three place settings.

By the time she heard the front door latch turn and Clive call, 'Hi, Chrissie! We're back,' she was engrossed in the Amsterdam tourist map spread across everything on the dining table.

'Hi,' she called over her shoulder. The narrow hallway amplified their footfall as they strode in.

'Hey, this is wonderful, Clive. So kind of you to invite me to your home.' The voice sounded mellow, the words from far back in the throat; English with a hint of a Dutch accent.

'Chrissie, this is Gert.' Clive stood aside so that she could see the Dutch inspector.

Chrissie had imagined he would be tall, but he was of average height, with short light brown hair and a neatly shaped beard and clean-shaven upper lip. He smiled and they shook hands in a relaxed informal way. She guessed he was much the same age as Clive, possibly a little older, mid to late forties.

While Clive went to get some bottles of lager from the fridge, Chrissie asked Gert how the case was going. She took care to keep her tone casual, more in the spirit of polite small-talk than a nosey probe.

'It's going OK, thank you. The dead man, Kinver Greane was Dutch, but I'm sure Clive will have told you.'

'Clive doesn't tell me much,' she lied. If this was a test she was determined to pass.

‘I see you’ve been looking at a map of Amsterdam,’ Gert said as he gazed across at the table.

‘Well yes, we stayed there on holiday a couple of weeks ago. It’s only a tourist map, but I just wanted to, well, make sure I could tell you where we stayed if you asked.’ She cringed inwardly, but she reckoned it was best if Gert underestimated her. He was more likely to relax his guard and let something slip. She pointed to the Swissôtel near Dam Square, central Amsterdam.

‘Clive tells me you’re a carpenter,’ he said looking at the spot she’d indicated on the map.

She didn’t get a chance to answer as Clive returned from the kitchen with glasses and bottles. Gert slipped the soft leather man-satchel from his shoulder and settled in the armchair; Clive sat on the sofa. It was obvious their minds were on the case, probably still mid-discussion about something important when they got out of Clive’s Mondeo. She sensed the two detectives would be more at ease, and happier to speak freely if she went into the kitchen and made food preparation noises. Clive probably knew she might hear what they said, but she reckoned as long as Gert didn’t realise, then Clive would be all right with it. Clive trusted her. At least that’s what she hoped.

Moments later, their voices played in the background while the kitchen tap gushed water into the butler sink. Splashing sounds rang out as she tipped in the potatoes. The volume of the exchanges in the living room rose, countering her potato-washing racket. Her strategy was working. She let the potatoes rest and concentrated on the voices in the living room.

‘We know Kinver Greane’s credit cards were used for nearly eight weeks after he was dead.’ Gert’s words resonated loud and clear.

'And we know Kinver died about seven weeks before Juliette Poels was killed,' Clive said, more softly.

'No identification, wallet, keys or cards were found on Kinver's body, yes?'

'Yes. I mean no. Everything had been taken, including his credit cards. It was one of the reasons identification was slow.'

'And we know while the real Kinver Greane lay dead with a fork in his chest, someone used his name and worked a short time as chef on the ferry to Hooke. Now my Dutch colleagues have traced his Visa card and Amex activity across Holland. But we find no activity on the cards since after your British news reported a dead body on a garden allocation in your Bury Edmund.'

'Yes, on a garden allotment in Bury St Edmunds.' Clive's voice faded.

Chrissie clattered a pan onto the cooker and made whisking noises as if mixing salad dressing.

'For the moment, Clive, we say this British John Brown is our killer, yes?' Gert's voice boomed.

'That's right. Kinver died in John Brown's allotment shed and we're guessing he took Kinver's wallet and legged it to Holland.'

'Legged it?'

'Just an expression, Gert. He ran away, caught the ferry. But it's the timing that interests me. John Brown resigned from Hyphen & Green Catering in May and hasn't been seen since. About one month later, the pathologist estimates June, Kinver is killed and then it takes another eight weeks before his body is discovered. But even now John Brown still hasn't been found. So – is John Brown even alive? And if he's in hiding, why go into hiding before Kinver dies? Yes, it makes perfect sense to go into hiding after he's killed Kinver, assuming he's our killer, but why before?'

'But we have to talk motive, yes Clive?'

'Yes.'

'Drugs, Clive. Kinver was drugs low-life. John Brown will be mixed up in it. You know it always comes back to drugs. I have informed you of Kinver's past activities in Holland. Yes, yes, I know we are more relaxed about drugs in Amsterdam than you are here, but we have our problems too - illegal drugs traffic through our borders. It's a popular route into Europe. So if we talk motive….' He dropped his voice.

Chrissie ran the kitchen tap again.

'But we've interviewed all John Brown's colleagues at Hyphen & Green. You've read their statements. You've even spoken to Sophie Hyphen this afternoon. John Brown wasn't a known drug user,' Clive said above the sound of the running water.

'Perhaps not, but I put a bet on it. Drugs come into it.'

'I don't know, I really don't. Hey, how about another lager?' Clive sounded weary.

*Another lager*? Chrissie flicked the cooker on under the pan of new potatoes and began to dice cucumber busily for the salad.

'Hey, Chrissie,' Clive appeared in the doorway, 'be a love and hand me another couple of lagers from the fridge would you? How's it going out here?'

'What? Out here? All good. Did you just ask for more lager?' She kept her voice low. She reckoned if Gert, still in the living room, couldn't hear her softly spoken words, then it followed he'd assume she, working in the kitchen, wouldn't be able to hear him speaking the loud side of normal in the living room.

'I promise we won't talk shop over dinner,' Clive murmured as she scooped more bottles from the fridge for him.

'Are you talking shop? I couldn't tell. I've been too busy getting things prepared,' she lied sweetly and quietly.

'Thanks, Chrissie.' He cast her a look, but she didn't know what to make of it.

'Hey Gert, I think it might be helpful if we talk to John Brown's mother again,' he said, as he retraced the couple of paces back into to the living room.

'If you think it will help, yes, OK, Clive.'

'Well, I wonder if John Brown ever visited Holland in the past. Maybe as a teenager? The connection with Kinver might have been made over there. You, being Dutch, well it might help to jog his mother's memory.'

'Yes, OK, if you think so.'

The second and third bottles of lager rapidly lent themselves to Chrissie's strategy. She no longer needed to make noise in the kitchen to get the two detectives to speak up. The alcohol did the job for her, freeing inhibitions and blunting fine tuning of their loudness. She chopped and diced, tossed and fried while their conversation flowed in the background like a radio play.

'What did you think of Leon? He's been a chef with Hyphen & Green for a couple of months or so, but he's from Holland. You read his statement, he's never met John Brown or Kinver Greane in the past. Do you believe it, Gert?'

'Leon Jansen? Yes a good Dutch name. Not everyone with a Dutch name is under suspicion, I hope! But you believe this most recent killing, Juliette Poels, is linked to John Brown and Kinver Greane, yes?'

'Her connection to Hyphen & Green Catering is too much of a coincidence. She has to be part of it, Gert. All three of them are connected to Hyphen & Green Catering. Two are dead and the third is missing or dead. But I don't think John Brown killed Juliette Poels; not if we believe he was the one using Kinver Greane's credit cards. The activity on them places him in Holland when she was murdered.'

'I tell you what. I will check our records when I get back to Amsterdam. I know it is not an official request from your British police, but I will take a look. I will let you know if we have anything on a Juliette Poels. OK?'

'Thanks, Gert. Oh, and maybe also on a Leon Jansen, as well?'

It was time to eat dinner and let some food slowdown the alcohol absorption, Chrissie decided as she carried bowls of cooked new potatoes and salad into the living room.

The conversation died as they bit into the deliciously tender meat. Dessert was a success; the locally grown strawberries looked small but were big on taste, an explosion of intense strawberry flavour.

'Ah, you have packets of couverture chocolate,' Gert said when he helped carry plates into the kitchen.

'Yes, I plan to make my own chocolate. I've never made it before,' Chrissie said.

'But you must speak to my wife! Nina makes chocolate. Of course it is a bit of a tradition in her family. Her grandfather was a chocolatier. I will give you her email and you must ask her anything about chocolate. Yes, and if you ever come to Amsterdam again, then you must meet and she will arrange a chocolate tour. It will be nice. Hey, what do you say, Clive?'

Clive nodded in the crowded kitchen as he spooned ground coffee into the cafetiere. 'Great idea, Gert. I'm making coffee if you'd like a cup? Hey, why don't you stay here tonight? It'd save you going back to the hotel. There's a bed made up in the spare room. It's more of a box room, but you're very welcome to stay with us if you like. Right, Chrissie?'

'Yes of course, but if you want to go back to your hotel, I'm OK to drive. You can both go on talking on the way there, and Clive will keep me company coming back.'

'No, no. Here is much nicer than a hotel. And I always carry a clean shirt in my shoulder bag. In this business sometimes you need an unexpected change of shirt,' Gert sighed.

# CHAPTER 18

It was the end of the week and Nick had spent the whole of Thursday and the best part of Friday working in the Willows & Son workshop. He'd used some of his breaks to craft his texting chat-up lines with Gacela; he had even suggested she meet him for a late Friday evening coffee or cocktail.

Dave had been working elsewhere – some final adjustments to one of the cherry wood kitchen unit doors in Nacton, and then an old customer in Needham Market needed a door rehanging after new carpets had been laid. When Dave arrived back after visiting a potential new client in Bucklesham, Nick was surprised to feel a wave of something akin to envy.

'How's it going?' Dave asked as he swept into the restroom-cum-office where Nick was sitting with Tim, one of the other carpenters, and taking a tea break.

'All good, but seeing you breeze in makes me… well, I've been stuck inside here too long,' Nick muttered.

'Then take your tea outside.' Dave grinned and threw a pad of paper down on the table. 'I better draw some plans while I've still got it all in my head. Mind you, I don't know why I'm bothering. I don't think Mr Gray really wants a car port at all.'

'Oh yeah? So what d'you think he's after?' Nick asked, his mind shifting from the great outdoors to the vagaries of customers.

'Storage space. You know, what goes on top of the car port.'

'Sounds like you're describing where I live. It's the

storage space over a garage, and it gets bloody hot in the summer, I can tell you.'

'Insulation. Sounds like you need a bit of lagging in the roof, Nick.'

'Maybe. But I don't think I'll run that past my landlady.'

'If you're talking car ports, they're pretty much open structures aren't they?' Tim chipped in before draining his mug of tea with a gulp. 'Right, that's me done,' he added looking into his empty mug with a wistful expression.

'How's the *giving up smoking* going, Tim? I've heard those electronic cigarettes and vaping are meant to be the way,' Dave said, as Nick rinsed the mugs in the sink.

Tim grunted and stood up stiffly.

'Don't remind him,' Nick laughed. 'He's been,' Nick paused mid-phrase. He was about to say, *like a bear with a sore head*, but Tim wasn't anything like a bear. He was tall and wiry thin, more of a middle-aged beanpole than a cuddly killer. 'He's been… sweetness and light,' Nick muttered, adopting a phrase he'd heard other's use. Nick didn't care if Tim wanted more sugar in his tea to counter the nicotine cravings, he just wished he'd stir it in properly; it might make him less cranky and the job of washing his mug easier.

Tim grunted again and walked through to the workshop.

'Talking of letting things get to you, how's your friend Chrissie?' Dave asked.

'Chrissie? Honestly? I think she's lost it a bit. She's coming round here at about four this afternoon. She wants to try something in our vacuum press system. It's an old writing box she's working on. A section of the rosewood veneer's lifted. I've told her she'd be better off using a warm iron, you know, making the old animal glue melt and re-stick it down. But she knows best, won't be told.'

'She's coming round here, you say?'

'Yes, in an hour or so. Hey no, Dave, you can't! I can see exactly what you're thinking, but if you ask her anything about the case, she'll think I've been talking. She'll kill me. Really she will.'

'OK, OK, Nick. But how'd you know I haven't something I want to tell her?'

'What? From your automotive network?'

Nick already felt unsettled, but this latest from Dave set the unease-bar higher. He knew Chrissie pretty well and if Dave waded in with his views on veneers and glues then he anticipated a pretty feisty response from her. He reckoned he was bound to get it in the neck for talking to Dave about her writing box, about Clive's case, about.... He gave up on the chain of consequences and walked back through to the workshop.

He had spent most of the day preparing wood for the wooden staircase, namely thickness planing the boards of French oak he would be using. He glanced at the set of figures written neatly on his plan: the total rise of the staircase, the rise height for each step, and finally the tread depth. The number of steps had been calculated to feel comfortable for ease of climbing within the space available for the staircase.

The final calculation had been tricky, namely the length of the stringers, the term for the planks of wood running on the underside of a staircase, following the incline and supporting each step. It was pure geometry; the length of the hypotenuse of a right angled triangle.

He picked up his carpenter's square, checked the stair gauges were set at the measurements he wanted and began marking out the cutting lines on the stringers. It was absorbing work.

'Hi, Dave!' Chrissie's voice carried from the restroom-cum-office and broke into Nick's consciousness.

Was Chrissie here already? He checked the time on the clock over the doorway. Five past four. Tim was about to go home; Dave should be leaving; Alfred the foreman and Kenneth, another carpenter would be returning in the Willows & Son van they'd had out all day. It was a time of bustle and clearing away. Better go through to Chrissie before Dave lands me in it, he thought.

'Hiya, Chrissie,' he called. He found Dave fussing with the kettle.

'Hey Nick, can you make the tea? I've still got these plans to finish,' Dave said and grinned.

Oh no, Nick thought, he's hanging around to see Chrissie. 'Really, Dave? So, it's tea for you, Chrissie, and… me.' He dropped teabags into mugs.

'Thanks for letting me re-stick the veneer down using your vacuum press. I hope I'm not going to be getting in the way.'

'No, no. It's after four now. What age is the box, by the way?' Nick asked. He glanced past the toolbox resting near her feet, and onto the table where she'd placed the repair project. Masking tape crisscrossed the lid, reminding him of medical strapping; sticky plaster crying out for sympathy.

'1880. It's late Victorian. Unfortunately it's had a bit of a rough life and I'm not the first to try and repair it. A warm iron didn't work so I'm guessing they used a PVA glue last time.'

'And if you scrape it all off you'll as good as destroy the old veneer,' Dave chipped in.

'Quite.'

Nick's cheeks flamed. He didn't know what Dave would be thinking of him after what he'd said about Chrissie losing it. He guessed he'd be raising an eyebrow. Nick kept his back to them and poured boiling water into the mugs.

'So how are you, Chrissie?' Dave pressed on, 'We all heard. It was in the news about that dreadful business of the woman found dead in a car near Tattingstone. You dropped by here with Ron Clegg the day she was found and, well word gets round. Nick said you'd been a bit shocked by it at the time. Are you OK now?'

No one spoke for a moment. Nick inwardly flinched, bracing himself for Chrissie's acerbic tones, but when she spoke she sounded relaxed.

'Yes, the poor women. Thankfully I didn't see anything, but it sounded horrific. I don't think just returning from holiday helped either. Nick's been pointedly not talking about it. Isn't that right, Nick? Sparing my feelings, but I'm fine now, thanks.'

'You see, Dave? I was trying to tell you that's why I don't know anything about the case.' Nick hoped he'd put the record straight, honour intact and all that.

'So, Dave, what's your interest in the case?'

'My Land Rover friends. The old wrecks we drive around – well, we get to talking about where to go for a professional paint re-spray job. One of my mates knew of old Cogger. He's one of the blokes working at the unit where that woman was found dead.'

'I thought it had been shut down. Isn't it still crawling with Health & Safety and forensic people?' Chrissie murmured.

'Yes, but Cogger's been moved by the boss to a

subsidiary in Hadleigh.'

'I shouldn't think he's too impressed with that commute to work,' Nick muttered.

'No he's not and the customers, and I mean the Hadleigh customers are getting pretty hacked off as well. It seems the way they're managing the extra work in Hadleigh is upsetting people. One of my Hadleigh mates has been waiting to have his Series IIA doors re-sprayed, but they keep telling him there's a problem finding the right colour match. His paint job's been cancelled several times now. And each time it's like it's a surprise and right at the last minute. Then they slip another car ahead in the queue. That Cogger bloke was quite short with him about it.'

'But if he wants an exact match, then, it's just bad luck, isn't it?' Chrissie said. Nick could see by the tell-tale frown, Dave had triggered her curiosity.

'Hmm, except my mate's spent quite a long time hanging around there just to get to talk to the staff and he thinks he's recognised one or two of the cars returning for a second paintjob.'

'Really? So what are you saying? Poor work and dissatisfied customers? What Dave?'

'I'm not sure, Chrissie. But… well maybe it's worth passing it on. Your bloke Clive's working on the case, isn't he? Cogger's been transferred there from the unit near Tattingstone. And lots of the cars have been moved over there as well. Something's not right. Perhaps you could drop Clive a word? No names, no mention of Land Rovers or my mates, right?'

'Yes OK, Dave. But I expect Clive already knows Cogger's been moved to Hadleigh. And–'

'Come on Chrissie, if you let Dave talk any longer about

cars you'll forget why you're here. Bring the mugs of tea; I'll carry the writing box and your toolbox. Let's go into the workshop. See you, Monday, Dave.' He led the way, pleased to escape.

It didn't take Nick long to select the right sized special polyurethane bag. 'OK, Chrissie, I'll put this grooved baseboard in first, then we can stand the writing box on it once you've glued up.'

'Oh yes, I remember. The grooves stop pockets of air getting trapped.'

'Yeah right. I'll set up the vacuum pump and everything else afterwards. So how do you want to do this with the glue?'

'I've already used a Stanley knife to incise where the veneer's lifted. You can see I used masking tape to protect it. So with any luck there's been no splitting and if the glue seeps out it won't get onto the veneer either.'

'You didn't have to bring your own pot of PVA with you – we do have glue here, Chrissie,' he said as she opened her tool box.

'Hmm, well I didn't know if you'd have a nice palate knife, fine artists brushes, syringes and blunt dispensing needles to get the glue under the veneer, so I've come prepared.'

They worked together, Nick feeling like the assistant nurse as he helped Chrissie load the syringe with some PVA glue. It was white and runny, the consistency of thick single cream. In the end the flat palate knife worked the best, slipping under the veneer and spreading the glue after she'd inserted a snail's trail with the syringe and blunt needle.

'Well, let's see if it works,' Chrissie breathed, as he held the special polyurethane bag open while she placed the writing box on the grooved baseboard.

He felt confident, in his element as he rolled the end of the bag, sealed it with a special slider, connected the suction tubing and switched on the pump. The polyurethane collapsed tight against the writing box as the air was sucked away.

'The theory,' he shouted above the sound of the pump, 'is the vacuum pulls the bag so tight against the veneer it presses out any air pockets trapped with the glue. It should give us a really good contact between the veneer and the carcass wood underneath. Brilliant isn't it?'

'Wow,' Chrissie murmured. 'So what happens now?'

'It stays like this overnight while the glue sets. The pump kicks in again if the vacuum doesn't hold and air starts getting back into the bag. Clever, isn't it?'

'Awesome.' Chrissie began to pack her PVA container and equipment back into her tool box. 'Hey, what's with all the nice wood over here?'

'Ah.' Nick made a flash decision to only partly tell. 'I'm going to make a trinket box with some of the leftover wood lying around in the workshop. I've got nice cherry offcuts from some kitchen units for a client in Nacton.'

'A trinket box? Cherry? That sounds nice. Is it a present for your mum?'

'No, not exactly.'

'Sarah? Your landlady?'

'God no!'

'A girlfriend?'

'I'm not saying,' but he felt his cheeks flame.

'Ah, so it's for a mystery girl. D'you have time for a drink after we've cleared up here?'

‘Yeah, it’s Friday isn’t it. But I can’t stay long and don’t think you’re going to get me talking about her.’

‘Of course not. Nags Head? Maybe catch up with the rest of the crowd?’

‘Yeah, but as I said, I can’t stay long.’ He reckoned if he played it cool and didn’t talk about Gacela, then he could play it casual with Gacela.

# CHAPTER 19

Matt sat on the bench seat and let the music from the jukebox wash over him. The Nags Head was beginning to come alive with the ripple and roar of voices as after work drinkers left and the early evening Friday nighters arrived. He had spotted Nick and Chrissie the moment he'd set foot through the doorway. They were in the snug area of the bar talking to Andy, an Utterly carpentry student they'd all got to know a couple of years before. Andy had been a first year while they were in their second year. Chrissie described it now as a kind of loose networking friendship.

By the time Matt had bought a lager, walked over to join them and slumped onto the bench seat, Andy had drifted away.

'Hiya, Matt. How are you, mate? Is Maisie waitressing today?'

'Nah, Nick, she's on a girls' night out. Cheers!' He half-raised his glass in a greeting before gulping slowly, drawing out the process and savouring the moment. The jukebox blared Ed Sheeran, as he rested back, engulfed.

'Andy hasn't changed much. He's still pretty solid in a weight-training kind of a way. D'you think he's still into swimming? Or was it rowing?' Chrissie asked.

'I kinda think it was rowing,' Nick said with a shrug.

The last chord faded and the jukebox fell silent. For a moment Matt sensed the atmosphere thin before voices and clinking glasses rolled across to fill the void. Now he could talk without shouting.

'I don't reckon Maisie were offered any waitressin' for today,' he said, then closed his eyes and pictured her email and the Hyphen & Green venue diary attachment.

'I thought Hyphen & Green were catering for a lunch party for an eightieth birthday out towards Felixstowe? Apparently the bloke used to play bowls, so half the bowls club will be there,' Nick said.

'Well Maisie aint told me anythin' like that. I reckon you're talkin' the Felixstowe Bowls Club venue, an' that's tomorrow, Saturday.'

'Are you sure, Matt?'

'Yeah.'

'That's odd. I could have sworn it was today.' Nick pulled his phone from his pocket.

They waited while he scrolled through his messages. Matt was about to repeat the venue details emblazoned across his visual memory, but Chrissie caught his glance, shook her head and frowned. *What? She thinks I've got the venue wrong?* He wanted to speak, deny any error but she put her finger to her lips.

'Oh right,' he whispered. Now he got it. *Keep quiet.*

'Sorry about that.' Nick looked up from his phone.

Chrissie raised her eyebrows. 'So?'

'So… I guess someone's messing with me, playing me along. I'm meeting her later on. I must remember to ask her how the bowls club lunch went today.' He slid, more than tossed his phone between the beer mats on the table and picked up his pint glass.

'Are you going to let on you know it's really happening tomorrow?' Chrissie asked.

'You bet I am.'

Something struck Matt. He knew Chrissie had done that *keep quiet* thing but maybe this new thought was important. He cleared his throat. 'Damon's come up with this phishin' trap for what he calls sophisticated searchin' to see if two people are communicatin'. How it works is – supposin' I send person A an email with some info like I can repair or up-cycle their sunglasses for a special knockdown price and with postage thrown in. But at the same time I send person B an email sayin' I can repair and up-cycle their sunglasses but it'll cost them and I don't offer special deals or knockdown prices. Then if B gets back to me sayin' they know the exact amount I've offered another customer as a special knockdown price and with postage thrown in - see then we know A and B have been talkin'.'

'I didn't know you gave out special deals and repaired sunglasses. Where's this going, Matt?' Chrissie's voice sounded tight.

'We don't. It's only kinda pretend things, stuff only we could've made up and specifically relevant to the person we're searchin'. See what Maisie were told is different to what you've been told, Nick. It's the kinda subtle stuff Damon and me might do.'

'Oh yeah? Subtle like it's the wrong day?'

'Nah, but it's like a sophisticated phishin' op. See, if your *someone* wanted to find out if you and Mais were talkin', then you lettin' on to your *someone* about you knowin' the bowls club thing is really tomorrow gives it away, don't it? You must've been talkin' to Mais… or me.'

'And it would work,' Chrissie added, 'because it's got you reacting. You're upset, angry? You said earlier you'll let whoever you're seeing later know that you know.'

'Yeah, but why'd anyone want to know if Maisie and I were talking?'

Matt couldn't answer the *why*, but he knew the whole Hyphen & Green scene made him nervous.

'Beats me, Nick,' he mumbled.

'So what are you saying? I shouldn't let on?'

'I dunno.' He looked at Chrissie and hoped she'd help him out.

Chrissie frowned and said, 'I think it all depends on how you feel about this person and, well playing it cool and not letting on gives you the advantage. And also some space to really make up your mind about her. I'm guessing we're talking about the mystery girlfriend, right?'

The words *mystery girlfriend* fired a connection in Matt's brain. 'Spanish goat! Are you talkin' Spanish goat, Nick? Mais said she reckoned she fancied you!'

'What?' Chrissie almost choked on her ginger beer.

'I've told you before. The name's Gacela. It's Spanish for a gazelle. And don't you dare go saying anything about this back to Maisie. Have you got that, Matt?'

'Yeah.'

'Right, well I'm done here. I need to change out of these work clothes and then I'm meeting… someone in Ipswich. Hey, and Chrissie, I'll be at Willows around ten tomorrow morning if you want to collect your writing box. See-ya.' He drained his beer in one final gulp, stood up and strode out of the bar.

'Well!' Chrissie puffed.

'He looked a bit red. Were he really angry?'

'More embarrassed, I'd say.'

They sank into their own thoughts. Matt felt confused. There were too many things to keep secret. He wasn't supposed to talk about the dead body he'd found, or tell Maisie she was an unwitting undercover spy at Hyphen & Green. And then there was his connection with Clive to consider. The DI had made it clear he wasn't to let on he was feeding information back to the police. Nor could he tell Damon that he was still searching into Sophie Hyphen by way of her boyfriend. And now this latest secret – he wasn't to say anything to Maisie about Nick and the Spanish goat. Blogspottin' hell! He was trailing Maisie tomorrow as an incognito protector. Where would it end?

'Are you OK, Matt? You look a bit serious?' Chrissie asked, interrupting his thoughts.

'Well it's just that… nah, it's nothin'.'

'By the way, thanks for sending me the link to the blog with a photo of the nightingale at Alton Water.'

'So what you think, Chrissie?'

'The photo could put Sophie Hyphen's boyfriend in the frame. I forwarded the link to Clive, but he's been really busy with the Dutch policeman all week. He hasn't said anything about it to me yet. I assume he got it.'

'You forwarded him me email?'

'Yes. Why, shouldn't I have?'

'But I didn't want Clive to know it were from me.'

'Why ever not?'

'In case Damon gets to hear I been sniffin' round Hyphen & Green, and the Sophie bird.'

'But why would he talk to Damon about it? OK, OK, don't get mad at me. I'll tell Clive not to let on it came from you if he ever gets to talk to Damon about it.'

'Thanks.' But the reassurance didn't quell the tightness in Matt's stomach.

•••

Matt watched the blue Fiat 500 drive away.

'Bye, Mais,' he called as he waved.

He had planned to wait thirty seconds and then follow Gacela's car, but of course when he'd pictured this the evening before, he hadn't realised how obvious and exposed he'd look. The Saturday mid-morning sun flashed tints of blackberry bubblegum off the Vespa's special edition paintwork. His full face white helmet with chin guard was like a beacon topping his torso. He was, by motorcycle safety design, high visibility. Not quite the stealth rider he'd envisioned.

He'd given the shadowing and tailing operation some thought. Firstly he'd stowed a change of jacket in the under seat compartment along with his small backpack and laptop. He reckoned if he slung the khaki backpack on his chest instead of back, it gave him another colour to wear and a different look and shape on the scooter. He would be Shadow Hawk, a superhero. Except now, as he surveyed the Copdock interchange supermarket car park, the Vespa's tints of blackberry bubblegum made him think oversized parrot rather than hawk. Frag 'n burn, he'd have to be Shadow Parrot-Hawk.

He started the Vespa and cruised slowly out of the car park. The blue Fiat would already be on the roundabout and taking the exit feeding onto the A14, the Orwell Bridge and eventually Felixstowe. It was the most direct route and Matt figured he could hang back and follow from a distance. The dual carriageway swept ahead and from time to time he spotted the pale blue paintwork of the bug-shaped car. He experimented with his lane positioning so as to get longer views ahead on the gently curving bends. He increased his speed, and then dropped back, never overtaking and always keeping several cars between his Vespa and the Fiat in front. He reckoned he was pretty Dos-in' awesome as Shadow Parrot-Hawk.

Tailing the Fiat was more of a challenge once they'd

turned off the dual carriageway and entered busy, congested Felixstowe. On the fast moving A14 his Vespa had been well out of range of the Fiat's rear view mirror. However in the town's sluggish traffic on a Saturday morning, he was barely fifty feet behind and risked being seen. When the choked roads finally began to clear as most of the cars took the main thoroughfares to the port area, the blue Fiat picked up speed and headed towards Old Felixstowe. Matt tailed behind, now with only one car separating them. He was too close. It was too risky. He nipped down a side turning and sped along residential roads to approach Crescent Road and the bowls club from the opposite direction.

The Felixstowe Bowls Club straddled the space between two parallel roads. The clubhouse itself faced onto Crescent Road and Matt positioned himself with his Vespa between cars parked on one of the streets close by. He reckoned he had a good angle to watch the entrance but not be seen, and sure enough he spotted the Fiat's distinctive blue bodywork as Gacela drew up outside the club.

It felt weird seeing Maisie get out of the car, jawing to Gacela, and all the while totally unaware he was spying on her. But who exactly was he watching? Gacela? Maisie? Or the others – Sophie and Leon?

He hadn't fully thought through his priorities. Was Shadow Parrot-Hawk a protector, an investigator, or simply not to be discovered? 'Blog Almighty,' he breathed as his stomach churned. He screwed up his eyes and remembered his plan. First blend in, then stake the joint.

He slipped his helmet off and stowed it with his jacket in the scooter's handy top-box. It only took a moment to retrieve his backpack from the under-saddle stowage, pull out his baseball cap and tug it down low so that the peak shaded his face. He felt the reassuring corner of his laptop as he slung the backpack over his shoulder. It was going to be OK, he reasoned as he ran through the plan in his head.

'Scam! Me phone.' He'd almost forgotten. If he was going to show himself, then he needed to walk holding his phone to his ear, as if deep in conversation. That way it would be easy to take a quick photo if needed. 'Grut lummox,' he mumbled, reverting to Suffolk and trying to hold his nerves in check. He pulled his phone from his jeans.

'Phew.' He was ready.

For a moment he was Shadow Parrot-Hawk, his camouflage-plumage now in sun-washed tones of khaki, grey and stony-blue. He squatted, rather than perched on the kerb, shielded from view between parked cars. He focussed and took a shot of Gacela and the Fiat. Emboldened, he strolled a few yards along the road, phone to ear and baseball cap pulled low to give himself a beak. He snapped the catering van. Moments later he stepped behind a car as Maisie, Gacela, and various other people trooped out of the club door and helped to unload boxes and catering equipment from the van. Who were these other people? He guessed one of them would be Sophie and another might be Leon. A half-second's work and they were captured on his phone camera.

'Now to case the joint,' he muttered as he pictured his list. It was time to glide on the warm up-currents rising from the sun drenched pavements, use his parrot-hawk vision to skirt the perimeter, and hover near the club's exit and entrance.

While his superhero soared high in his mind, Matt made a circuit of the area on foot. He kept to the shade cast by impressive three-storey high Victorian and Edwardian houses – semi-detached, built of red brick and faced with upper walls of pebbledash. They edged the rectangle of roads and hemmed in the bowls club. A church on the circuit attracted his attention. It had a colourful border of flowers and a cool, stone-faced open porch. He reckoned it would be the ideal place to sit while he waited and made internet searches on his laptop. Unfortunately it was the wrong end of the rectangle to watch directly over the club's exit and entrance, but that was OK. Shadow Parrot-Hawk could do a circuit from time to time. He figured it would draw less attention than him sitting on the pavement at the front of the club for five or six hours.

Matt settled in the porch and scrolled through his photos. He wanted the ones he'd taken with faces caught sharply in focus. If a Google facial recognition search was to have any chance of finding the names of the people unloading the van, then he needed to use his best full face pictures. Profiles wouldn't do. He chose four good shots; one each of Gacela, Sophie, the bloke – probably Leon, and an unknown waitress. If he sent an email to himself from his phone and attached the photos, then he reckoned once he'd opened his emails on his laptop he could use Google image search to identify the faces. He pulled his laptop from his backpack and waited for the emails he'd sent to arrive.

'Bloggin' hell, this is takin' forever.' His Wi-Fi connection was proving sluggish.

'I reckon I'll start with you. Yeah, you'll be the easiest,' he murmured as he eventually copied and pasted the full face shot of Gacela into the Google image search function. For a moment he studied her features. Her eyes were striking; black eyelashes, dark eyebrows and a head of rich dark brown hair pulled back into a neat waitressing pony tail. But he knew it was the biometric measure of her facial features, such as intercanthal distance and underlying facial bone structure which really counted. It added up to something like 80 nodal points for a computer to use. He tried to imagine the complexity of the algorithm the Google programmers must have written, analysing the relative proportions between all the interconnecting measurements. He waited while his laptop took its time.

'A-hah! Seems Google reckons she's got several possible matches.' He squinted at the search results – several photos of similar faces but with different names. He saved the page and started with the Google result named Gacela; no second name, simply Gacela like a statement.

'Now that's interestin',' he murmured when he finally scrolled through her public access Facebook page. 'There aint nothin' from before this year. Right, let's try the next one.' He typed Megan X into Facebook and waited.

Megan's face looked similar to Gacela's in both shape and proportion, except her eyebrows were paler and her hair was a curly short bob. Her Facebook page had no new entries after November 2012, and what she had posted was mainly about riding and horseracing over the course of one year starting in 2011.

'Right, the next one Google's matched.' He typed Cassia Muttosh in the Facebook search box. She had the same shaped face with similar proportions.

'Hmm, but she looks a touch older an' shorter.' Or was it just the way she was dressed and the shoes she favoured? Her latest entry was only a week ago, and judging from the mention of Iran in one of her posts, he reckoned she couldn't be a double for the Spanish goat.

He decided he could forget about Cassia, just as he could dismiss Stella Starlite, the final Google search result. She also had the same shaped face, but she looked too young to be the Spanish goat. Moreover, judging by the home page, she lived in Cornwall.

Frag 'n burn, what did it mean? For a moment he wished he was back in the Balcon & Mora office with Damon and could tell him what he'd just found. Damon would do that arm stretch thing and then suggest they discuss it over a coffee and chocolate milkshake break. Just imagining the routine centred Matt's thoughts.

So were Gacela and Megan twins? Or were the odds stacked more in favour of them being one and the same person. In other words, had Megan changed her name and hairstyle and reappeared as Gacela? And if so, why? Matt felt a hand tighten on his guts. This was spammin' scary.

He reached for his phone, ready to call Clive, but something more urgent flashed through his mind. He hadn't made a circuit of his stakeout for at least an hour. Gacela could already have abducted Maisie in the blue Fiat, or one of the others could have imprisoned her in the catering van. He needed to check the club entrance and exit. And fast.

With his backpack slung loosely over one shoulder, baseball cap pulled low and phone in one hand, he hurried along the warm pavement and made a circuit to take in the front of the clubhouse.

'The crate with the sparklin' water? Yeah, yeah, I got it,' Maisie's voice rang out from the other side of a wooden fence.

'Thank blog,' Matt breathed as relief surged through his veins. Maisie was OK. She was out at the back of the clubhouse and close to the bowls green, shielded from the road by the fence. He slowed his pace and walked along Crescent Road. Some elderly guests were already arriving and the catering van and blue Fiat were still parked outside.

Back in the church porch once again, Matt assessed his plan. The Wi-Fi connection was frustratingly slow and his laptop's battery wasn't going to last another four hours. At this rate he wouldn't be able to check out the whole catering crew. So was it to be more of the Spanish goat or make a start on the bloke he reckoned might be Leon?

He chose his photo of the tall blond-haired man he'd seen help unload the van. 'Yeah, I reckon you could be Leon coz you certainly aint anythin' like Sophie's bloke, Lang Sharrard,' he murmured as he pasted the square-jawed face into Google's image search.

He waited and waited. Eventually a result match named Leon Jansen loaded onto his screen. 'Yeah, wicked!' He'd guessed right, he was a bloke named Leon. However when he tried Facebook, the page seemed to freeze. After waiting forever and with still no result, Matt gave up. Instead he simply typed the name Leon Jansen into the general Google search box.

'Scammin' hell,' he griped when a series of results mainly in Dutch loaded at snail-pace onto his screen. It was hopeless. His luck was running out. He needed better internet speed and the Balcon & Mora computer with the language translator app. Leon would have to wait.

The afternoon flew as Matt made sporadic circuits and aborted internet searches. He sent Maisie a text reminding her to bring back some high-end chocolates, and took a short walk to find somewhere to buy a sausage roll and can of cola. He lingered between parked cars and watched the guests leave before finally taking more shots when the catering crew loaded up the van.

His plan was simple: change his jacket from the blue denim to his spare old black one; follow Gacela with Maisie in her Fiat until she took the Copdock interchange exit off the A14; hang back from taking the exit himself and initiate phase two of his plan. The idea, or rather the phase two part, had come to him in the church porch.

He reckoned once he knew Gacela and Maisie were definitely heading for the car park, he couldn't just follow in and arrive a few seconds behind. It would be so obvious he'd been tailing them. Hence phase two. He'd stop, shed his jacket into the stowage, sling his backpack to rest against his chest, text Maisie to say he'd be slightly late, wait ten minutes, then take the Copdock interchange exit, and ride into the car park from its western approach.

The plan went like a dream. He cruised across the car park while Maisie waved excitedly.

'Where's Gacela? You aint been waitin' here long 'ave you'?' he asked as he pushed up his visor.

'She couldn't wait. And nah, I aint been here long.'

'Right. So how'd it go? Did you have a good time?'

'I weren't a guest, Matt. I aint been to no party. I were workin'.'

'Right, Mais.'

'An' me feet are killin' me.'

'D'you fancy goin' for a drink?'

'In this? I'm wearin' me waitressin' stuff.' She pulled at the collar of her blouse.

'Right.'

'Nah, just take me home an' I'll die for a bit. Maybe I'll call later.'

She slipped on a helmet and got up behind him on the Vespa while he waited, disappointed.

‘I got you some chocolates,’ she squealed over his shoulder.

‘Really? Ta, Mais,’ he shouted when she squeezed his ribs and stretched further to slip something into the top of his backpack.

They eased onto the feeder roundabout and sped along the A14 to Stowmarket before taking the quieter roads to Stowupland and her parents’ home.

He felt empty as he watched her shut the front door, a quick half-wave and then she’d gone. She still filled his thoughts, even if he couldn’t see her. He had spent the whole day fretting, watching over her and anticipating abduction scenarios while she.... Well, wasn’t that the whole point? She was blissfully unaware.

‘Blogspottin’ hell!’ His head was going to explode with it all. He decided to ride on to Woolpit on the off chance Clive and Chrissie were in.

# CHAPTER 20

*Rat-at-at-at-at-at!* The metallic notes of the doorbell rang out.

'OK, OK, I'm coming,' Chrissie called as she hurried through her narrow hallway. She knew it wouldn't be Clive because he had a key. Could it be her friend Sarah, Nick's landlady, popping over with an excuse for a natter and angling to share an early Saturday evening glass of wine?

'Hey Matt!' she cried in surprise as she opened the door and took in his dishevelled figure. A backpack hung low across his chest. He clasped his helmet to one side of it, tight against his belly. His short sandy hair had lost its reddish tones where sweat had moistened and clumped it together. He radiated clammy unease.

'Are you OK? Where's your scooter?' she asked, catching his agitation and peering past him.

'I parked it just there. Is that alright?' He indicated the kerbside beyond the handkerchief patch of grass behind him, all the while clutching his helmet.

'Yes, it'll be fine there. Come on in. So what's going on?'

She led the way to the sitting room, leaving him to close the front door and tramp behind. She sensed he'd try to veer from the hall into the comfort zone of her kitchen.

'No come straight in here, Matt. There's more space for your helmet and backpack. The kitchen's completely cluttered up.'

'Right. Is Clive around?' he asked.

She checked her watch. 'Well he should be, it's six thirty and it's his weekend off. Did you want him? Has something happened?'

'Kind of. See I got somethin' to tell him,' his voice wavered.

'Well he should be home soon. He nipped out after lunch. He's got loads of paperwork to catch up on and there was a whole lot of stuff to pass on from Dave. You remember Nick's old trainer? It's all because of this awful case, and the Dutch policeman being over here for a few days. He's been rushed off his feet.'

'Yeah, but Clive's comin' back, right?'

'Yes of course, except he promised to drop by Tesco on his way home. But he shouldn't be long now. Take a seat. Do you want something to drink? There's a lager, or if you prefer, elderflower cordial in the....' She didn't bother to finish. It was obvious he wasn't listening. He'd pulled off his backpack and tipped the contents onto the sofa.

'Hey, what are you doing? There's no need to throw your stuff everywhere,' she said, grabbing an empty drinks can and sausage roll wrappings. She eyed a crumpled green paper napkin binding a small bundle.

'I'm gettin' me laptop, Chrissie. See I've found some stuff Clive ought to see.'

'OK, but slow down. If it's really urgent I can ring him, let him know you're here. Do you want me to get him to come straight away?'

She watched, searching Matt's face for clues. She'd got to know his moods and the way he coped, slipping into his own world, reeling off facts or plunging into comic-strip fantasy. He was definitely stressed, but the way he was acting seemed more extreme than usual; it felt different. Cold dread reached into her stomach. Had he found another body? He hadn't said last time, at least not directly to her although he had told Clive. She'd been left to work it out for herself. So was this a repeat; another dead body waiting to be reported to Clive?

'You seem upset. Would it help if you talked to me? You don't have to, of course.'

'Sorry, Chrissie but I don't know any more who I can tell or what I can say.' His voice spiralled upwards.

'It's OK, Matt. I think I'll ring Clive anyway and… let's tidy up this mess.' She reached for the green paper napkin. It loosened and fell away from something.

'Hey, what have you got here? This looks a bit special, Matt.'

She stared at the clean lines of a small shiny-white cardboard box. She sensed quality. The swirly gold writing on the side suggested exclusive luxury. She held the box up to inspect it more closely.

'*Choc…ol…atier*,' she read out, deciphering the gold lettering, '*Ver…vol…gens. Amsterdam*. They're Dutch chocolates! Hey Matt, where did you get these?'

'Er what? Oh them. That were Mais. She said she'd got me some chocolates from the lunch do she were waitressin' today.'

'Oh yes, the Felixstowe Bowls Club. But wow, have you tried one? What are they like?' All thoughts of phoning Clive evaporated.

'No, I aint had one yet. I didn't know she'd put 'em in me backpack, otherwise I'd 've tried 'em by now.'

'Can I open them?' Chrissie asked, focussing on the box and picking up a rich chocolaty aroma.

'Yeah, go on then.'

A gold paper disc joined the top flaps. Chrissie caught its edge and eased the sticky fastener away. She opened the box, relishing the warm rush of cocoa scents.

Six chocolates, rounded like balls, nestled amongst white and gold crinkled paper cases. Fragments of something buttery-bronze adhered to the milk chocolate casings. They begged to be eaten, each chocolate the right size for one mouthful, no biting required. She proffered the box to Matt and he took one.

'They all look the same so we don't have to choose. I wonder if they're truffles,' she murmured, feasting her eyes.

When she popped one straight into her mouth, the outer fragments melted into strong flavours of salted caramel, then blended with rich chocolate as the shell began to melt on her tongue. She crushed the softened casing against the roof of her mouth and released the smooth, salty chocolate-caramel centre.

'Bit salty, aint it?' Matt muttered.

'Hmm… I'll make a coffee. Did you want a cold drink? You never said when I asked earlier.'

'Well yeah, I'll need one if I'm gonna have another of 'em chocolates.'

She laughed. She was right. She'd always known chocolate soothed the soul and already Matt was thinking of his next chocolate rather than fretting where Clive was.

There seemed no need to hurry as she walked happily into the kitchen. She took a couple of small bottles of lager out of the fridge. She didn't know why, but she'd changed her mind about the coffee. She just didn't have the energy to switch the kettle on and spoon out the coffee granules. It was so much easier to scoop a bottle opener from the cutlery drawer and not worry about glasses or cups. She carried the opened bottles back into the sitting room, handed one to Matt and set the other one on the coffee table.

'A lager, that's more like it, Chrissie. Better than elderflower,' Matt said, and took a long swig from the bottle.

'Well budge up a bit and then I can see whatever's so important on your laptop.' Chrissie flopped down heavily beside him on the sofa.

'Me battery's got no charge left on it.'

'Oh right.' They sat in companionable silence for a few minutes.

'Aint you goin' to ring Clive?'

'Oh yes I was, wasn't I.' Chrissie retrieved her mobile from the coffee table and flicked through her favourites and recent calls. She pressed Clive's automatic dial number and listened to the ring tone. It seemed to ring for an eternity, before switching into the messaging service.

'Hmm, I'll text him,' she murmured, feeling no particular frustration or curiosity because he hadn't answered her call.

Her fingers moved across the phone's keypad with clumsy, sluggish movements. She struggled to control and co-ordinate her thumbs until the effort became too great. It didn't worry her. The predictive text would be able to make sensible words from her bumbling finger stabs. She giggled when she tried to read what she'd written. It was hopeless, she couldn't pull the letters into focus. And as for the words, they were just one long fuzz… fuzz… fuzzy….

'What you laughin' at, Chrissie?' Matt asked very slowly.

'I don't know. I just feel so… so….' Her eyelids weighed so-o-o heavy.

‘Really?’ Matt mumbled, his head lolling forwards.

‘I….’ The words died in her throat, but she didn’t care. She felt no anxiety or fear, merely a fleeting dizziness. And when she closed her eyes she sank into profound nothingness.

‘Hey wake up! Chrissie, Matt! What the hell’s been going on here?’

Clive’s voice reverberated as he paced around the sitting room, angry concern bouncing off the walls one moment, only to be muffled by the sofa the next. The sounds penetrated Chrissie’s head, the words stirring her into reluctant wakefulness.

She opened one eye, and struggled to focus. ‘Hi.’ She didn’t have the strength or inclination to say more. ‘Hmm.’ She sank back into oblivion.

•••

The quiet sound of voices played in the background. Chrissie moved her head. Muscles twinged in her neck. She groaned and her mouth felt dry. She rubbed her eyes and then her nose.

‘You’re awake at last. Was it a good trip?’ Clive’s voice cut into her consciousness.

‘What?’ She blinked and glanced across to where he sat in the armchair. The TV screen flickered with an Attenborough wildlife programme.

‘Have I been asleep? You should have woken me. Hey and my neck’s got a crick.’ She rubbed it. She didn’t remember sitting down or feeling sleepy, let alone drifting off. She couldn’t even recall walking into the sitting room.

‘How long have I been out?’

Clive didn’t answer. He flicked the TV off with the remote control. She was conscious of him watching her, a frown concentrating his stare.

Something on the sofa snorted beside her. Startled, she crooked her neck. 'Matt? What's he doing here?' she mouthed at Clive.

'I was hoping you were going to tell me, Chrissie.'

'Hey, Matt! Wake up.' She dug him in the side with her elbow. 'Hey Matt!' she bellowed. He stirred and snorted.

'So what's been going on here, Chrissie?' Clive asked quietly.

'I don't know.' She frowned with the effort of thinking back, except there wasn't anything to think back to. She tried her earlier question. 'How long have I been asleep?'

'I don't know before I got home, but you've both been snoring for the last three hours. If you hadn't woken soon, I'd have had to start thinking about calling an ambulance.'

'Calling an ambulance? But why, Clive?'

'Because it's pretty damned clear you've both taken something. Your breath doesn't smell of alcohol, Chrissie, but Matt has probably had a lager. I'm guessing that small one, judging by the empty bottle on the floor.'

She gazed at the full uncapped bottle of lager on the coffee table and the empty one lying on its side on the geometrically patterned rug at her feet.

'Did you get those lagers from the fridge, Clive, because I didn't?'

'No, Chrissie. This is how I found them when I got home.'

'So Matt must have got them out of the fridge? The cheeky anorak.'

'Possibly. But what's the last thing you can remember, Chrissie?' His tone seemed to change.

She thought back. 'The doorbell… yes, I remember

thinking it couldn't be you because you've got a key.'

'So who was it, Chrissie?'

'Matt... yes that's right. I asked him where he'd parked his scooter.'

'And was Matt alone? Was there anyone else?'

'No, he was by himself. And he seemed upset, he was asking for you.'

'Is that why you texted me?'

'Did I? No I don't remember texting anyone.'

'Hmm, what happened after Matt arrived?'

'Nothing.' She focussed for a moment, searching back through the sequences in her memory. It was blank.

'Nothing happened,' she repeated.

'What do you know about these? They were on the sofa.' He held up a small white box with swirly gold lettering. 'They're chocolates. Do you remember eating any of them?'

'No, and I love chocolate. I'd remember if I'd eaten any.'

'Hmm... did Matt eat any?'

'How'd I know, Clive? I don't think I've ever seen that box before. Hey maybe...? Now you're starting to make me doubt myself. Let me have a closer look.'

He got up from the armchair and walked over. When she looked into the box a delicious aroma of cocoa seeped into her nose. The crinkly gold and white paper stirred a memory, just as the buttery-bronze fragments holding fast to the four milk chocolate globes made her think... caramel.

'This is really weird. I don't know if these are salted caramels because I can smell them or because I've eaten one. Are you playing some kind of mind game with me?'

'No Chrissie. I think you've taken some kind of a drug. I've been watching the pair of you sleeping it off and I'm guessing from the way you can't remember much, it's got to be something like Rohypnol or GHB.'

'What? What's Rohypnol or GHB? What are you talking about?'

'They're the so-called date rape drugs.'

'What? But when? And how? And you think Matt as well? I don't get what you're saying, Clive.'

'Hmm, I'm going to make a call, have a chat with the duty police doctor. They're bound to have seen a lot of this kind of thing and they'll know how to test for it.'

She gasped, lost for words.

He looked weary, his shoulders sagging as he walked from the sitting room. She guessed he'd want to make the call from the kitchen, no doubt feeling less inhibited without her in his eye line. But hell, if he was going to be talking about her, she had a right to know what he was saying. She checked her watch. It was eleven o'clock.

'Eleven o'clock?' She'd lost over three hours of her life, wiped clean from her memory.

She started to stand to follow Clive, but Matt snorted and stirred in his sleep. Torn between Clive's call and Matt she slumped back onto the sofa and gave Matt a shake. If only he'd wake up, maybe he could tell her what was going on.

•••

Chrissie sat in the sunny bedroom she shared with Clive and sipped her morning mug of tea. She was propped against comfy pillows. Clive had been up for a while, hence the tea. She could hear him pottering around in the kitchen and a faint smell of frying bacon wafted through the cottage. A radio droned its Sunday morning programme in the background, but Chrissie had already blocked out any meaningful sound with her own thoughts.

She was making a simple calculation. She estimated three to four hours had been wiped from her memory by a so-called date rape drug. What had the doctor called it? GHB - Gamma Hydroxy Butyrate?

Oh God! What if it causes more problems? One small hole in her memory was bad enough, but a rampant moth attack was terrifying. Her stomach lurched. If she could recall the latter part of Saturday evening then she'd know her memory was working again. She had to find out. And so, there and then, right that second she forced herself to picture the evening as it played out just after Clive had made a call from the kitchen. If she wasn't able to do this, then she knew life would never be the same.

'Our police duty doctor says she'll see you,' Clive had said, as he'd walked back into the sitting room.

She remembered feeling reassured by his announcement, but apprehensive. She recalled how together they'd woken Matt up, and persuaded him to stagger to the Mondeo where he slouched into the backseat. He dropped off to sleep and snored for most of the journey. Clive had driven them to the police investigation unit, just off the slip road into Bury St Edmunds. She could still picture the clean, modern medical examination room where a middle-aged female doctor took her pulse, temperature and blood pressure. The doctor had been interested in her eyes, shone a light into them and asked lots of questions, some intimate. She'd taken a blood sample, a few strands of hair from her head and told her to pee into a container. She could even remember the uniformed police constable, probably doubling as a chaperone. And that was all there had been to it.

Afterwards she'd sat in a small anteroom with Clive while the doctor saw Matt. The curiosity and emotion came back to her now.

'What have you done with the box of chocolates?' she'd asked him.

'Ah, well the box and contents are in an evidence bag. I'll get them to Forensics tomorrow for analysis.'

'But what about Matt? Do you think he'll be OK by himself tonight? I don't reckon his mum would notice if the house burned down around them. Shouldn't we offer him a bed? Let him stay the night?'

'Yes OK, Chrissie. You said he wanted to tell me something, so this way he'll have a chance to get whatever's bugging him off his chest. We can talk in the morning.'

'I have a feeling it was something on his laptop.'

'His laptop? It was on the sofa when I got home. I had to rescue it before it fell on the floor. There's no battery left.'

Had Clive sneaked a look? The jolt of curiosity flipped her right back to the present.

She almost slopped her tea onto the sheets. Matt! He'd still be in the spare bedroom where he flopped down once they'd come back from the investigation unit.

She gulped down the rest of her tea. Matt was the key piece in the jigsaw. It was time she got up, showered and launched into the day.

'Hey, good morning! How are you feeling?' Clive said fifteen minutes later, as she walked into the kitchen.

Her hair was towel-dried and damp after her shower. It cooled her head, like a revitalising head rub. She'd thrown on a clean tee-shirt and cropped linen trousers. She felt ready to face the day.

'I'm afraid Matt's already beaten you to the bacon. Do you want me to fry you some more?' Clive asked.

'Yeah, I'll 'ave some more if you're offerin?'

'No, not you Matt. Chrissie hasn't had any yet.'

'Toast would be nice. Hey, good morning, Matt. I see you've made yourself at home.'

She watched him for a moment as he sat at her narrow kitchen table. Her laptop had been pushed to one side to make room for his. It took central position, its flex trailing. His empty plate was out of the way in second place.

'Clive said it was low on battery. Lucky you had your charger on you.'

'Well I aint. Clive picked this one up for me while we were at the investigatin' unit last night.'

'Really? So how do you feel? Any ill effects from whatever we took?'

'Nah. Me head seems OK. Hey Clive, this is what I wanted to show you,' Matt said, his eyes firmly glued to his screen.

She stepped out of the way so that Clive could lean in and read whatever Matt had loaded. Instinct made her gravitate close. She couldn't help but catch a view of the names against various Facebook photos and profiles.

'Matt, I don't get what you're trying to show us,' she said.

'Well I do.' Clive straightened his back and stood tall.

'When we did a preliminary check on all the Hyphen & Green employees, we were working from a list of names, not photos. The team will have started with police records, previous convictions, and then Facebook etcetera. But if a name doesn't flag up as having any previous, and we don't have any photos, we're only entering names.'

'I still don't get it,' Chrissie repeated.

'Matt used the photo of Gacela he took yesterday and reverse searched. In other words, he started with the photo and not her name. My team didn't have a photo of Gacela for their preliminary checks. It seems Matt's Google facial recognition search has come up with several possible matches for her photo.'

'So?'

'So it appears the waitress who calls herself Gacela may not be who she says she is. And if that's the case, it's a safe bet it's not her real name either. Of course it might not mean anything, but I don't like it. Not in a murder investigation.'

'So you're saying she's not who she says she is? But what about Nick? I mean, she's like… his new girlfriend.' Chrissie tried to keep the alarm from her voice.

'Yeah, and Mais. She's the one brought back them chocolates for me.'

'Hmm, I'm going to have to go to the station. I need to get the team onto this fast.'

'That's great, Clive, but in the meantime what do we do? Shouldn't we warn Nick and Maisie? I mean how did Maisie come by those doctored chocolates in the first place? Do you reckon they were intended for her? And if she nicked them, someone's going to notice they've gone.'

'Now both of you listen to me. Don't tell anyone about this until I've had a chance to check it out. Stay here, have a lazy morning and I'll get back to you with how I want you both to play this. Have you got that? Chrissie?'

'Yes.'

‘Matt?’

‘Yeah, but I don’t get it, Clive. What if Mais phones me this mornin’? What do I say?’

‘Nothing.’

‘Yeah, but see I know she got another waitressin’ gig this evenin’.’

‘You say nothing, Matt. Nothing until I get back to you. OK?’

‘Yeah, OK if you say so.’

Chrissie’s stomach churned. It was getting seriously scary.

# CHAPTER 21

It was Sunday morning and Nick let his head rest on the pillow with his eyes closed and his mind drifting between images. A melody played somewhere deep inside his head. It came from nowhere and he liked it. When he was fully awake he'd write it down or sing it into his phone's record function, but for the moment his eyelids were too heavy and his pillow too comfortable.

It was often like this after playing a gig, the music going round in his head on a never-ending loop with images and memories coming back to him from the previous evening, and fragments of conversation slipping past like minnows in a current. If he snatched the phrases and pressed them into the rhythm of the new melody, he could try to sing it; maybe fix it in his memory. The effort of thinking it through disturbed the harmony and lifted him closer to waking.

*Ping!* A text alert intruded further. *Ping!* It cracked the shell still holding him in sleep.

'Ugh,' he groaned and reached back over his head for his mobile. His fingers brushed against the slope of the garage attic ceiling before finding his phone on the low drawer unit, its side doubling as a bedhead. 'Ugh,' he groaned again. He'd have to open his eyes and he didn't know if he was quite ready yet. But try as he might, further dreamy-state sleep eluded him.

Curiosity took over and he peeked between his eyelashes. Sunshine streamed through the small end window. He focussed on his phone's screen. 11:30. 'Almost midday,' he breathed and opened the text message, sender

ID – Gacela.

*Sorry I didn't make it to Frasers. Hope gig awesome triumph last night. Fancy a late Sunday brunch? Pin Mill? G x.*

'Hmm… that's nice.'

It had been fun meeting her for cocktails again on Friday night; he'd felt more relaxed than on their first cocktail date. Of course it would have been better without the question *why* constantly running in the back of his mind.

'What's your game?' he sighed, now fully awake. He was drawn in.

He hadn't expected her to make it all the way to Frasers, a nightclub in Bury St Edmunds. His band had been playing a gig there the previous evening. He'd dared to hope, but he'd been wise enough not to expect. She had already told him she'd be at her mother's birthday lunch on Saturday, and she anticipated the family celebration would spread late into the day. He had known she was lying and that she'd be in Felixstowe with Hyphen & Green, waitressing with Maisie for a birthday lunch at the bowls club.

Why all the lies? If Chrissie and Matt were right and it was all an elaborate plan to see who was talking to whom, then it made no sense to him. Gacela had great looks. He reckoned she was much more likely to have another bloke on the go and she'd probably spent Saturday evening two-timing him with this other bloke. Except two-timing implied he and Gacela were already an item, which somewhat overstated the situation.

So how should he respond to her brunch suggestion? Pin Mill was on the River Orwell, a small hamlet with a waterfront pub on the Shotley peninsula. It was a long way to drive to meet someone who might simply be playing him along. He thought for a moment and texted back: *Great idea. How about somewhere closer – there's a nice pub near Fox's Marina? N x.*

Her reply pinged back almost by return. *OK. What time? G x.*

They settled on one o'clock.

He was surprised she'd agreed to his suggestion. So far, he'd got the feeling she liked to be in charge of any arrangements. And he wasn't going to admit it, but he was finding the whole deception thing exciting. It added an energising frisson, a sense of danger rather than nervous tension. As Chrissie had said, it gave him the edge, helped him hold back and keep his heart safe until he knew the whole score. This was a game he reckoned he could play without getting hurt. A late Sunday brunch was going to be fun; he'd enjoy quizzing Gacela about her supposed family celebrations.

It didn't take him long to shower and dress. Casual in a French-blue tee-shirt and pale stone-coloured cargo shorts, he drove his old Ford Fiesta from Woolpit and headed for Fox's Marina on the outskirts of Ipswich. He turned off the A14 before the Orwell Bridge crossing, and traced the road past the pub for a short distance along the banks of the Orwell. The tide was in and salty water covered the mudflats, widening the look of the estuary and surrounding the bases of the soaring bridge supports. The effect was stunning.

He parked and strolled back towards the pub close to the marina. He reckoned Gacela wouldn't be expecting him to arrive on foot and he drank in the smell of the estuary as he walked. The sound of halyards clinking against masts set a rhythm playing in his head. Pausing, he gazed at the boats lifted from the water onto the marina's hard standing for repair and maintenance. The whole scene fascinated him.

A quick scan of the car park told him Gacela hadn't arrived, at least judging by there being no sign of a blue Fiat 500. He approached the pub's side entrance and made his way to the main bar.

'A half of your Adnams on tap, please. And are you still serving Sunday brunch?' he asked the barman.

'Sorry, last orders for brunch finished five minutes ago. Ghost Ship OK for you? It's a pale malty ale with a touch of citrus.'

'Yeah, sounds good to me.' Disappointed to be missing out on bacon and egg in a toasted bun, he sat on a bar stool and looked round. There were plenty of Sunday drinkers, but no one resembling a Spanish beauty with rich dark brown hair and striking eyebrows and lashes. So, Gacela hadn't slipped in while he was ordering at the bar. He sipped his beer when it came, and tried to ease the knot of developing tension.

He spotted Gacela before she saw him. He smiled and waved as he caught her glance.

'Hi, Nick!' she mouthed and wove around a family group to join him.

'Hi!' He kissed her lightly on the cheek and looked pointedly down at her feet, her toes seemingly cool and free in minimal strappy sandals. 'Hey, I reckon you must've been abusing your feet again in those black pumps yesterday,' he murmured suggestively.

He knew she'd pick up the inference to her waitressing footwear worn the previous afternoon. He figured guilt would make her over react and deny his insinuation that she needed to ease her feet and let her toes recover. It was all part of the game – did he or did he not know she'd lied to him? He'd keep her guessing.

'What are you talking about, Nick?' Her tone rang sharp, and then she appeared to relent as she added, 'I tried out some new nail colours yesterday and silver matched my dress. I rather like it. What do you say?' She wiggled her toes as if to show off the silver nail varnish. He recalled they'd been a burgundy colour when they'd met in the cocktail bar.

'Silver's nice. Goes with your necklace. So what would you like to drink? Your usual Cosmo? How was the family celebration yesterday?'

'Woa, slow down. One question at a time.'

'OK then, first - what to drink?'

'Something long, like a spritzer.' She settled for sparkling soda water and white wine in a tall glass with a slice of lime.

'Come on, let's find a table outside.' Nick carried their glasses and led the way while she brought a menu card.

The beer garden was partly covered in patio tiles and the rest had been given over to rough-cut grass and a children's play area. Trestle tables with bench seats and sun-bleached umbrellas on pedestals completed the look. It was hardly a sexy venue.

'I thought we could walk along the footpath next to the Orwell after we've eaten,' he said, hoping he'd added a touch of suggested romance to the meeting.

'That would be nice. I was hoping we'd walk. That's why I put on my sandals,' she murmured.

'Yeah, of course.' He smiled, but he wasn't convinced. Nice recovery on her part, he thought.

They chose a table in a quiet area of the garden and

studied the menu.

'Hmm, I'm going to have something light. The smoked chicken salad sounds nice,' she said, her eyes still on the menu.

'That doesn't sound very much. Hey, are you OK?'

'Yes, of course. You're forgetting I ate loads yesterday. Mum's birthday, remember?'

'Oh right. So what did you have?'

'Too much!'

He laughed. 'Well I think as the bacon and eggs are off, it'll have to be a burger for me.'

'Here, I've got some photos if you want to look.' She leaned towards him and held her phone so he could see.

'A hog roast? How big was this party?'

'My mum's side of the family is pretty extensive. Lots of cousins. I told you.'

He studied the image. The hog roast was the focus of the shot, and the few people caught by the lens had their backs to the camera as they faced the roasting spit.

'Are you in any of the shots?'

'No, I don't do selfies.'

'The hog roast looks awesome. Now I get the family interest in food.'

'Yes, sometimes it can be a real burden,' she laughed, 'but tell me, how was your gig in Bury last night?'

She looked up, still holding her phone for him. He noticed how her dark eyelashes added smoky tones to her eyes. She's hot, he thought, but she's lying. It was fun to flirt. His problem was that he rather liked her.

'I'll go and order the food,' he said and flashed a smile.

When he was back at the table and they waited for her salad and his burger, she asked him again about the gig the evening before.

He couldn't help it, but when he talked to her about music and the band, he slipped into a different world and relaxed into his usual self. The first time they'd met, it was his passion for carpentry that filled the conversation. This time it became music. She had a knack of getting him to talk.

'But what about you?' he asked finally, 'You've hardly said a word.'

'I've been listening to you. Hey, but remember last week when I asked you about drugs and bands and if it was a problem for you? I told you I'd noticed a guy, probably a dealer with ecstasy hanging around your band when we first met. In Freston? So, have you noticed any dealers now I've pointed it out to you?'

He thought for a moment. 'No, I can't say that I have. Mind you I haven't gone looking. What made you suddenly ask?'

'No reason. But the other things I said? About drugs not always being in pills or powder form? You know, drinks, smokes, hashish cakes… chocolates? Have you noticed or come across anything?'

'Now that's a weird question. What are you getting at?'

'Nothing. I'm just looking out for you, that's all. You see some of the venues I waitress at… well we get to see all sorts. People ask for all kinds of things.'

'I bet they do! But you can't be serious about chocolates. It's not the type of thing doing the rounds in the nightclubs round here, at least not the sort we play!'

'It's what's in the chocolates, I'm talking about.'

'Oh, right.' He stared into his glass and thought for a moment.

‘Do many waitresses become dealers, then?’

‘Of course not. And before you ask, I’m not a dealer or a user. Got that?’

‘OK. But what about the waitress from Hyphen & Green who was killed? Was she a dealer?’

‘I’ve no idea. Hey, I think this is our order.’ She waved to a teenager in a black tee and skinny jeans, a plate of food in each hand and scanning the beer garden.

They didn’t say much while they ate. Nick was hungry and wanted to concentrate on his burger and chips. When he’d eaten his last mouthful he watched Gacela as she picked over the remains of her salad. The bunch of charm-like silver dragonflies, enamelled blackberries and leaves swayed on her silver necklace as she leaned over her plate.

‘Aren’t you going to finish that? Was it OK?’ he asked.

‘Yes, it’s nice. I didn’t expect so many radishes.’

‘Don’t you like radishes?’

She shrugged. ‘Not today.’

‘Cool necklace, by the way.’

‘Hmm, I got it in a shop in Woodbridge recently.’

He didn’t say anything. It was the first spontaneous thing she’d told him about herself and when he thought about it, she hadn’t really told him anything at all.

He waited for her while she went to freshen up, his mind filled with the idea of inlaying a design of dragonflies, blackberries and leaves on the trinket box lid. When she returned she looked serious and carried her mobile in her hand.

‘Do you want to take a walk by the water? It’s pretty beyond the bridge. I think the path goes all the way to the Wolverstone Marina, if you want,’ Nick asked.

‘It sounds really nice, but I’m sorry, Nick. I’ve just had

a call. It seems they're a waitress down for this evening. I'm going to have to leave now.'

'What? Really? But… this evening doesn't have to start now. It's only just turned half past two. We could take a shorter walk if you like?'

'Sorry, Nick. I have to get back. By the time I've showered and changed… and also I'm needed early to help set up.'

'Well OK, but at least I can walk with you to your car?'

She seemed preoccupied as they threaded their way back through the main bar and out to the car park.

'It was a great idea of yours, brunch by the Orwell,' Nick said as she unlocked her car.

'Hmm, and I was looking forward to the walk as well.'

'I know; you came in your sandals. But music, waitressing, it all seems rather–'

'The service industry is antisocial, Nick. We work unsociable hours. It's just how it is.' She delivered the line deadpan, as if it was some kind of mantra. He tried to read her face and detected a trace of agitation. What was really going on?

'Bye, Nick. See you again soon.' A fleeting kiss, a frown and then almost as an afterthought she asked, 'But where's your car? You are all right to get back?' The Fiat engine leapt into life before he could answer. It was obvious she wasn't offering a lift.

He stood to one side and raised his hand in a half-wave as she drove away. He got the impression she didn't even look back in her mirror, as if all her thoughts were on whatever lay ahead. He would have liked to have followed, seen where she was going, but of course it was impossible. Instead he considered the more practical options - another beer or a solitary walk. But, there was also a third possibility.

# CHAPTER 22

Matt slumped on the sofa in Chrissie's living room, his recharged laptop on his knee. He couldn't settle to anything, his mind was in too much turmoil. Clive had left a few hours earlier and so far there'd been no word back from him.

'Clive will come back here, or ring us? I mean he aint forgotten us, has he?' he asked Chrissie, his anxiety spiralling.

'Of course he won't forget. As long as nothing else comes along and side-tracks him,' she soothed.

'So you're sayin' you think he could've forgotten. Should I give 'im a call, then?'

'No. Give him a bit longer. He'll only get irritated if we hassle him. Where's Maisie waitressing this evening?'

'It's,' he pictured the file Maisie had emailed, 'today is Sunday, 1st September. So it's in Framlingham, Castle Street.'

'Framlingham Castle?'

'Nah, not exactly, but close. It's for some kinda history or genealogy group. A special celebratory meetin'. It don't say exactly what. But the pickup point for lifts is the Copdock interchange car park, 5:15 pm.'

'Is it Gacela giving the lifts again?'

'Yeah, the Spanish goat. Well it don't call her the Spanish goat on the spread sheet, but yeah.'

'You've met her, haven't you? Do you think she could be a killer?'

'I don't know. We aint really said much, but Mais likes her.' He sank into his own thoughts, adding, 'An' Nick likes her.'

'Hmm, it's frightening. You'd think the police would have rounded up all the Hyphen & Green people and checked them out really thoroughly by now. Clive says they've all been interviewed, but I still don't think they know the first thing about some of them. It's almost as if no one's telling the police anything.'

'You mean like one of them conspiracy theories, Chrissie?'

'Yes, I suppose so.'

'That's interestin' because for me, see recent, when I've been searchin' people on the net, I keep comin' up against websites an' postin's in Dutch. But I don't speak no Dutch.'

'What? You think you've got a Dutch virus on your computer?'

'Nah, me searches 've been for people turnin' out to be Dutch. I'll just 'ave to wait till I'm in Bury tomorrow and can use Damon's translator app, that's all.'

'Right, well I reckon Gert, he's Clive's Dutch police contact, is pretty much like your translator app, except it'll take him a lot longer. This is turning out to be more far-reaching than anyone imagined, what with the Dutch connection. I'm starting to think what's happened here could be just the tip of the iceberg.'

He didn't speak for a moment. He needed to think it through, but talking with Chrissie while surfing the net at least helped assuage some of his fear. It was how he'd spent most of the morning after Clive had left to set the investigating team onto Gacela.

Matt turned his attention back to reading about the various date rape drugs. 'We had a shedload,' he muttered. But was it Rohypnol, Ketamine or GHB? And did it really matter now that it was all over and out of his system?

His stomach and guts still felt gripey, but Chrissie had said it was probably just anxiety or too much fried bacon. Either way, he wasn't hungry for lunch. She had also told him the doctor's best guess was GHB, pending the results, but knowing that wasn't going to stop him searching. His mind was too restless to settle.

*Mixing GHB with a sweet drink masks the salty taste*, Matt read. What had Chrissie said about caramel? It was basically pure sugar, admittedly not a drink but still very sweet and when combined with GHB it was a confectionary winner. He reckoned you'd have to be a chef or confectioner to have thought up something like that.

'Epibotics! No wonder it were called *salted* caramel. If I hadn't been here with you, I'd 've eaten the whole box,' he muttered.

'We don't know yet if all the chocolates were laced with the drug, Matt.'

'Yeah, but if they were it could've killed me. You know Damon says, when you reach a dead end searchin' a person you should switch to searchin' about somethin' related to 'em, like a possession or one of them hobbies.'

'How do you mean? Are you saying we should start searching for GHB or chocolate suppliers?'

'Nah, but we've reached a dead end coz all the info's in Dutch, right? So what if we start searchin' for their possessions?'

'Like what?'

'Like Kinver Greane's car. I mean I'm guessin' he had a car. So what do you reckon happened to it? Where's it now?'

'But Matt, if Kinver had a car, the police will have

traced it and checked it over.'

'Yeah, but what if it were a stolen car. It won't 've been registered in his name. It kinda covers his tracks. Have you asked Clive?'

'No I haven't but I'm sure they'll have gone through all his things. He probably had a Dutch driving licence and a Dutch registered car.'

'Yeah, and he were already known to the Dutch police, right?'

*Beep-itty-beep! Beep-itty-beep beep!* Matt never heard Chrissie's reply as he grabbed his phone and read the caller ID.

'Oh no! It's Nick and Clive aint got back to me yet. Do I tell 'im 'bout the Spanish goat?' he wailed.

'Answer it, go on answer it, Matt! Hey, put him on loudspeaker. Then I can help you if you don't know what to say to him.'

Matt swallowed hard. 'Hi,' he muttered and pressed the loudspeaker setting.

'Hiya, mate. Are you OK to talk?' Nick's voice travelled around Chrissie's living room, amplified and tinny-toned.

Chrissie nodded and Matt followed her signal, 'Yeah, go on then,' he said cautiously.

'Look, you said Maisie gets a lift with Gacela to the waitressing jobs after you've dropped her off at the pickup point.'

'Yeah.'

'And you pick Maisie up at the drop-off point when Gacela brings her back afterwards, right?'

'Yeah.'

'So, would you be able to follow Gacela after you've

picked up Maisie? See where she's going? What she's up to?'

'What?' Matt didn't need to look at Chrissie. Horror gripped him. 'But Maisie'd be on the back of me scooter. It'd be obvious we were followin'.'

'Yeah, I get that, but say I picked Maisie up and then you followed Gacela?'

'But aint you and Mais not meant to be talkin'? Weren't that what all the bowls club thing were about?'

'Right. Do you think Chrissie would pick Maisie up instead and then you followed Gacela?'

Matt looked at Chrissie. She shook her head; waved her hands.

'I don't know. You'll 'ave to ask her yourself.' He was about to hand his mobile to her, but she was still waving her hands and mouthing *no*. 'Why'd you want her followed?' he asked, curious.

'I've just had brunch with her. There's something going on and she's not telling me and I don't even know if she's even part of it. I'm kinda worried about her. She may not be safe. If I was the one following her it would just seem creepy, like I'm some kind of weirdo stalker. I thought it'd be the kind of think you're into, Matt, what with all your searching and tracing stuff you've done on her. What d'you say?'

'Like I'm a weirdo stalker?'

Chrissie closed her eyes and shook her head.

'No, Matt. You're,' Nick's voice dropped, 'well you're a kinda investigator not a stalker. Look, just think about it, OK?'

Chrissie drew her finger across her throat repeatedly, like a knife.

‘Err… cut. I-I’ll get back to you if I change me mind. OK?’ Matt whispered, anxiety squeezing his voice, not sure whose throat he was supposed to cut.

*End the call*, Chrissie mouthed at him, but Nick had already gone.

‘There, that wasn’t so bad was it,’ Chrissie said.

# CHAPTER 23

Chrissie stood at her front door and waved as Matt scootered away. He seemed to have coped surprisingly well with unwittingly taking a shedload, as he'd called it, of date rape drug. She, on the other hand, couldn't shrug off the outrage of it all. And now, following Clive's reassurance, he was riding off to collect Maisie and take her to the Copdock interchange pickup for a lift with Gacela. She was worried about him and frightened for Maisie.

'It'll be OK. Bye,' she called, more to herself than him, her words taken on the warm afternoon breeze.

She caught the faint scent of late flowering chrysanthemums just coming into bloom near her front door. It helped to calm and steady her nerve.

'Oh God,' she sighed, hoping they were doing the right thing. But what choice did they have? Clive had told them to take Gacela at face value and to forget about her alternative name and persona used a year or so previously. He'd said they needed to watch out for themselves but not to behave any differently towards her. If they showed their distrust then Gacela might realise they were onto her.

Chrissie wasn't very good at taking instructions without being given a reason, and Clive had been less than transparent with his explanations. She figured it was time to press Clive for more information now that Matt had gone.

Back in her living room once again and ensconced on the sofa with a mug of tea, she faced Clive across the coffee table. He sat in the armchair, eyes closed, as if weary. Chrissie knew from his frown lines and tension in his face that he was nowhere near sleep. She guessed he was concentrating on the case and shutting his eyes to lock out distraction.

'What are you thinking?' she asked.

'I'm trying to see the bigger picture, and no puns about being in the dark, please.'

She smiled, despite her angst. 'Well I'm hoping you know a lot more than you've told us, Clive, because you haven't told us much. I mean we're taking it in good faith that Maisie will be all right. What if you're sending her back into a hornets nest? What if she–'

'Gets stung? Don't you think I'm well aware of that? Look, I didn't want to say this while Matt was here in case he told Maisie, but I spoke to the chief today about Gacela. You know the kind of thing - should we pull her in for questioning again, maybe arrest her, or at the very least track her? He got back to me, warned me off. We're to steer well clear. There's a bigger investigation going on and we could jeopardise it by sniffing around Gacela.'

'What bigger investigation?'

'I don't know. He wouldn't say.'

'Wouldn't say, or you're not going to tell me?'

'He couldn't say. Information sharing at high level only.'

'But you're investigating two murders. What's not high level about that? And what about Maisie? What happens to her while you're trying not to upset some other investigation? And open your eyes, for God's sake. It's really irritating talking to you with your eyes closed.'

'OK, OK.' He opened his eyes. 'What you don't know is that I had already asked Matt last week to tell me everything Maisie tells him about Hyphen & Green.'

'Like that's going to protect her? And don't say you can

use her as a spy. I mean you have met her, haven't you?'

'It'll be fine, Chrissie. You know Maisie's safer if she has no idea what's going on. Her ignorance of the whole business is her best protection. I certainly don't fancy her chances if she tries to use any guile. And if she doesn't turn up this evening, well they'll know she stole the chocolates.'

'Or ate them. But what about Nick? He had brunch with Gacela today. We already told you he rang while you were out. I think he's keen on her, and he must be worried because he asked Matt to follow her. And Matt really did say no, by the way.'

'Good. At least Matt is following instructions. Nick is more difficult.'

Chrissie opened her mouth, about to fly to Nick's defence, but it was obvious Clive was going to be right about Nick over this. She changed track. 'Matt told me today that when he and Damon are doing their internet people tracing, if their usual avenues don't come up with anything, then they concentrate on searching the subject's possessions and hobbies. So I was wondering, what happened to Kinver Greane's car, if he had one? I mean I'm assuming he drove to the allotments in Bury where he was murdered, right?'

'Yes, he was known to drive a blue Toyota GT86 which turns out was a re-sprayed stolen car. It finally surfaced in the long stay car park at the Harwich ferry passenger terminal. It came up on the car park system as not having been collected after about 4 weeks. Since then it's taken the best part of another 4 weeks to connect it with Kinver Greane. The forensic team are taking it apart as we speak!'

'But if it was a stolen car, how did the car park people connect it to Kinver?'

'They didn't. The number plates were cloned ones; copies of genuine plates belonging to a similar blue 2012 registered Toyota GT86, but owned, taxed and insured by someone living in the London area. The London owner, when presented with a huge parking and collection bill, was able to show he had his car with him and give the genuine chassis and engine number.'

'And of course the ones on the Harwich long-stay blue Toyota were for a different Toyota. The stolen one.'

'Exactly, by which time we knew from the Dutch police that Kinver's credit cards had been used in Holland for the best part of a couple of months after he'd died and he'd supposedly travelled there on the ferry from Harwich. After that it was a case of old fashioned police work and checking for cars abandoned in or close to Harwich.'

'But how did you know John Brown hadn't taken the Toyota with him on the ferry?'

'We didn't, but there was no record of Visa or Amex payment on Kinver's cards for a car crossing on the ferry. Also Gert has CCTV footage from a gas station where Kinver's Visa was used to pay for fuel in Holland. It shows John Brown with a different car.'

'But–'

'And also we were lucky. Luck always plays a part. We're expecting Forensics to confirm from fingerprints and hair evidence etcetera, that it was Kinver's car. Hopefully they'll find some other interesting stuff in it as well.'

'Hey, I wonder where his car was re-sprayed. I suppose it would be too much of a coincidence if…,' Chrissie murmured, her thoughts running off at a tangent.

'Hmm, now that was a really heavy-handed hint, Chrissie; even for you.'

She looked at him with her eyebrows raised and tried to maintain an offended innocent expression.

'Yes, I know you're itching to be told if anything's come of Dave's observations about the Hadleigh car body repair outlet. But give us a chance. You only told me yesterday morning and I passed it straight on to Stickley. He's been trawling through that side of things since Juliette Poels' murder. So now I've got him looking into the current cars going through the Hadleigh outlet as well.' He held up his hands in a mock hold-your-fire gesture.

'I suppose it's still only Sunday today. It just seems to have been a very long day, that's all.'

'Hey, it could have been worse, Chrissie.'

She watched him stand up and negotiate his way around the coffee table before sitting down next to her on the sofa.

'And there's no reason to expect any lasting harm. So come on, try to stop worrying about your memory. If it helps any, I think… well your brain seems to me to be as sharp as ever. But you need to give it a rest now.'

'You're probably right. It's still only Sunday.' She finally allowed herself to relax and leaned sideways, resting her head on his shoulder.

•••

Monday morning in the Clegg & Jax workshop started in pretty much the same way as on most Monday mornings of the year. Chrissie parked her TR7 outside the old barn at around eight o'clock and hurried inside, but on this occasion she carried the veneered writing box. Ron was already sitting at a workbench. 'Good morning, Mr Clegg,' she called by force of habit. He was busy, as always at this early hour with a particularly delicate piece or some precision carpentry, a mug of tea close to hand.

‘Good morning, Mrs Jax. I see you’ve got the writing box with you. Bring it over; let me see how well the vacuum press worked.’

‘I think it’s good. Nick set the vacuum to last overnight.’ She could have also said that Nick hadn’t been particularly communicative when she’d collected it on Saturday morning. At the time she’d supposed it was the after-effects from too much alcohol and his Friday evening date with Gacela, and so she hadn’t asked him how the date had gone. Now she felt a flash of regret for her lapse.

She set the writing box down on Ron’s workbench and stood back while he ran his hand over the highly figured rosewood veneer. It followed the contours of the underlying carcass wood, and when he tapped it with his gnarled finger, there were no papery tones. It sounded as one solid piece of wood, veneer and carcass united without air pockets or space between.

‘I’d say that’s pretty good. What d’you think, Mrs Jax?’

‘I think it worked like magic. I have to say I’m rather tempted, but I need to work out the cost first. In the meantime I’m putting the kettle on for a mug of tea. Do you want a refill, Mr Clegg?’

Chrissie had anticipated Ron’s positive response the moment she’d collected the writing box on Saturday morning. But he wasn’t a businessman and neither was she. At least with her accountant’s hat on she knew she couldn’t be swept along by enthusiasm alone. She waited for the kettle to boil and tried to keep her mind on the day ahead. But what would she say if he asked about her weekend? Be logical, she thought. It wasn’t Ron’s way to ask, he usually waited to be told. So she’d be OK and she wouldn’t have to lie.

‘Will you need any help with delivering Mrs De Vries’ games table?’ Ron asked, pulling her thoughts into tighter focus.

‘I should be fine, thanks, Mr Clegg. But if you’d give me a hand lifting it into the van, then her husband can help me unload when I get there. Mrs De Vries said any time after five o’clock, so I’ve got all day for polishing. We don’t need to load up for ages.’

Her words turned out to be surprisingly accurate. Her day centred on her favourite dark brown polish - beeswax mixed with carnauba wax and turpentine. She worked for ages, applying it and then once the coats had hardened, burnishing it with a furniture brush. The final polishing with a clean duster seemed endless.

‘It looks magnificent, Mrs Jax,’ Ron said as they carried it through the barn workshop and out into the sunny courtyard. She flung open the rear doors of the firm’s smart ex-Scottish Forestry Commission van and together they lifted in the table.

‘We’re doing OK, Mr Clegg. The business is doing OK.’ She patted the yellow stripe along the side of the forest-green Citroen van. *Clegg & Jax. Master Cabinet Makers and Furniture Restorers* was printed where once it had read *Forestry Commission, Scotland*.

She took her time as she drove along the rough track from the workshop to the airfield perimeter lane. She was careful to avoid any sharp swerves around potholes, and there was no rocking & rolling across the ruts. The special Citroen van had high ground clearance and great traction, but she was conscious of the table loaded in the back. The return journey could be another matter, she told herself.

Mrs De Vries lived to the east of the workshop, about

seven miles as the crow flies, but whereas a crow could fly across the Wattisham airfield, Chrissie had to drive around it and that added several miles to her journey. She hadn't been to Mrs De Vries' home before, it was somewhere out towards Great Blakenham and she reminded herself of the address. The house was called Rozenhof, obviously a Dutch word sounding like roses. She hoped it would be easy to find and pictured an idyllic cottage tucked away in some secluded spot.

The miles sped by as she wondered about the people who might have sat around the table and played dice and card games. She guessed there would have been many, if she counted all the ones since it had been made in Holland over 250 years earlier. It was an absorbing train of thought and it kept her from worrying about Maisie or Nick.

Rozenhof turned out to be a modern house with a manicured front garden. The only nod to roses was a metal trellis with a pale pink climbing variety close to the front door. Chrissie parked in the drive and got out of the van.

'Mrs De Vries?' Chrissie called by way of a greeting as she watched a middle-aged woman approach from the side of the house.

'Yes, hello, you must be Chrissie. We spoke on the phone. My husband should be here any moment.' Almost on cue an open topped jeep turned into the drive.

'Ah, and here he is. The YA 66. It's his pride and joy. You won't see many around. I think they only ever made about twelve hundred. This one's from 1975.'

'It's a DAF, isn't it?' Chrissie said, reading the letters on the centre of the radiator grille. 'They're Dutch aren't they?'

'Yes, are you interested in cars?' Mrs De Vries asked as

they watched her husband jump down from the jeep.

It looked ex-military with its khaki coloured bodywork. Chrissie couldn't help but notice the fishing gear loaded into the back. She recognised the shape of the rod cases and spotted a fishing keep net. It all looked pretty similar to the kit she'd watched the man in the Alton Water car park load into his car. She spoke without really thinking.

'Hello Mr De Vries. I must say I love the DAF jeep. Have you been out fishing?' And then she realised how she must have sounded and her face flamed.

'Darling, this is Chrissie from Clegg & Jax. She's here with your mother's old games table. You're just in time to help carry it inside.'

'Yes, of course. I have been looking forward to seeing it back to its old splendour.' He spoke with a hint of a Dutch accent as Chrissie threw open the rear van doors, loosened the tie down straps and slipped the dustsheet off the old games table.

He took one end and she the other, while his wife led the way along the flagstone path between the side of the house and a double-length garage. They followed the path through a flower garden of roses. It was flanked by the main body of the house and a rear wing, together forming an L-shape.

'The roses are magnificent!' Chrissie exclaimed.

'Yes, this is our rozenhof,' Mr De Vries said.

'Hof?' she queried.

'It's Dutch for yard, or court.'

'This way,' Mrs De Vries said and opened French windows into a light summery living room. 'We keep it just here.' She indicated the spot.

Chrissie saw the imprints left on the plush carpet where the table's feet had rested. Hadn't she guessed a thick pile carpet had some part to play in damaging the swivel-out legs used to support the table flap? For once she held her tongue as she helped position the table.

'Mamma would be so pleased. This looks wonderful now,' Mr De Vries said. He stepped back, a smile creasing his kind face and revealing uniform white teeth. He struck Chrissie as being at least ten years older than his wife. His hair, no doubt once blond was thinning, now a short indeterminate gravel colour, and his square shoulders drooped slightly.

'Were you the one to work on this?' he asked, lifting the table flap and swivelling out the support legs.

'Yes. It's a quality piece, and unusual to be made of teak. I managed to use old teak in the repair, and of course a good wax polish always brings out the beautiful tones in the wood.' She couldn't stop herself from adding, 'If you put up the flap frequently, it might be easier on those swivel legs if the table wasn't standing on such a luxurious thick pile carpet.'

She watched his face to see if she'd caused offence.

'You like old cars too?' he asked.

'Well, I have a bit of a weakness for a classic car. I drive a 1981 TR7.'

'That's why you noticed the DAF jeep. And do you fish as well?'

'No. I don't have the time.'

'Fishing is good. I am a member of the Gipping Valley Angling Club. There's good fishing in the flooded gravel pits around here. It's very pretty along the Gipping Valley.'

'You mean like Needham Lake? Do you ever fish at Alton Water?'

'Alton Water? No, it is too far. Why go when I have so

much here?'

'What did you catch today, darling?' Mrs De Vries asked, as if she'd only just noticed the conversation.

'A small carp and some roach and bream, dear.'

Something Matt had said while they waited for Clive to get back to them on Sunday pinged into Chrissie's mind.

'Pike? What about pike?' she asked remembering him mention John Brown or someone called Mr Risotto cooking a summer treat of pike and rice for his garden allotment friends. He'd apparently caught one in the River Lark.

'Pike? Yes, there are many. They like plenty of vegetation in the water, which we have here. They like to collect in the weedy areas such as in the Alderson Lakes, but no one fishes them at this time of year. They are very aggressive in the summer. They would have your hand off.'

'Oh, right,' she said. 'So no one fishes pike in the summer?'

'Well, I can't speak for everyone, but none of my angling club. Why risk getting hurt? Pike don't taste good enough for it.'

When Chrissie drove home, she found herself replaying the conversation about pike fishing in her mind. She tried to recall the last time she'd seen pike on a menu, and couldn't summon up even one occasion. Was a summer-caught pike the trophy of a man trying to show he was hard? It sounded too crazy to be the rite of passage for an underworld gang, and unusual as a warning or message. No, it was more likely a random chance catch, except from the sound of it, hooking and landing a pike in the summer wasn't an act of random chance. She was curious.

# CHAPTER 24

‘Hi, Nick.’ Matt’s voice sounded thready over the airwaves as he answered Nick’s call.

‘Hiya, Matt! Have you had a chance to think about that favour I asked you to do for me? You know, the one I called you about yesterday, Sunday? To follow Gacela?’ Nick sat in his Fiesta in the supermarket car park and spoke into his mobile. He waited for a reply, but all he got was silence.

‘Hey Matt, can you hear me?’

‘Yeah, I can hear. Look, I’m sorry mate, but I can’t. I just can’t.’

‘OK, no need to get upset. Your voice cut out for a moment back there. You sounded… well I mean you’re all right, aren’t you?’

There was no answer and Matt’s silence irritated him. He doubted it was all down to poor reception, more likely Matt not knowing what to say. Why the hell couldn’t he just speak?

He changed his tone; ‘Hey, it’s OK, Matt. I suppose it was a bit weird me asking you to follow Gacela for me. Anyway, forget it. Subject closed. See you in the Nags Head on Friday, or before if you fancy a pint sooner.’ Nick ended the call, but instead of feeling some kind of closure, he was overwhelmed by a tide of frustration.

Perhaps it was just a response triggered by a long Monday in the Willows workshop. He’d been working on the French oak staircase. The stringer he’d started on Friday required finishing and another identical one cut, and then there were the treads and kickboards for the steps. By the end of it he felt as if he'd cut a pile of oblongs for a fiendish puzzle or giant parquet flooring, and the stringers looked like a pair of massive frame saw blades with over-sized teeth.

'I see you've been busy,' Dave had said when he'd poked his head into the workshop at the end of the day. Nick had responded by grinning and throwing a polishing rag at him.

The memory made Nick smile as he slipped his mobile back into his pocket and started the Fiesta.

He'd dropped by the supermarket on his drive home from Willows. He needed to stock up with essentials: a box of a dozen bottled beers, a loaf of bread, a slab of cheese and a readymade meal for the microwave. He hadn't thought about Gacela all day, at least not until he walked past the flowers and newspaper stand on his way back to his car. The sight of them brought her crashing back and hence his call for an update from Matt.

So, he thought as he eased the car out of its parking space, the situation hadn't changed. Matt wasn't going to play ball and follow Gacela for him. It was hardly a surprise. He reckoned he'd just have to play it cool until he'd worked out what the girl was up to. And playing it cool meant he needed to rethink the trinket box project.

Making something from wood for her was personal; it was supposed to be a statement about wood, carpentry and his skill. Did he really want to spend his time on something like this simply to impress someone he didn't understand?

Furthermore, incorporating a design of inlayed blackberries, silver dragonflies and leaves, similar to the ones she wore on her necklace, suited Chrissie's skillset better than his. Wouldn't it be quicker and easier if he simply went to the shop in Woodbridge and looked for something with blackberries on it? He was tempted. Why even make a trinket box, he asked himself. And why drive all the way to Woodbridge when he might be able to buy something featuring blackberries much closer to home?

His thoughts flew around as he headed for Woolpit and his garret bedsit. It was only as he carried his box of beers up the outside wooden steps and unlocked his door that he realised he had a very good reason to go to Woodbridge. How else would he know if Gacela had lied to him again? If the shop didn't exist, had never existed, then he'd have his answer.

# CHAPTER 25

Matt sat in the airless Balcon & Mora office and gazed at his screen. It was late Tuesday morning and he planned to leave by midday. He needed to catch the photographer at Utterly Academy. He'd already missed the Monday afternoon photo session and Tuesday afternoon would be his last chance to update his mug shot for his pass.

'You don't seem to be doing much,' Damon said from his desk behind Matt.

'Yeah well I've already worked through me list of names.' He heard the creak, knew the moves. 'You're doin' that arm stretch thing, aint you? If you're stoppin' for another coffee, can I have one them cans of Coke?'

'Right, if we're taking a break, you can tell me what you were doing with the translator programme yesterday. Leon Jansen? He wasn't on the list of names to trace for the credit card company.'

'Ah, well it were a bit complicated.' How much to say, Matt wondered. He ran through his checklist of who he wasn't supposed to tell and what he'd been told not to spill. Leon's name didn't feature.

'I followed Maisie like you said, to check she were OK waitressin' at the bowls club on Saturday. In Felixstowe.'

'You really did it?'

'Yeah, and see I took some photos of the caterin' crew without them knowin'. One of them photos came up as Leon Jansen when I ran it on Google facial recognition.'

'And he's Dutch?'

'Yeah, and the Dutch stuff I found with the translator were about cookin' an' fishin'. He were holdin' a big fish he'd caught.'

While Matt talked, Damon moved quickly around the office, handing him a can of Coke and then returning to his own desk with a mug of coffee. Within seconds Matt heard him tapping on his keyboard.

'Hey, it seems coarse fishing is big in Holland. Not surprising with all that water. They're awash with canals in Amsterdam and this site keeps mentioning *polders*,' Damon said.

'Polders? What you lookin' at?'

'Here, I'll send you the link. I think it's a Dutch word.'

'*Polder*,' Matt read out, '*a low-lying swathe of land enclosed by dikes* and yeah, *the dikes are filled with water*. It's… like flooded land reclaimed from the sea? Hey, there's pictures of polders with windmills on the edge.'

'It says something here about *monstrous pike* and *big fishing* around the polders.'

'Yeah, and *lazy chair anglin'* for roach, tench & bream.'

'Well Matt, judging by the picture of Leon Jansen on this Dutch site, he's more into big fishing than lazy chair angling. That looks a pretty vicious fish he's holding.'

'Yeah, accordin' to this site, *sport fishin' is the third most popular sport in the Netherlands*,' Matt murmured as he scrolled through the search results. Would Kinver Greane have been into big fishing as well, he wondered.

Something stirred in the back of his mind. Pike. The memory came flooding back, just as it had on Sunday when he'd told Chrissie. There'd been an old man in a flat cap, the one he'd spoken to when he'd ridden his Vespa to the allotments in Bury St Edmunds on that fateful day. Matt remembered asking where Flodden Drive was and the way to Poachers, which had turned out to be John Brown's shed.

The old man had told him about a pike and a Mr Risotto before giving him directions. But the memory sequence didn't freeze there. It rolled on so that he relived the shed and the nightmare played again.

'Are you OK, Matt?' Damon asked.

'Yeah, just somethin' you said set me rememberin'. An' Chrissie did the same thing the other day when she talked about fishin' and Alton Water. Funny, but I aint thought about it for a couple of weeks and then twice in a couple of days.'

'You've thought about fishing?'

'Nah the dead man. It's like a kinda sequence. I aint s'posed to talk about the dead man. Seems fishing and pike are OK to talk about, but it sets me head off.'

'OK, then let's not talk about p-pi fishing. Tell me about following your girlfriend.'

Matt explained his strategy – the variations with his helmet full face visor up or down, the different jackets, sweatshirts, and backpack positioning. 'See, there aint no number plate on the front of me scooter and I were real careful.'

'I'm impressed. But your Vespa must stand out. Didn't you say special edition?'

'Yeah, blackberry bubblegum.'

'Could you dull it down a bit?'

'Hey, what you sayin'?'

'If the colour was grey or black you'd be less noticeable.'

'Yeah, well I like the colour of me scooter. It's retro.' He knew it stood out. It was his statement. Retro Italian. Cool.

'Hmm, well you still managed to get those photos. It

may be an area we should expand into. See how this one goes first, hey?'

'Yeah.' Matt let his eyes drift back to his screen and the scenic shot of glassy water-filled dikes and a windmill. How, he wondered, could John Brown have been into *big fishing* and he not find a single reference to any kind of fishing when he'd searched about him? Even his foodie blog hadn't been particularly heavy with fish.

'Why are you rushing back to the Academy this afternoon?' Damon asked.

'What?' Matt dragged his mind onto Damon's track.

'Why the Academy today? I thought you said you were helping in the practical sessions on Thursday mornings?'

'Yeah, well I am. Today it's me ID pass photo.' He could also have said he was meeting Maisie mid-afternoon. She was working a short shift in the retro-clothes shop in the centre of Stowmarket and she'd wanted to meet him for *a bit of a talk*, afterwards. He hadn't liked to ask what it was about.

He fumbled around his neck and tugged on the blue lanyard. The plastic card on its end appeared at his throat. He flipped it outside his tee-shirt and let it drop and dangle like a giant pendant from the 60s.

'Let's have a look.' Damon held out his hand.

'Err… yeah, OK then.' Matt slipped it over his head and tossed it at Damon. He hadn't wanted to take it off. It was like a talisman, a badge of honour: *Matt Finch, Utterly Academy, Computing & IT Department. Assistant Demonstrator*. It also had a face shot of a serious eighteen year old fresher caught with unblinking gaze and smooth skin. It was the most important thing he'd ever worn around his neck.

‘Hah! You haven’t got a beard on this. It makes you look kind of different. If they give you a new one, keep this. It could be useful if you’re going to do more of this real world tracing,’ Damon said.

•••

Matt rode into the centre of Stowmarket. He was making good time. It seemed to him that fate intended he meet Maisie, mid-afternoon, three thirty, just as she’d instructed. He’d half hoped it would take longer to be photographed at the Academy. It would have given him an excuse to be late. He’d assumed there’d be a re-run of when his mug shot was taken in 2009, but of course he’d partly forgotten. Back then he’d been a fresher, too shy to ask the way. It had taken him hours; a journey of discovery around the Academy site. Unfortunately this time he’d had his photo taken quickly and efficiently. He reckoned it was fate playing with him once again.

And why did Maisie want to have *a bit of a talk* with him? And about what? She was always talking. It seemed odd to tell him in advance she was going to talk.

He parked his scooter along Church Walk, behind the market place. It was a tranquil spot, tucked away from the thoroughfare and where a narrow road, barely the width of a car, encircled shady grass. He guessed it had once been a busy graveyard to the imposing old flint church, but in more recent times cleared of headstones for ease of mowing. It struck him as more like a pocket-handkerchief of parkland than a graveyard. He pulled off his helmet and inhaled the immediate sense of calm.

He sauntered towards the John Peel Centre, once the old Corn Exchange. The afternoon sun warmed its pale old Suffolk clay bricks, bringing it to life as he paused to gaze up. Footsteps echoed from the alley close by, an ancient shortcut threading behind buildings fronting the main shopping area.

‘Hey Matt!’ Maisie’s screeching call was unmistakable.

‘Mais? What you doin’ walkin’ along there?’

‘It’s a shortcut? Why shouldn’t I?’

She hurried to join him, her heeled gladiator sandals clipping the stone. ‘Hey, let’s find a spot nearer the library. I don’t fancy sittin’ on any of them dead people.’ She tilted her head at the park-like graveyard, then linked her arm with his and together they ambled back along Church Walk.

He knew he couldn’t rabbit on about this ’n that, not while at the back of his mind he knew she wanted to tell him something. There were too many trains of thought to follow; park one, drive the other, he decided. It was something he’d heard Damon say.

‘So what you want to talk about, Mais?’ he asked, biting the bullet like a superhero in his comic-strip books.

‘You aint said nothin’ about them chocolates, Matt. I could’ve lost me job gettin’ them and you aint even said thanks.’

He stared at her, panic gripping his guts.

‘And don’t look at me all innocent like, an’ say you don’t know what I’m talkin’ about.’

He saw the lines creasing both ways on her forehead.

Her voice hardened; ‘Hey Matt! You gotta remember. Saturday? You picked me up after the lunch do at the bowls club in Felixstowe. I were on the back of the Vespa. I said I’d got you some chocolates and slipped ’em into your backpack.’

He took a deep breath. ‘I think they must’ve fallen out, Mais. You can’t ’ve put ’em in proper.’

‘What? How’d you mean not put ’em in proper?’

‘Well, I don’t remember findin’ any.’

‘So why didn’t you say?’

‘I didn’t like to.’ He dropped his gaze. It was difficult to lie but at least the not-remembering bit was partly true.

‘Oh, Matt – that’s sweet.’ She slipped her arm around him.

He tried to read her face, focussing on her eyes, then her mouth.

‘C’mon, let’s sit on the grass,’ she squealed.

They found a patch of grass on one side of the library. Matt flopped down on his back, hands behind his head so he could see Maisie’s face. She sat, cross-legged beside him.

‘You said you could’ve lost your job. No one saw you take them chocolates, did they Mais?’

‘I don’t think so. But they noticed they were missin’ because Gacela asked me about ’em when we were drivin’ to Framlingham on Sunday.’

‘How’d you mean?’

‘Well, she asked if I knew anythin’ about a box of chocs goin’ missin’. See, the box I took were small. I spotted it with the cool boxes in the van, not with the caterin’ sized cartons of them ones to eat with the coffees. I reckon she were tryin’ to catch me out. So I said, “What? One of them huge great boxes went missin’?” like I didn’t know about them smaller ones in the van.’

‘An’ she swallowed it?’

‘I don’t know. She looked at me funny, but when Leon asked if I’d been in the van, I knew to say no, I’d just carried stuff what were handed me, and I weren’t involved with loadin’ it inside.’

'Were there lots of them smaller boxes of chocolates in the van, then?'

'Why you askin'? You want a box?'

'Bloggin' hell no, Mais. An' I don't want you in no trouble either.'

'Hmm, well I aint sure they're the same as the ones in the cartons. I don't do no Dutch, but I reckon the name on the outside don't look the same.'

Matt let her words settle in his mind before he tried a different angle.

'So what's this Leon bloke like? You said he can slice a tomato, but what else?'

'Well he don't say much, but when he do he looks at you like he's….'

'Fishin'?' Matt finished for her.

'That's a weird thing to say. So what kind of a look is a fishin' look?'

'I don't know, maybe kinda mean if you're a big fish?'

'Mean? I don't know 'bout big fish. It were more like he suddenly noticed me.'

'What? Like he fancies you?'

'Nah, it were spooky.'

'Spooky? Is he always there or are there other chefs round?'

'I've only waitressed three times so far.' She counted off on her fingers, 'Bank Holiday Monday lunch at Wickham Market; this last Saturday, Felixstowe; and Sunday in Framlingham. That's three. Yeah, he were the only chef at all three, but Sophie said *see you in a week* to him when we were clearin' up.'

'So you reckon he'll be away for a week?'

'Yeah, and Sophie don't do no cookin' so there's got to

be another chef fillin' in. Gacela said he does this regular like – you know, going off for a week at a time.'

'Why's that then?'

'How'd I know?'

'Has Sophie got a bloke? Maybe he can do the cookin'?'

'That'll be Lang, I reckon. He don't have anythin' to do with the business.'

'Yeah, too busy watchin' birds, more like.'

'Watchin' birds? Where'd you get that from?' A gust of wind caught a tendril of her bleached hair. She straightened her back.

'I-I don't know,' he lied.

Bloated malware, had he fragged it?

He watched her rigid back, toyed with the idea of sneaking his arm around her waist, and then changed his mind. He figured it was time to bite another bullet.

'I reckon I must've read somethin', Mais. See, when you said you were workin' for Hyphen & Green, I searched 'em online. It's what I do.'

'So if you know everythin', why you askin' all them questions?'

'There weren't no Leon on their website.'

'Yeah, but you knew Sophie's bloke were called Lang, and he's into bird watchin'. So why ask if Sophie's got a bloke, like you don't already know? What else aint you tellin' me, Matt?'

'Nothin',' he lied and then added, 'honest, Mais.'

He was uncomfortable. All this obfuscation was on Clive's order, and it made him feel uneasy. Should he tell Maisie he was following her? He wanted to, but did he have the guts? He closed his eyes and tried to shut it all out.

'Hey, Matt,' Maisie wheedled, 'let's get a pizza later

and watch a DVD. One of the girls at the shop lent me The Sapphires. It's about a girl-singin' group back in the 60s. Come on, it'll be fun. We can go back to your place. What you say?'

# CHAPTER 26

Chrissie put a glass of iced tea on the coffee table and sank into her sofa. It was Wednesday early evening and already over halfway through her working week. A sudden thought struck. She hadn't given Matt a call to see how he was getting on. She'd assumed he'd be all right as far as any after effects from the GHB were concerned. Clive had kept reassuring her, and as she felt back to normal, she supposed all was well with him. But she didn't actually know.

She scooped her mobile from the table and pressed automatic dial for his number. She waited. There was no answer. She sighed and fired off a text message: *Hi Matt. Are u ok? Let me know. Good luck with the computer supervising session tomorrow. x C.*

There wasn't any more she could do short of driving round to his mother's bungalow on Tumble Weed drive, or hunting him down in the Academy library. Even she knew it would be overkill, but it didn't stop her worrying. What if…? Her mind sifted through worst case scenarios. What if he'd planted himself in the library, surfed the net about date rape drugs so obsessively that he'd let his guard down, drawn suspicion on himself and somehow come to the attention of the Utterly Academy Computing Director? What if–

A key grated in the lock as the front door catch released.

'Clive?' Chrissie called as she heard the front door open.

'Hi, I'm home,' he called back.

'I've collapsed on the sofa and I'm drinking iced tea. If you want a glass, there's a jug in the fridge.'

'Are you OK?' The sound of footsteps quickened

through the narrow hallway. A blend of concern and mild amusement coloured his voice as he stood in the doorway and surveyed the scene, 'Hey, it's not like you to collapse so early.'

'Well thank you very much. Hey, and leave me some iced tea,' she said as he stooped to pick up her glass, 'and a kiss would be nice!'

He laughed. 'Well, you sound pretty much like your normal self. Have you had a busy day?'

'Yes, but in a good way. I've got an 18th century four-poster bed frame to repair. It's a first for me. How about you? You sound pretty cheerful.'

'I am.' He sat down beside her and gave her a kiss.

'You've cracked the case?'

'No, but the results of the chemical analysis of Juliette Poels' urine and stomach contents are starting to come through. And guess what? Gamma hydroxybutyrate, that's the GHB–'

'The date rape drug? It was found in the dead waitress?'

'Yes. There were very high levels in her urine. Some of it may be down to post mortem changes, and of course the process of her being overheated in the paint-curing oven complicates it. But it would also fit with Juliette being drugged.'

'So what about our box of chocolates?'

'Well, they were easier for the lab to test than poor Juliette Poels' bodily fluids. And yes, they had GHB in the salted caramel flakes. And before you ask, GHB is easy to make – apparently you just have to mix a couple of ingredients, so it lends itself to a cottage industry, so to speak.'

'Like chocolate making. So was it sprinkled on all of the

ones left in the box?'

'Yes, and again before you ask, GHB was detected in your urine. And also in Matt's. The levels were high enough to fit with you ingesting the stuff.'

'So it's what you thought all along. We got a dose when we ate the chocolates.'

'Yes, but I'm not supposed to tell you yet. I think either your GP or the police doctor is supposed to be the one who tells you. And in case you're wondering, yes I have asked them to specifically look for evidence of chocolate in Juliette's stomach contents. Cocoa, to be more precise.'

'Right.' She sat for a moment and let the information settle. 'Wow, and wow again. It kind of gives you a handle on the case, doesn't it?'

'Yes, and there's more. Kinver Greane's car from the ferry terminal long stay is giving up a few secrets. Hmm yes, it's all starting to build a picture.'

She waited for him to say more, but his eyes told her he was miles away, focussed on the middle distance. 'Hey,' she said and nudged his shoulder, 'come back. You can't start building a picture and not describe it to me.'

'What? Oh yes, well the auto crime technicians and Forensics have as good as stripped out the inside of his car and they've found matches for some of the hair fibres and fingerprints. We can now confirm it was Kinver's car, or rather he'd been driving it.' Clive paused and swigged back the last of her glass of iced tea.

'But there was never any doubt was there?'

'No, but it was originally stolen and there's no documentation to say it was his. This is proof he was driving it. We have to go through the motions. Anyway, as well as Kinver's prints and hair fibres, guess who else we've matched so far?'

'Well I imagine John Brown. You said he'd driven off in the car after he'd killed Kinver. So come on, Clive. Stop being a tease and just say.'

'Yes, John Brown. Except we haven't got formal prints for him yet, but when we do I expect they'll match ones from his shed and the car. No, more interestingly we've lifted Juliette Poels' prints from the car.'

'Juliette Poels – the dead waitress again?'

'Yes, and her hair fibres. So it makes me wonder, could she have been Kinver's girlfriend, or John Brown's girlfriend? Or did she have a fling with both of them? It could be a motive for killing.'

'But surely you already know? You've interviewed all the staff at Hyphen & Green. Someone would have known if the chefs were going out with any of the waitresses. That kind of thing doesn't stay secret for long.'

'No, Chrissie, we don't know. We asked, but no one was willing to say. It looks like we're going to have to interview them all again.'

'Is it common to have to keep interviewing people?'

He frowned.

She hadn't meant it to sound critical, she'd assumed police questions would get straight answers. 'I suppose it implies there's something to hide, right Clive?'

'Not always. People forget things, or just don't want to get involved. You'd be surprised what people suddenly "remember" on a second interview.'

'You mean like with Gert, your Dutch detective? Didn't you get him to interview John Brown's mother again on the off chance she'd remember something when a different person asked the questions?'

‘Exactly and when she spoke to Gert she remembered her son had spent his first summer after leaving school over in Amsterdam.’

‘Really? But that gives you his Dutch connection. Do you think that’s when he might have first met Kinver?’

‘Maybe, it could explain a lot.’

‘I wonder… and if Kinver was dealing in drugs when he met him–’

‘Almost certainly he was dealing, and he probably tried to introduce him to weed and no doubt a whole lot more.’

‘Like fishing. But weed? Didn’t you say his mother told you it set off John Brown’s asthma?’

‘Yes, that’s what she said. But why did you just say fishing? What made you say Kinver might have introduced John Brown to fishing? His mother said he’d never fished.’

‘I wonder….’ Something stirred in the back of Chrissie’s mind. A connection, a tipping point. But it was too vague, too fleeting. It needed to brew awhile.

‘Hey, I’m hungry’, she said, ‘Why don’t we drive over to Hadleigh? I’ve heard there’s a great gastro pub there. It’s on one of those little roads off the High Street, you know, leading down to the church and guildhall.’

‘It sounds great, but Hadleigh? Hey, just a second, Chrissie. Is this one of your ulterior motives again? An excuse to go sniffing around? You know damned well the car body repair place is in Hadleigh. I told you it’s where work from the unit near Tattingstone has been sent since it’s been temporarily closed.’

‘Has it been temporarily closed?’ she said in mock surprise.

‘Careful. Remember you passed on Dave’s info about the Hadleigh outlet. So that innocent look won’t wash. Why can't we just walk down to the White Hart?'

She toyed with the idea of pushing the Hadleigh gastro pub again but saw the serious edge behind his smile. It was obvious he'd said all he was prepared to say.

'OK, that's a better idea, Clive. We'll walk to the White Hart.'

'Good, let's support our local.' He grinned and the edge vanished.

The early evening air felt pleasantly warm as they strolled along the lane and headed towards the centre of Woolpit. Her active mind was distracted by the scent of roses from a front garden, the long shadow cast by a large ash tree, the sight of hedgerows and the green expanse of playing fields. As she walked her appetite grew. She linked her arm through Clive's and ran through her favourites on the White Hart menu.

'I hope they're serving sweet potato chips,' she murmured.

'And the quarter-pound Red Poll beef burgers.'

'Hmm….' But despite all the distractions Clive's words had triggered images, ones of the school leaver John Brown first meeting the drug dealer Kinver Greane in Amsterdam. The images half-connected with an idea. And just like an itch, she had to keep scratching at it.

'So did Kinver start out as a chef?' she asked, hoping if she kept her tone neutral and mild, Clive would answer.

'Yes, I think so.'

'Then I wonder if their link was more about cooking than drugs?'

'It might well have been. But drugs corrupt. They'll have come into the equation eventually.'

'So if the two men were linked because of their interest

in cooking and John Brown never fished, it's more likely Kinver rather than John caught the pike to make a risotto for his allotment friends. Matt said something about a pike risotto. We had a lot of time to kill on Sunday while we were waiting for you.'

'Yes, but I don't know where you're going with this. It's very circumstantial and doesn't add anything to the case. We already know they both worked as chefs for Hyphen & Green.'

'But catching pike in the summer isn't what anglers do. At least not our local ones here. It's apparently particularly difficult and not without personal risk. So do you think it's a Dutch thing? Or gang stuff – rite of passage, macho man stuff?'

'Pike fishing? Since when have you been interested in pike fishing?'

She bit her lip. 'Just something I heard on the radio.' Her tongue had run ahead of her brain.

She was about to embellish her radio listening lie when a blue Fiesta drove towards them. For a moment she thought it was Nick. The car slowed, its indicator winking before swinging across in front of them and into the parking area for the playing field. She concentrated, taking in the driver's face and features. It wasn't Nick. It was a woman. Clive, his arm still linked with hers, must have sensed her reaction.

'I know, I thought it was Nick's car for a moment as well,' he said.

She glanced up at him. The old flint and stone church dominated the skyline with its spire. The sight of it choked her with thoughts of mortality.

How could Clive be so sure Nick was safe dating

Gacela? It didn't make sense. What if Gacela had just done something awful to him and she was the one driving his car, disguised in a wig and getting rid of the evidence?

'You're frowning. What are you thinking?' Clive asked.

'It wasn't someone else driving Nick's car, was it?'

'Not unless they've changed the number plates. It doesn't have the same year of registration prefix as Nick's Fiesta.'

'Right.'

'You get used to noticing number plates if you're a policeman.'

She knew it was a dig. A reminder she wasn't an official investigator, merely an amateur with a voracious curiosity.

'Well I don't have a photographic memory like Matt.'

'Spot-on. You're not in the least bit like Matt. But you're right. A photographic memory would be a help. You know Stickley, my DS only ever tries to remember the year prefix and the last few letters for the area code. He reckons the make, colour, year and area code narrow it down pretty well if you've only got a few seconds to memorise it. When you try to remember the complete number plate, well it gets away from you.'

'How's Stickley getting on looking into the cars going through the car body repair place?' The question just popped out, but she sensed from his arm and unbroken stride that he wasn't irritated.

'It's just Stickley's kind of thing. He's been matching the car number plates recorded passing through customs at the Harwich and Felixstowe ferry terminals with the number plates on the cars having bodywork paint repairs at the two units we're investigating.'

'And?'

‘There are a surprising number of matches. Too many to put down to pure coincidence. And before you ask more, I’m in the middle of two murder investigations and I don’t need anyone nosing around the bodywork repairers and making them guess we’re onto them. Have you got that, Chrissie?’

‘Yes, but you know I’d never say anything to anyone.’

‘I know,’ he said softly, ‘but that’s why we’re eating here in Woolpit, not over in Hadleigh.’

They’d reached the centre of Woolpit and the White Hart came into view. A large half-barrel planted with pale pink geraniums brightened the pavement outside its front.

‘Come on Chrissie, let’s give the case a rest for a moment. I want to enjoy my meal.’

‘Right.’ She tried to keep disappointment from her voice.

‘And if you’re worried about Nick, why not text him? Set your mind at rest once we’ve ordered our food. Now come on, try and relax.’

But she couldn’t. Relaxed wasn’t on her menu.

# CHAPTER 27

Nick pulled his mobile from his pocket. He was sitting in the pub in Sproughton, a pint of beer in one hand and Dave perched on a bar stool next to him.

'Is it something important?' Dave asked.

'I don't know.' He glanced at the sender ID, 'It's a text from Chrissie.' Disappointed it wasn't Gacela, he began to slip it back into his pocket.

'No, wait. It could be something important about the car stuff I told her. You've got to read it. Come on, Nick.'

'What? Why would she text me about that?' He looked at Dave's open face; curiosity and excitement were written plainly across his tired smile.

It had been a long day. Together they'd worked late to finally complete the on-site construction and fitting of the oak staircase. It had been a two-man struggle and he'd been grateful for Dave's help. His own measurements had been accurate, but there was no accounting for the warp and vagary of an old timber frame cottage. And this one stood in the heart of Sproughton near the old tithe barn and the bridge crossing the Gipping.

Tired, dusty and hungry, they'd retired to the closest pub for a drink and a bite to eat.

'Come on Nick. You've got to read it,' Dave said firmly.

'OK, but I'm telling you it won't be anything to do with cars.' Nick opened the message and focussed on the text.

*Hi. I'm eating in the White Hart with Clive. He's close to a break thru with his case. Are u ok? Let me know. Be careful. See u drinks Friday? x C*

‘Well?’

‘Like I said, there’s nothing about cars. She just wants to know if I’ll be drinking at the Nags Head on Friday.’

‘Oh.’

He fired off a reply: *Hi. All good. See you Friday. N x*

‘Right, Dave. Last drink. A toast to the staircase!’

‘I swear that cottage was breathing; a breath in, a breath out.’

‘Yeah, it’s the only explanation for the changing measurements.’

Dave laughed, ‘There’ll be some local history, mark my words. There always is around these old places.’

The next day Nick drove the Willows van back to the cottage in Sproughton. It was a one-man job to apply sanding sealer followed by a liquid wax polish to the French oak staircase. He reckoned the sanding sealer would only take an hour to dry, so by the time he’d finished applying it he’d be ready to start rubbing on the lightly stained wax polish. It was simply a case of working from top to bottom; firstly the banisters – straight, plain oak to reflect the timber frame structure of the old walls; and lastly the steps, tread side first followed by the underside.

The grain in the wood seemed to come alive with warm shades as he brushed on a coat of sanding sealer and later, liquid wax polish. Time passed quickly as he worked up and down the banisters, treads and then underside.

By mid-afternoon the job was complete. A sense of achievement washed over him as he loaded the last of the dustsheets into the van. This had been his project. Admittedly Dave had been on hand, but the cottage had stood for three or four hundred years and a staircase, like a fireplace, was an integral focus. His staircase, as if in the spotlight, led directly off the main living room. Thankfully the old wormed beams exposed in the ceiling and walls were a warm burnt honey colour. He reckoned they'd been sand blasted during a previous renovation; less imposing than jet-black gloss or matt paint used to replicate tar and years of smoke. It would have been heart breaking to have had to paint the beautiful oak staircase black to match.

Feeling proud of his carpentry skills, he eased the Willows van away from the cottage and onto Lower Street and across the Gipping. Within minutes he was on the A14, but rather than head back towards Needham Market and the workshop, he chose to skirt around Ipswich and drive east. He hadn't fully thought through a visit to Woodbridge yet, it was more a gut feeling than logic guiding him. But buoyed by confidence, he needed to know what Gacela's game was before he wasted any more emotion.

He was familiar with the town; there was the Oak & Oyster where he'd performed with the band, and the canoeing club on the banks of the Deben. A quick left turn off the quayside road and he drew into the car park close to a supermarket. He locked the van and headed on foot into old Woodbridge. He followed the gentle curve of a thoroughfare between close set buildings, dominated by shop windows reflecting the age and higgledy-piggledy fronts from earlier centuries. Which shop to try? What should he say or ask?

Windows of shoe displays, clothes, leather goods, cakes and books were easy to dismiss. He reckoned it wasn't likely he'd find them selling silver necklaces and hurried on. The arty shops, the ones selling pictures and prints, fancy pottery and jewellery – those must surely be his target.

He pushed at a glass panelled door and stepped down into a narrow shop. The smell of scented joss sticks tickled his nose. A display of filmy scarves brushed against his shoulder.

'Hello? Can I help you?' a middle-aged lady asked. She wore her glasses on the end of her nose as she arranged a selection of painted pebbles in a display cabinet. She stood back to survey the result before eyeing Nick.

'I-I was looking for a necklace for my girlfriend.' He cast around the shop, feeling uncomfortable referring to Gacela as his girlfriend.

'My girlfriend,' he repeated, his cheeks flaming, 'she said she'd seen one she liked; a silver chain with silver dragonflies and enamelled leaves and fruit hanging from it.'

He sensed the scrutiny of his work trainers splattered with dark wood stain and spotted with sanding sealer. He waited.

'No, I don't have anything like that. Enamelled silver? It sounds the kind of thing Livia might stock. That'll be a few shops along that way on the other side of the road.' She indicated the direction before adding, 'I don't suppose your girlfriend would like a painted pebble?'

He made his escape and hurried to a double fronted shop displaying framed scenic photos and prints. When he stepped inside he spotted glass display cabinets. They were filled with jewellery and formed an island in the middle of the floor space.

'Hello, are you looking for anything in particular or are you just browsing?' An Indian woman in her thirties sat behind a counter towards the rear of the shop. She wore a pastel print silk scarf loosely draped around her head and shoulders.

‘Just browsing, thank you,’ he mumbled, thankful to be let off the *I’m looking for my girlfriend* hook.

Various pieces of artwork hung on the wall. Some of the mounted photos caught his attention. He peered at one more closely. The background seemed familiar.

‘Is that a view of Alton Water?’ he murmured, more to himself than expecting an answer from the lady with the headscarf.

‘Yes, I believe so. The photograph is really about the foreground shot of those mallards coming in to land. It’s amazing how the photographer’s caught the water splashing and rippling.’ She got up and walked over to stand beside him and gaze at the photo.

‘Wow, yes. And the light across the water. What a camera to get a shot like that!’

‘It will have been static; the camera will have been on a tripod. Then he’ll have set up the shot and shutter speeds etcetera, and then waited. He’ll have taken hundreds to get that one perfect shot.’

‘You talk as if you’re a photographer.’

‘I am, well kind of. I’m on a photography course at the Suffolk New College in Ipswich. I help out here part time.’

‘So what’s the name of the photographer?’

‘Lang Sharrard. He’s local to Ipswich. We’ve several of his photographs here – all birds. And what’s amazing is that one of our local jewellery makers uses his photos of birds to work from and cast in silver.’

‘Really?’

‘Yes, we’ve some of her work in this case. Over here, if you’re interested.’

He was interested but frowned, hoping to play it down as he walked over to the showcase. He didn’t want to appear too keen. This had to appear natural.

'Awesome,' he breathed, as he let his eyes wander over a display of silver birds, some enamelled and hanging in bunches from silver chains, some mounted as earrings or brooches.

'Hey, that's a green woodpecker, isn't it? My girlfriend has a necklace that reminds me of this jewellery, but hers has fruit on it. A blackberry, yes a silver enamelled blackberry and a dragonfly,' he said, forcing his words to sound relaxed and conversational.

'Ah, that will have been her woodland phase. Nuts and berries, leaves and dragonflies. Then she started doing birds, initially in plain silver, and now enamelled. We have lots of people who come in wanting her woodland jewellery, but she won't make any more. Apparently she's moved on to her bird phase.'

'It sounds like she's more artist than businesswoman.'

'Possibly, but it's driven up the value of her work.'

'Ah, but that's not so good for me if I'm buying. If my girlfriend wears her necklace a lot, do you think she'd want another one but with bunches of birds?'

'It depends if she likes birds or just likes this jeweller's work generally. If it's valuable and in short supply it drives up desirability.'

'So how long has she been making these?'

'A while, but the woodland ones were phased out and the birds have only been for the last couple of years.'

'A couple of years?'

He needed to think. Gacela's words *I got it in a shop in Woodbridge recently* played back in his head. Recently had to imply a short time ago, and in his experience timespan, when used about shopping, was generally measured in weeks or months. Not in years.

‘Right, so my girlfriend must have got her necklace ages ago.’

A thought struck. ‘Does anywhere else…? Sorry, that came out wrong. If I’m not back this way, do you know if I’d be able find this jewellery anywhere else?’

‘No, and the maker is pretty exclusive. But she has a website, it may list other outlets. Feel free to take one of her cards.’

‘Thanks.’ Gacela had confounded him again. At least this time it was a part truth she’d spun, just the timings were blurred. He pocketed a card the size of a postcard with photographs of the jewellery on it.

‘I really came in to look at your artwork, not jewellery. I think I’ll take a closer look at the Lang Sharrard photographs, if that’s OK?’

‘They’re a limited edition, like a numbered print run, so they’re numbered, signed and dated. I think there are going to be a hundred of each.’

Nick moved around the shop, viewing the art displayed on the walls. Lang’s photographs were certainly striking. As well as the mallards landing on Alton Water, there was a heron stalking fish and a green woodpecker colourful against the bark of a tree. He pictured the little silver and enamelled birds – mallards, herons and woodpeckers, but there hadn’t been any nightingales. He was sure he’d heard Chrissie say something about nightingales and Alton Water. But then nightingales weren’t known for their striking or distinguishing looks, hardly a subject for a necklace; it would be difficult to cast their song in silver. The thought made him wistful, pensive.

‘This week’s been crazy, and it’ll be Friday tomorrow. I

think… well maybe I'll just settle for showing my girlfriend the card. I'll tell her I've been here and let her say if she's interested in the birds. At least I'll get credit for trying!' He smiled at the lady in the delicate headscarf.

'It's a good plan. This particular jewellery is part of our regular stock, so you can always drop in if you're passing this way again.'

'That's great, and thanks for your help. Bye.'

On impulse he pocketed a couple of Lang's business cards. He made a mental note to pass one on to Chrissie. They'd all be meeting up for the regular end of week drink the next day, so he could give it to her then. He knew she was interested in everything pertaining to the murder in the paint-curing oven, and by association Alton Water.

It was only as he drove the van back to Needham market, that he realised he'd missed a trick. He hadn't thought to look at the dates on the photographs. Chrissie was bound to ask when they'd been taken. *Where* was interesting but *when* was fundamental.

Damn, damn, damn! Well he wasn't going to turn round and drive back. If she wanted to know, she'd have to find out for herself. If he drove back now, the shop assistant would probably think he was making a play for her, and the foreman would have to hang around late before locking the secure parking for the van. Success plunged into frustration. He decided he'd send Matt a text once he was back at Willows and see if he wanted a drink. It would have been his first day at the Academy helping out in the computer lab with the new intake of students. Nick reckoned he might be glad of a pint.

# CHAPTER 28

Matt sat in the Utterly Academy library and considered his options. A pint with Nick sounded exactly what he needed, but there was trouble with Maisie. He had sensed a slight souring of the air between them following the box of chocolates incident. He'd denied ever finding them in his backpack and at the time she'd appeared to believe him. Perhaps his mistake had been in following up his denial with questions about Leon and Sophie Hyphen's boyfriend, Lang Sharrard.

Since then Maisie had clammed up when he asked about her waitressing with Hyphen & Green.

'Why'd you ask when you already know?' she'd snapped the previous evening.

It was true. He already knew her work schedule because she'd previously forwarded the email with the September venues to him, but Clive had said to keep reporting back, and so Matt knew he had to keep checking for updates.

And then Maisie had surprised him: 'I got somethin' for you. A new tee. To wear like for good luck tomorrow, your first day lecturin'.'

'Hey Mais, that's real cool. But I aint really lecturin', I'm helpin' them freshers out in the computer lab,' he'd said as he unfolded the tee-shirt.

Excitement and disappointment struck. New wasn't entirely accurate. Yes, the tee-shirt was new to him, but it obviously wasn't new in itself. It must have belonged to some other student, luckily a size large and probably barely worn since a previous year. It began to make sense when Maisie explained she'd bid for it on an online auction site.

‘But it says *ALUMNA UTTERLY ACADEMY 2009 – 2012*. That aint right for me years at Utterly. Me dates finished this July, 2013,’ he’d said.

‘So? It’s a leaver’s tee. It’s retro, aint it?’

‘Yeah but it’s meant to reflect me.’

She’d stood up. ‘But you are goin’ to wear it, right? You aint gonna start sayin’ stuff like I never gave it you? Like them chocolates?’

Her words stung.

‘No, course not, Mais.’

‘Right, well we both got a busy day tomorrow. I think it’s time I got home.’

‘OK, then,’ he’d said.

And those had been the last words from her, either spoken or texted.

At first it hadn’t bothered him too much. He’d had more pressing things on his mind such as logging into the Academy computing and IT site to make a final check through the student programme. But now, late Thursday afternoon, after the student session in the computer lab and almost twenty hours since she’d said *I think it’s time I got home*, she still hadn’t answered any of his text messages. Was she cross? Was she OK? Or more likely, was it because somehow she knew he hadn’t worn the tee-shirt?

He’d kept it in his backpack to prove he wasn’t lying but instead had sported his more powerful and relevant good luck talisman, his Assistant Demonstrator ID with the old photo dangling from the blue lanyard around his neck.

‘Are you OK, Matt?’ a familiar voice murmured.

He crashed back from his anxious reasoning. ‘What? Hey Rosie!’ He blinked at his favourite library assistant. She must have walked over while he was miles away on his mind flight. Of course, he was in the library.

'I thought I'd come over and say hi. You've hardly moved for ages, and look, even your screen's gone to saver.'

'What? Ah right.' He looked at the screen on his computer station. 'Yeah well I were considerin' me options. I reckon I may have messed up.'

'Why d'you say that?'

He glanced up at the ceiling with its gothic styled beams, then focussed on a wisp of auburn hair escaping from Rosie's loose pony tail.

'See I figure I should have worn a tee I were given for this mornin'.'

'Well that's OK. Take a selfie in it and then post it.'

'Post it?'

'Yes, on line. The selfie.'

'Right. I aint thought of that.'

She moved away, silent in her summer pumps.

'That's genius,' he breathed.

He pulled the crumpled tee-shirt from his backpack near his feet and shook it out to read the words and dates printed across its front. Who might the Alumna student have been? He had to check; after all, tracing people was what he did. He logged into the Academy Alumni site.

'Why aint we called former students?' A few clicks and another glance at the tee told him the previous owner must have been a bird. Alumna was the female version of the Latin word. He as a bloke was the male version, an alumnus. If he was pleural and mostly male, he was alumni.

'Fraggin' Latin.' Not only was the tee the wrong year, it was girlie as well. He stared at the writing on the cotton. He reckoned he was going to have to change it.

'Yeah *ALUMINA*, that's aluminium oxide.' It only needed the letter I between the M and N. And if he wrote the chemical formula above the student years, then the number 3 against the O for an oxygen molecule in oxide would make the 2012 look like 2013. Blogspot heaven! He could fix it to blokey, his years, and suitably techy. He hoped Maisie would approve.

He scrabbled at the bottom of his backpack for a permanent marker pen and set to work.

'Wicked,' he murmured when he'd completed his efforts. A quick wrestle with the cotton fabric and he'd slipped it on over the grey tee-shirt he was already wearing.

Rosie glanced across from her desk near the photocopiers.

'What you think?' he mouthed at her.

She gave him a thumbs up sign.

He flipped out his Assistant Demonstrator ID which had become trapped between the tee-shirts and let it dangle in full view below the words on his chest. He aimed his phone camera at himself. Click! It was the work of a moment. Seconds later he'd sent the shot with a text message to Maisie. *Yay! Thanks for the T. All good. x*

He reckoned the lucky ID pass would help to tip the scales for him. Along with his selfie it was bound to sweeten Maisie. The thought set him wondering when he'd see her next. He closed his eyes and visualised her schedule, the one she'd forwarded from Hyphen & Green with her timetable for the month. It looked promising; she wasn't booked to be waitressing tomorrow so hopefully she'd be free to spend the evening with him. He opened his eyes and fired off another text: *See you Friday, Nags Head?*

Feeling lucky and girl-savvy he turned his attention to

the text still waiting on his phone, the one from Nick suggesting a pint thirty minutes ago. *Yeah, see you in 20* he replied.

True to his word, Matt found Nick in the Nags Head about twenty minutes later. It was quiet for early Thursday, even the jukebox was silent. Nick sat with a half of Land Girl at a table near the old quarry tiles in front of the dead fireplace. Matt paid for a pint of lager and ambled over to him.

'Hiya mate. How'd it go today?' Nick raised his glass in a greeting.

'OK. Yeah, it went OK. Cheers!' Matt sucked a centimetre of lager from the top of his dripping glass before setting it down on the table. He slumped onto a chair.

'What the hell have you written across yourself?' Nick asked.

'Oh this?' He dried one lager-moist hand across his outer tee-shirt.

'Yeah, the graffiti? What's it about?'

'It's Maisie's good luck present Thought I'd better wear it. What d'you think?'

'Well from here it doesn't say good luck.'

'Course not. It's the formula for alumina.'

'What?'

'Aluminium oxide. Maisie's been buyin' retro again. But see, this leaver's tee - it's meant for a bird an' the year's wrong. *ALUMINA* fits. So I changed it.'

'And Maisie was OK with you writing all over her retro find, was she?'

Matt let Nick's question settle between them. It struck him as an odd thing to ask. Personalising something was like putting a stamp of approval on it. Everyone knew that, didn't they? Maisie would likely giggle. *It's all Greek to me* is what she usually said if she ever saw a chemical written as its component elements. The thought of her set him worrying again.

'You look a bit serious. Did today really go OK?' Nick's voice pulled him back to the Nags head.

'Yeah, yeah,' Matt said in an absent way, then gulped some lager.

'Look, I know you don't want to do any following people. You're strictly keyboard and cyber. You've said it and I get it. But I reckon Gacela is just as caught up in the Hyphen & Green thing as Maisie and well... if you personalised the Vespa–'

'Personalised?' Matt cut in. Was it thought transfer? Hadn't he just been thinking about how he'd personalised the tee-shirt?

'Yeah, I was thinking. How about some vinyl wrap? You must've seen the kind of thing on the side of vans? The go-faster stripes along the side of cars?'

'What?'

'Well, you could buy some vinyl graphics or stripes and stick them to the face and front mudguard of your Vespa. Something to dull the colour, like a black or a camouflage pattern?'

'But I like me blackberry bubblegum finish. Mais likes it too.'

'Yeah, but the vinyl isn't permanent. You can take it off again. Just warm it up and peel it off. The idea is to make the scooter look different for a short while. Less obvious it's you following.'

'Followin'? I'm strictly cyber, mate. I already told you.' But the idea of personalising the Vespa appealed, and Nick didn't know he'd already been trailing Maisie on her waitressing jobs.

'Yeah, so tell me more about them vinyl stripes. How'd I put 'em on? Say I were dropping Mais off an' I'm on me blackberry bubblegum, then what? I get a sticker out me backpack and whack it on?'

'Hmm, I suppose so. But I think you have to use a plastic spatula, a kind of spreader to smooth the vinyl on as you pull the backing paper off.'

'What? So how long d'you reckon it'd take me?'

'A couple of minutes. Depends on the size of the sticker.'

'And gettin' it off again?'

'Ah, that could take longer. Hmm, I wonder if some masking tape might work better. You just pull a strip off the roll and press it on. And as long as it doesn't get too hot, you should be able to whip it off without leaving adhesive all over your paintwork. Too cold, of course and it loses its stick. I think we have some special extra wide masking tape in the workshop.'

'Hey, but I keep sayin' I aint doin' no followin' for you. I aint no cookie for Gacela.'

'A cookie for Gacela?'

'Yeah, like them computer cookies used on websites. They track your browsin' and tailor the ads. Except I'd be on the road. I aint goin' to be no motorised cookie trackin' Gacela. I aint followin' her, mate. It's too risky.'

'Yeah, you said.'

They lapsed into silence. For a few minutes Matt was hardly aware of Nick or the handful of other drinkers in the bar. He was too busy thinking about his secretive mission for Clive. He reckoned Maisie still had no idea he'd been following her. But what about Gacela? She'd be looking at the traffic on the road behind as well as in front of her car. Nick's suggestion of sticking something over his bright paintwork might come in useful.

'Would maskin' tape look odd on the front of me scooter?' he said, part-voicing his thoughts.

'Yes, but at least the tape's a kind of custard colour, one of the old classic Vespa shades. You might get away with it.'

'Yeah, except I won't be findin' out,' he said and made a mental note to slip a roll of masking tape into his backpack. His cheeks burned as he looked away. He downed a huge mouthful of lager and hoped his face didn't betray him.

*Ping!* A text alert sounded from his pocket.

'Phishin' hell,' he choked, as he grabbed his phone.

'Is it Maisie?' Nick asked.

'Yeah, she must've got me selfie.' He opened her message, his thumb moist with lager and sweat. Relief washed over him as he read: *Wicked pic! See u Nags Head 2morrow. Xxx.* She was OK. No shouting capitals and three kisses. 'Yeah, she's good,' he murmured.

'When's she waitressing next? I expect Gacela will be working the same,' Nick asked.

'Saturday. An early afternoon wedding reception in the old guildhall in Hadleigh,' Matt reeled off as he recalled the timetable.

'Hmm, so nothing tomorrow?'

'Friday? I don't think so.'

'Well I'm seeing Gacela tomorrow night. More Friday cocktails. I wonder if she'll spin me a yarn about her Friday or the Saturday wedding in Hadleigh.'

‘How’d you mean?’

‘She might say the wedding reception is an evening do, or… I don’t know.’

Matt sensed the uncertainty and felt confused. He waited, watching Nick’s face for clues, but he didn’t catch any. ‘When’s your band playin’ again?’ he asked to fill the silence.

‘Saturday night at the football club, Stowmarket. Jason’s brother is a member. That’s how we got the gig. Jason plays drums, his brother follows football.’

‘Right. Yeah, well maybe Mais an’ me’ll come along.’

# CHAPTER 29

It was Friday and Chrissie was looking forward to the end of the week. Usually it crept up on her, surprising her when it was finally time to lay down her tools and sweep up the wood shavings around her feet, but this Friday was different. She felt exhausted. She knew she should be excited by the prospect of repairing the four-poster bed. It was going to be a first for her and she was due to collect it on Saturday morning.

'Are you sure you'll be all right dismantling the four-poster tomorrow, Mrs Jax?' Ron asked.

'Mr Airs said he'd give me a hand. He's dismantled it before when he moved to Bury St Edmunds a few years ago. So he should be OK helping me tomorrow. It's only held together with bolts going through the posts into the bearers.'

'If you're sure, Mrs Jax.'

'Yes, because I might need the front passenger seat to give me extra length in the van for the posts. It's late $18^{th}$ century, so at least the posts aren't chunky oak. The foot end ones are slender mahogany and the head ones are beech. It'll be OK, Mr Clegg.'

'And the headboard?'

'I was surprised. It's pretty basic and not particularly tall. There'll be no problem loading it into the van.'

'And the cornice?'

'Stop worrying, Mr Clegg. It's a simple frame. I think the bed was really all about the drapes.'

She wanted to accept his offer of help, but she was determined to appear self-reliant. It was that spark of independence again. It flashed through her despite her fatigue. Sometimes she wasn't even sure who she was trying to prove herself to. Perhaps her weariness was clouding her judgement. Had Ron sensed it too?

'It's been a long week,' Ron said, as if reading her thoughts.

'It's my mind. It's as if I've got hundreds of things running in the background sapping my energy.'

She wasn't going to tell him all the things on her mind. How could she? He'd understand she'd be worrying about Nick getting caught up with Gacela, and Maisie being pulled into the Hyphen & Green web. But Ron was pragmatic and realistic. He didn't know about the chocolates laced with date rape drugs. She hadn't told him and without that knowledge he was bound to be dispassionate and reasonable and say to leave it to Clive and the authorities.

And if only those things had been the sum total running in the background, perhaps she could have been dispassionate and reasonable too. But what about the other thread in her personality? The one others politely called nosiness? How could she leave it to Clive when it was so obvious to her where the police should be directing their enquiries? Meddlesome, yes Clive would call her meddlesome.

'A penny for them?' Ron said, his voice cutting through her flight of introspection.

'You'd think there'd be a position; someone, or a bank of people like independent consultants.' She gave up. How could she voice the gist of her idea when she couldn't even find the right words for it?

She looked across at Ron and shrugged.

‘It’s Clive’s big case, isn’t it? You always get like this when there’s a murder investigation going on, Mrs Jax. But the thing is, it often appears simpler when you don’t have expertise around your subject. Take the four-poster. We know it will have been altered to fit a modern mattress, the headboard may have been remodelled because down the ages an owner no longer wanted drapes at the head end, and the posts may have been shortened to lower the height. Then someone comes along with a little knowledge and realises the bed’s been altered and isn’t quite right for its original age. But they don’t know when, what or why those alterations were made.’

‘So you’re saying you need real expertise to recognise when a headboard isn’t original to the bed; that it’s made from two pieces - a section of age appropriate 18$^{th}$ century wall panelling and a length of Victorian carved panel from a choir stall. Is that what you mean, Mr Clegg?’

‘Yes, but more than that. A real expert will read deeper still; he, or she, can work out from the clues in the construction and marks in the wood etcetera, what’s been done in the past and why. The time sequence is crucial. And I’m guessing, in order to bring a successful prosecution, the police need the complete picture and time sequence.’

‘And I’m not a police expert.’

‘Well I didn’t want to say that, Mrs Jax, but you have to admit you aren’t. Sometimes it’s best to do what you do best and let others do what they do best.’

‘Hmm.’ She wasn’t convinced but there was no point in arguing.

‘You’re looking tired, Mrs Jax. Go home. Things will seem better after a good night’s rest.’

‘You’re probably right. I said I’d see my friends for a

drink, but maybe I'll give the Nags Head a miss. Go straight home.'

'Are you going to take the van now?' Ron asked.

'You mean leave my car here now? Yes, I suppose that would make sense, then I can drive straight to Mr Airs in the morning. Right, that's decided. I'll skip the Nags Head and take the van home. Thanks, for suggesting it, Mr Clegg.'

'I'll be here in the morning if you need help unloading the van,' he murmured.

'Thanks.' She swung her bag over her shoulder, picked up her toolbox and headed for the door. 'Bye, Mr Clegg,' she called back to him.

One of the hundreds of things milling around in her head took sudden form. It must have been the gentle rocking as she drove the van along the rough track from the old barn workshop.

Hadleigh! It had only been the other evening when Clive vetoed her suggestion of a meal there. And here she was, the green nose of the Citroen Berlingo van pointing onto the Wattisham Airfield boundary lane. If she turned to the left she'd be in Hadleigh in fifteen minutes. A right turn and she'd be in Woolpit and home. From where she sat, perched far higher than in the driving seat of her TR7, she was on top of the world. Invincible. She indicated and turned left.

Her route was simple. She followed the road down into Bildeston, then joined the old Hadleigh road as it climbed up and swooped down from Semer before winding alongside the River Brett to Hadleigh. Hedges and trees obscured most of her view across the countryside, but she caught glimpses of earthy fields, the crop-stubble already ploughed in and the soil planted with winter wheat and barley. She determined to concentrate on the road and focus her plan, except she didn't have a plan. It was more of a gut feeling, a need to see the paint spray body repair unit. 'And then what?' She didn't have an answer.

Dave had given her vague directions as part of the information for Clive about cars being repeatedly re-sprayed while others were pushed to the back of the queue. He'd told her the unit was located on the west or southwest outskirts of the town, somewhere out towards Polstead.

She spotted a sign for the Hadleigh industrial park and turned towards it. 'This can't be right,' she muttered. She was still on the northern aspect of the town and the polar opposite direction to Polstead. She pulled off the road and considered her options. This was crazy. Short of turning into the industrial park and asking for directions, she'd have to go home. Feeling hot and foolish, she opened her window.

'Hey, excuse me,' she called to a man who happened to be walking past, 'can you help me? I'm looking for a car body repair unit.'

'Try the industrial estate.' He waved his hand in the direction she'd been heading.

'I was told it wasn't in the estate but out towards Polstead.'

He frowned and cast a glance at her van. She could have sworn he was looking for a dent or scrape along its side.

'I think there's somewhere out along the main road west of here. As if you're heading for Sudbury.'

'Sudbury?' She had hoped he'd say Polstead.

'Well not as far as Sudbury. From this direction it's maybe a mile along the main road and then it's a turning to your left. It's easy to miss.'

She looked at him for a moment and tried to gage his reliability. Did he appear like someone who might know? But what choice did she have? At least it was west. That was something. 'Thanks,' she said.

Back on the main road once again, but this time heading along it in the Sudbury direction, the hedgerows seemed to disappear and the fields fanned out as far as her eye could see. 'Easy to miss,' she muttered as she flew past a lane to the left. She slowed, not sure if she should turn back, but then passed two more turnings to the left in quick succession. 'The man's a joker.'

It was time to track back. 'Hey, a signpost!' She approached with caution. It was another road off to the left but this time she was in luck; it was signposted to Polstead Heath. So should she follow the road because it might lead eventually in the direction of Polstead or should she double back and take one of the earlier turnings she'd missed? The futility of her search struck home. She needed both the name of the car body repair place and a map. It was just as Ron had said. She was nothing but an amateur. At least he'd dressed it in kinder words.

Feeling downcast and silly, she turned the van and headed cross country on quiet roads back home to Woolpit.

Later, when the evening was beginning to draw in and she'd part-prepared an evening meal, she sat at the small table in her kitchen and searched on her laptop for car body repair businesses in the Hadleigh area. The sweet rich smell of her Bolognaise sauce filled the air, as a pan gently simmered on the cooker. Clive would be home soon, and she knew she'd better hurry up with her online search. She didn't want him to find her in the act of meddling. But it wasn't going well. So far, using postcode locations to narrow down the businesses listed, she wasn't having much luck. It would likely be quicker to text Nick and ask him for the name, or failing that, Dave's number so she could text him direct.

The front door latch grated. She caught the unmistakable click and rustle as the door opened. Clive was home. She was out of time.

'Hi,' she called.

'Something smells nice.' Clive's footsteps sounded through the hallway.

She closed the search window, flipped down the screen, grabbed her phone and began texting: *Hi Nick. Long day! Sorry couldn't make it for drinks.*

'You've been busy. Are we having spaghetti?' Clive said as he walked into the kitchen and made a beeline for the fridge. 'Ah good, some cold beer. Do you want one as well?' he asked.

'No thanks, but you could put a pan of water on for the spaghetti.'

'Right. Everything OK?' He gave her a kiss.

'Yes. Just end-of–week weary. I even skipped drinks at the Nags Head. The beer's just reminded me I haven't let anyone know I wasn't coming. They'll have been expecting me.' She indicated her phone, 'I thought I better text.'

'Yes,' he laughed, 'better let them know otherwise they'll turn up here worried something's wrong.'

While he filled a pan with water, Chrissie fired off the rest of her text message to Nick: *What's the name of the car body repair place Dave was on about in Hadleigh? It may be easier just to give me Dave's number? C x.*

'I see you've got the van parked outside,' Clive said as

he gave the Bolognaise sauce more of a prod than a stir.

'Yes, I've got to pick up a four-poster bed from Bury tomorrow.'

'Did you drive out to Hadleigh this afternoon? I could have sworn I saw you on the bypass.'

'What?'

'It's a pretty distinctive van with its yellow stripe along the side. And of course the names Clegg & Jax are a bit of a give-away.'

'Really?' She tried to hold her voice steady, 'You saw the van? Where? I didn't see you.'

'No, you were driving quite slowly. You seemed to be looking off to the left as I passed. I was coming the opposite way.'

'Why?'

'I was on my way back from paying Misters Isledon and Cogger another visit.'

'Who?'

'The blokes working at the car body repair unit near Tattingstone before we closed it for the forensic and safety investigations. They're working at the unit out Hadleigh way rather than be laid-off.'

She felt him watching her face as he spoke. Her cheeks flamed.

'Oh yes, I-I'd forgotten their names.'

'Are you all right, Chrissie?'

'Yes. Why?'

'You don't seem quite yourself. So where were you off to in the van when I passed you?'

She'd known the question was coming, but knowing hadn't helped find her an answer; one he'd believe.

'I-I thought….' Her words failed. He must have guessed

she'd been nosing around. Why else delay asking what brought her to be driving near Hadleigh? It was interrogation technique, pure and simple and he was the detective. How could she be so stupid?

'I-I was out that way visiting a customer and then….' She stopped. There was no point, he'd sense if she was embellishing a lie.

The pan with the spaghetti bubbled up and broke the silence as water spat and sizzled on the element. She turned the heat down, thankful for an excuse to avoid his gaze while she marshalled her nerve.

'It'd be easier if I just came clean, wouldn't it?' she said, slipping into *suspect* role. 'It's a fair cop… I was out that way for a customer but I thought, while I was there I might just as well have a quick nosey around… except I couldn't find the car body repair place, so I headed back home instead. Honest, Gov. Sorry.' She raised her hands as if being arrested.

'What? I should have guessed. God, Chrissie. You're like a dog with a bone. It would have been easier if we'd gone to the gastro pub the other evening. You really are impossible.'

'I know.'

'So did you find it?'

'No. I thought it might be somewhere out west or southwest of Hadleigh, but I hadn't a clue and gave up.'

'West, southwest? Since when have you been up to speed with compass directions?'

'Exactly. I rest my case.'

He laughed and shook his head. 'As long as you never found it, that's the main thing. We're this close to cracking the case.' He held up his hand as if pinching the air and leaving barely an inch between index finger and thumb.

'Really?'

'Yes, so keep your nose out of it, OK?'

'Of course. It's just today I feel as if my brain's scrambled and my head will explode. Tell me I haven't completely lost it. Was there anything, anything at all of relevance about fishing to the case?'

'Possibly, but let's eat. I'm hungry.'

'OK then,' she said and gave him a hug. She couldn't believe he'd taken her meddling so well.

They ate their spaghetti Bolognaise in large pasta bowls on the small kitchen table, for once not talking but instead each concentrating on their own thoughts. Chrissie felt relaxed as she stacked the dirty dishes in the sink and followed Clive into the sitting room. 'They can wait till later,' she said.

'So, will telling you some fishing news unscramble your brain?' Clive asked as she sat down beside him on the sofa.

'I don't know. It depends what you tell me.'

'Hmm, well nothing to go beyond these four walls, OK?'

'Of course. But you know I never tell anyone what you've told me in confidence. I may be nosey but I don't gossip.'

'Right, well we've gone back through the fishing club members again and interviewed all the fishing permit holders for Alton Water. This time we've also asked for the names of the people with keys for the car parks.'

'Night fishing?'

'Something like that. Anyway, a couple of people can't account for their keys. One key seems to have been genuinely lost and the other was lent, via a contact of a contact, to Lang Sharrard and not returned.'

'Lang Sharrard? He's the one who posted that photo of nightingales on his blog site, isn't he? *Taken at Alton Water*, according to his blog. I told you Matt had found it and forwarded the link to you. But why'd he want a key? It's a daytime photo.'

'I know, and he isn't an angler. But the key helps tie him into the location. Time & place, and all that. He's Sophie Hyphen's live-in, so the coincidences are building up.'

'What? Do you think he could have killed Juliette Poels?'

'I don't know, Chrissie. Let's just say, I'm looking forward to formerly questioning him tomorrow.'

# CHAPTER 30

Nick walked slowly to his car. It was early Friday evening and he'd just enjoyed a pint of Land Girl with his mates, but he had Gacela on his mind and it was time to leave. He wanted to get back to Woolpit, shower, change and head out on his date with her. For once he felt prepared. He'd decided to take her the maker's publicity card for the jewellery he'd seen in Woodbridge, but more importantly he was armed with the knowledge of her Hyphen & Green waitressing schedule. Not knowing quite what to expect from her was thrilling. A frisson of excitement tweaked his stomach.

*Ping!* A text alert sounded from his pocket.

'Oh no, don't say you're standing me up.' He extracted his phone and checked the sender ID. It was only Chrissie. Now what, he wondered and opened her message.

*What's the name of the car body repair place Dave was on about in Hadleigh?* he read. He didn't know, and in all honesty didn't care; right now he had other things on his mind. He skimmed through the rest of Chrissie's message. Sending her Dave's number could wait.

He unlocked his old Fiesta and settled into the driver's seat. His mind flicked to the evening ahead as he started the car. He wondered how Gacela would react when he told her about the jewellery. But the thought brought other memories back too: the shop in Woodbridge; the framed photos; mallards landing on Alton Water at dusk and a heron fishing. He had planned to tell Chrissie when he saw her in the pub, but then she hadn't turned up. Damn! Well it would have to wait. He'd text her in the morning about the

Alton Water photos along with Dave's number.

An hour later, back in his garret bedroom Nick had showered and changed into clean jeans and pale coffee-coloured tee-shirt. Ready to leave, he slipped the jewellery card into his pocket, and carried a sweatshirt to the car in case the evening turned cool. Gacela had wanted to meet him at Sandlings cocktail bar again. He hadn't suggested somewhere different because it was an easy starting place for the evening. The drive into Ipswich didn't take him long, and as he parked in a car park a couple of roads back from the waterfront, it occurred to him that by choosing the same place again to meet she was being mysterious. She'd avoided letting him know more about herself, a closed book. Selecting a different venue might have told him she was partial to Indian or Greek food, or interested in a particular genre of movie or theatre.

More intrigued than ever and now on foot he hurried towards the waterfront. One-way streets and narrow pavements made him glance back and forth. Around him old and new were in juxtaposition; red brick and timber frame. He caught a sudden glimpse of a quiet leafy corner hiding the old swimming pool building with its porthole-sized windows and the word BATHS etched in the stone. On the skyline in the distance there were cranes and a tower block.

The pavement became busier with people out for a Friday night as he dived down a narrow alleyway leading to the waterfront. The cocktail bar looked out across the Orwell, the water glassy smooth. He didn't waste a glance on it or soak up its timeless fascination but strode inside. He guessed he'd find Gacela on a barstool at the counter, her back to the entrance, one elegant leg straight so that her toe rested on the foot rail. He paused and smiled at her. He knew she'd have seen him in the mirror behind the bar. She raised her glass to his reflection and mouthed *hi*.

'Hiya,' he murmured. It felt theatrical but he was happy to play. 'Are you drinking a Cosmo?' he asked as he took a couple of steps and stood next to her.

'Hmm, yes. Do you want your usual?'

'You mean a Black Russian? It's too early for laced black coffee. I think I need a beer. Are you hungry?'

'Laced? Now that's an interesting word to use. I don't think I'd describe a cocktail as laced. A dash or splash of things, yes. A blend or a mix even, but laced? The word suggests something spiked, drugs.'

'Yeah well you know what I mean. I don't need a vodka and coffee right now.' He caught the barman's eye. 'What beers do you have?' he asked and settled for a bottle of Adnams.

'Don't look so disappointed. You can hardly expect a beer on tap. This is a cocktail bar, Nick.'

'I know, but it's been a long day,' he said, echoing the opening words from Chrissie's text message an hour and a half earlier, a phrase giving nothing away but at the same time making an excuse for everything.

He watched her eyes, framed by her dark lashes; he saw the uncertainty and then something more akin to appreciation, possibly even amusement. It took one to know one, and he figured she'd recognised his information but no information trick. She smiled and this time he detected genuine warmth, no play-acting.

'Hey, but I haven't asked you how your day's been,' he said. A deliberate question dressed as an observation. This time he laughed and gave her a fleeting kiss. 'Come on, two can play at not really saying stuff. Let's take our drinks outside where it's quieter. But you know I was being serious when I said I was hungry. Do you fancy going for something to eat later?'

Outside with their drinks, they sat at a table under one of Sandlings' bottle green umbrellas. Cool river air drifted up from the Orwell. It lifted salty estuary scents over the low wall separating the cocktail bar and restricted road from the boardwalks and gantries for the boats. Nick shuffled his chair closer to Gacela. 'I left a sweatshirt in my car. I wish I'd brought it with me now.'

'It's the first week of September, Nick. The evenings are drawing in.'

'Talking of bringing things reminds me. I had a bit of time to kill on Thursday while I was waiting to visit a customer in Woodbridge.'

'Woodbridge? Nice place. I don't suppose you had time to look at any of the shops?'

'Well yes I did. I had a bit of a wander round and spotted somewhere selling jewellery like your necklace, the one with silver dragonflies and enamelled blackberries and leaves.'

He sensed her tense and ploughed on, 'I would have got you something, but I didn't know if you'd like the silver birds. They aren't making the dragonflies and fruit anymore. In fact the woman in the shop said they haven't been for some time.'

He let his words sink in. Gacela was bound to pick up on the significance of the *not for some time*. He'd keep the *not for a couple of years* back for the moment. He drove his fingers into his pocket and pulled out the jewellery information card. 'I brought this for you. It's a bit crumpled, but I thought you might be interested in the current stuff.'

'Thanks.' She took the card and appeared to look at the pictures.

'I thought the mallards were rather comical, their feet out as if coming in to land.' He leaned closer and pointed to the silver mallard pictured on the card. 'Apparently it's based on a photo of mallards landing on Alton Water.'

'It's sweet… and so are you. But I already have a necklace, and well I don't really need another.'

'Yes, but time for a change, maybe? You must have had yours a while.'

'What? Why d'you say that? Have you noticed chips in the enamel then?'

He knew she was guiding the conversation away from how long she'd had the necklace. Should he run with it or get her back on track and force a showdown?

He considered his choices while she took her mobile from her handbag and flicked through her messages, as if she wasn't interested in his answer.

'I'm sorry, Nick but this isn't working for me.'

'Your phone isn't working?'

'No. This… us.' She indicated the pair of them with a casual gesture.

'But I thought we were getting on great. Is it something I've said? Or not said? Are you OK? Has something happened?'

She didn't answer.

'Well aren't you going to tell me?'

She looked at him, a hard expression tightening her face.

'I like you, Nick. Don't get me wrong. But you're getting too close. You're a nice bloke, but it's not the right time for me.' She stood up. 'Bye, Nick.'

'But Gacela....'

Without a backward glance she walked from the table to the restricted road and away.

God, he hadn't wanted it to end like this.

# CHAPTER 31

‘Bye, Mais,’ Matt shouted as he watched Gacela’s little blue Fiat 500 drive away. It was just before midday, and the Saturday sunshine dulled her indicator lights.

He figured she’d likely take the most direct route from the Copdock interchange roundabout to the wedding reception in the Hadleigh Guildhall. It would be the A1071 – the main road straight from Ipswich. It skimmed past the northern outskirts of Hadleigh on its way to Sudbury.

Trailing the Fiat without being rumbled had been easy on the busy dual carriageways of the A12 and A14. But how would he fare on a quiet single track road for eight or ten miles in broad daylight? He wasn’t so sure.

He had already offered to take Maisie from Stowmarket direct to Hadleigh on his scooter.

‘Nah,’ she’d squealed, ‘I like Gacela. She aint stuck up. It’s like gettin’ a lift with one of me mates. We ’ave a bit of a natter an’ a laugh. Can’t do that on the back of your scooter. Not in helmets.’

‘Natter? Careful, Mais. Don’t go sayin’ nothin’ ’bout them chocolates.’

He’d thought through his mission, both his route and dress. He’d whizz off the roundabout, take the A12 towards Colchester and almost immediately turn onto the small roads, speed cross country and pick up the A1071 and blue Fiat at Hintlesham. From there he’d follow them to Hadleigh. He could see it in his mind as plain as anything.

He’d layered his clothing, putting his personalised alumina tee-shirt on to please Maisie, but slipping it over a dark purple one. He’d doubled up on his jackets again, wearing blue denim but stowing the old black one with his khaki backpack and laptop under his seat.

And the scooter? The blackberry bubblegum? He'd rung Nick for masking tape first thing, but there'd been no answer. He'd sent a text and then given up. In exasperation he'd used his Computing & IT Assistant Demonstrator pass to slip unnoticed into the Academy buildings. Old Blumfield, director of the carpentry department, was a stickler for tradition, and Matt reckoned he wouldn't have changed the carpentry workroom code on the keypad lock. It turned out Matt was correct. He'd pressed the sequence of numbers held in his visual memory from way back, and seconds later he was into the workroom and searching through a familiar drawer stocked with masking tape.

It was odd, but when he thought of the roll of masking tape now stashed in the Vespa's handy top-box, a pang of guilt twisted his guts. 'Sorry, Mum, I'll put it back,' he mumbled. But DOS-in' hell, what made him think of her? She'd once told him everything he did was a waste of time.

Matt twisted the handle-grip accelerator. The Vespa's four-stroke engine responded with a metallic growl and he streamed off the roundabout. Uninhibited by passenger or surveillance techniques, he swooped and wove, rode a tail wind and darted between lanes. He made good time along the winding, cross country route. He might be clumsy on his feet, but on wheels he was an athlete. The god of good timing must have ridden on his shoulder as he sped into Hintlesham because just as he paused at a junction concealed by a sharp bend, the Fiat 500 drove past on the A1071.

The rest of the journey was slower, a lot of hanging back and speeding up as he avoided being seen in Gacela's rear view mirror. The centre of Hadleigh was Saturday morning busy with shoppers and cars, and Matt peeled away to park in the library's drop off and restricted parking area. He reckoned his scooter would be OK there. In fact it was DOS-in' ideal; Wi-Fi in the library and only a stone's throw from the guildhall. He could thread on foot along the old pavements and alleyways, and in less than a minute he'd be able to watch the rear of the guildhall.

He shed his distinctive alumina T and changed his blue denim for his old black jacket. Helmet safely stowed, he pulled on his baseball cap. He slung his backpack over a shoulder, and armed with his mobile phone in one hand, set off to case the joint.

He hurried along an old pavement cutting past the Victorian Town Hall, and approached the 15$^{th}$ century guildhall's rear aspect. It appeared to partially adjoin the town hall buildings, and at one end it had what he supposed was a walled garden. He might not be able to see beyond its wall, but he'd be able to hear. In front of him the ancient guildhall rose, timber-framed and three storeys high, each storey jutting out further than the one below. Warm sandy coloured wash blended with old brick base extensions on either side. A massive Tudor brick chimney dominated a rear side wall.

Voices carried on the air. 'Are these for the garden?' Maisie asked shrilly.

He relaxed. Maisie was OK. But where were the van and blue Fiat? Somewhere round at the front? He walked on.

The front of the guildhall was open and exposed, facing onto a grassy graveyard and ancient flint and stone church. He circled in front, keeping close to the church side of the graveyard. He supposed the guests would be arriving soon, but they'd have to be on foot because the road stopped well short of the guildhall. There were no cars parked anywhere and their entry was blocked.

At the far end of the guildhall he spotted the Hyphen & Green van parked behind bollards. Gacela's blue Fiat had been drawn up alongside, together with a couple of other cars in what appeared to be a restricted parking area at the rear of the town hall buildings. But how had the van and cars got there, and more importantly how were they leaving? There was no obvious vehicle access from where he was standing.

He sidled out of view and waited. Ten minutes later the van had been unloaded and its doors slammed shut. He hung on for another five, but no one came out to the van or cars. It seemed safe to sneak between the bollards, line up his phone camera and take a shot of the car number plates.

'I still don't get how the van got in here,' he breathed. It was time to investigate, and he hurried along a tarmacked track and pavers between pale brick Victorian buildings. There was no one around and he slowed his pace as the way led him on. A few more yards and he stepped into Market Place, a narrow street passing along the front of the town hall. So this was the way in and out for the van and cars.

He was in luck. The far end of Market Place curved and led directly into the street where he'd parked his Vespa outside the library. He reckoned if he positioned the Vespa just right, he'd be ready to tail Gacela's car the moment he saw its nose poke out between the town hall buildings and drive into Market Place.

The afternoon passed quickly as he made repeated forays on foot to listen for Maisie amongst the guests in the walled garden, and then backtrack and creep along the vehicle access route he'd discovered to watch the van and Gacela's car. He made sure to avoid the exposed area in front of the guildhall.

Between forays he worked on the Vespa outside the library and covered every last inch of the blackberry bubblegum front plate and mudguard with masking tape.

'Yeah, DOS-in' cool,' he said as he stood back to admire his handiwork. He'd transformed the front of the scooter into the pale scaly leg and foot of Shadow Parrot Hawk, complete with a wheel and black tyre for a talon.

A little before six o'clock it was over. The civil ceremony and lunch had ended and the bride and groom left to the sound of clapping and shouts of *good luck*. It all seemed a bit tame from where Matt skulked close to the walled garden, but the glimpses he caught of the happy couple told him they were ancients. 'Yeah, well I s'pose that explains why there aint no serious drinkin' an' partyin'.'

Without a wild late night bash to cater for, the Hyphen & Green team began to clear away and load the van. The guests started to drift off and Matt concentrated his surveillance on the vehicle access end of the guildhall. He hid between the town hall buildings but kept within earshot.

'Just leave the box of empty bottles by the van, Maisie. Lars is loading up today. It's a one man job and you'll only get in his way.'

It was Gacela, the Spanish goat's voice. He recognised her from the Copdock interchange drop-offs and pickups.

'OK. I were only tryin' to help. I'll put'em here.' Maisie's screechy tones were unmistakeable.

But who was Lars? Was he the chef standing in for Leon? Matt decided he'd get a shot of him for Clive.

Van-loading chatter echoed between the brick and stone buildings as he crept closer. He aimed his phone. Click! He'd captured Lars, full-face just as he reached out to take a plastic crate being handed into the van.

It had only taken a second and Matt stepped back out of sight. Something moved in his peripheral vision, off to his left; now almost behind him.

He froze, his eyes scouring the buildings. Nothing. All he could hear was the sound of Maisie and Gacela as they carried crates to the van. He waited. Five minutes, an eternity, but nothing moved. Had his imagination played tricks? Shaken, pulse racing, he retraced his path back to the library and his scooter.

It didn't take him more than a moment to stow his backpack and shove on his helmet. He started the scooter and rode slowly to the widely paved area linking the far end of Market Place to the library road. He waited, shielded by the buildings, his eyes trained on the entrance and exit gap. And then he saw the pale blue Fiat 500 appear. Gacela was at the wheel and Maisie in the front passenger seat. The car turned onto the road and headed slowly away from him and towards the High Street. Out of nowhere, a man stepped into its path.

'That's bloody Leon,' Matt muttered as red brake lights flashed and Gacela stopped. Leon bent to say something through the car window. He opened the passenger door and stood while Maisie got out and then into the rear seat. Leon glanced around before slipping into the front passenger seat. The Fiat moved off again.

'He must be wantin' a lift as well,' Matt reasoned, unease tempered by curiosity.

The odds had changed with Leon in the car. Three pairs

of eyes increased the chance of him being spotted. Was Leon a threat to Maisie? Either way, he daren't get too close. Thank scam spotters' luck he'd transformed the front of his scooter. And the black jacket and purple T he was wearing didn't look anything like the blue denim he'd worn when he dropped Maisie off for her lift and tailed her to Hadleigh.

He reckoned he could outwit them and watched as the Fiat indicated right and turned onto the High Street. It was the obvious direction back to the A1071 and Ipswich. Matt, still at the far end of Market Place made a quick decision. It would appear less suspicious if he joined the High Street from the library road. He turned the scooter.

'Fraggin' hell,' he yelped and jolted to a halt.

'What's she doin' comin' down the library road? Where's she goin'?' The blue Fiat sped past his nose. A second earlier and he'd have turned directly into its path. It was heading in the wrong direction for Ipswich and if he didn't get a move on, he'd lose it.

Pulse hammering, Matt twisted the accelerator. The Vespa surged forward. He steered hard right, leaned into the turn and followed the Fiat. He swept out of Hadleigh over a narrow bridge and the River Brett; a sharp left, a hard right – the narrow lane twisted and turned. Gacela drove fast; so fast he almost lost her as she raced up a steep hill. High hedges, sudden bends, forks in the road – it was a rollercoaster of a chase through the hilliest Suffolk countryside. Did she realise he was following? He didn't know; he was too busy keeping up. More than one bend between them and she'd have escaped him.

Within minutes he lost all sense of direction. He hadn't seen any road signs, houses or farm buildings. Ahead he only had eyes for the Fiat's blue paintwork and tail lights. When he glanced to either side, it was only to help steer him round tight bends.

Another corner loomed. This time the Fiat swung off the road and onto a track. He followed, hitting gravel and stones at speed. The track slopped away. Now there were ruts. He kept his eyes on the ground but he was gaining speed. Another bend. He braked.

'Woa,' he screamed and slewed sideways. Wham!

The scooter slid into the back of the Fiat. 'Frag!'

•••

Nick rubbed his eyes and groaned. God, what time was it? He was meant to be at a Saturday lunchtime band rehearsal. Heaviness pressed the back of his eyes. A mild nausea threatened to rise in his throat. The previous evening was a bit of a blur, at least the bit after Gacela walked out of the cocktail bar. She'd said he was *getting too close*. What the hell was that supposed to mean?

He'd downed his beer and left. The cocktail bar wasn't the place to get drunk, there were too many associations with her. He'd walked to his car and driven back to Woolpit to wallow alone in his garret and drink his collection of bottled beers. He'd slipped into alcohol soaked sleep.

Daylight finally forced itself on him. It compounded the hammering inside his head and the turmoil in his guts. He sat up, regretted the movement and layback. Time drifted. Sunshine streamed through the roof space. He had to get up if he was ever going to make Saturday band practice.

When he'd rinsed out his mouth and drunk a pint of water, he checked his mobile. There weren't any messages from Gacela. It was hardly a surprise but the pang of disappointment hurt. He opened Matt's message, more as a distraction than anything else.

‘What?’ he barked as he read the text, ‘You want masking tape? If it means you’ve changed your mind and want to follow Gacela - well, she’s ditched me, mate. You can forget it! You’re too bloody late!’

He didn’t know why he was raising his voice or who he was shouting at. Not Matt; he probably thought he was being helpful, although he hadn’t mentioned Gacela by name and for once he’d omitted the Spanish goat jibe. Well, the masking tape text could wait. Nick didn’t want to think about Gacela, and he certainly didn’t want to spell out her name. He closed Matt’s message. For the moment he couldn’t bring himself to reply.

# CHAPTER 32

The moment of impact with the stationary Fiat played out in slow motion for Matt. He squeezed the brakes. Front, then rear locked in an emergency stop. He clutched the Vespa's handlebar grips and pressed his feet into the footrest.

The tyres skidded on gravel, slewing the scooter sideways towards the rear of the car. 'Woa,' he screamed.

The Vespa leaned over horribly. Matt fought to hold it upright but it was too heavy. Instinctively he threw his weight to counterbalance the tilt. It was hopeless. Wham! The scooter fell onto its side as Matt let go of the handle grips. The momentum carried him forwards. He half-stepped half-leapt off the scooter. When his feet hit the ground, he hopped and ran. He veered away, missing the Fiat's tail lights by an inch. He tumbled over. By some miracle he landed in a heap on the ground, out to the side and clear of both car and scooter. 'Frag!' he yelped.

The scooter, now on its side, all forward thrust and energy spent, slid unhurriedly under the rear of the Fiat's back bumper.

Matt lay motionless, feeling no pain but his mind on fire as he assimilated the collision.

Car doors slammed. Voices shouted.

'I told you this would happen if I just stopped like that.' Anger fired through Gacela's voice.

'Is he all right? Who is he?' Maisie screeched.

'Get back in the car, Maisie.' It was a male voice, the manner cold, the words slow.

'Yeah, but why we here? Where we goin'?'

‘I said to get back in the car.’

There was silence and then the Fiat’s door opened and closed.

Matt, his head cocooned in his helmet felt strangely separate from his surroundings.

‘I thought he’d have spun off into those trees,’ the cold voice said. ‘Hey you! Are you alive?’

The toe of a shoe dug into his shoulder. ‘Ugh,’ Matt grunted in surprise.

‘Yes, he’s alive.’

‘Thank God,’ Gacela said, ‘but he must have hurt himself. And look at my car! His scooter’s half under my bumper. Why did you tell me to lead him here? Couldn’t you have just asked him why he was creeping around the van? Save all this drama?’

Blog almighty! So someone had seen him amongst the town hall buildings. It must have been that flash of something in the corner of his eye. His guts twisted.

‘Sometimes it’s good to teach a lesson. Now let me get a look at his face.’ The voice chilled.

Matt heard the rustle as someone crouched down. He wanted to play unconscious, but a hand grabbed his chin guard, scratched at his visor. Instinctively he struggled as his helmet was yanked up. The chinstrap held. The visor flipped open and he stared into the eyes of a square-jawed man.

It was Leon. He’d guessed it would be. There was no mistaking his blond hair or the face of the man from the Dutch fishing site.

‘Big fishin’,’ Matt breathed, in recognition.

‘What?’ Uncertainty flickered across Leon’s face.

‘I said pike. Big fishin’.’

‘Pike? Who the hells are you? Come on, get up.’ The Dutch accent was more obvious to Matt’s ear now his visor was open.

An iron grip clamped his upper arm and an unstoppable force dragged him to his feet.

‘Frag! Me scooter.’

His eyes flew around the blackberry bubblegum bodywork. ‘What’ll I scammin’ do?’ he moaned as he gaped at the Vespa lying on its side.

Little shreds of masking tape peppered the grit close to the Fiat. Fragments of wing mirror glass glinted on the gravel. Grief snatched his breath, punched his stomach. His legs buckled and he doubled up, at least he would have if it hadn’t been for the iron grip on his arm.

‘Stand up! Who are you? Why are you saying pike fishing?’

‘But me scooter,’ Matt whimpered. He pulled away from Leon. He was desperate to get a closer look at his Vespa.

Its wheels had slid under the Fiat, but the wider parts - the front plate, footrest and exhaust pipe had simply come to rest against the car’s back bumper.

Gacela took hold of the handlebar and tugged. ‘I don’t think the scooter’s trapped.’

‘No, stop. Don’t pull it out. You’ll scratch it even more,’ Matt wailed, ‘me paintwork’ll be ruined.’

‘OK, OK. I’ll move my car forwards. Then you should be able to stand it up without dragging it over the ground.’

‘Thanks, Gacela.’ He watched her get into the Fiat.

‘Gacela?’ Leon said sharply, ‘So you know each other, do you?’

‘What? No. I’m Maisie’s bloke. Gacela gives Maisie a

lift.'

'But you have a scooter. Why not give her a lift yourself?'

The Fiat's 1.2L engine burst into life, cutting across further talk. Exhaust fumes gusted over the scooter as Gacela edged the car forwards.

'That's far enough. You're clear now,' Leon shouted and banged the car with his open hand. 'And the back of your car looks all right. Hey Maisie, stay in the car!'

Matt grabbed a handlebar and began to heave the scooter. Leon stood on the other side and between them they lifted it upright.

'Scammin' malware,' Matt groaned as he took stock of the Vespa's scratched paintwork. 'It's all dented and bent along them edges. Why'd you spammin' stop like that?' He ran his hand over the front plate, footrest and bodywork along one side. 'How'll I get it home?'

'Will it start?' Leon asked.

Sick with anxiety, Matt pressed the ignition and twisted the accelerator. The Vespa spluttered into life then stalled. He tried again and this time kept the revs going.

'Right,' Leon shouted, 'Gacela – drive slowly. I'll walk next to the scooter. Its only fifty yards around this bend and then we're at the back of the car paint and body repair unit.' He turned to Matt and added, 'You can get it fixed there. Come on.'

Maisie waved and mouthed something at him through the rear windscreen. She looked excited, almost desperate as she screeched, 'Matt!' But he couldn't make out what else she said. His mind was fixed on his Vespa. The dents and scratches seemed brutal. How would he get it repaired? How much would it cost? Misery tore through his body. It sapped his strength and froze his guts. His life, his focus, his world narrowed to only his Vespa. He could barely even feel the bruising on the back of his calf and elbow.

He rode slowly behind the Fiat while Leon walked briskly alongside. Leon was tall, six feet tall, and his arm had a long reach. He simply held Matt by the back of his jacket collar. At the time it struck Matt as an act of matey guidance. 'We don't' want any more falls,' Leon said.

The approach was shielded by trees, and it was difficult to make out the size of the warehouse from the rear aspect. Wide metal roller doors closed off the end of a single storey building. Large air vents and flues punctured the galvanised metal construction.

Leon whisked the keys from the Vespa's ignition.

'Wait!' he barked, and hurried to open the roller doors for the Fiat to drive inside.

'Now you get off and push it in,' Leon shouted at Matt.

There were no windows and the inside gloom only deepened when the roller doors clattered shut behind them. He screwed up his eyes, adjusting to the darkness that swirled beyond the Fiat's headlights.

Leon flipped a switch. Matt blinked in the sudden brightness of the overhead lights. Concrete floor stretched away from him. A panel of dials and controls ran along the side of a unit the size of a small lorry container jutting into the warehouse space. Huge metal ducts ran into its roof from a heater the size of a giant boiler. Observation windows gave a view into the unit, except from where he stood all he saw was darkness on the other side of the thick glass. Something struck Matt as odd. The place seemed deserted. There were cars in various stages of panel strip down with wings and doors missing, and cars still untouched but waiting with dented and scratched bodies for attention. He saw welding equipment, heat lamps and trolley racks of tools. But there were no people, no one in overalls.

'Where are the repair blokes? I need to show me scooter to someone,' he wailed.

'What? I can't hear you properly with your helmet on. The chin guard squashes your cheeks. Please to take it off, then we can talk. No misunderstandings,' Leon said quietly.

Matt hesitated, suspicious and unsure what to do. But there was something in Leon's manner which reassured, and when he dropped his voice, Matt couldn't catch all he said.

'OK then,' he muttered and wrenched his helmet off.

The Fiat doors flew open and Gacela got out, quickly followed by Maisie.

'Matt! Are you OK? Are you hurt? Hey, and what you been doin'? Why you been spyin' on me?' Maisie screamed, and rushed over, almost knocking the wind out of him with the exuberance of her hug.

'Hey, careful, Mais. What you just say? Spyin' on you?' Matt stepped back to make more space for the helmet between them.

'OK, so you are Matt and I can see Maisie is your girl. OK.'

'Leon's the chef,' Maisie said, 'he's amazin' choppin' tomatoes. But he aint me boyfriend.'

'So Matt, tell me. If you were not spying on Maisie, who were you spying on?'

'What?'

'I saw you snoop around the van. You watch it all afternoon. What is your interest in the van?'

‘Nothin’.’

‘Ah, but then I must think you are interested in what is *inside* the van.’

‘Inside the van?’

‘Yes. I think your girlfriend takes something from the van last week. Now you want more, and you come looking.’

‘What’s ’e talkin’ ’bout?’ Maisie screeched.

‘*Houd je kop*,’ Leon snarled.

‘Don’t go talkin’ no foreign stuff at me. I know when someone’s tryin’ to blame me for somethin’ I aint done. It’s a stich-up. Anyway, what I s’posed to take?’ She flung the words at all of them.

‘Is this about the chocolates that went missing last week, Leon?’ Gacela asked.

Leon looked surprised, as if he’d forgotten Gacela was there. ‘Yes, of course,’ he said.

‘All this about a box of chocolates? My car could have been wrecked over a simple box of chocolates?’

‘But this is about more than a simple box of chocolates. I am still waiting to hear Matt explain his interest in the van.’

•••

Nick checked his mobile. It was close on seven o’clock in the evening and he should have been on his way to the Stowmarket football club. The rest of the band would be setting up for the Saturday night gig, but he’d delayed leaving his garret room until the very last minute. Would Gacela call or text him? She’d have finished work by now and returned from waitressing at the lunch reception in Hadleigh. He couldn’t imagine taking a call from her in front of his mates, not after the cocktail bar brush off.

But he was out of luck. There was nothing new from her in his messages and no missed calls. Matt's unanswered text remained at the top of his messages screen. Its very presence seemed to reproach him for not responding. 'Oh God,' Nick sighed as he pictured Matt. Had he been serious? Was he following Gacela at this very moment? Guilt spurred his fingers and he thumbed in a quick reply.

*4get the masking tape and trailing Gacela. You're 2 late, mate. She's,* he was about to write *ended with me* but it felt too final. He considered for a moment, deleted *She's* and keyed *We've split.*

He pressed send and slipped his mobile into his pocket. It was time to leave.

•••

*Ping!* The text alert sounded, deep in Matt's pocket. Leon, Gacela and Maisie all heard it too. For a split second it froze time inside the car body repair unit.

'It is OK. Go on, answer it,' Leon said.

Matt felt confused. In all the movies he'd watched, phones were taken from hostages and captives by their kidnappers and hijackers. A captive with a mobile was like a prisoner with a weapon, but Leon had just said he could use his, so everything must be all right. Except if everything was all right, why did Leon make him feel so nervous? Why had the roller door been closed? And why wasn't he talking to a bloke about fixing his scooter instead of Leon still?

'OK,' he said slowly, and unzipped his jacket. He pulled his mobile from an inside pocket and tapped in his PIN. Nick's message filled the small screen. *4get the masking tape and trailing Gacela. You're 2 late, mate. We've split*, he read.

‘Is it something important?’ Leon asked.

Before Matt had time to look up or answer, a hand smashed down onto his wrist and flicked his mobile from his fingers.

‘Hey! What you doin’? That’s me phone.’

‘Yeah, give it back,’ Maisie screamed.

‘*Houd je kop*. I will read your message. *Masking tape and trailing Gacela*? The message ID is Nick. Who is Nick?’

‘What? Did you say Nick? Let me see that,’ Gacela said and stepped towards Leon.

‘Stay. Wait, Gacela. Ha! I must read the message thread. And yes, now the photos. I have it all here. Shots of the cars and Lars today. And me! These ones were taken of the van, Gacela and Maisie last week. It is obvious you have been snooping for some time.’ He spoke as he scrolled through the photos.

‘Scammin’ malware. You can’t go lookin’ through me photos. It’s me phone. Hey give it back.’

‘But you unlocked your phone for me, Matt. It would be rude not to look. Who is Nick?’

‘What?’ Matt stalled.

‘Go on, tell ’im, Matt. He’s one of your mates. Now give back the phone,’ Maisie squawked, her voice cracking and rasping.

‘This message implies you work for Nick, but now you’ve split. Was he an associate? Does he fish for pike too? And Gacela? Your name is in this message. How do you know this Nick?’

‘See, I were right,’ Maisie croaked, ‘I knew you fancied Nick. Is that what this is about? Leon’s gone all jealous?’

Gacela ignored Maisie and directed her words at Leon;

‘I met him at Freston. Hyphen & Green were catering for a party there. He’s asked me out on a couple of dates, but he’s not really my type. I don’t plan to see him again. Anyway, what’s it to you?’

‘I’m curious, that is all. He probably hoped to vet you for information. So now you are a subject for surveillance, it seems.’ Leon turned his attention back to Matt.

‘I don’t think you’ve told me all about yourself yet.’ He half-sprang at Matt and grabbed his throat, squeezing hard with one hand. Matt fought for breath.

‘Oi! Leave ’im alone,’ Maisie rasped and ran at him. Gacela stepped into her path and blocked her. ‘Hey get out me way, Gacela.’

A couple of seconds of crushing pain, a pulse pounding in his ears, and then Matt felt the pressure release. He coughed and spluttered, hardly aware as Leon, in one deft movement pulled at the blue lanyard around his neck. The Computing & IT Assistant Demonstrator pass flipped out from under his purple tee. It dangled in plain view for all to see.

‘Ha! You don’t look anything like this ID pass. You have a beard. You are not this Matt Finch!’

‘What?’ Maisie squealed.

‘Tell me, what do you want, Matt? A turf war? No one muscles in on my territory. Who do you work for?’

‘What? I don’t work for anyone.’

‘I know you work for Nick, but who is behind Nick? His name is not on the street. Gacela, what do you know about this Nick?’

‘Nothing. He wouldn’t talk about himself.’

Leon didn’t say anything, just stared at her. Matt ran a finger around the neck of his tee-shirt and eased the cotton fabric away from his bruised skin.

Gacela broke the silence. ‘Look, Leon, I’ve done my bit. You told me to drive here and Matt just happened to follow. So I’ve done nothing wrong and I’ve broken no law. But I’m not part of this.’ She spread her arms in an expansive catch-all gesture.

‘But you are part of this. You are here, Gacela and therefore you are involved, fully implicated. Remember what happened to Juliette Poels. I have to decide what to do with Matt. Do we play him or dispose him? I must make some calls. It may take me time to get an answer from Holland.’

‘What you mean, play me or dispose me?’ Matt’s voice rose in panic.

‘Juliette Poels were found dead, right?’ Maisie rasped.

‘Juliette didn’t understand to, how do you say it… turn a blind eye? She was stupid enough to get curious and ask questions. I told her to forget Kinver and his car but she would not do as she was told. She had to be taught a lesson. Everyone learned the lesson. That’s what happened to Juliette.’

‘Well then I aint curious,’ Maisie said.

‘Good girl, you are learning. But I’m curious to speak to Nick. Matt, you will call him and tell him to come here.’

‘No I scammin’ aint. He’ll have his phone off by now.’

‘Yeah, his band’s playing at the football club gig in Stowmarket tonight. I were really lookin’ forward to a bit of bop an’ a rum n’Coke. And now all this has happened.’ Maisie’s face flushed in the harsh overhead lights. ‘I-I shouldn’t have said that, should I? Sorry Matt.’

‘No Maisie, you are being good girl. If you will not call Nick, Matt I will text him using your mobile. He will think it is you texting him.'

'Oh scammin' hell.'

'Right. It is time for action. Gacela, help me put these two somewhere safe. We will lock them in the paint curing booth.'

'What? You aint lockin' me in no booth,' Maisie squealed.

'*Houd je kop!*'

# CHAPTER 33

The band was taking a break midway through the gig in the football clubhouse in Stowmarket. The first set had gone well but Nick didn't have the heart to drift up to the bar with its crush of girls excitedly ordering drinks. His stomach was too raw. He'd had more than enough to drink the previous evening, what with his cocktail bar brush off and split with Gacela. The rest of the band were chatting to Jason's brother and hanging around the low platform crowded with speakers, amps, keyboard, drums and guitars. Nick craved his own company and wandered outside with a bottle of water.

A large roughly gravelled car park filled the space between the long wooden clubhouse and road. He ambled to his car and leaned against it in the darkness, diluted by arc lamps and passing car headlights. He knew there was no point in checking his mobile again. She wasn't going to call.

With a sudden compulsive need to know he pulled his mobile from his pocket and checked again for new messages and missed calls. There was nothing from Gacela. The disappointment cut deep, just as deep as the last time he'd looked. But there was something from Matt.

'Now what's he's up to?' he murmured and opened the text.

*Nick – you must come quick. My scooter is crashte. I am at…* Nick skimmed across the details.

Had Matt had a smash, an accident? But what could he do? He was part way through the gig and there was no way he could leave. He looked at the location again. Trust Matt to use the postcode as a locater. He opened his Google maps app, and for once had signal. What was the postcode? Damn, he'd forgotten. He flicked and pressed to get back to the text.

'Hell, Matt. You know I can't reel off letter and number sequences like you.'

This time he concentrated harder. He held the start of the sequence in his mind as he went back into the Google maps app. 'It's a Hadleigh postcode! Why the hell couldn't you just say somewhere in Hadleigh?'

Oh God, but Matt must have damaged his scooter. And he was in Hadleigh. What if he'd gone to that dodgy garage place?

Nick's emotions unravelled. 'I can't deal with this now,' he breathed. He pressed his finger on Matt's message, chose the *more* option and forwarded it to Chrissie. He pressed her automatic dial number, barely able to wait for her to answer.

'Hi Nick.' She sounded surprised.

'Chrissie? I-I've just forwarded you a message from Matt. Look I can't deal with it now. I'm in the middle of a gig.'

'Yes something just pinged on my phone, but I can't open it while I'm on the call. Is it important? Has something happened?'

'I don't know. Can I just leave it to you? I'll call you after the gig. OK?'

•••

'Is everything all right?' Clive asked as he carried coffee into their cosy living room.

Chrissie sat on the snug two-seater sofa and concentrated on her phone. 'I don't know. Nick's forwarded me a text from Matt but it seems a bit odd. What do you think?' She handed him her phone with the text message open for him to read.

'So you think this is odd? You do know that Matt and odd go hand in hand don't you?'

'Hmm, but this is odder than usual.'

'*Nick – you must come quick. My scooter is crashte*,' he read out slowly.

'Exactly, it just isn't Matt's style, Clive. And *crashte*? Is that a typo or deliberately spelled with a T and an E? I'll get my laptop.'

It didn't take her a moment to fetch her laptop from the narrow pine table in the kitchen. 'You see, I think….' She let her words drift as she sat down again, flipped up the screen and typed *post code identifier* in the search box.

'This is interesting. It's in Hadleigh, or rather a bit outside Hadleigh, more towards Polstead,' she muttered.

'What? What have you found? Oh no, the bloody fool. He's given the postcode for the car body repair place. The one we've had our suspicions about.'

'Really? So that's where it is. Hey, I've just had a thought.' She typed *crashte* into the search box, 'I was right, it's a bloody Dutch word. A slip of the tongue for crashed, if you're Dutch.'

Clive's phone shrilled with a sudden ringtone.

'What?' Clive stood up and paced around as he took the call.

Chrissie watched, anxiety taking hold. She didn't need to ask, it was obvious something serious was happening.

He ended the call. 'We've had a tipoff. I've got to go, Chrissie. Don't call me, I'll call you. Radio silence, and all that. This is big.'

‘What? Hey, for God’s sake be careful,’ she called after him. But it was too late; the front door had already slammed.

•••

Matt sat on the concrete floor inside one of the paint spray and curing units. It had felt like forever. Maisie sat clinging to him.

‘I don’t think you ought to have hit Leon with me helmet, Mais,’ he murmured.

‘Why not? He had it comin’.’

‘Yeah, but the thing is, you go smashin’ around with me helmet and well, it can damage its structure.’

‘Can it?’

‘Yeah. An’ now he’s got me helmet. Thank blog me scooter’s with us in here. I’d be worryin’ he were goin’ to ride away on it. You know, steal it.’

‘Ride it? How about we ram the doors and break out on it?’

‘Coz we aint got no scammin’ keys, Mais. Leon’s kept ’em. He’s locked me scooter, top-box, everythin’. All we got is scammin’ maskin’ tape hangin’ off the front plate.’

They lapsed into silence. The bruising on the back of Matt’s calf ached and his shoulders and ribs hurt from fighting the Vespa when he’d tried to stop its fall. He felt empty, drained of emotion. If Maisie hadn’t been clinging to him, he’d have curled into a ball and escaped into his world of comic-strip heroes.

‘What d’you think Leon’s doin’?’ Maisie asked.

‘I reckon he’ll be callin’ Holland. Askin’ for orders.’

‘Do you think he’s goin’ to kill us?’

Matt’s stomach lurched. He couldn’t answer.

‘What’s that grill for?’ she said.

A strip of metal grating ran the length of the floor. Matt had noticed it when they were thrown into the chamber, but he'd been too distressed to check it out. He stood up and walked over to look more closely. It was about nine inches wide, and if he peered through it he could see a steel channel running beneath, about four inches deep.

'I reckon it's either for water or it's ductin'. Floor ductin'. And that up there,' he pointed at a large box unit, like an air conditioning unit high on one wall, 'I reckon that blows in air. Then it's sucked out through the ductin' on the floor down here.'

'Why?'

'Well, I reckon it's for ventilation. Takes away all them paint fumes, an' if the air's warmed by them units up there, it'll be drawn down past whatever they're workin' on. Helps with the dryin'.'

'What's paint curin' then, Matt?'

'I reckon it's about paint hardenin' as well as dryin', but I aint really sure, Mais.' He didn't want talk about heat and temperature or think about ovens. Fan assisted ovens.

'Gacela's a sneaky bitch,' Maisie said and stood up to take a peek through the viewing window. 'I can't see her out there. I can't really see anythin' out there. What d'you think she'd doin'?'

'I don't know, Mais.'

'Just wait till I get me hands on her.'

*Crack! Crack! Boom!* Brutal sound tore through the silence. It came out of nowhere, heart-stopping, visceral, terrifying.

Maisie screamed and threw herself at Matt. The lights cut out. They dropped to the ground.

'What's goin' on?'

‘Shush, Mais. Keep quiet.’

Matt held onto her, a crouching bear hug of panic. He closed his eyes and shut out the darkness. And waited, heart pounding.

Sounds from the main part of the repair warehouse travelled through the walls of the chamber. Matt strained to hear, listening for voices, but all he picked up were vibrations and dull thuds.

Someone, something rattled the chamber door. His guts twisted. Maisie whimpered. He held his breath. There was a clunk right outside, then scratching as whatever had been used to jam the door handle was detached. The door opened. Matt steeled himself for a blinding shaft of light. There was nothing, just darkness. They clung to each other. He heard footsteps, slow, measured, relentless. They headed straight for him.

‘Police! Hands in the air where I can see them,’ a voice hissed, distorted.

Maisie disentangled her arm from his while Matt held his hands high.

‘Names!’ the voice demanded.

‘Matt Finch.’ His eyes stung.

‘Yeah, an’ I’m Maisie,’ she coughed.

‘I’ve got ’em. Last package complete, Sir.’

The lights flashed on. Matt blinked at a man dressed in black and wearing a flak jacket, helmet, night vision goggles and breathing mask. He held an automatic weapon.

‘What’s goin’ on, Matt?’ Maisie whimpered.

‘It’s scamming tear gas getting’ in,’ Matt wheezed and rubbed at his eyes, while his nose streamed. ‘Shut the fraggin’ door, can you!’

# CHAPTER 34

Chrissie sat on the grass outside the Alton Water visitor centre and gazed at the October sky. It was a Sunday morning and Clive was on a circuit around the reservoir. 'A run of seven and a half miles,' he'd said. She assumed it was his way of purging the case from his psyche because he'd been emphatic when he'd dismissed the idea of cycling the route again. 'Not enough of a challenge.' And so she was happy to sit and daydream and wait.

It had been over a month since the raid on the car body repair and paint spray unit, the one she'd never managed to locate between Hadleigh and Polstead. It had taken her a while to get her head around what the paint sprayers had been up to. Clive had explained the bones of it; the cars returning from the ferry for repeat re-spraying; the forensic discovery of "repaired dents" in the bodywork; and the even more surprising discovery of what had been used as "filler" to repair the dents.

Analysis of the "filler" had revealed crystals mixed with paste. The paste was water soluble and turned out to be a mix of white flour and water. The crystals were crack cocaine.

In the end it had been Matt who'd talked about the chemistry in a way Chrissie could understand.

'See Nick had been tellin' me about disguisin' me Vespa with vinyl wrap,' he'd explained to her over a lager in the Nags Head.

'Then when I'd sat with Maisie in that scammin' paint booth for ages, she kept askin' questions. It set me thinkin' 'bout coverin's and paint curin' and critical temperatures.'

‘It must’ve been a nightmare.’

‘Yeah it were. But somethin’ kind’ve clicked in me mind when them policemen walked us out through the front of the spray place.’

‘How d’you mean? What clicked in your mind?’

‘Coverin’ car bodywork. See, why cover it unless you’re hidin’ somethin’? And then it were all over the news about them bein’ arrested for smuggling crack cocaine.’

‘So?’

‘So I started researching, you know, netsurfin’. I reckoned the paint sprayin could mean they’d been hidin’ crack cocaine in the bodywork.

‘But how?’

‘You said Clive had mentioned flour and water, but you didn’t know why. Well I reckoned they’d found they could mix the crystals with a paste of water and white flour and fill the dents with it. No sniffer dog could’ve smelled it under all them coats of primer, paint and clear top layer.’

‘Why not use vinyl wrap?’

‘Too eye-catchin’ I reckon.’

‘So it was all about transporting cocaine? Is that what you’re saying, Matt?’

‘No. Crack cocaine. It’s crystalline, not a powder like cocaine and it’s got higher street value, coz weight for weight it’s stronger then cocaine. See, the important thing about the crack is temperature and not being soluble in water, well not unless the water’s acidic, like with lemon juice.’

‘Temperature?’

‘Yeah well it were critical if they were goin’ to hide it like filler in them car dents and spray paint over it. See the booth temperature for rapid curin’ re-spray paintin’ and clear coats is around 60° C. And that's OK coz crack don't melt and vaporise till just below 100° C. And also the flour in the paste don't ignite or burn until even higher temperatures.'

'And what's so important about not being soluble in water?'

'Yeah, well, it makes sense. Wash off the paste and sieve out the crack crystals.'

'Like panning for gold?'

'Yeah, as long as the water aint acidic.'

'I assume flour and water isn't acidic, then?'

'Nah, white flour is kinda bleached so that aint acidic. You gettin' another lager, Chrissie?'

'You know, it sounds very like something you'd dream up in a kitchen,' she'd said. And it made sense to her because John Brown, Kinver and Leon had all been chefs.

Outside in the fresh October air Chrissie daydreamed and waited for Clive to complete his run. She closed her eyes and half dozed as the pieces of jigsaw moved in a slow motion dance. Two murders - Juliette and Kinver; two chefs - Leon in custody, John Brown detained since last week in the Netherlands; two drugs - crack cocaine and a date rape drug. There was a kind of symmetry to it all, while on the periphery Alton Water shimmered, and if she peered beneath its rippling surface, she saw pike, night keys, photos of nightingales and Gacela. She shivered.

'Are you OK?' It was Clive.

She opened her eyes. 'Have you run all the way round already? That was quick.' She blinked.

He stood looking down at her, his head framed against the pale sky. Beads of sweat dripped from his nose and trickled down his temples. He breathed fast, mouth open, face flushed beneath his auburn hair.

'Have I just woken you up?' He slumped down on the grass and sat, forearms resting on bent knees while he caught his breath.

'Well it's puffed you out. Do you feel any better?'

'Yes, it kind of helps drive away the frustration.'

'You mean the Kinver and Juliette killings?'

'Yes. It's been bad enough working the case, but having a covert op running in the background is the final straw. Why the hell they couldn't just keep me in the loop, I'll never know.'

'Bloody Gacela,' she muttered, 'Matt calls her the Spanish goat, and Nick's still pretty pissed off with it all.'

'Gacela wasn't the problem. It's the precious organised crime unit and its command line. Throw in the National Crime Agency, this year's name for what used to be the Serious Organised Crime Agency plus a whole lot more… and what do you get?'

'Chaos? The right hand doesn't know what the left hand is doing? A raised blood pressure?'

He laughed. 'Thank God she tipped us off when she did. Leon had just received orders from his gang bosses in Holland. He was told to dispose of Matt, and by association, Maisie.'

'What?'

'To liquidate them. That's when Gacela knew she had to act fast, but she couldn't risk blowing her cover. We have her to thank her for Matt and Maisie.'

'Hmm.' Chrissie wasn't quite so sure. To her way of thinking, Gacela was a mixed bag of contradictions. Maisie was convinced she was a scheming bitch and still swore she'd scratch her eyes out if she ever saw her again. And

Maisie had been in the car with Leon and Gacela when Matt was trailing them. Surely as an undercover operative she could have thrown Matt off her tracks if she'd really wanted?

'Come on, you'll get cold after all that running. Let's walk to the car and get you home. I think you probably want a shower,' she said.

'Did you mind coming out to Alton Water with me?' Clive asked as they walked to his Mondeo.

'I thought I might, but no; it's good to lay things to rest. There's still a whole lot I don't understand about the case though.'

'Would it help to lay your demons to rest if you knew?'

'I think so.' But would it, she wondered. Certainly her mind kept returning to fret over unanswered questions. It was like a compulsion to scratch an itchy spot; the more she scratched the more it itched. But laying her demons to rest? That would be nigh impossible.

'OK, ask away,' Clive said as they got into his car.

He drove on minor roads from Alton Water and headed east past fields of sprouting winter wheat and barley. Radio Suffolk played in the background, a male voice sandwiched between comfortable easy listening music. They joined the A12 at Capel St Mary and Chrissie waited until they were smoothing along the dual carriageway before she asked her first question.

'Why was Juliette Poels murdered?'

'Ah, to answer that you need to understand what happened to Kinver.'

'And to understand what happened to Kinver, I need to understand what happened to John Brown. Right, Clive?'

'Yes, so I'll try and tell you how I think it happened. I

believe John Brown met Kinver in Amsterdam when he spent his first summer there after leaving school. John wanted to experiment with marijuana, and Kinver was a small time dealer and a chef. John found he couldn't smoke it but he could eat it. I think their shared interest in cooking laid the foundation to a friendship.'

'OK, but roll on the years, Clive.'

'John developed his signature chocolate bars. Marijuana chocolate, and Kinver was his specialist marijuana supplier. He in due course joined John at Hyphen & Green. Then the bigger guys in Amsterdam muscled in on the act. Maybe they wanted to add date rape drugs to his chocolates? Who knows exactly, but John left the catering firm. There must have been an argument, tempers flared and John drove a garden fork into Kinver, a fellow chef who had been a friend.'

'No wonder he ran. But you think it was basically a falling out among thieves, so to speak?'

'I don't know yet but I'll be going over to Holland to interview John as soon as the paperwork is sorted.'

'Well go on. Don't stop there, Clive. Juliette Poels? What about her?'

'The pretty waitress with Hyphen & Green? It would be difficult to imagine she hadn't fallen for Kinver, the worldly Dutchman. I think she started nosing around after he disappeared and asked too many questions. Leon had meanwhile come over from Amsterdam, sent by the gang to replace Kinver as chef at Hyphen & Green. He's ruthless, a professional. He was to expand the crack cocaine business along with growing a network of paint spraying body repair units.'

'And Juliette was nosey, getting too close?'

'Hmm, that's what I guess.'

'The keys to the night parking! That's how Leon got her. Am I right?'

'I'm still piecing it together. The Organised Crime lot have been questioning Leon and I think he's cutting a deal with them if he sings about the gang.'

'Oh God, so he turns informant and gets away with it? Walks free, no prison, just community service or protection and a new identity? You are kidding me aren't you Clive?'

'We've a lot of circumstantial evidence, but no forensics to nail him. We know Lang Sharrard, Sophie Hyphen's live-in boyfriend borrowed a key for the Alton Water car park from a fishing club member. He parked there while he took photos of waterfowl. Sophie says he left the key lying around at their home but it disappeared after Leon dropped by for something. I'm guessing he stole it.'

'And the Dutch chocolate wrappings?'

'I don't know if the chocolate wrappings you found were left by Lang Sharrard or Leon.'

'So, you think Leon asked Juliette to meet him in the Alton Water car park late one evening?'

'Yes, Chrissie. I reckon he spun her some yarn about discovering Kinver's car, or maybe he just proposed a romantic evening with her. He's a good looking bastard.'

'So she drives to meet him. He gets into her car and then she drives with him to the car body repair and spray unit. It's barely a five minute drive away.'

'And at some point he gives her a chocolate laced with date rape drug like the one you ate, except he likely persuaded her to eat several.'

'They were delicious, Clive.'

'I can believe it. But then with her drugged it would

have been easy, a short journey into the paint spray booth. He jams the temperature controls on maximum, overrides the timer and locks the exit. We know the rest.'

'Poor Juliette Poels.'

And again it struck Chrissie how chefs seemed to run like a thread through everything. It would have been second nature to Leon as a chef; he'd have been fully conversant with temperature controls, timers and ovens. What a bastard.

# CHAPTER 35

'Cheers!' Chrissie stood in her kitchen and sipped her glass of sauvignon blanc.

'To chocolate making!' Her friend Sarah whooped and raised a glass in exuberant mood, 'Chrissie, it's about time we cracked this. Have you really had all this chocolate making stuff for weeks and not had a go with it yet?'

'Hey, that's not fair. I had a shot at….' She waved an arm expansively and abandoned the thread. It would have been too complicated to explain.

Her friendship with Sara dated back well over five years. They'd first met at the fencing club in Ipswich and the bonds of friendship had cemented when they discovered they both lived in Woolpit. Sarah, unlike Chrissie, was still a member of the fencing club. She had a big personality and Chrissie's small kitchen was beginning to feel hot and claustrophobic.

'I thought you told me Clive was going to help you. Chocolatiers together, and all that,' Sarah said over the rim of her glass.

'He was, but this last case of his has been grim. He's done bloody well though, coping with the Dutch Korps Nationale Politie, our government's National Crime Agency and then the regional Organised Crime Unit.'

'Well if he can juggle that lot it sounds to me like he's in line for a–'

'He's over in Amsterdam again.'

'I was going to say, in line for a promotion.'

Chrissie smiled. 'Who knows? Now don't get me side-tracked. Why don't you read the instructions on tempering chocolate before that wine goes to your head? I'm going to put a pan of water on to boil. We can melt the couverture chocolate in this.' She pointed to a heatproof bowl just the right size to go on top of the pan.

While they waited for the water to heat, she busied around, setting out her marble slab and laying the palate knife and thermometer close to hand.

'Do we have some moulds to pour the chocolate into?' Sarah asked.

'Hmm, somewhere in one of these carrier bags, I think.'

'Hey, why don't we add something to the chocolate before it goes in the moulds… like nuts or–'

*Rat-at-at-at-at-at!* The doorbell's metallic notes sounded down the hallway.

'Now who's that?'

'It's probably Nick,' Sarah said. 'He drove in as I was leaving home. I shouted something to him about you and chocolate, if he wanted to come along. I didn't think you'd mind if I asked him, but to be honest I wasn't sure he'd heard me.'

'That's great. I'll let him in. No Sarah, stay here, you haven't read all those instructions yet. I know you!' Chrissie left Sarah with a densely printed A4 sheet.

'Hey!' Chrissie said as she opened her front door, 'this is a nice surprise, Nick. We're in the kitchen. There's wine already opened or there's beer in the fridge.'

She followed him as they walked past the stairs and narrow hall table, and into the kitchen.

'Hi.' Sarah flashed him a smile and flicked her sleek black hair so that it swept forward to complement the curve of her chin; an expensive cut, short at the back, longer at the front.

‘Hi. So this is the chocolate factory, is it Chrissie?’ Nick’s eyes swept around the kitchen.

‘Hardly a chocolate factory. Right Sarah, once it’s melted we cool it down to 28° C, yes?’

‘That’s what it says. It’s why you pour it onto your slab. It says to *work it across the marble slab–*’

‘With the palate knife?’

‘Yes, until it’s cooled to whatever temperature we just said and then you scoop it back into the bowl and warm it to 31-32° C’

‘Critical temperatures. It’s about critical temperatures. Right, so are we all up to speed with tempering milk chocolate?’ Chrissie laughed.

‘I don’t know if I am. I wasn’t really–’

‘So who’s the latest girlfriend?’ Sarah cut in.

Nick looked surprised. ‘There isn’t anyone in particular. I’m not really in the market at the moment, Sarah.’

‘I thought you had some Spanish girl you were keen on?’ Sarah persisted.

‘Spanish? No, not any more. It seems I never really knew much about her.’

Sarah, stared at him for a moment, and then sipped her wine.

‘You know if we’re messing about with chocolate, let’s have some fun with it and try out some different ingredients. You’ve said nuts, Sarah. How about stem ginger? Come on, any more suggestions either of you?’ Chrissie asked.

‘I think I’ll have a beer, if that’s OK.’ Nick opened the fridge. ‘Hey, I don’t suppose you could put beer in chocolate, could you?’

‘I’m not sure it would work, Nick. But we could set

some aside and try if you like?'

She didn't say, but something flashed through her mind; the image of Kinver and a youthful John Brown throwing marijuana into chocolate. She could see them laughing and experimenting, friends like her friends in her kitchen now. What was it about kitchens and cooking and chefs, she wondered. Even the macho gang ethos from Amsterdam had been represented by something that could be stuffed and served as a dish, as well as mounted on a wall. Too bad it had to be a vicious pike.

'But you're not upset are you? Not now? I mean you are over her aren't you?' Sarah asked, her eyes on Nick, and her voice dragging Chrissie back from her reflections.

'I'm fine, Sarah. Why shouldn't I be when the only genuine thing I knew about Gacela was she didn't like radishes.'

He reached across her for the instructions.

'Hey – I wonder what radishes are like dipped in chocolate,' Sarah said.

*The end.*

Lightning Source UK Ltd.
Milton Keynes UK
UKHW021818081019
351238UK00005B/145/P